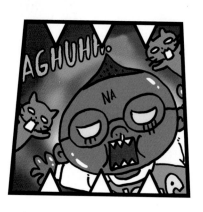

YASUNARI NAGATOSHI

I've finally fulfilled my dream of writing about Zombie Boy after fourteen years!! Well, that may sound like an exaggeration, but I had really been hoping to write this story ever since I first got the idea for it years back!! Please cheer me on!!

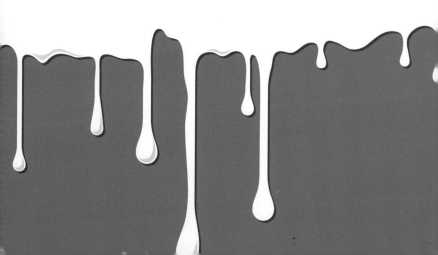

ZOMBiE BOY'S METAMORPHOSiS COLLECTiON

LARVA ZOMBIE BOY

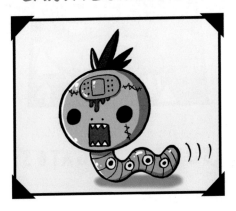

As the name suggests, this is Zombie Boy during his larval phase. After this, he turns into a pupa, and then transforms into Zombie Boy. Some say the true form of the mythical demon snake Tsuchinoko might actually be this phase of Zombie Boy. But then again, Larva Zombie Boy is also an extremely rare creature...

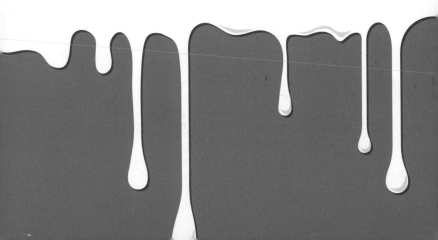

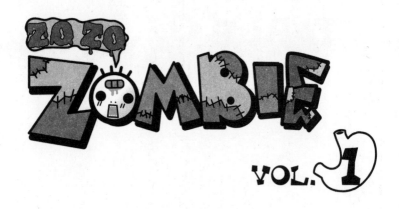

VOL. 1

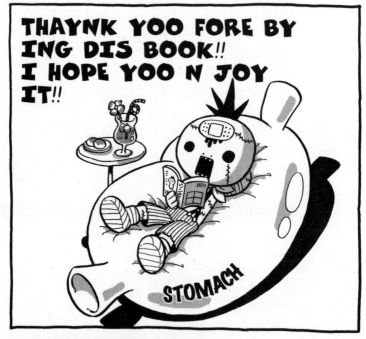

THAYNK YOO FORE BY ING DIS BOOK!! I HOPE YOO N JOY IT!!

STOMACH

YASUNARI NAGATOSHI

TABLE OF CONTENTS

MANGA

FOUR-PANEL COMIC

EXTRAS

THE ZOMBIE ATTACKZ!

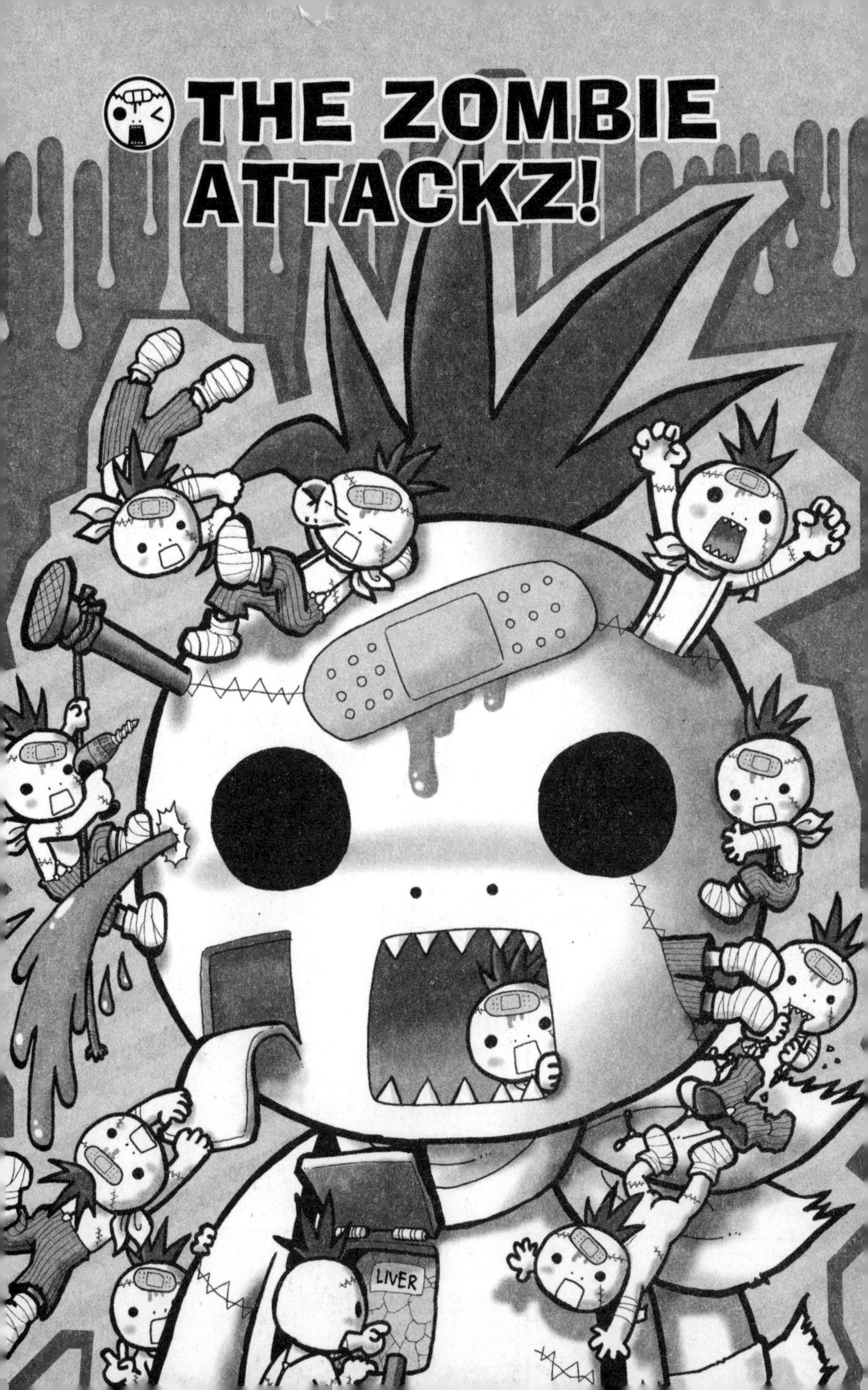
LIVER

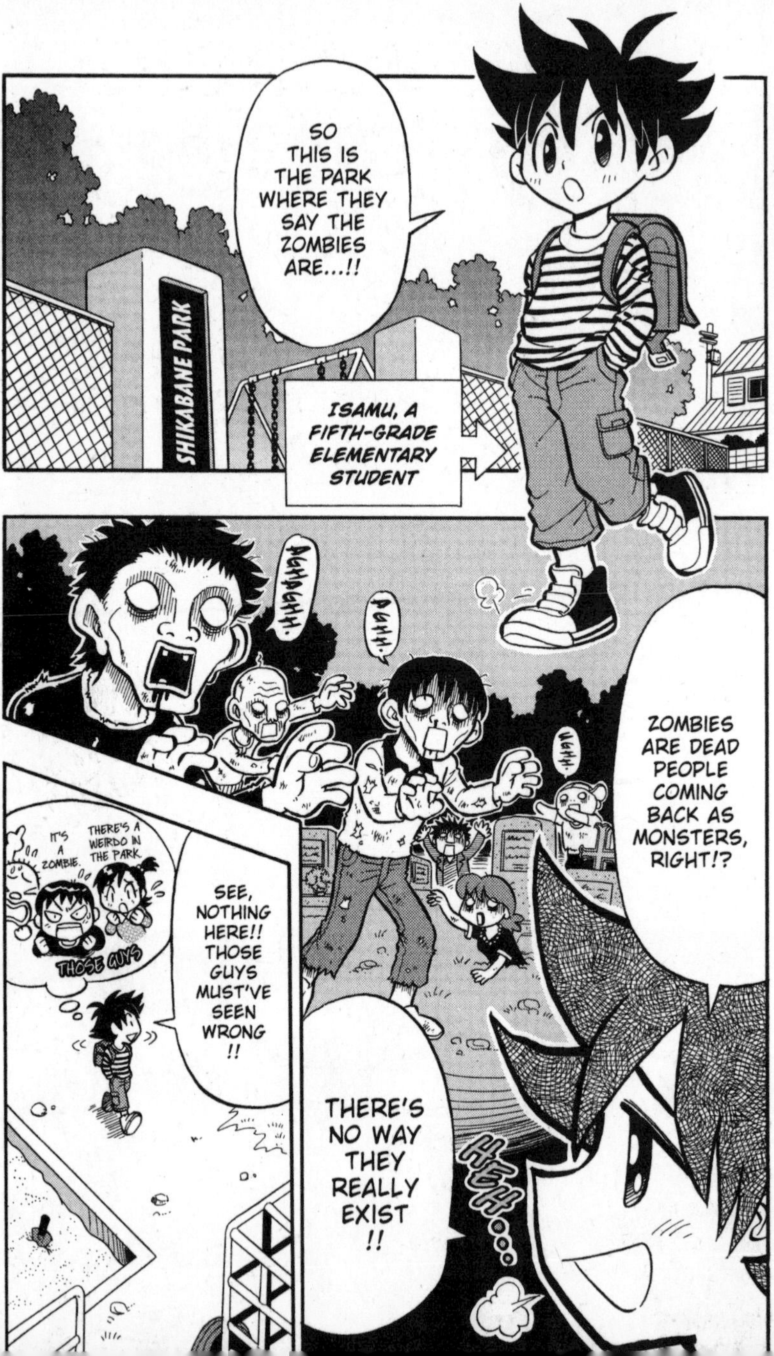
SO THIS IS THE PARK WHERE THEY SAY THE ZOMBIES ARE...!!
ISAMU, A FIFTH-GRADE ELEMENTARY STUDENT
SHIKABANE PARK
ZOMBIES ARE DEAD PEOPLE COMING BACK AS MONSTERS, RIGHT!?
UGHH.
AGHH.
AGHAGHH.
THERE'S NO WAY THEY REALLY EXIST!!
HEH...
SEE, NOTHING HERE!! THOSE GUYS MUST'VE SEEN WRONG!!
THERE'S A WEIRDO IN THE PARK.
IT'S A ZOMBIE.
THOSE GUYS

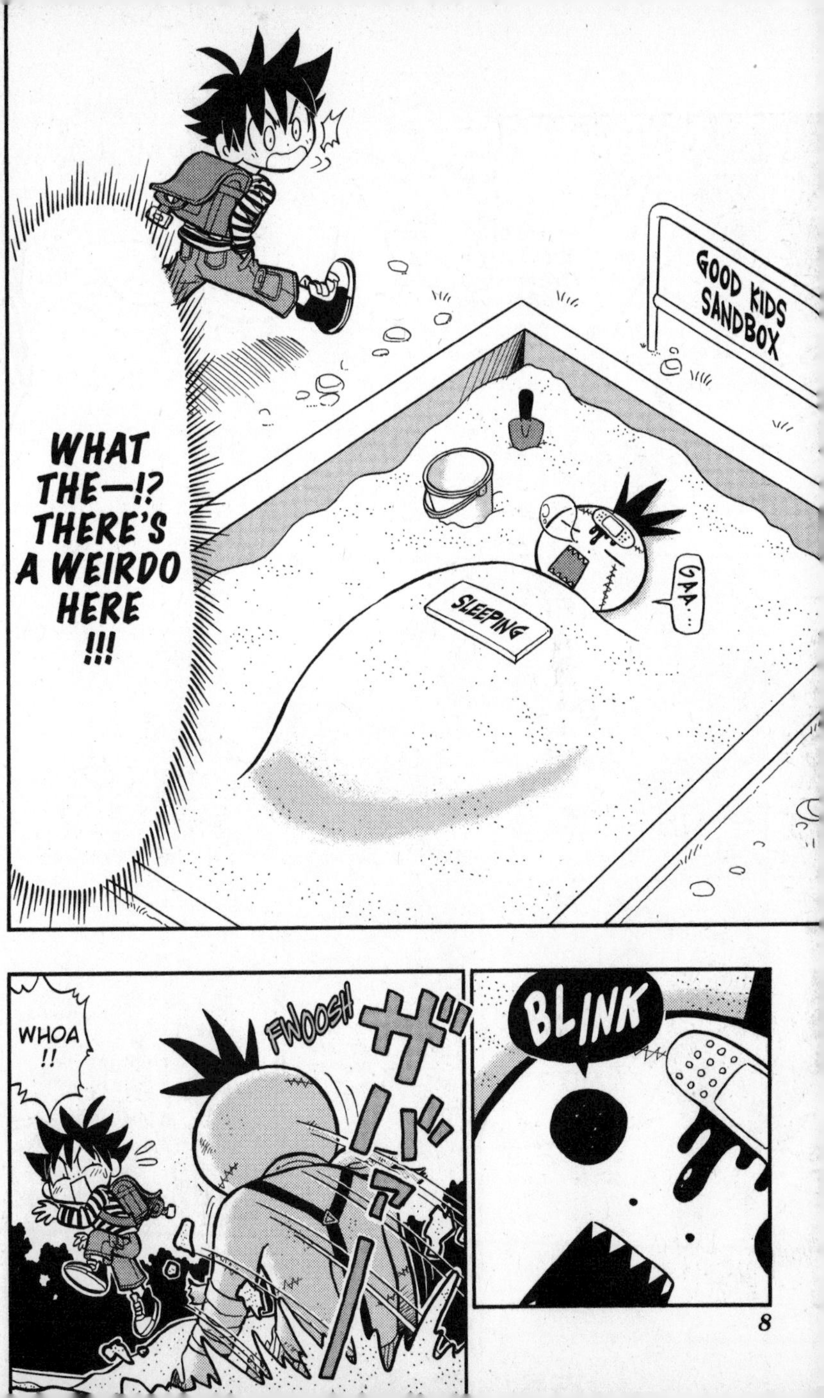

GOOD KIDS SANDBOX
WHAT THE—!? THERE'S A WEIRDO HERE !!!
SLEEPING
GAA...
BLINK
FWOOSH
WHOA !!

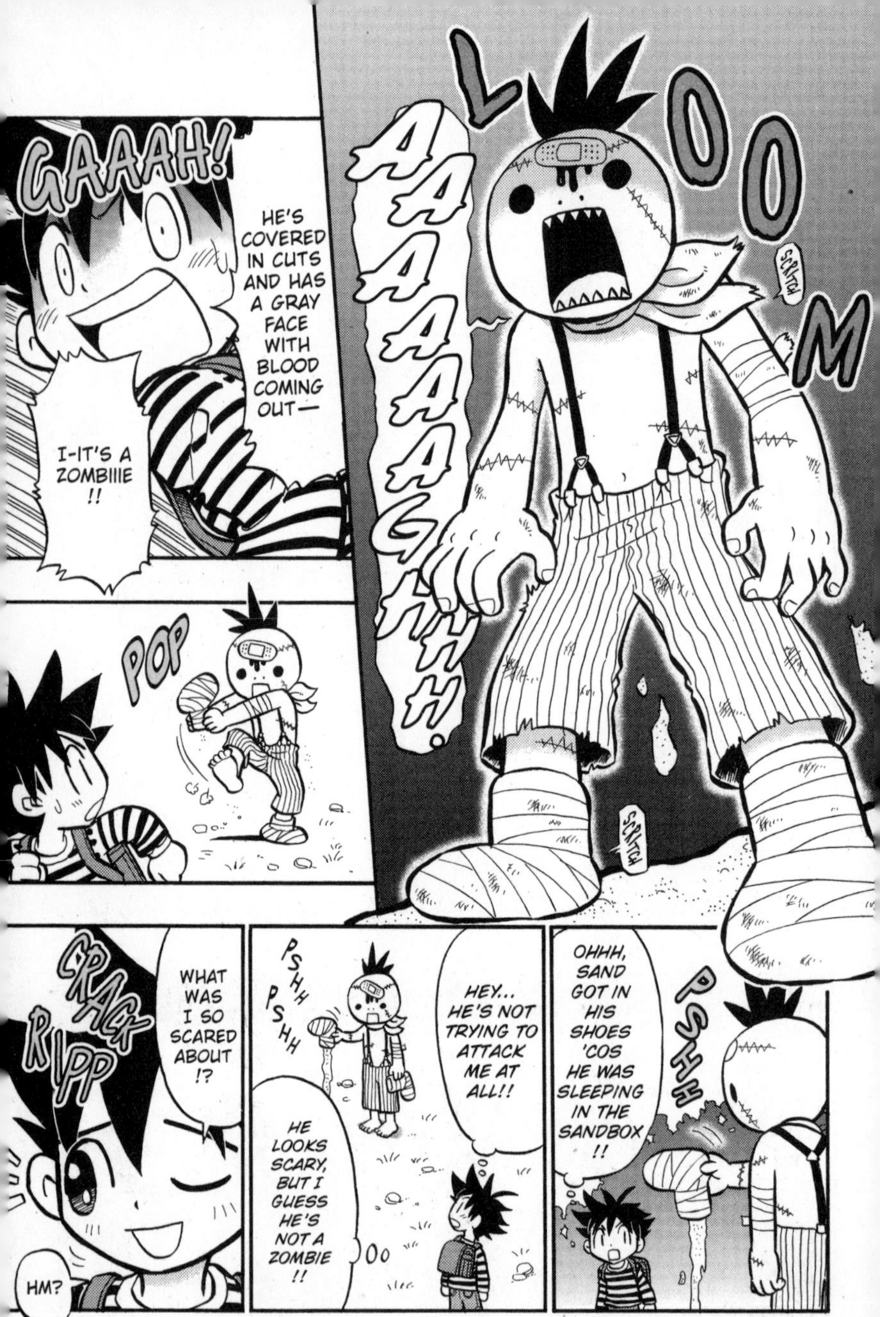
LOOOM
SCRITCH
AAAAAAAGHHH.
SCRITCH
GAAAH!
HE'S COVERED IN CUTS AND HAS A GRAY FACE WITH BLOOD COMING OUT—
I-IT'S A ZOMBIIIE!!
POP
OHHH, SAND GOT IN HIS SHOES 'COS HE WAS SLEEPING IN THE SANDBOX!!
PSHH
PSHH PSHH
HEY... HE'S NOT TRYING TO ATTACK ME AT ALL!!
HE LOOKS SCARY, BUT I GUESS HE'S NOT A ZOMBIE!!
CRACK RIPP
WHAT WAS I SO SCARED ABOUT!?
HM?

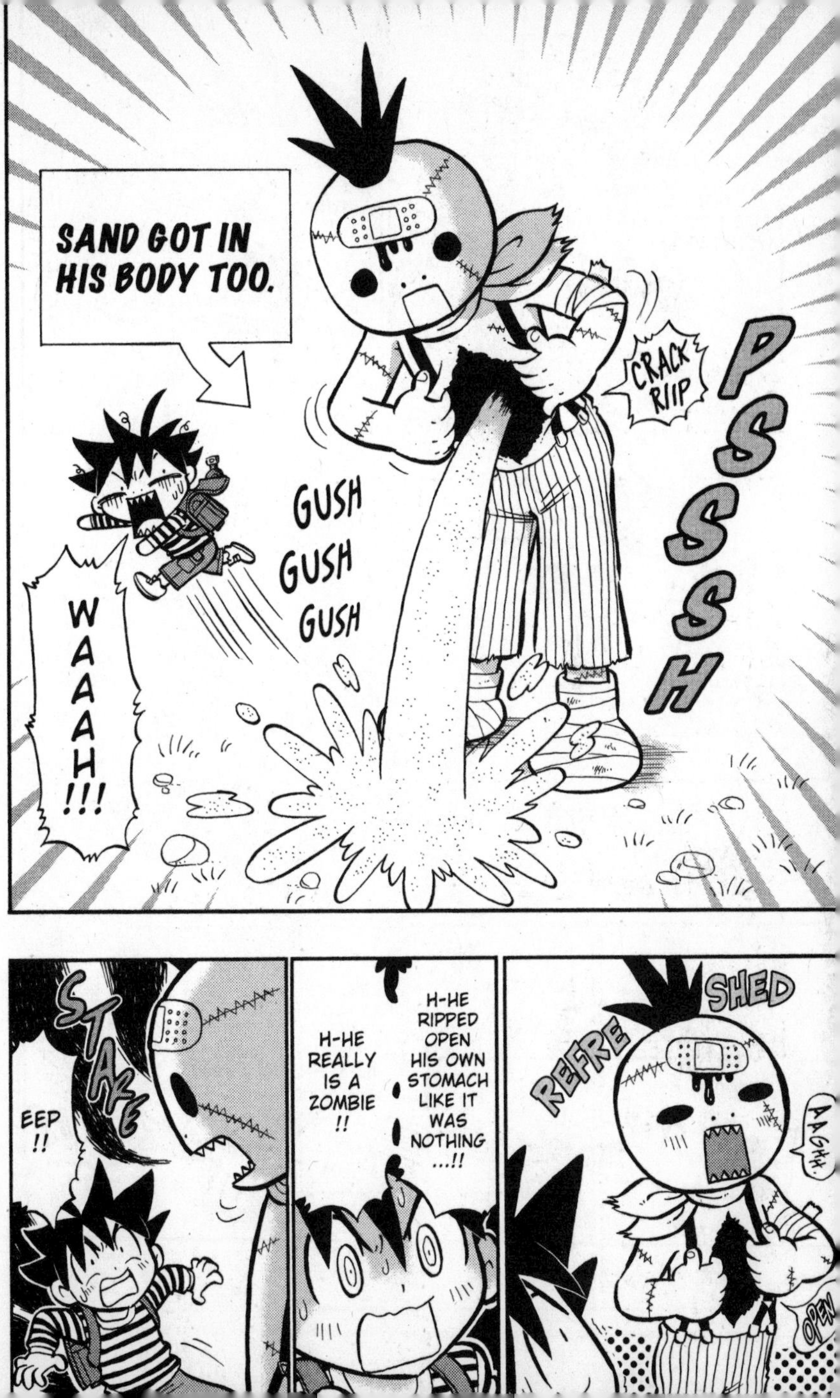
PSSSH
CRACK RIIP
SAND GOT IN HIS BODY TOO.
GUSH GUSH GUSH
WAAAAH!!!
REFRESHED
AAGHH.
OPEN
H-HE RIPPED OPEN HIS OWN STOMACH LIKE IT WAS NOTHING ...!!
H-HE REALLY IS A ZOMBIE!!
STARE
EEP!!

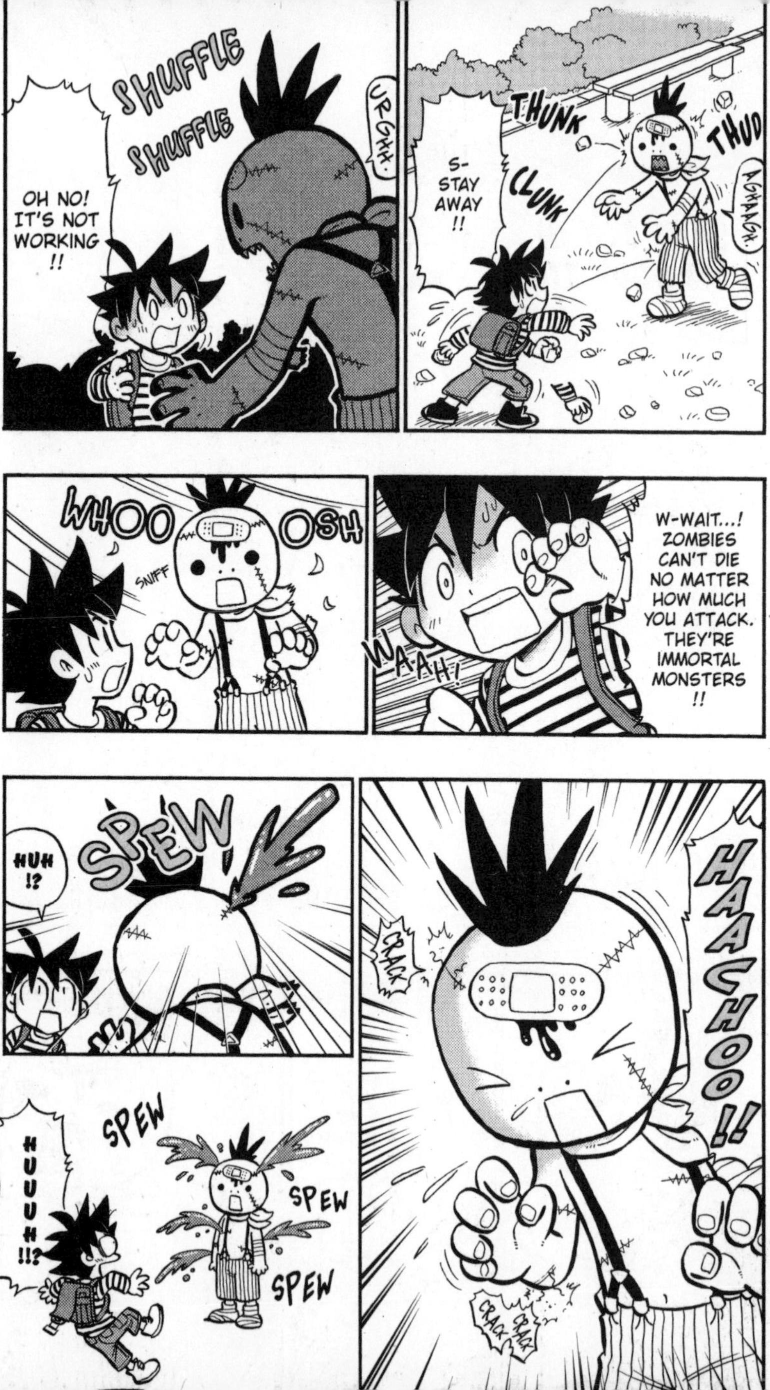
S-STAY AWAY !!
THUNK
CLUNK
THUD
AGHAAAGH.
URGHH.
SHUFFLE
SHUFFLE
OH NO! IT'S NOT WORKING !!
W-WAIT...! ZOMBIES CAN'T DIE NO MATTER HOW MUCH YOU ATTACK. THEY'RE IMMORTAL MONSTERS !!
WAAH!
WHOO OSH
SNIFF
HAACHOO !!
CRACK
CRACK CRACK
HUH !?
SPEW
HUUUUH !!?
SPEW
SPEW
SPEW

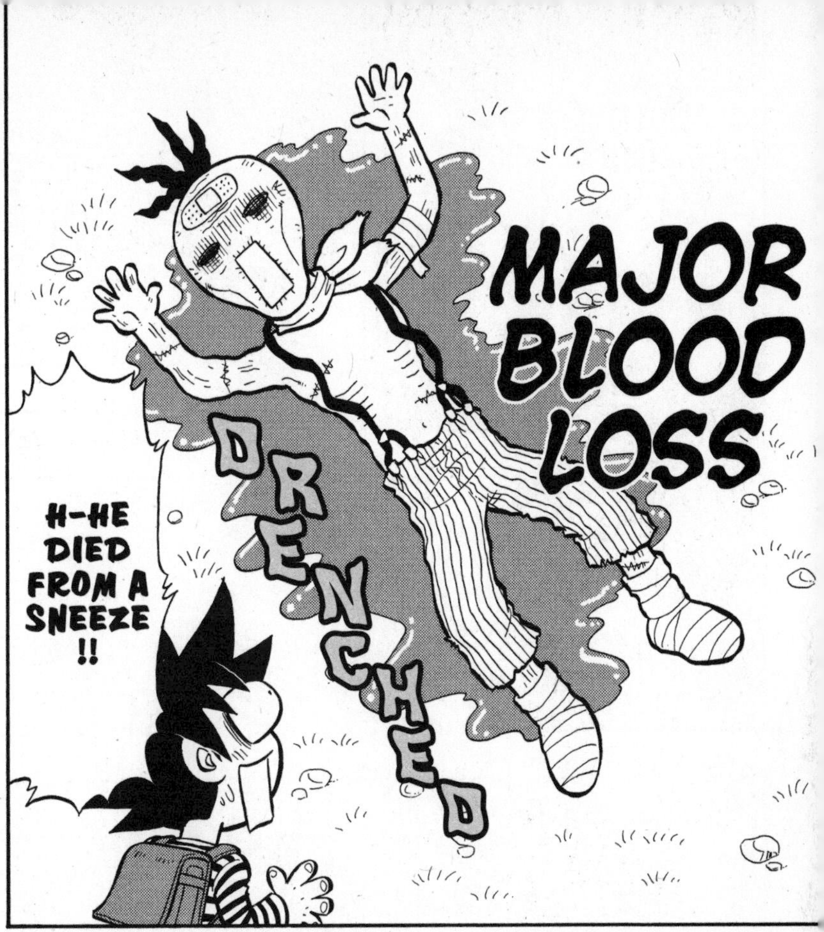
MAJOR BLOOD LOSS
DRENCHED
H-HE DIED FROM A SNEEZE!!

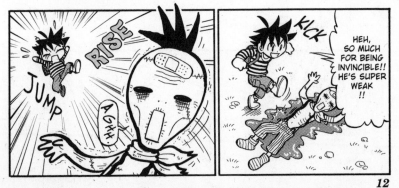

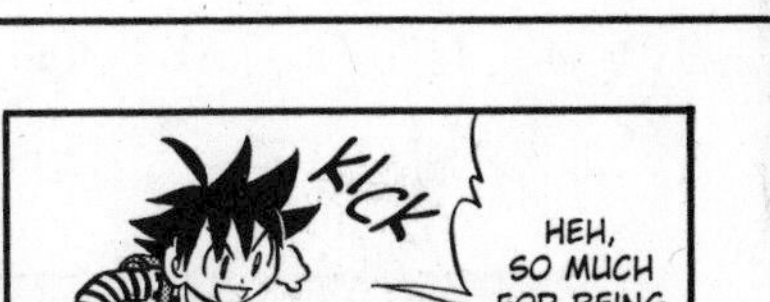
KICK
HEH, SO MUCH FOR BEING INVINCIBLE!! HE'S SUPER WEAK!!

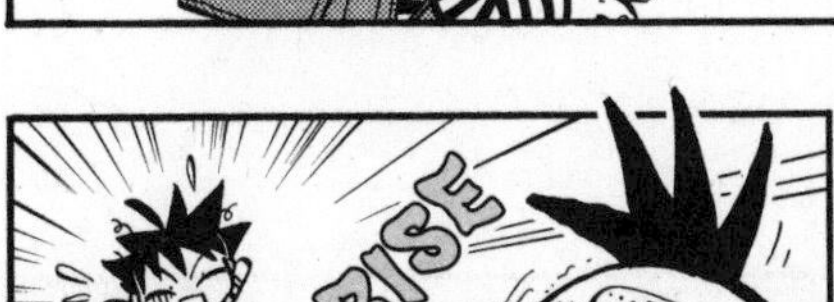
RISE
JUMP
AGHH.

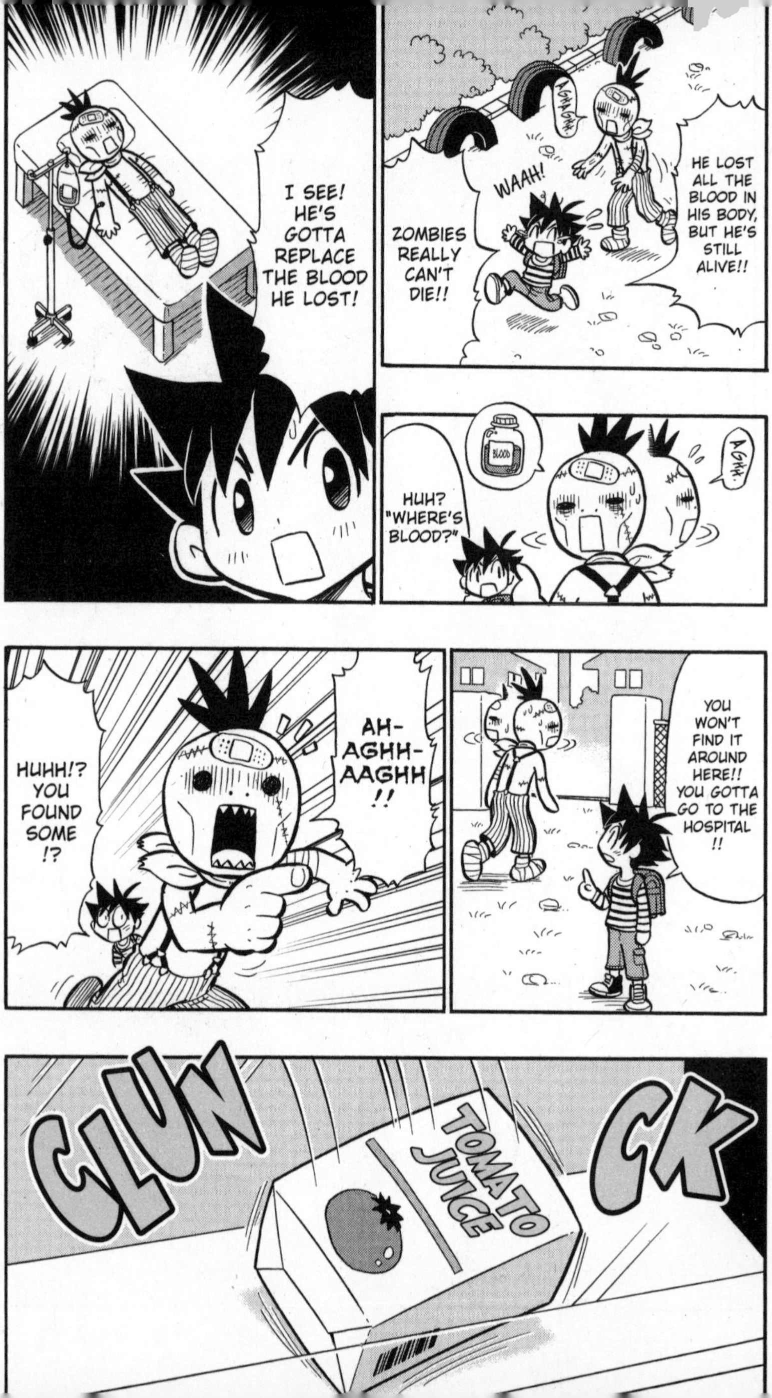
AGHAGHH.
HE LOST ALL THE BLOOD IN HIS BODY, BUT HE'S STILL ALIVE!!
WAAH!
ZOMBIES REALLY CAN'T DIE!!
AGHH.
BLOOD
HUH? "WHERE'S BLOOD?"
I SEE! HE'S GOTTA REPLACE THE BLOOD HE LOST!
YOU WON'T FIND IT AROUND HERE!! YOU GOTTA GO TO THE HOSPITAL !!
AH-AGHH-AAGHH !!
HUHH!? YOU FOUND SOME !?
CLUN CK
TOMATO JUICE

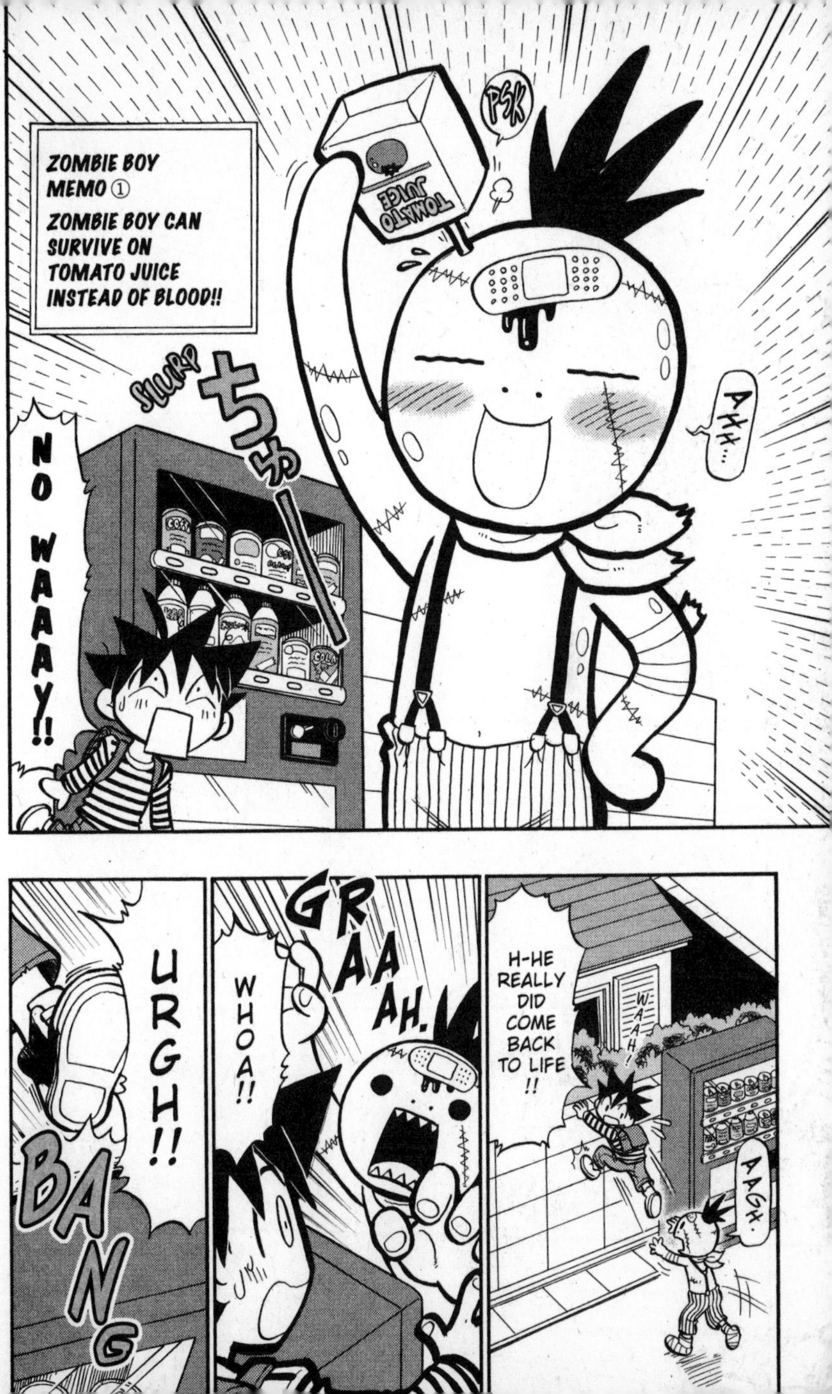
PSK
TOMATO JUICE
AHH...
ZOMBIE BOY MEMO ①
ZOMBIE BOY CAN SURVIVE ON TOMATO JUICE INSTEAD OF BLOOD!!
SLURP
ちゅ
NO WAAAAY!!
H-HE REALLY DID COME BACK TO LIFE!!
WAAAH!
AAGH.
GRAAAH.
WHOA!!
URGH!!
BANG

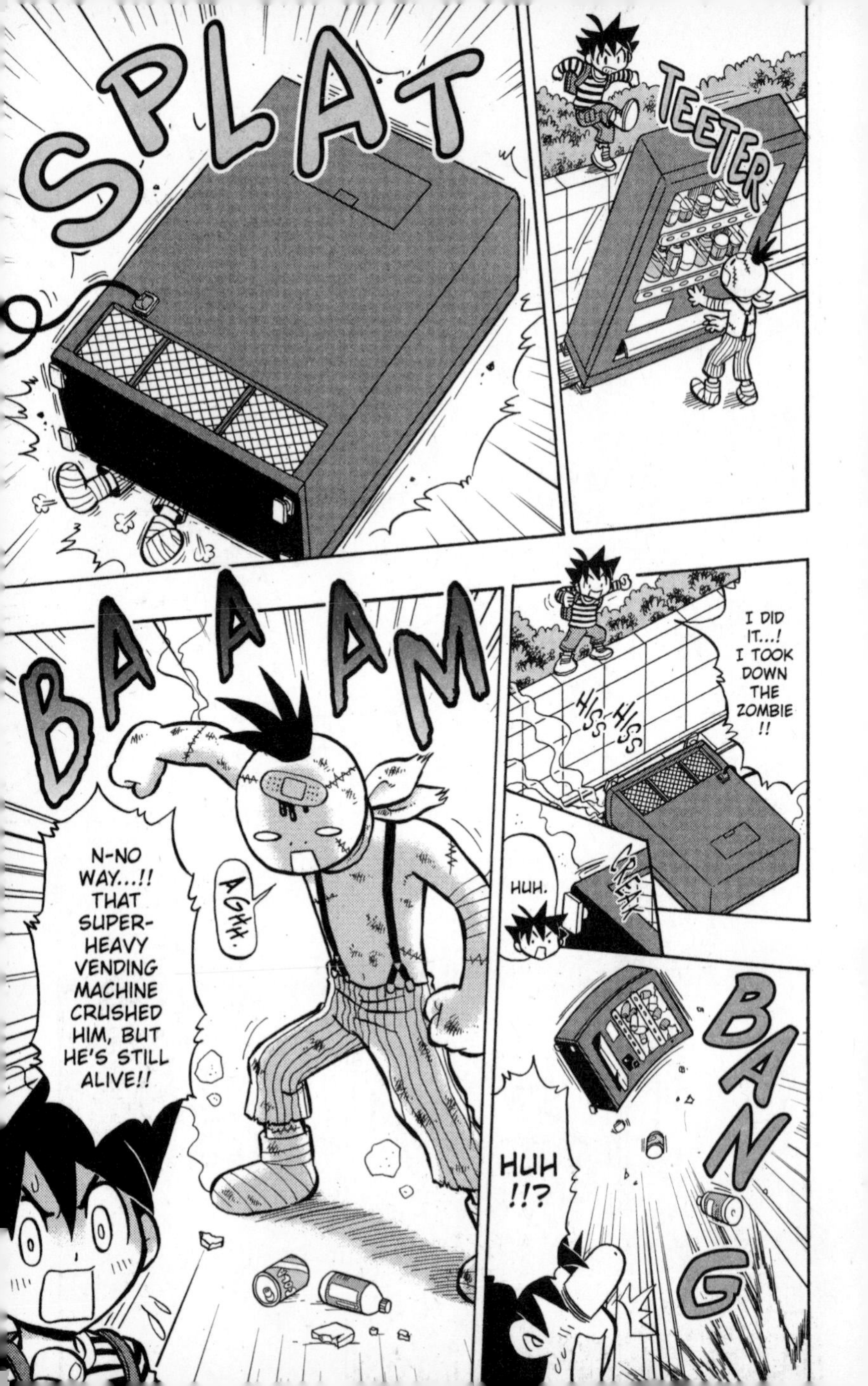
TEETER
SPLAT
I DID IT...! I TOOK DOWN THE ZOMBIE !!
HISS HISS
CREAK
HUH.
BANG
HUH !!?
BAAAM
AGHH.
N-NO WAY...!! THAT SUPER-HEAVY VENDING MACHINE CRUSHED HIM, BUT HE'S STILL ALIVE!!

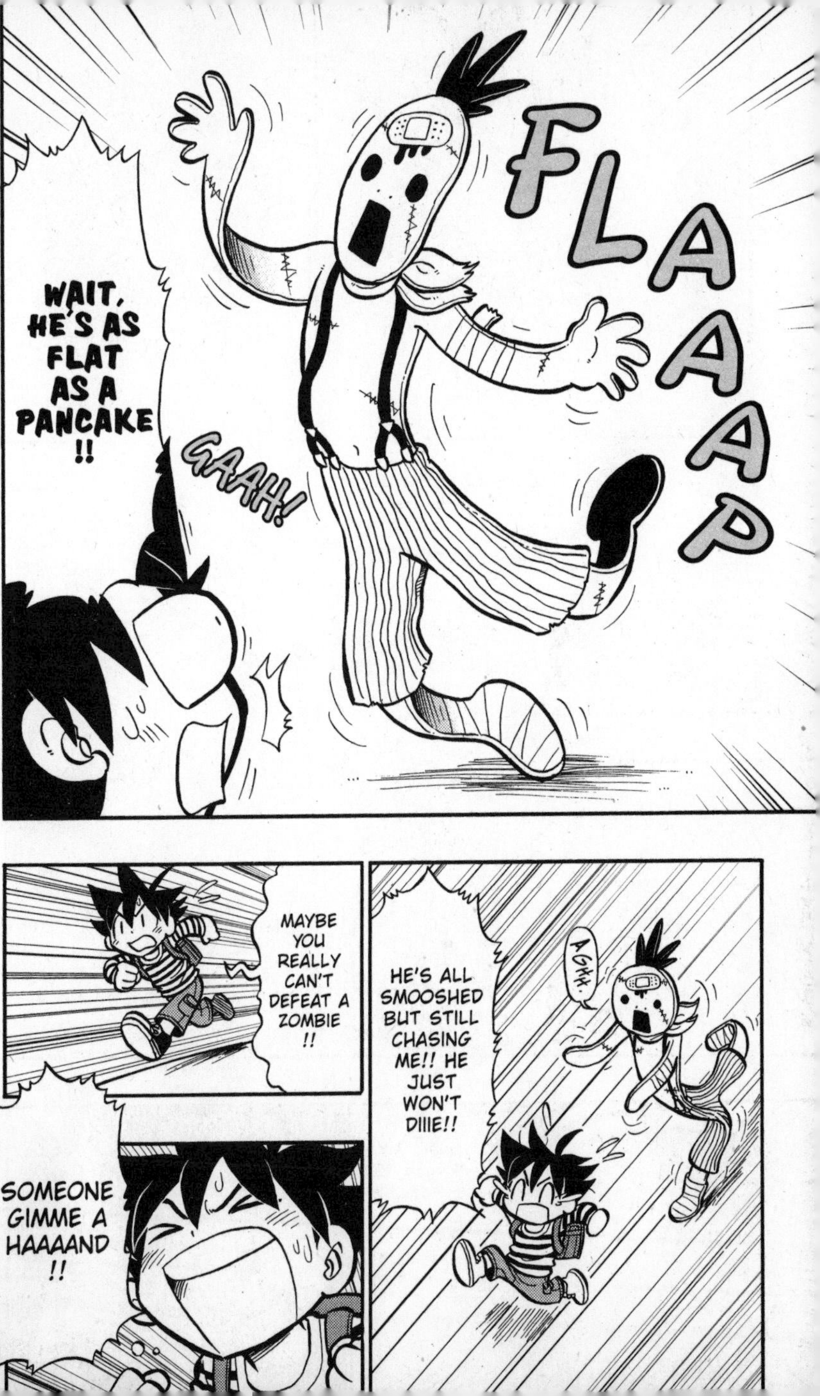
FLAAAAP
WAIT, HE'S AS FLAT AS A PANCAKE!!
GAAH!
AGHH.
HE'S ALL SMOOSHED BUT STILL CHASING ME!! HE JUST WON'T DIIIE!!
MAYBE YOU REALLY CAN'T DEFEAT A ZOMBIE!!
SOMEONE GIMME A HAAAAND!!

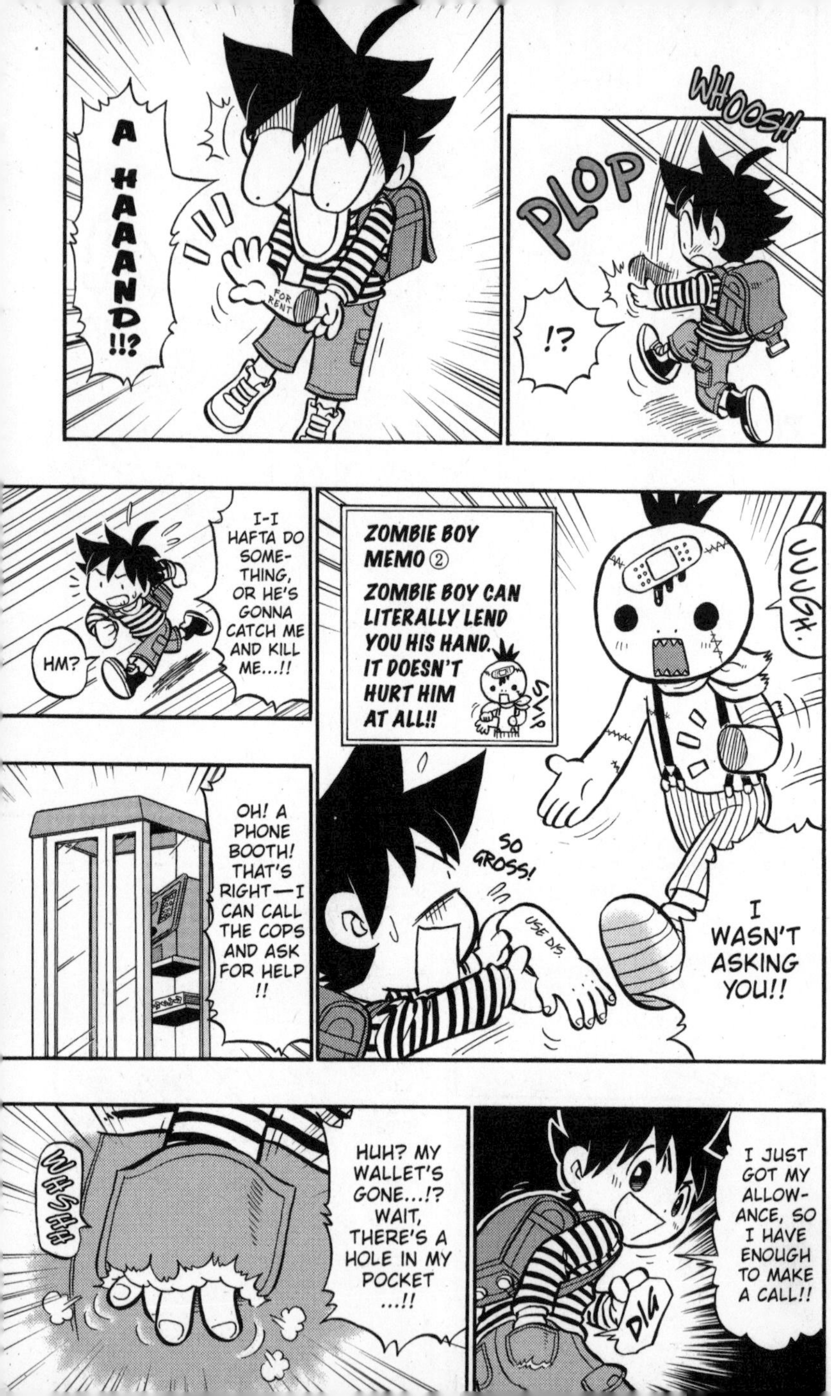
WHOOSH
PLOP
!?
A HAAAAND!!?
FOR RENT
UUUGH.
ZOMBIE BOY MEMO ②
ZOMBIE BOY CAN LITERALLY LEND YOU HIS HAND. IT DOESN'T HURT HIM AT ALL!!
SLIP
SO GROSS!
USE DIS.
I WASN'T ASKING YOU!!
I-I HAFTA DO SOME-THING, OR HE'S GONNA CATCH ME AND KILL ME...!!
HM?
OH! A PHONE BOOTH! THAT'S RIGHT—I CAN CALL THE COPS AND ASK FOR HELP!!
I JUST GOT MY ALLOW-ANCE, SO I HAVE ENOUGH TO MAKE A CALL!!
DIG
HUH? MY WALLET'S GONE...!? WAIT, THERE'S A HOLE IN MY POCKET...!!
WHSHH

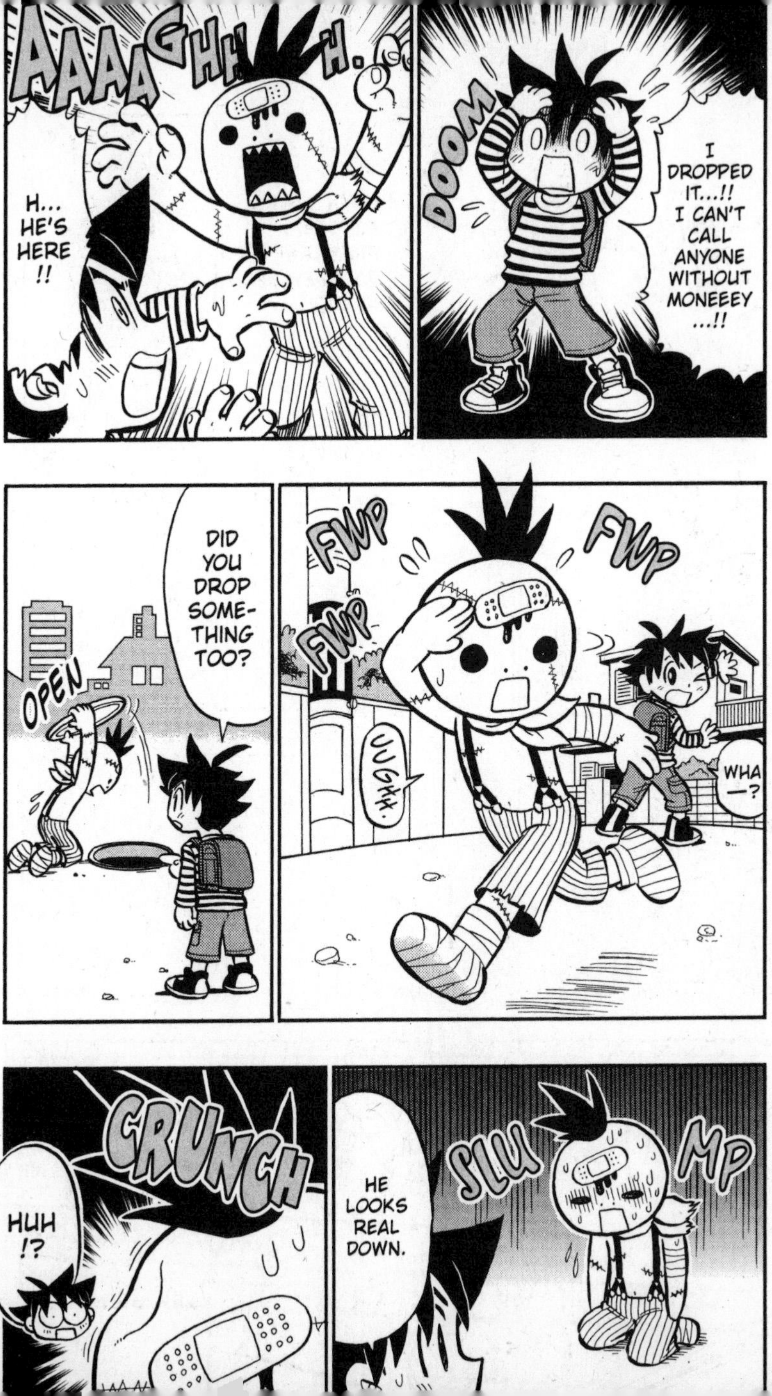
DOOM
I DROPPED IT...!! I CAN'T CALL ANYONE WITHOUT MONEEEY...!!
AAAAGHHHH.
H... HE'S HERE !!
FWP
FWP
FWP
UUGHH.
WHA—?
OPEN
DID YOU DROP SOME-THING TOO?
SLUMP
HE LOOKS REAL DOWN.
CRUNCH
HUH !?

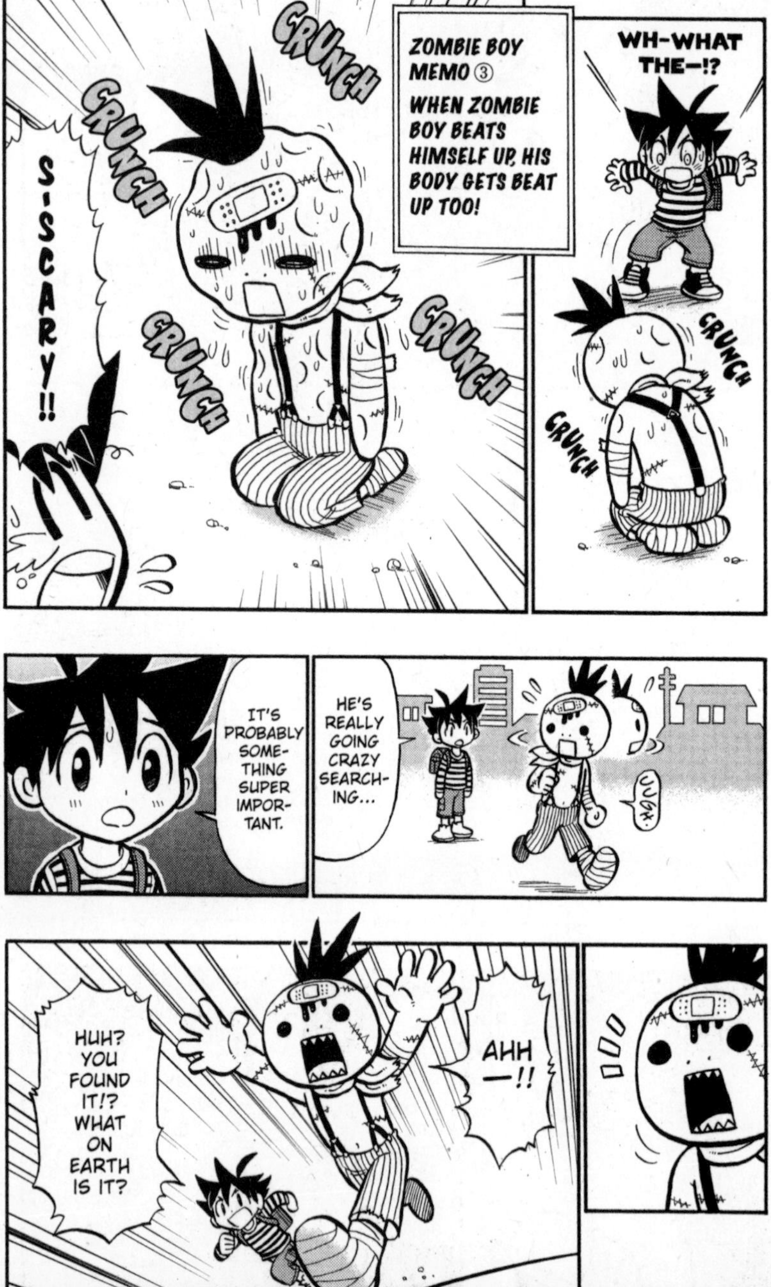
WH-WHAT THE–!?
CRUNCH
CRUNCH
CRUNCH
ZOMBIE BOY MEMO ③
WHEN ZOMBIE BOY BEATS HIMSELF UP, HIS BODY GETS BEAT UP TOO!
CRUNCH
S-SCARY!!
CRUNCH
CRUNCH
CRUNCH
HE'S REALLY GOING CRAZY SEARCHING...
IT'S PROBABLY SOMETHING SUPER IMPORTANT.
AHH—!!
HUH? YOU FOUND IT!? WHAT ON EARTH IS IT?

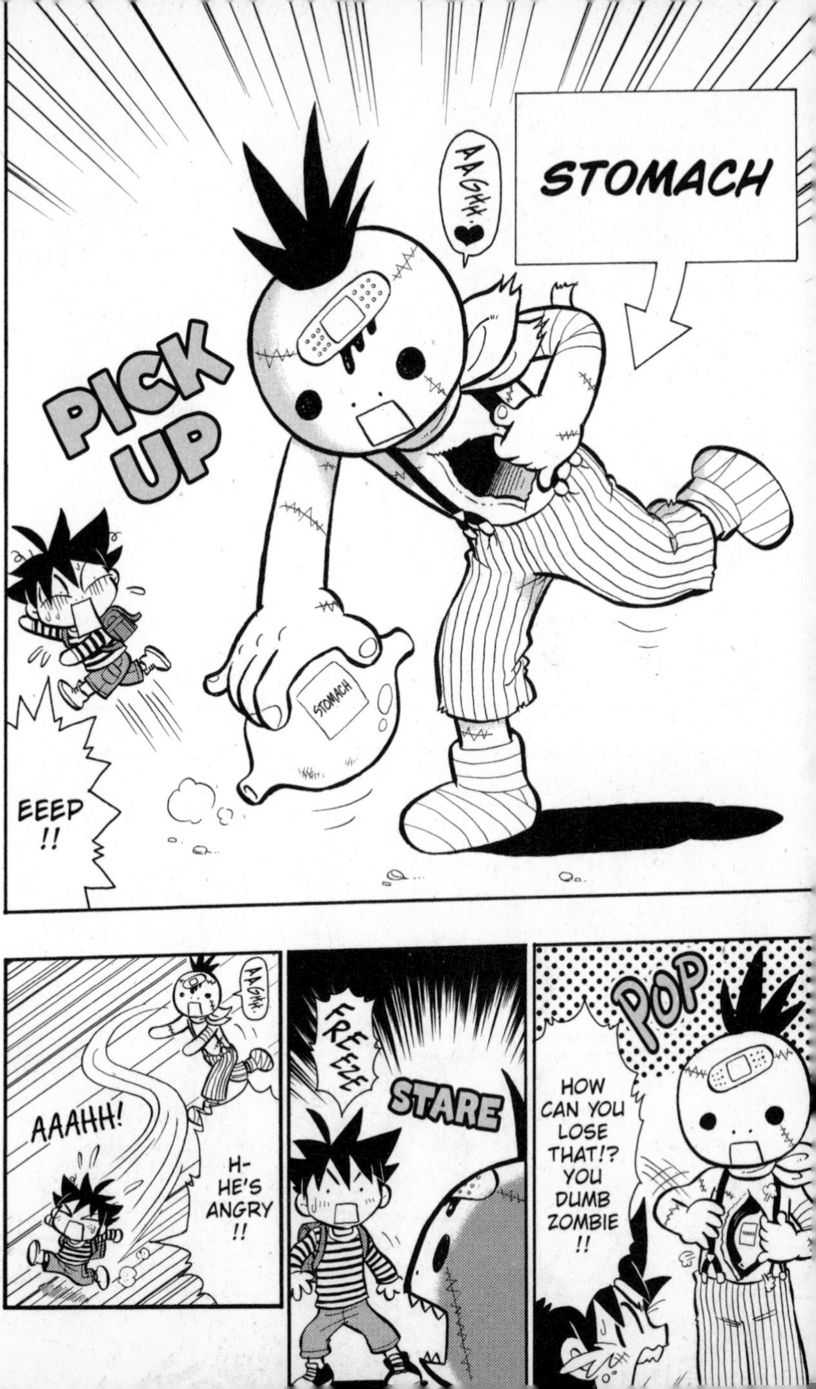
STOMACH
AAGHH.♥
PICK UP
STOMACH
EEEP !!
POP
HOW CAN YOU LOSE THAT!? YOU DUMB ZOMBIE !!
FREEZE
STARE
AAGHH.
AAAHH!
H- HE'S ANGRY !!

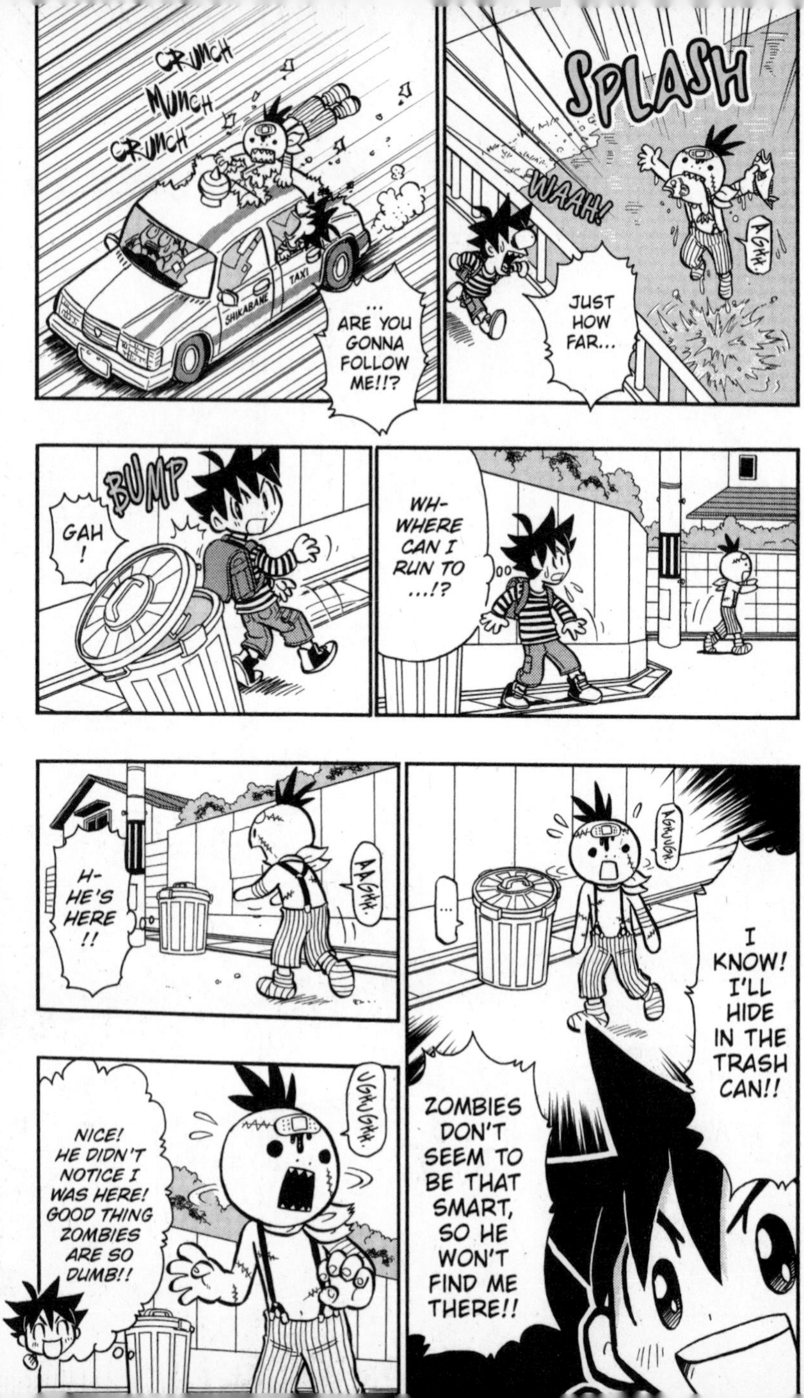
SPLASH
WAAH!
AGHK..
JUST HOW FAR...
CRUNCH
MUNCH
CRUNCH
... ARE YOU GONNA FOLLOW ME!!?
WH-WHERE CAN I RUN TO ...!?
BUMP
GAH!
AGHUGH..
...
I KNOW! I'LL HIDE IN THE TRASH CAN!!
ZOMBIES DON'T SEEM TO BE THAT SMART, SO HE WON'T FIND ME THERE!!
H-HE'S HERE!!
AAGHK..
UGHUGHK..
NICE! HE DIDN'T NOTICE I WAS HERE! GOOD THING ZOMBIES ARE SO DUMB!!

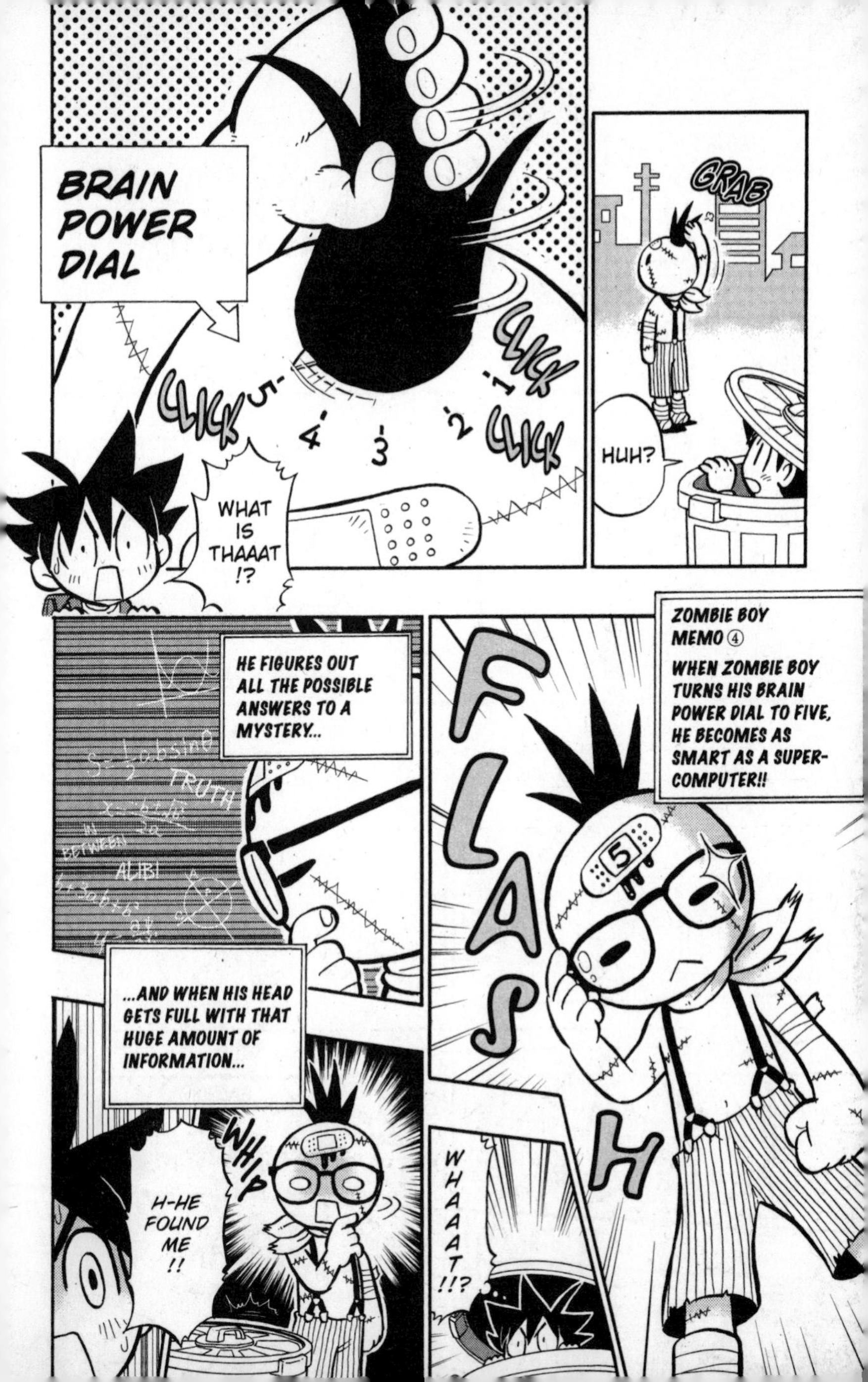

GRAB
HUH?
BRAIN POWER DIAL
CLICK
CLICK
CLICK
1
2
3
4
5
WHAT IS THAAAT!?
ZOMBIE BOY MEMO ④
WHEN ZOMBIE BOY TURNS HIS BRAIN POWER DIAL TO FIVE, HE BECOMES AS SMART AS A SUPER-COMPUTER!!
FLASH
5
HE FIGURES OUT ALL THE POSSIBLE ANSWERS TO A MYSTERY...
TRUTH
IN BETWEEN
ALIBI
...AND WHEN HIS HEAD GETS FULL WITH THAT HUGE AMOUNT OF INFORMATION...
WHIP
H-HE FOUND ME!!
WHAAAAT!!?

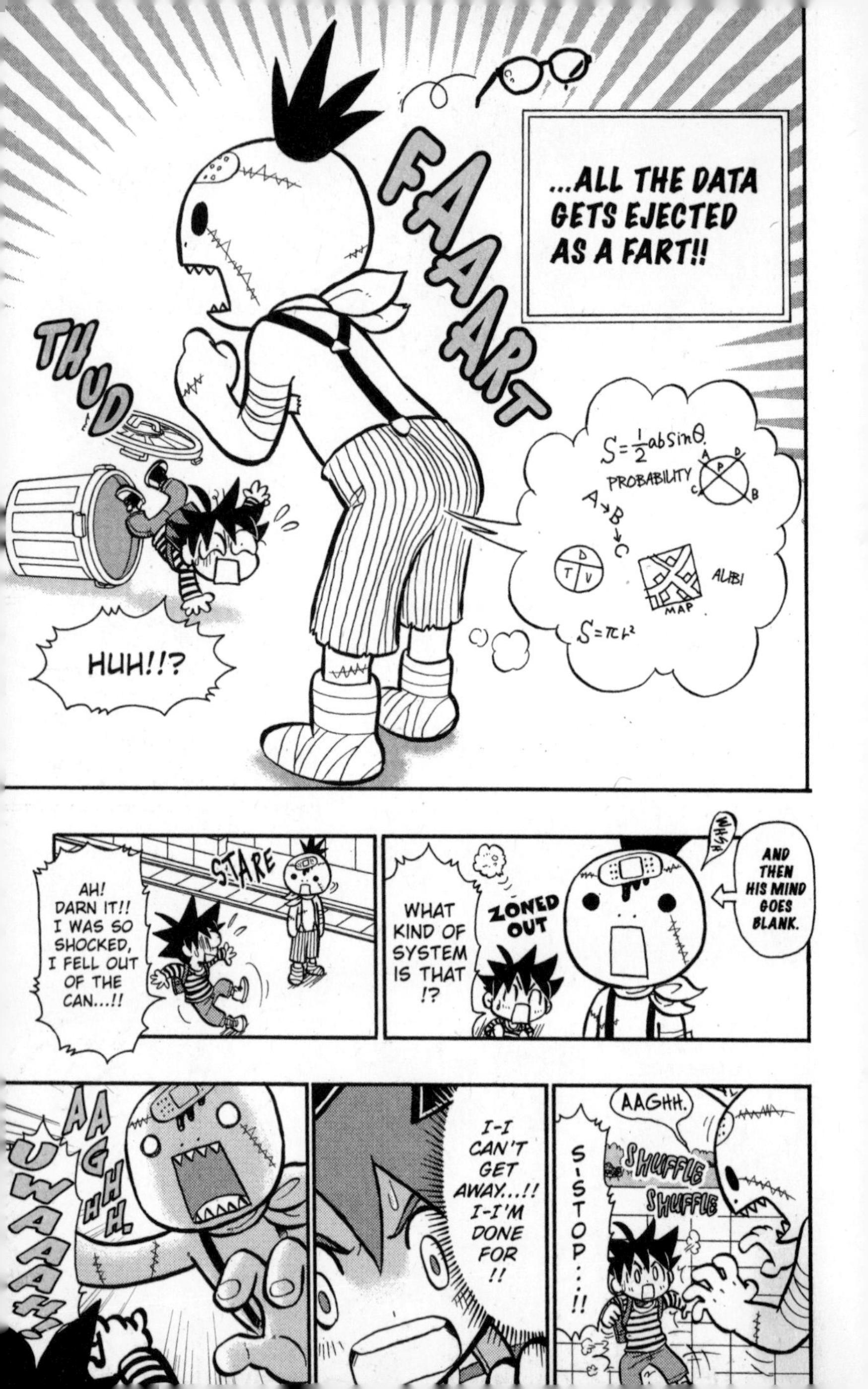
...ALL THE DATA GETS EJECTED AS A FART!!
FAAART
$S=\frac{1}{2}ab\sin\theta$
PROBABILITY
A P D C B
A→B→C
D T V
ALIBI
MAP
$S=\pi r^2$
THUD
HUH!!?
WHSH
AND THEN HIS MIND GOES BLANK.
ZONED OUT
WHAT KIND OF SYSTEM IS THAT!?
STARE
AH! DARN IT!! I WAS SO SHOCKED, I FELL OUT OF THE CAN...!!
AAGHH.
SHUFFLE
SHUFFLE
S-STOP...!!
I-I CAN'T GET AWAY...!! I-I'M DONE FOR!!
AAGHH
UWAAAAH!

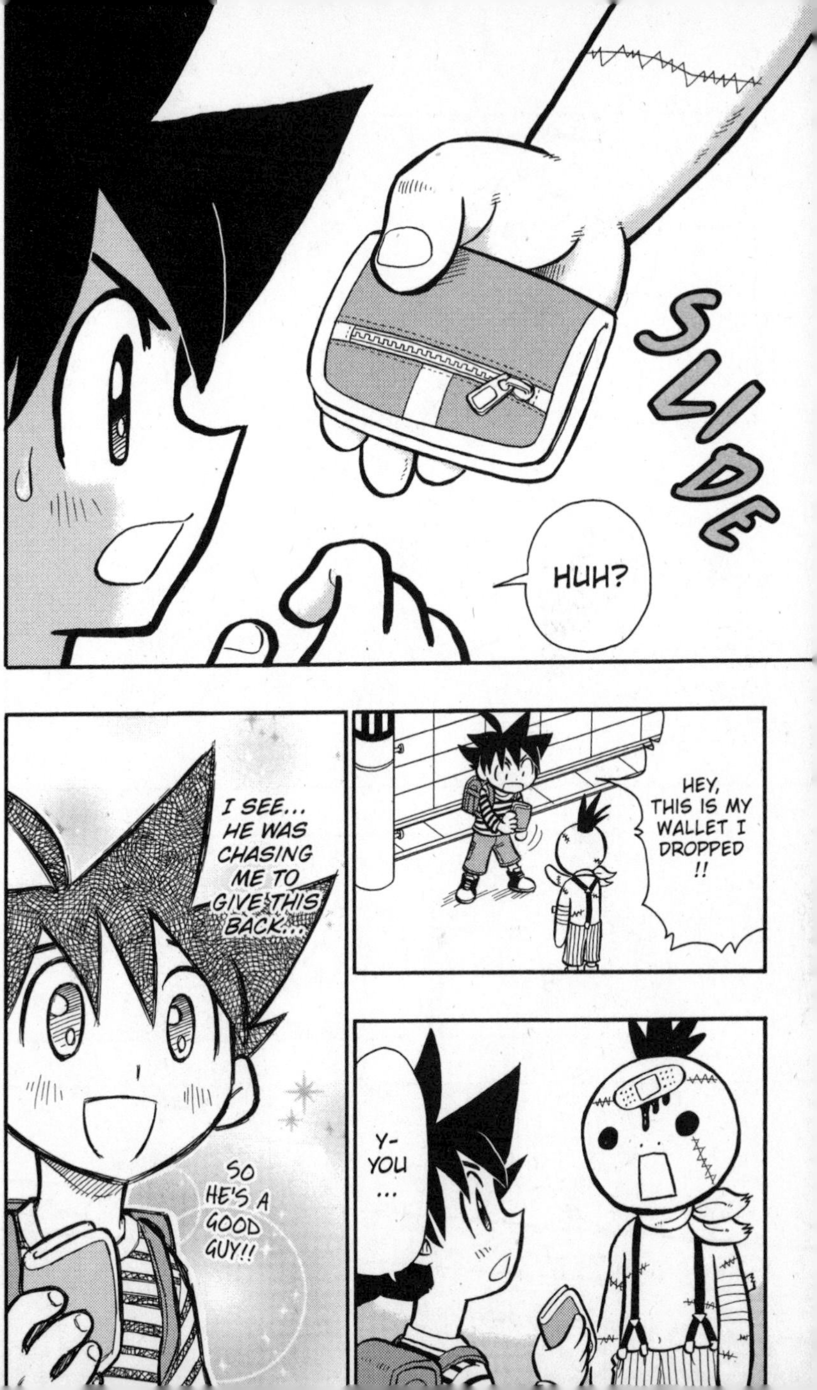
SLIDE
HUH?
HEY, THIS IS MY WALLET I DROPPED!!
Y-YOU...
I SEE... HE WAS CHASING ME TO GIVE THIS BACK...
SO HE'S A GOOD GUY!!

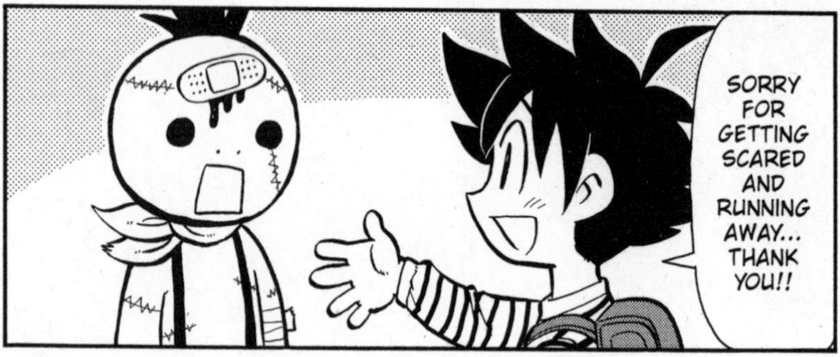
SORRY FOR GETTING SCARED AND RUNNING AWAY... THANK YOU!!

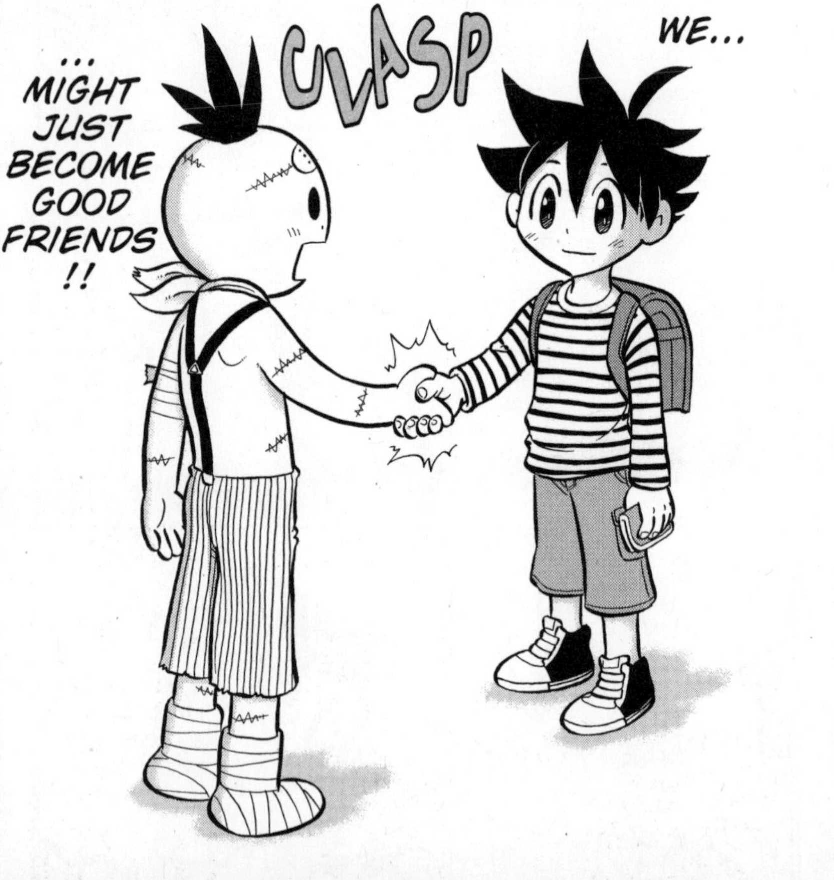
WE...
CLASP
...MIGHT JUST BECOME GOOD FRIENDS!!

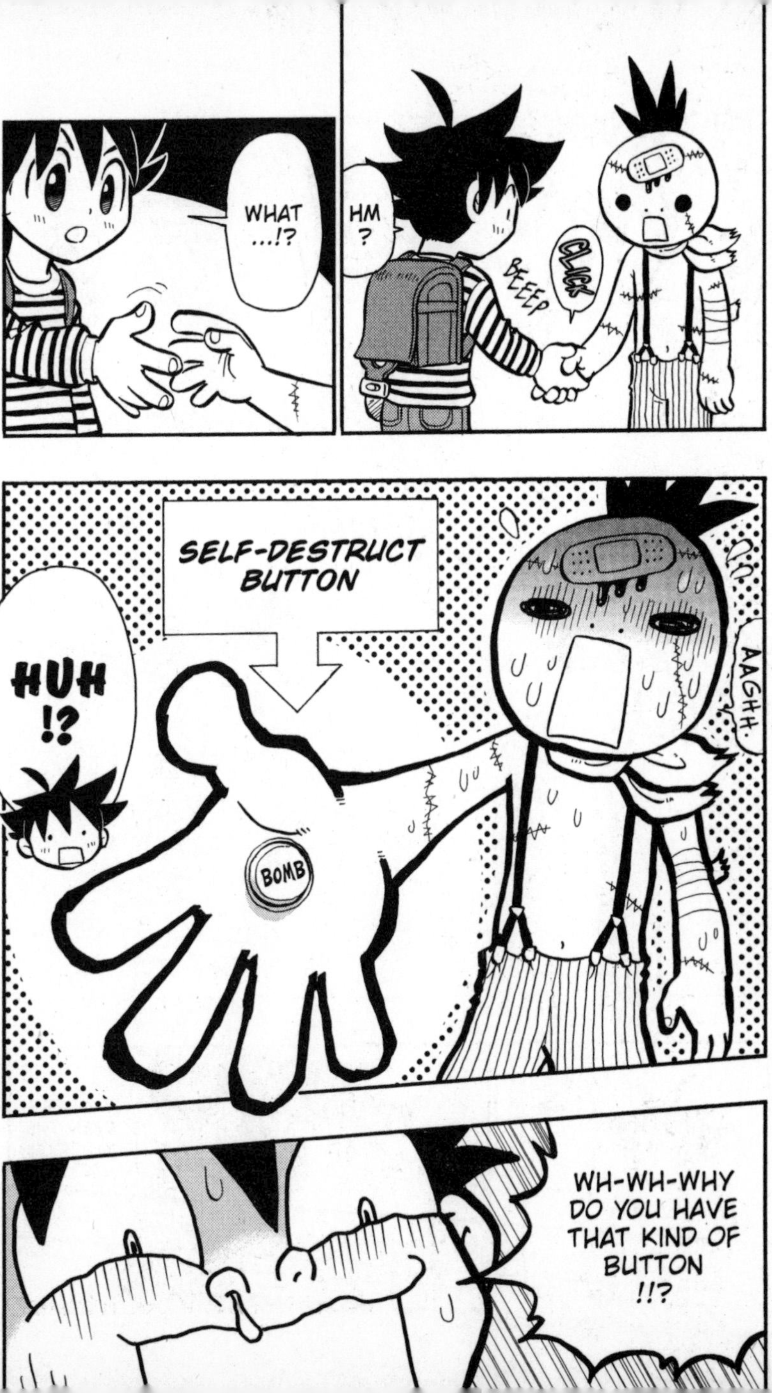
HM ?
CLICK
BEEEEP
WHAT ...!?
AAGHH.
SELF-DESTRUCT BUTTON
HUH !?
BOMB
WH-WH-WHY DO YOU HAVE THAT KIND OF BUTTON !!?

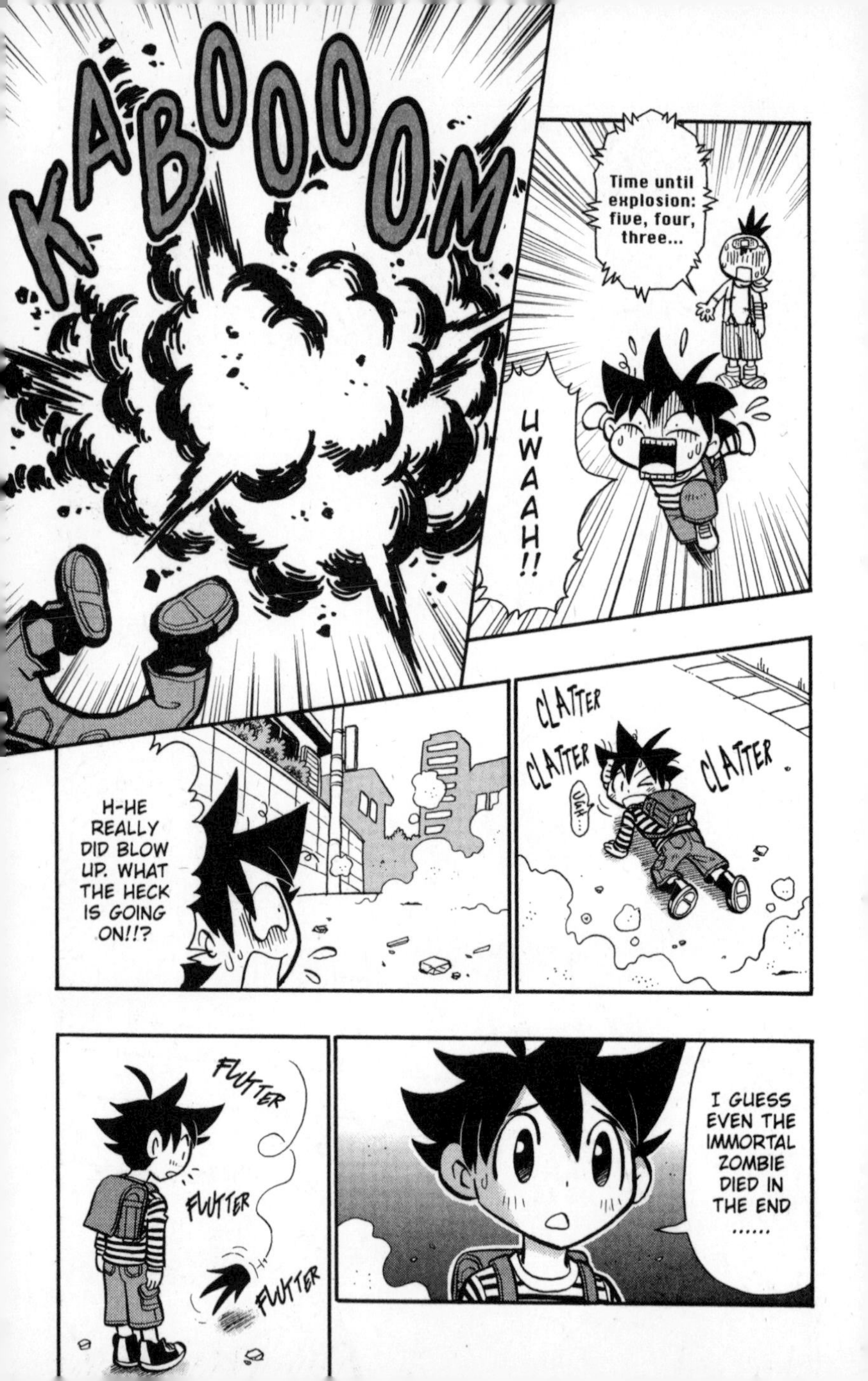

Time until explosion: five, four, three...
UWAAAH!!
KABOOOOM
CLATTER
CLATTER
Ugh...
CLATTER
H-HE REALLY DID BLOW UP. WHAT THE HECK IS GOING ON!!?
I GUESS EVEN THE IMMORTAL ZOMBIE DIED IN THE END ......
FLUTTER
FLUTTER
FLUTTER

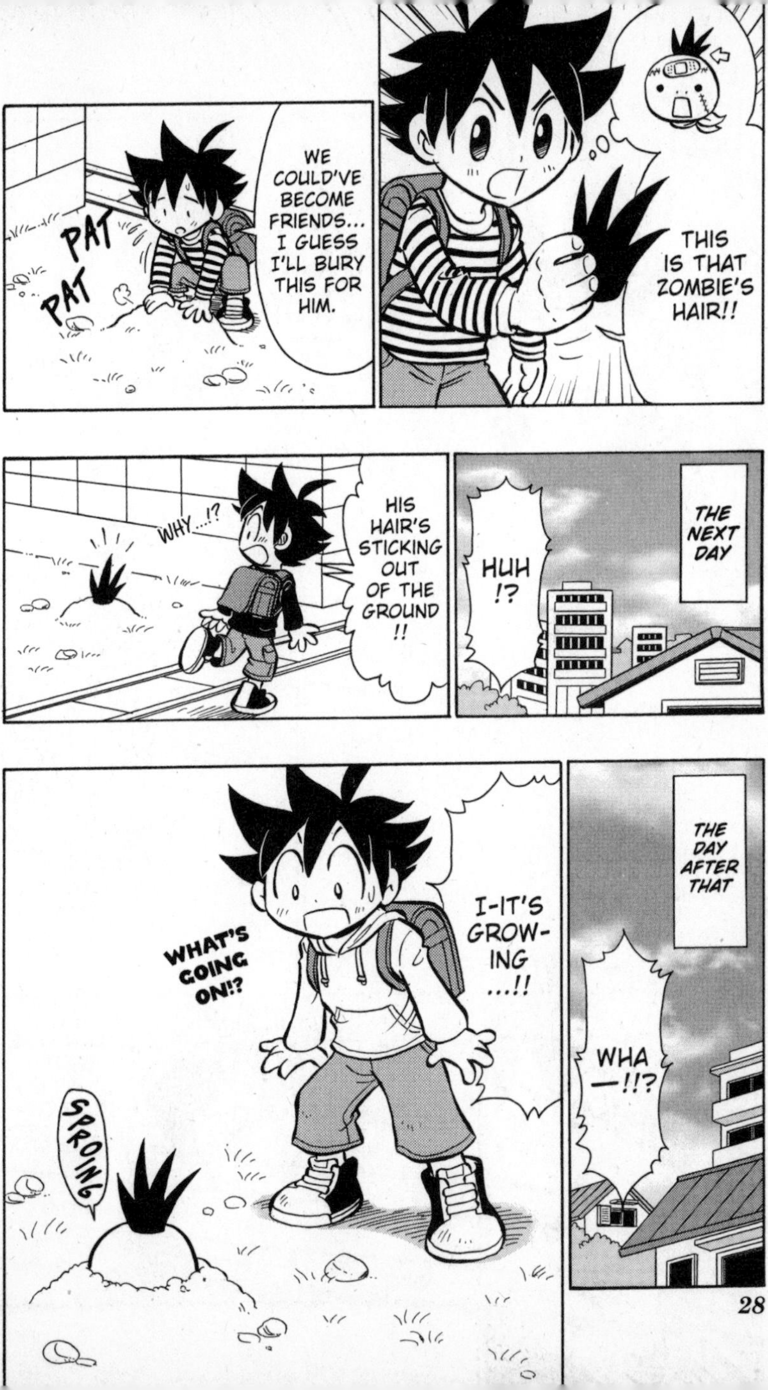
THIS IS THAT ZOMBIE'S HAIR!!
WE COULD'VE BECOME FRIENDS... I GUESS I'LL BURY THIS FOR HIM.
PAT PAT
THE NEXT DAY
HUH!?
HIS HAIR'S STICKING OUT OF THE GROUND!!
WHY...!?
THE DAY AFTER THAT
WHA—!!?
I-IT'S GROWING...!!
WHAT'S GOING ON!?
SPROING

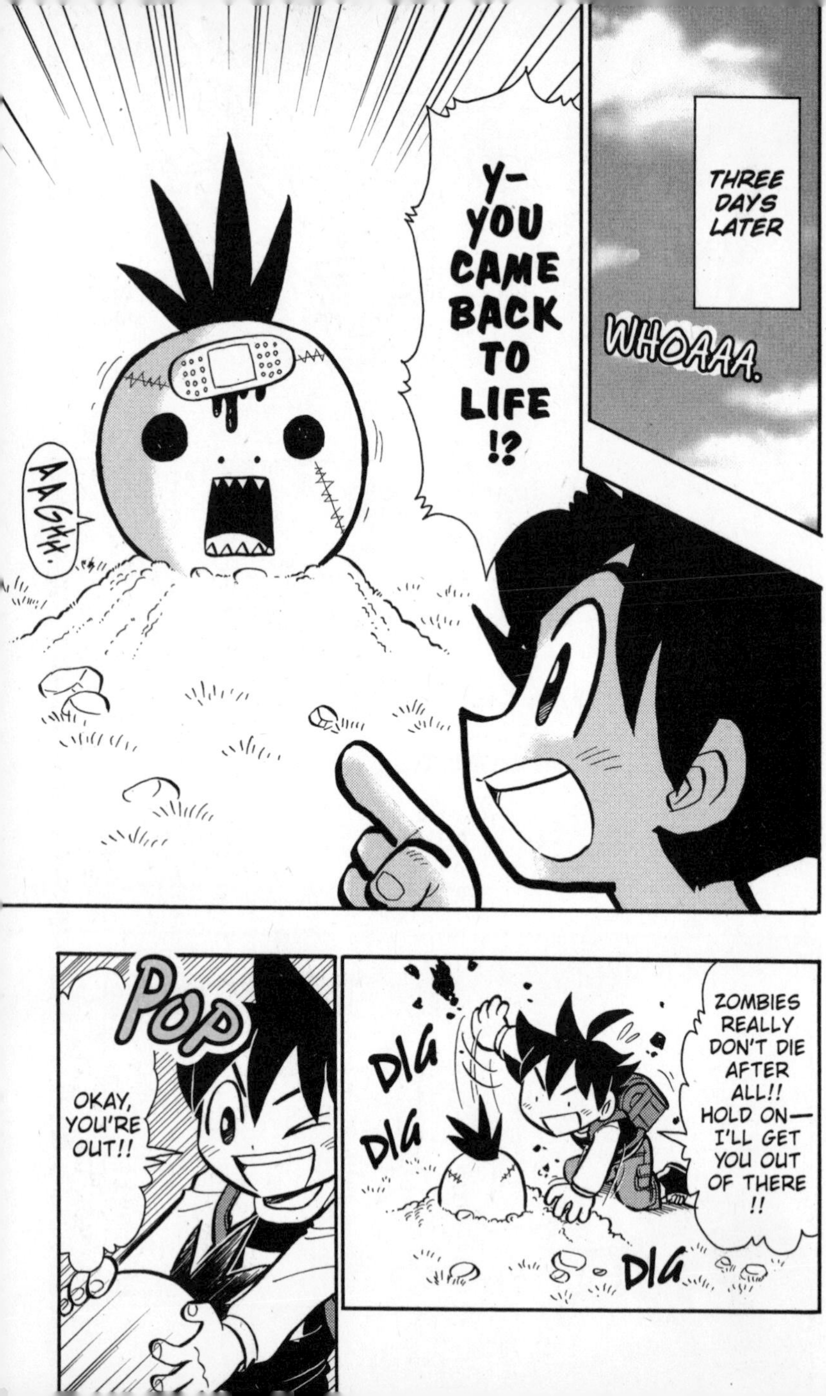
THREE DAYS LATER
WHOAAA.
Y-YOU CAME BACK TO LIFE!?
AAGHH.
ZOMBIES REALLY DON'T DIE AFTER ALL!! HOLD ON— I'LL GET YOU OUT OF THERE!!
DIG
DIG
DIG
POP
OKAY, YOU'RE OUT!!

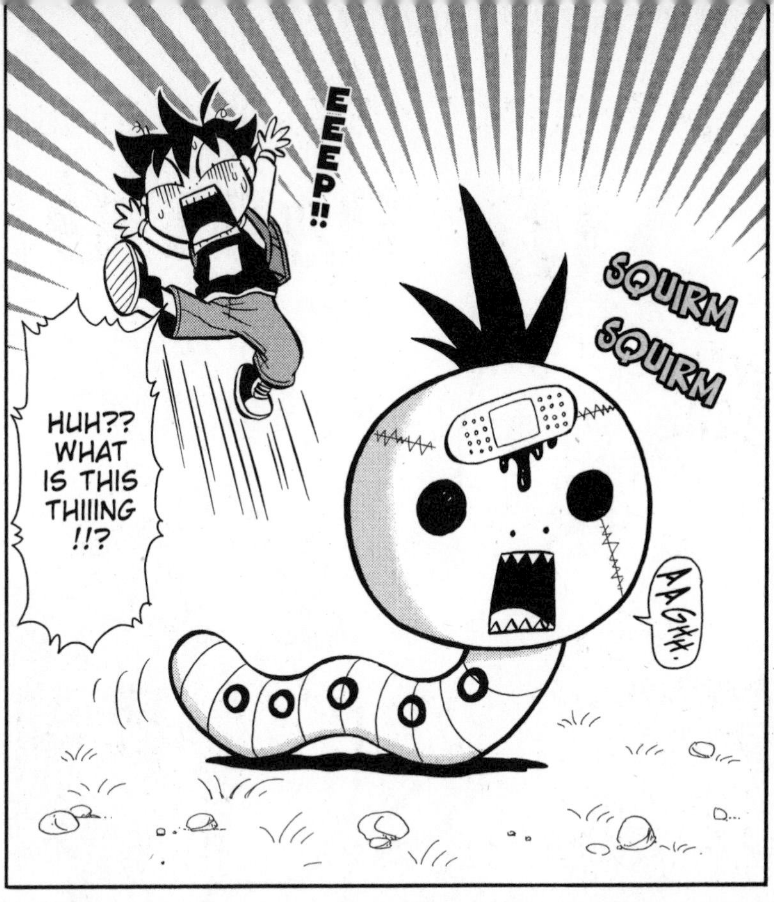
EEEEP!!
SQUIRM SQUIRM
HUH?? WHAT IS THIS THIIING!!?
AAGHH.

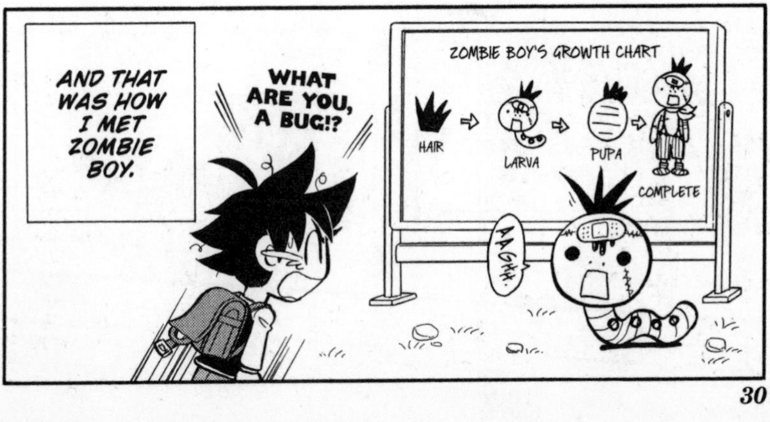
ZOMBIE BOY'S GROWTH CHART
HAIR
LARVA
PUPA
COMPLETE
AAGHH.
WHAT ARE YOU, A BUG!?
AND THAT WAS HOW I MET ZOMBIE BOY.

SPECIAL FOUR-PANEL COMIC

PART 1

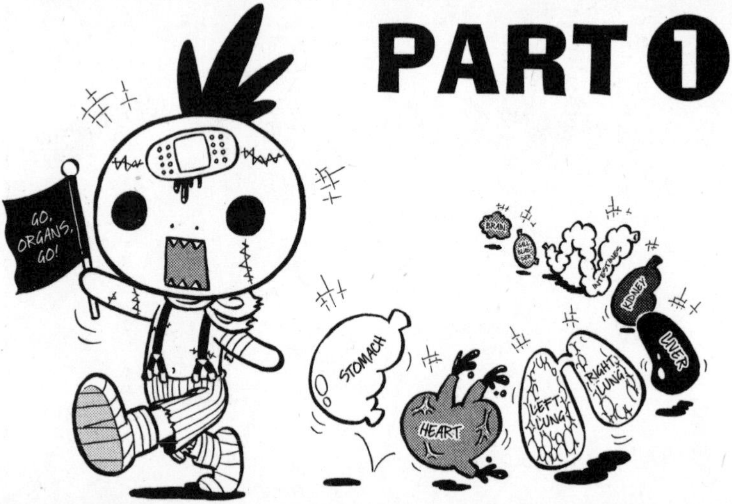
GO, ORGANS, GO!
BRAIN
GALL-BLAD-DER
INTESTINES
KIDNEY
LIVER
RIGHT LUNG
LEFT LUNG
HEART
STOMACH

SAVING SEATS

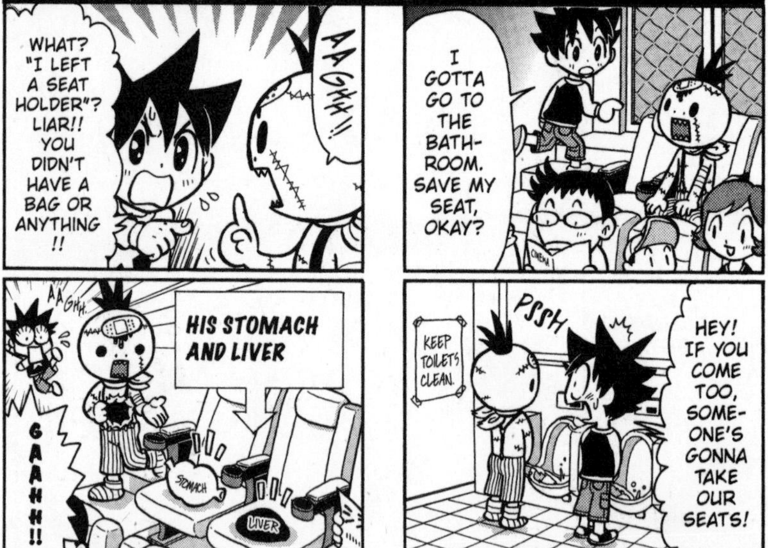
I GOTTA GO TO THE BATH-ROOM. SAVE MY SEAT, OKAY?
CINEMA
HEY! IF YOU COME TOO, SOME-ONE'S GONNA TAKE OUR SEATS!
PSSH
KEEP TOILETS CLEAN.
AAGHH!!
WHAT? "I LEFT A SEAT HOLDER"? LIAR!! YOU DIDN'T HAVE A BAG OR ANYTHING!!
HIS STOMACH AND LIVER
AAGHH
GAAHH!!
STOMACH
LIVER

INVESTIGATE THAT ZOMBIE, AZAP!

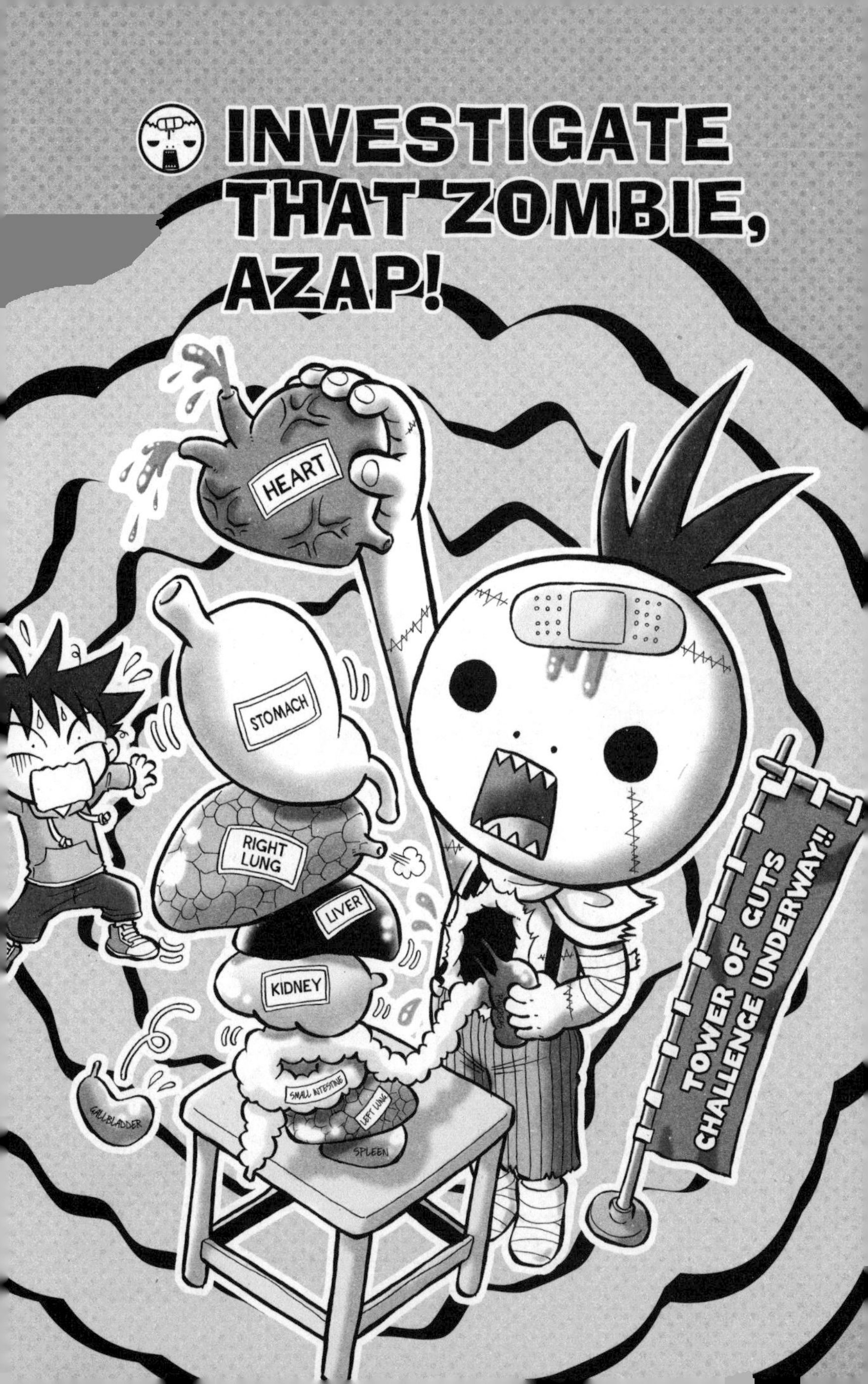
HEART
STOMACH
RIGHT LUNG
LIVER
KIDNEY
SMALL INTESTINE
LEFT LUNG
GALLBLADDER
SPLEEN
TOWER OF GUTS CHALLENGE UNDERWAY!!

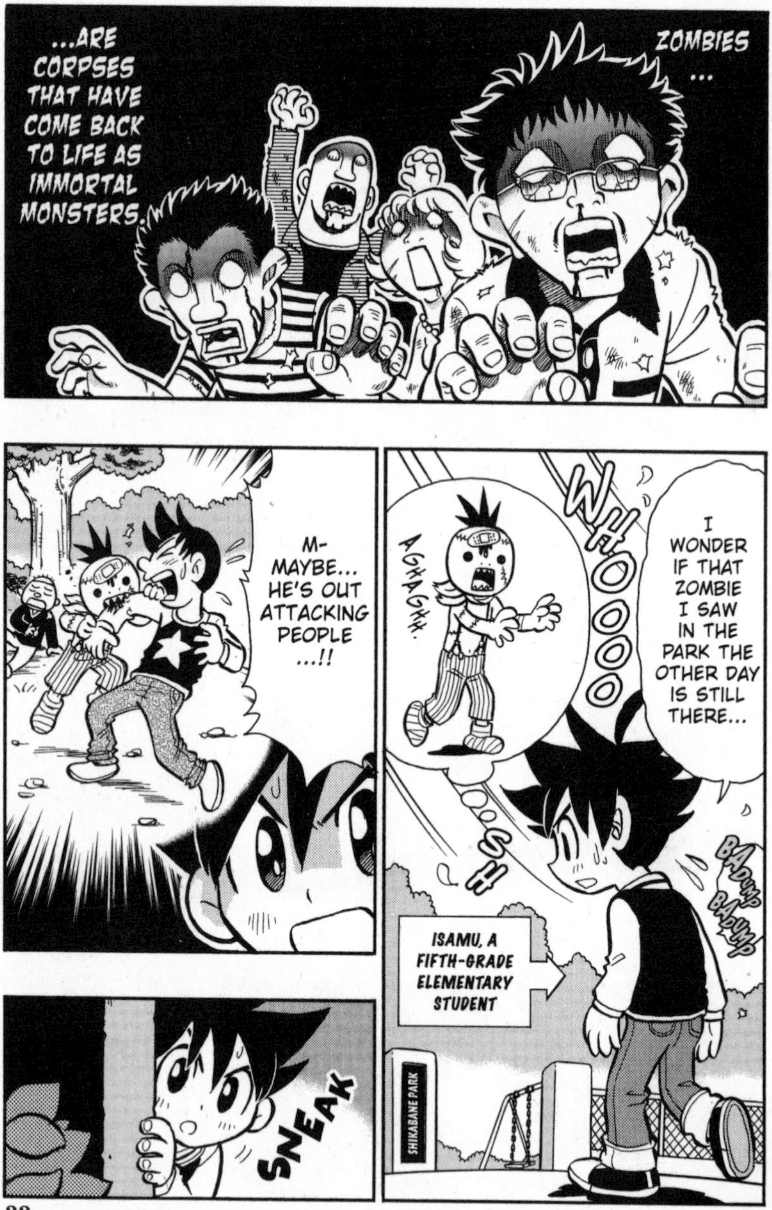
ZOMBIES ...
...ARE CORPSES THAT HAVE COME BACK TO LIFE AS IMMORTAL MONSTERS.
I WONDER IF THAT ZOMBIE I SAW IN THE PARK THE OTHER DAY IS STILL THERE...
WHOOOOOSH
AGHAGHH
BADUMP BADUMP
ISAMU, A FIFTH-GRADE ELEMENTARY STUDENT
SHIKABANE PARK
M-MAYBE... HE'S OUT ATTACKING PEOPLE ...!!
SNEAK

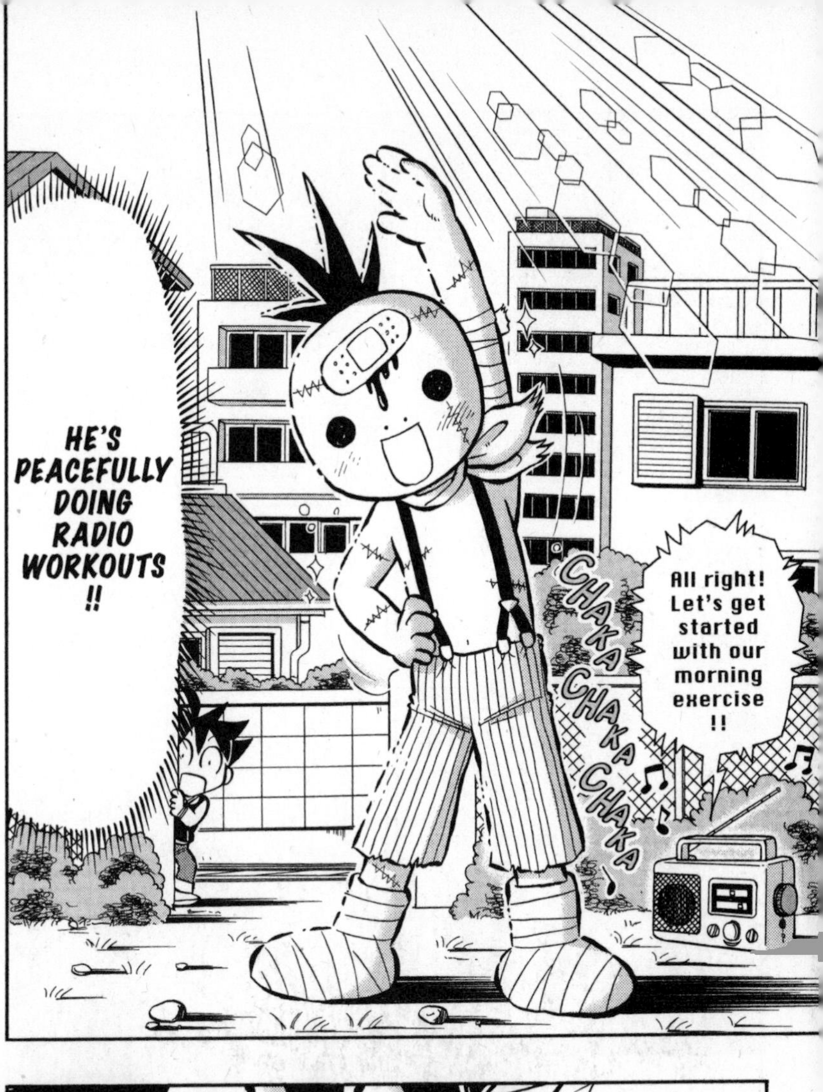
All right! Let's get started with our morning exercise !!
CHAKA CHAKA CHAKA
HE'S PEACEFULLY DOING RADIO WORKOUTS !!

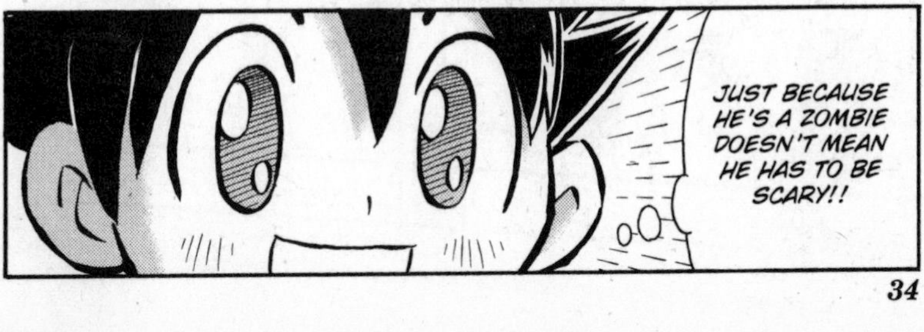
JUST BECAUSE HE'S A ZOMBIE DOESN'T MEAN HE HAS TO BE SCARY!!

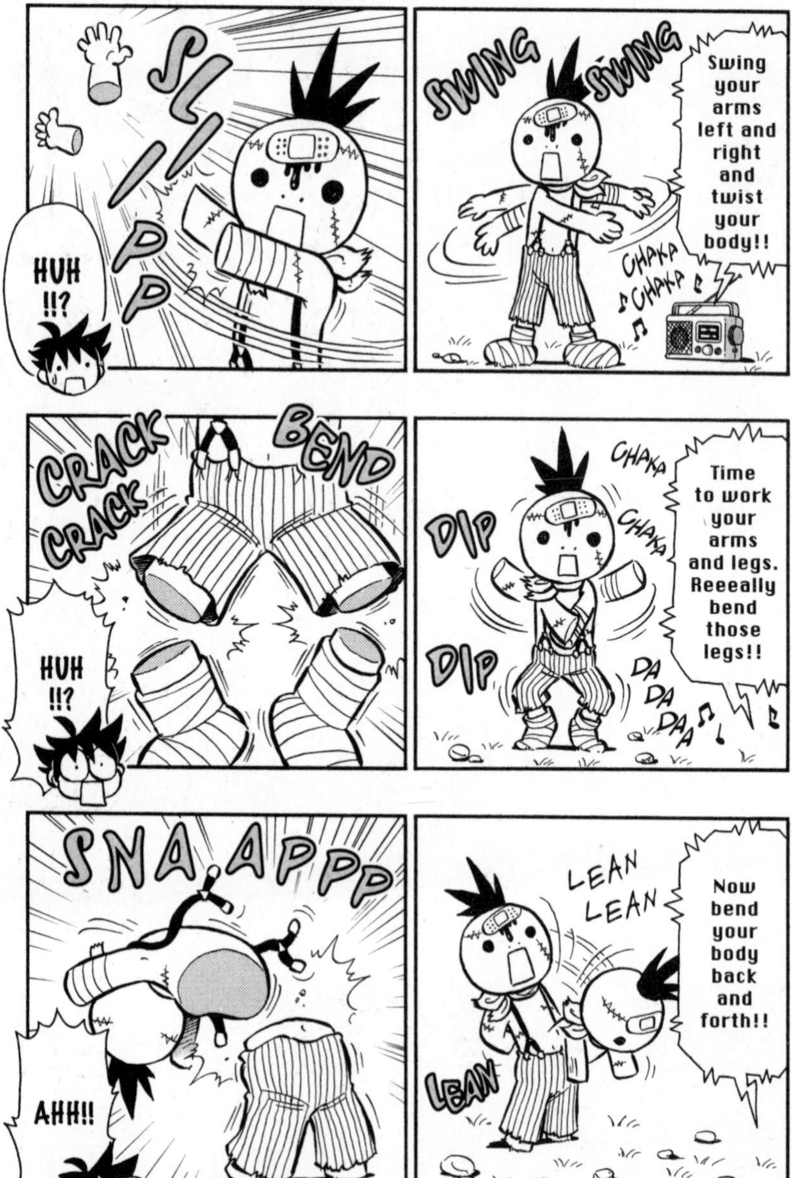

Swing your arms left and right and twist your body!!
SWING
SWING
CHAKA CHAKA
SLIPP
HUH!!?
Time to work your arms and legs. Reeeally bend those legs!!
CHAKA
CHAKA
DIP
DIP
DA DA DAA
BEND
CRACK CRACK
HUH!!?
Now bend your body back and forth!!
LEAN LEAN
LEAN
SNA APPP
AHH!!

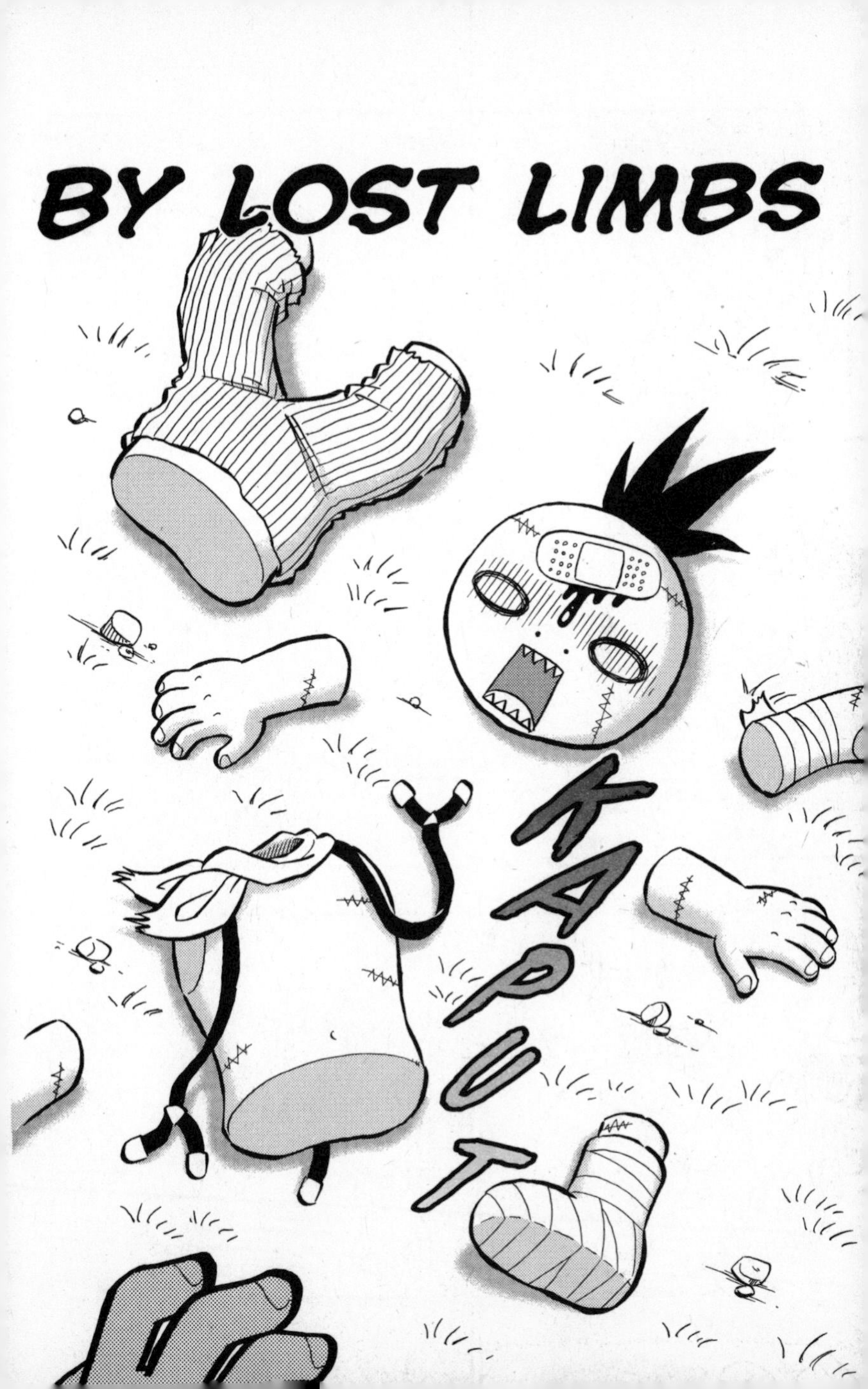
BY LOST LIMBS
KAPUT

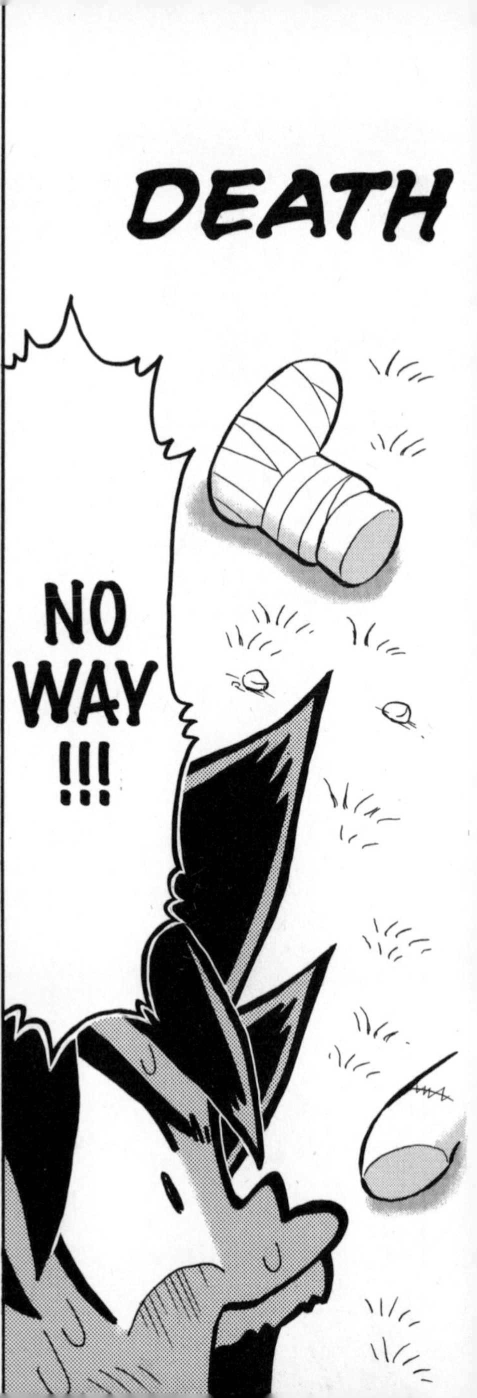
DEATH
NO WAY!!!

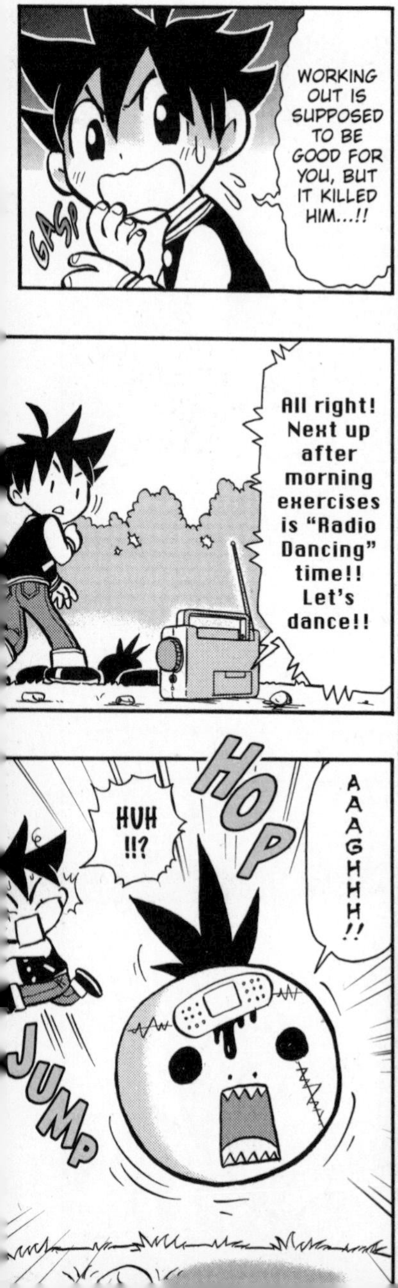
WORKING OUT IS SUPPOSED TO BE GOOD FOR YOU, BUT IT KILLED HIM...!!
GASP
All right! Next up after morning exercises is “Radio Dancing” time!! Let’s dance!!
AAAGHHH!!
HOP
HUH!!?
JUMP

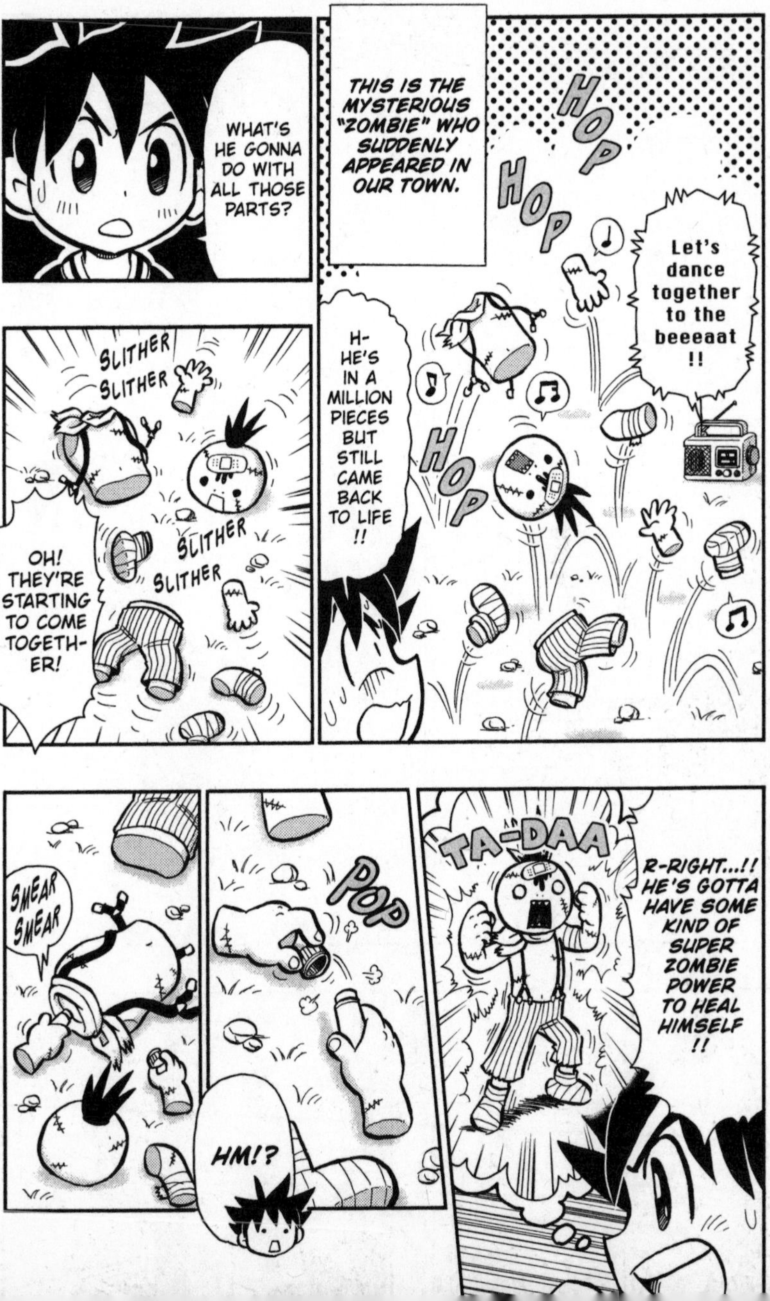
THIS IS THE MYSTERIOUS "ZOMBIE" WHO SUDDENLY APPEARED IN OUR TOWN.
HOP
HOP
Let's dance together to the beeeaat !!
H- HE'S IN A MILLION PIECES BUT STILL CAME BACK TO LIFE !!
HOP
WHAT'S HE GONNA DO WITH ALL THOSE PARTS?
SLITHER SLITHER
SLITHER SLITHER
OH! THEY'RE STARTING TO COME TOGETH-ER!
TA-DAA
R-RIGHT...!! HE'S GOTTA HAVE SOME KIND OF SUPER ZOMBIE POWER TO HEAL HIMSELF !!
POP
HM!?
SMEAR SMEAR

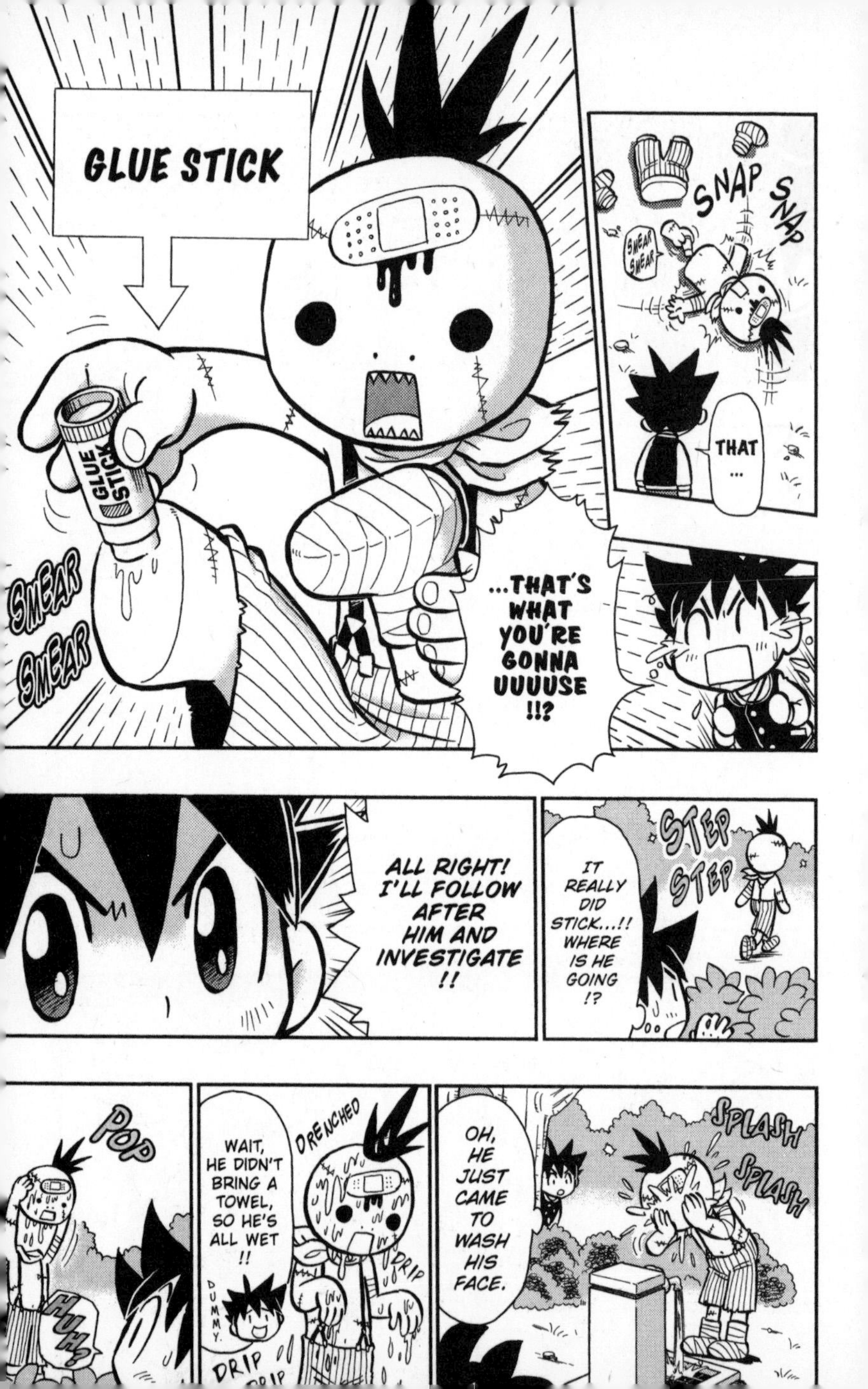
SNAP SNAP
SMEAR SMEAR
THAT ...
...THAT'S WHAT YOU'RE GONNA UUUUSE!!?
GLUE STICK
GLUE STICK
SMEAR SMEAR
STEP STEP
IT REALLY DID STICK...!! WHERE IS HE GOING!?
ALL RIGHT! I'LL FOLLOW AFTER HIM AND INVESTIGATE!!
SPLASH SPLASH
OH, HE JUST CAME TO WASH HIS FACE.
DRENCHED
WAIT, HE DIDN'T BRING A TOWEL, SO HE'S ALL WET!!
DRIP
DUMMY.
DRIP DRIP
POP
HUH?

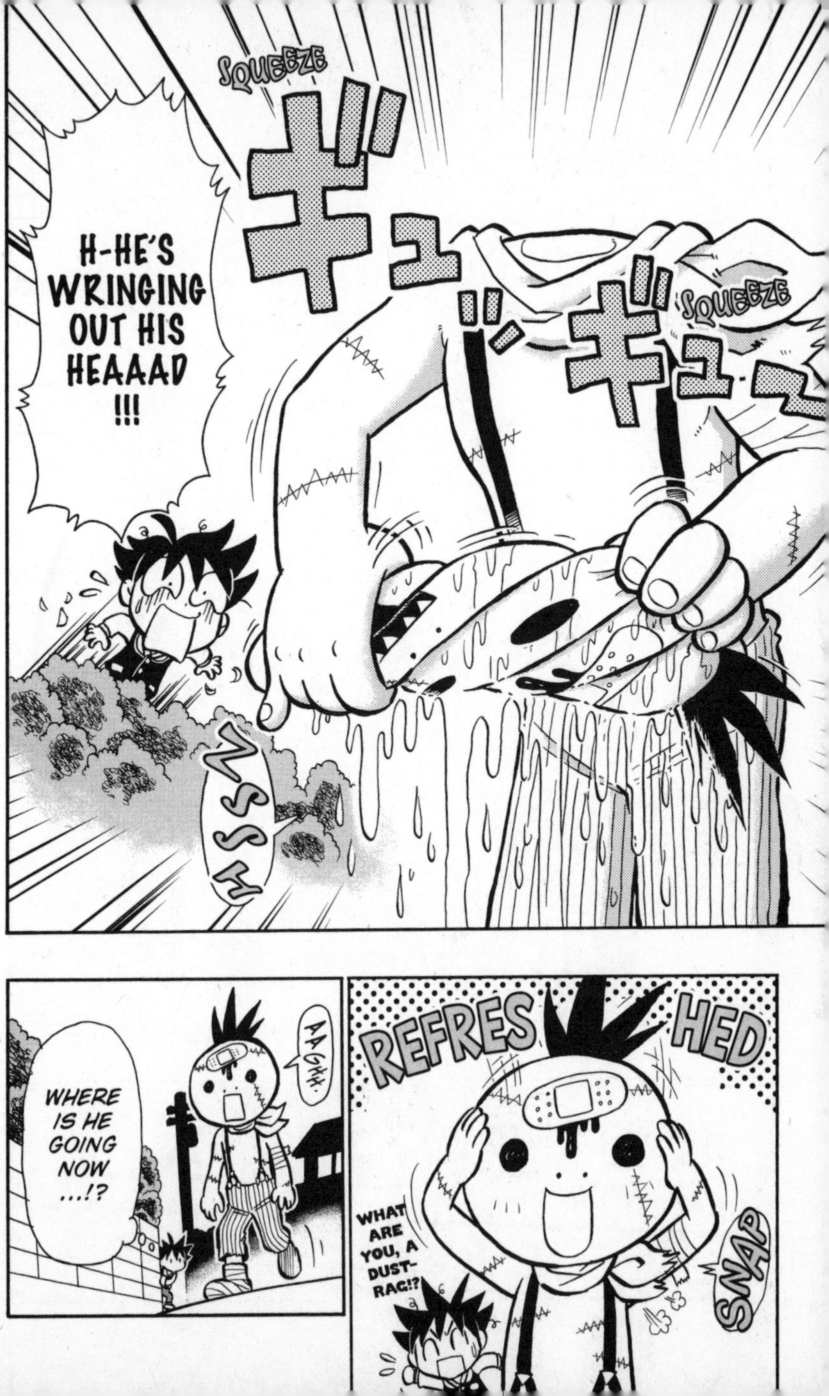
SQUEEZE
SQUEEZE
H-HE'S WRINGING OUT HIS HEAAAD!!!
HISS
REFRESHED
SNAP
WHAT ARE YOU, A DUST-RAG!?
AAGHH.
WHERE IS HE GOING NOW...!?

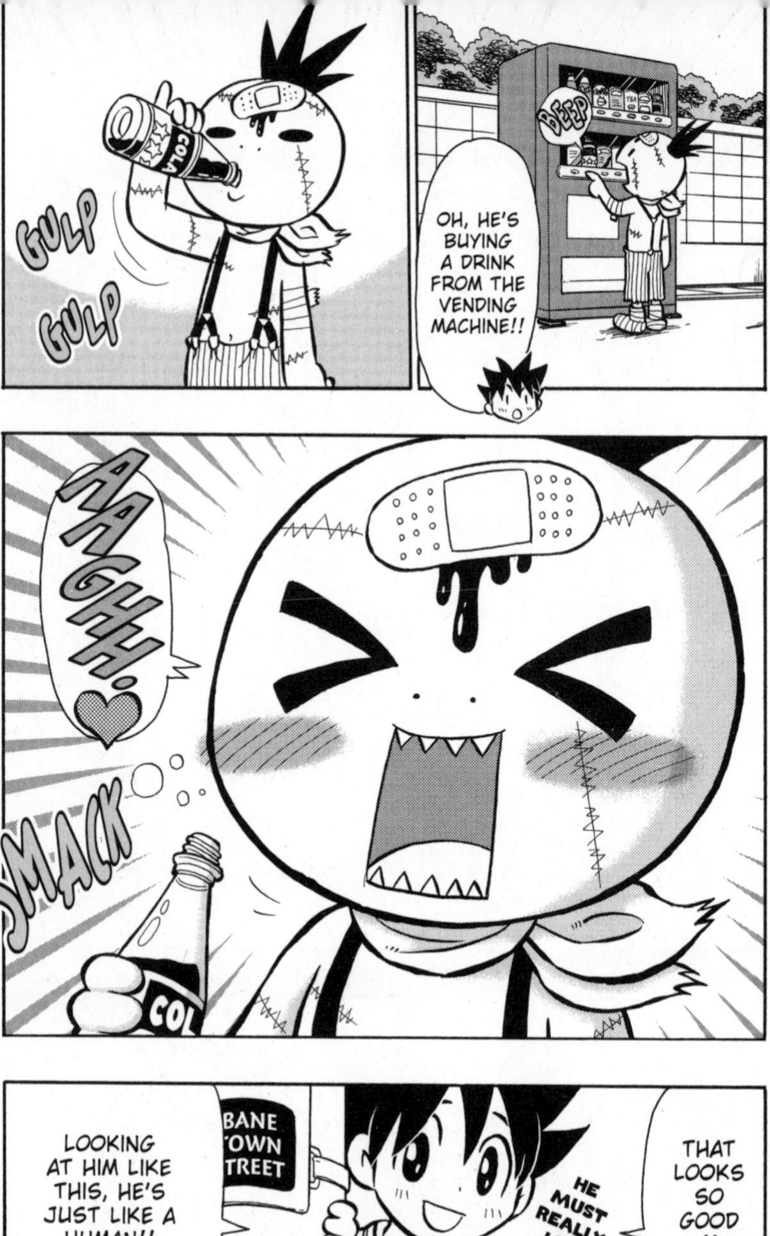
BEEP
OH, HE'S BUYING A DRINK FROM THE VENDING MACHINE!!
COLA
GULP
GULP
AAGHH!♥
SMACK
THAT LOOKS SO GOOD!!
HE MUST REALLY LIKE COLA!!
LOOKING AT HIM LIKE THIS, HE'S JUST LIKE A HUMAN!!

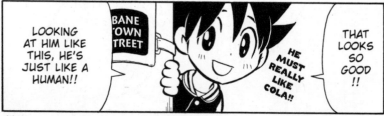

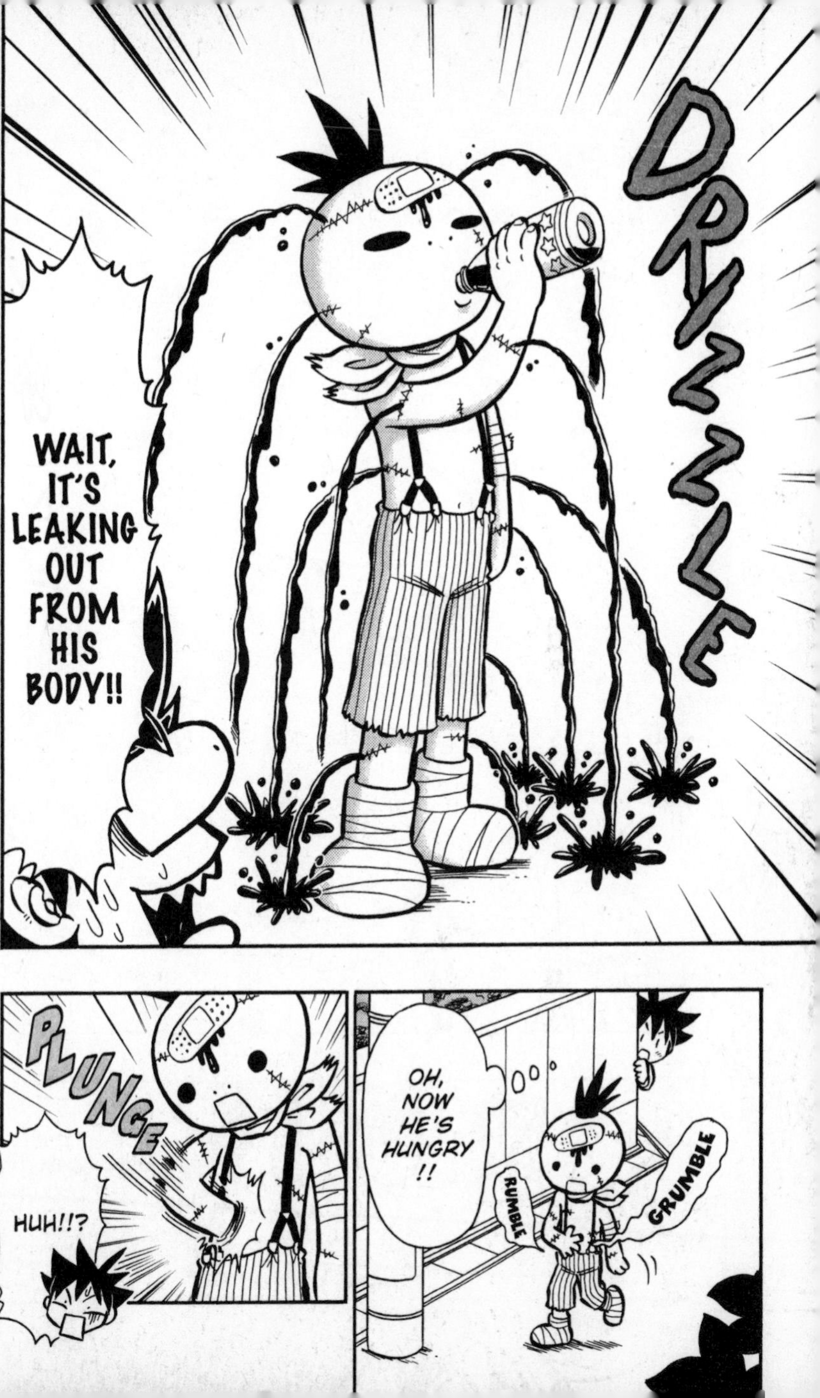
DRIZZLE
WAIT, IT'S LEAKING OUT FROM HIS BODY!!
OH, NOW HE'S HUNGRY!!
GRUMBLE
RUMBLE
PLUNGE
HUH!!?

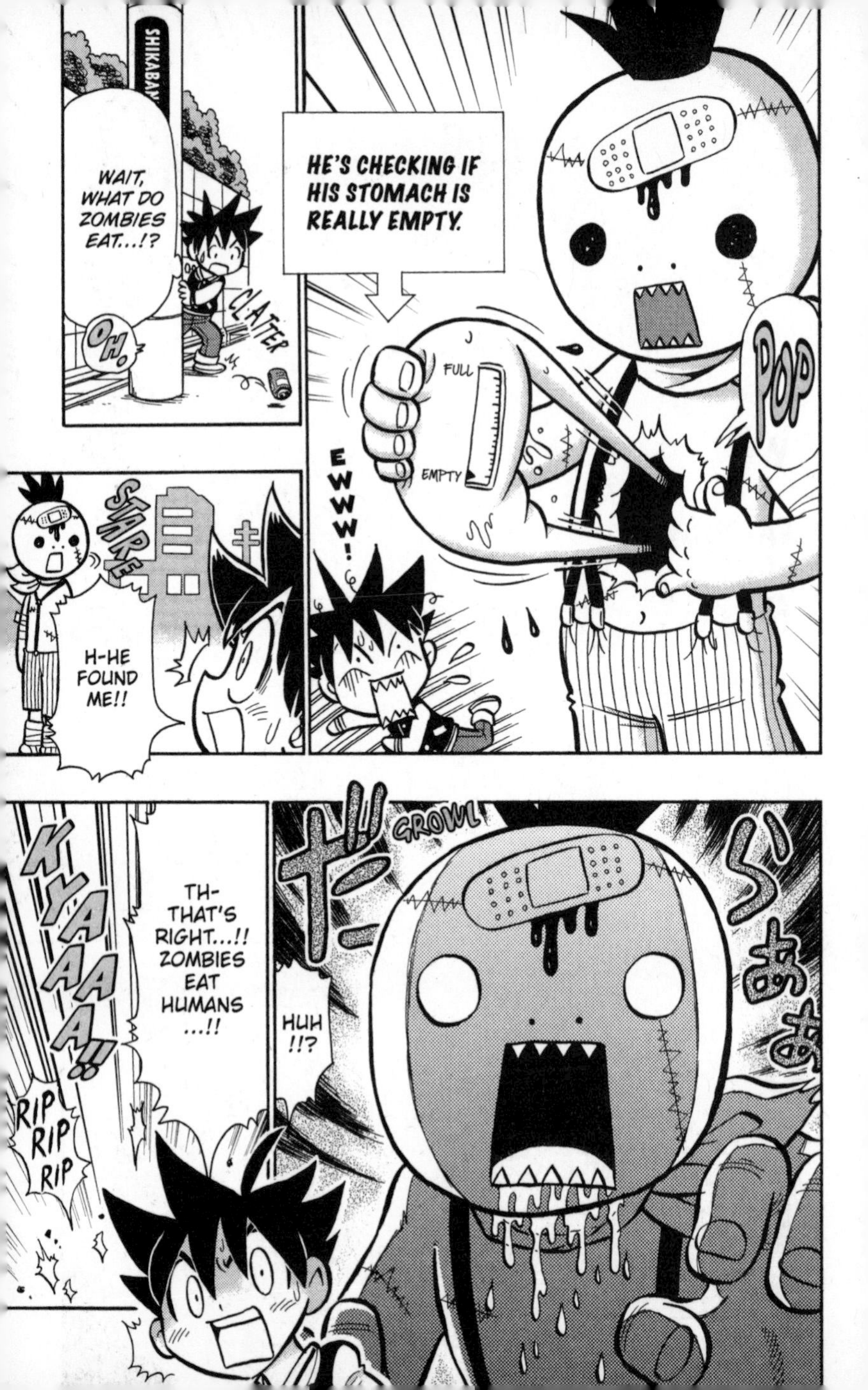
HE'S CHECKING IF HIS STOMACH IS REALLY EMPTY.
FULL
EMPTY
POP
EWWW!
WAIT, WHAT DO ZOMBIES EAT...!?
OH.
CLATTER
STARE
H-HE FOUND ME!!
GROWL
HUH!!?
TH-THAT'S RIGHT...!! ZOMBIES EAT HUMANS...!!
KYAAAAA!!
RIP RIP RIP

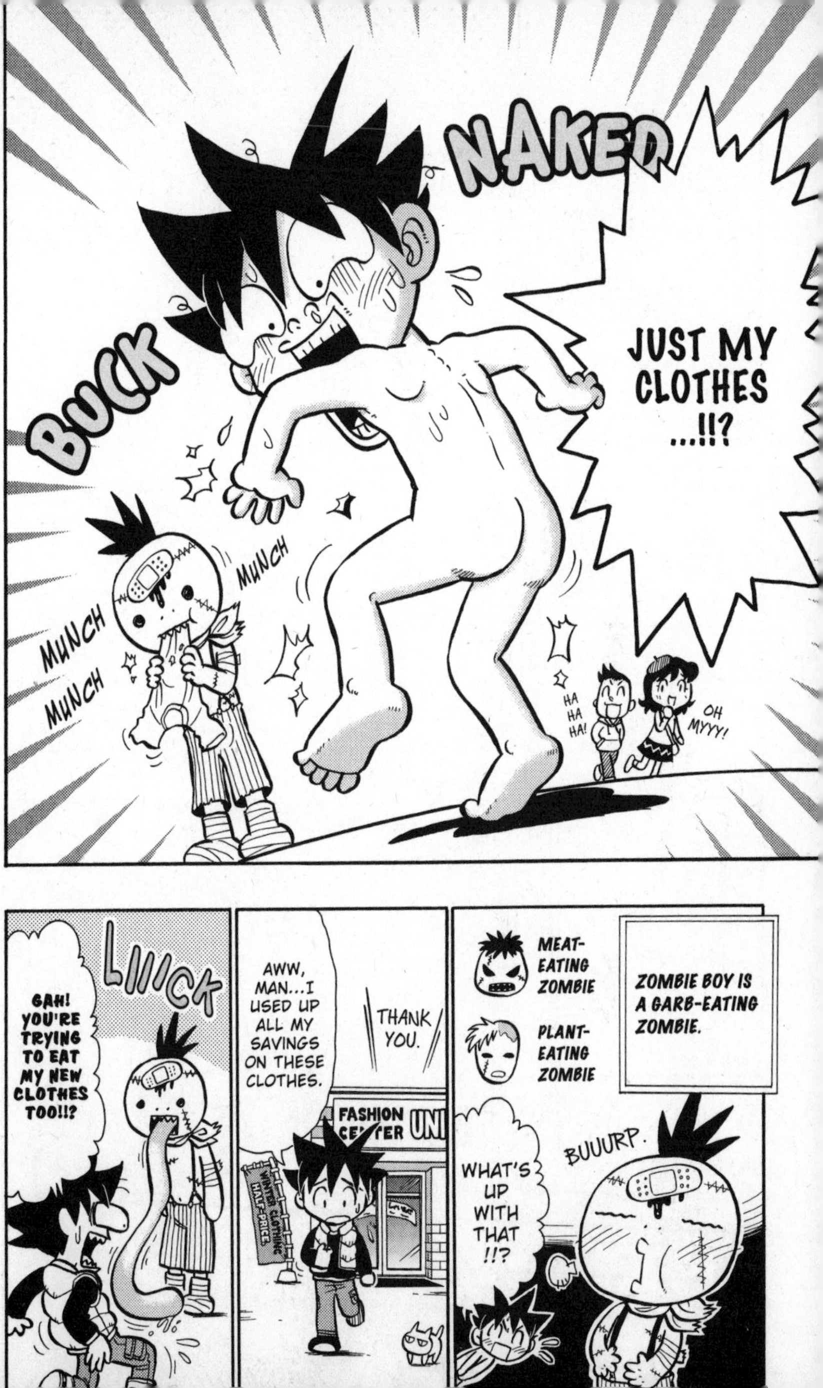
NAKED
JUST MY CLOTHES ...!!?
BUCK
MUNCH
MUNCH
OH MYYY!
HA HA HA!
MUNCH
MUNCH
ZOMBIE BOY IS A GARB-EATING ZOMBIE.
MEAT-EATING ZOMBIE
PLANT-EATING ZOMBIE
BUUURP.
WHAT'S UP WITH THAT !!?
THANK YOU.
AWW, MAN...I USED UP ALL MY SAVINGS ON THESE CLOTHES.
FASHION CENTER UNI
WINTER CLOTHING HALF-PRICE
LIIICK
GAH! YOU'RE TRYING TO EAT MY NEW CLOTHES TOO!!?

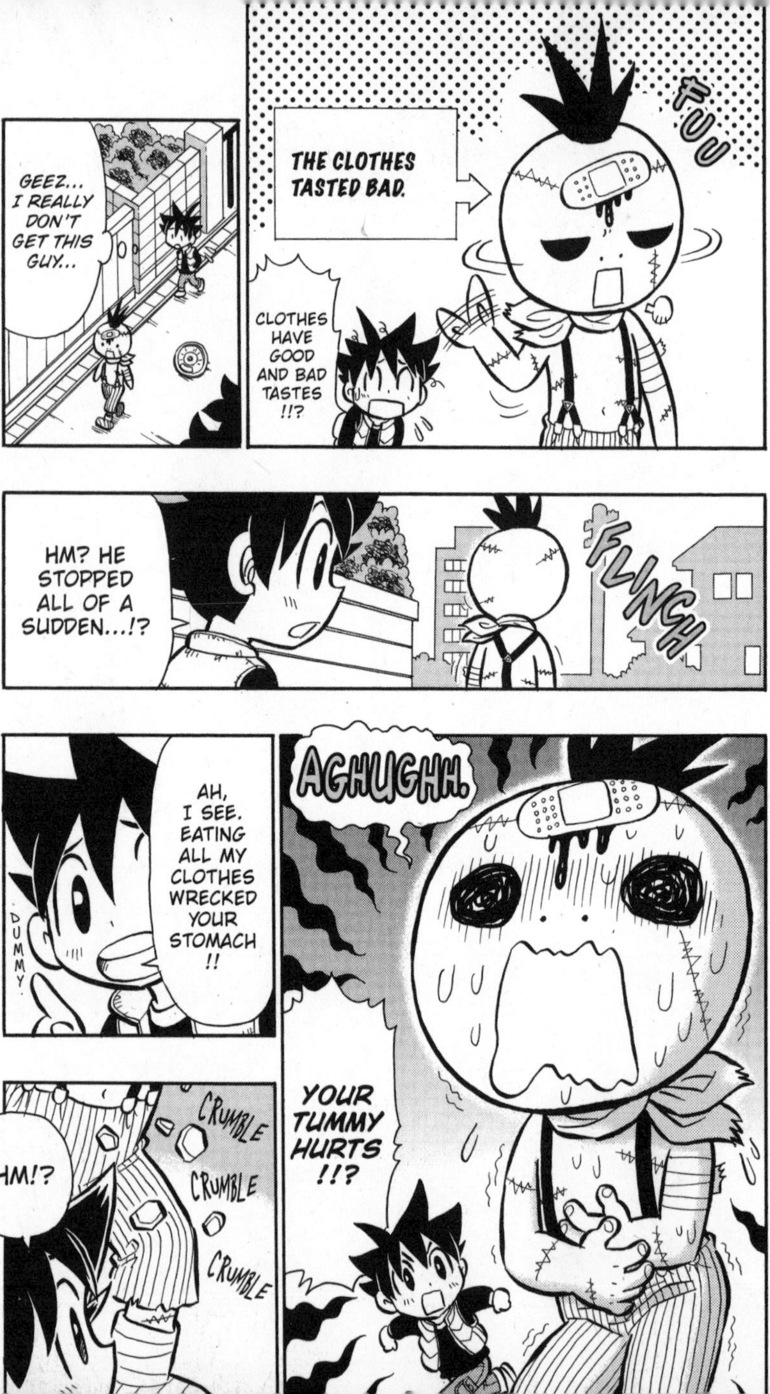
FUU
THE CLOTHES TASTED BAD.
CLOTHES HAVE GOOD AND BAD TASTES !!?
GEEZ... I REALLY DON'T GET THIS GUY...
FLINCH
HM? HE STOPPED ALL OF A SUDDEN...!?
AGHUGHH.
YOUR TUMMY HURTS !!?
AH, I SEE. EATING ALL MY CLOTHES WRECKED YOUR STOMACH !!
DUMMY
CRUMBLE
CRUMBLE
CRUMBLE
HM!?

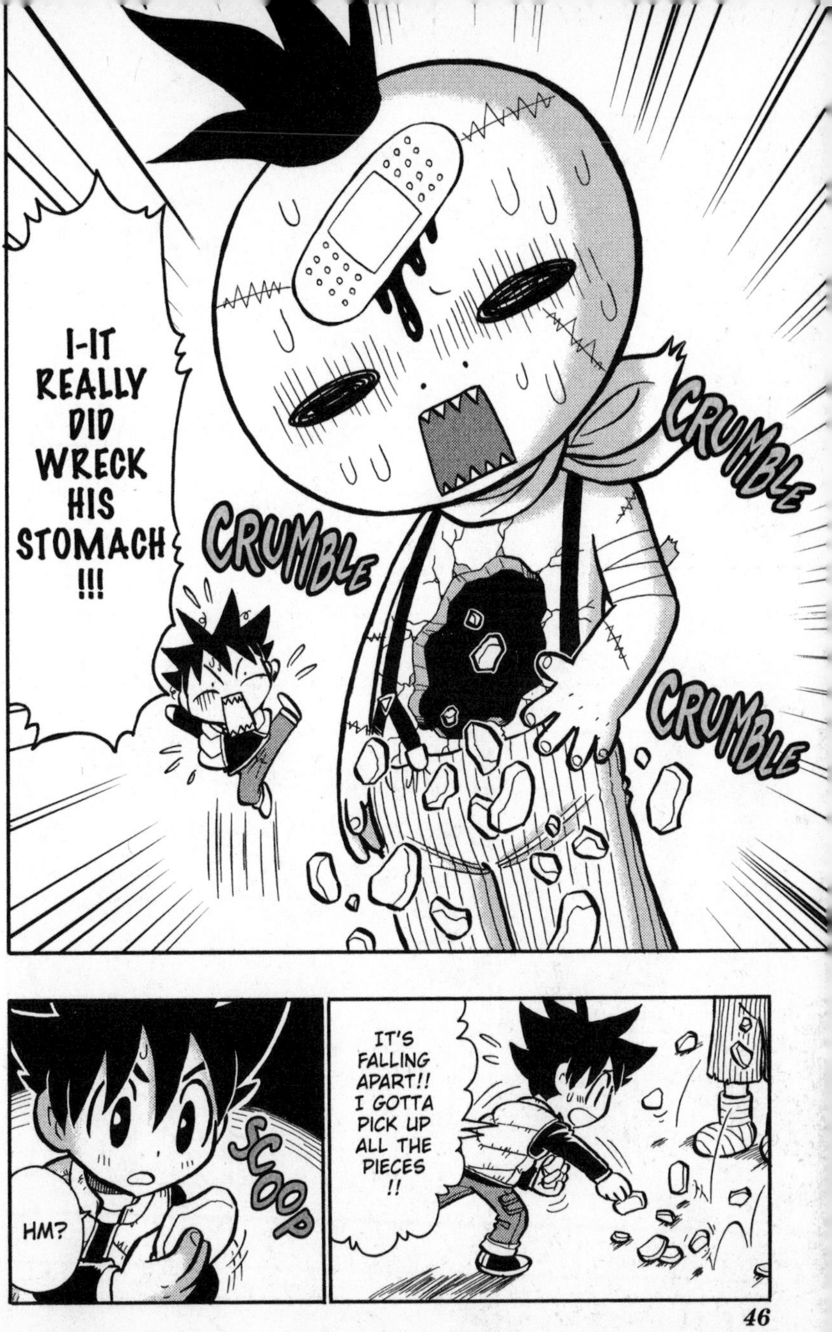
I-IT REALLY DID WRECK HIS STOMACH!!!
CRUMBLE
CRUMBLE
CRUMBLE
IT'S FALLING APART!! I GOTTA PICK UP ALL THE PIECES!!
SCOOP
HM?

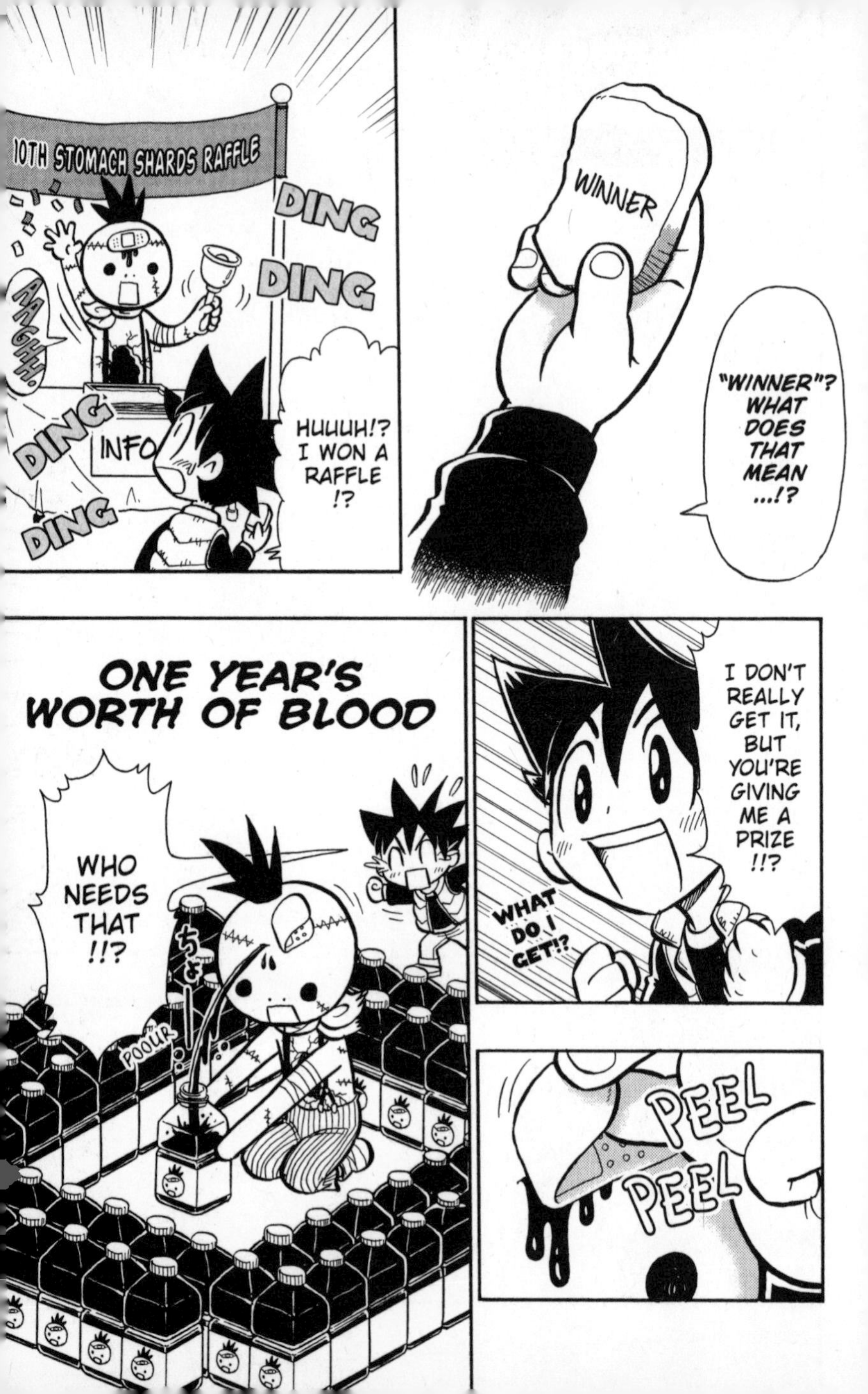

WINNER
"WINNER"? WHAT DOES THAT MEAN ...!?
10TH STOMACH SHARDS RAFFLE
DING DING
AAAGHH.
DING DING DING
INFO
HUUUH!? I WON A RAFFLE !?
I DON'T REALLY GET IT, BUT YOU'RE GIVING ME A PRIZE !!?
WHAT DO I GET!?
PEEL PEEL
ONE YEAR'S WORTH OF BLOOD
WHO NEEDS THAT !!?
POOUR

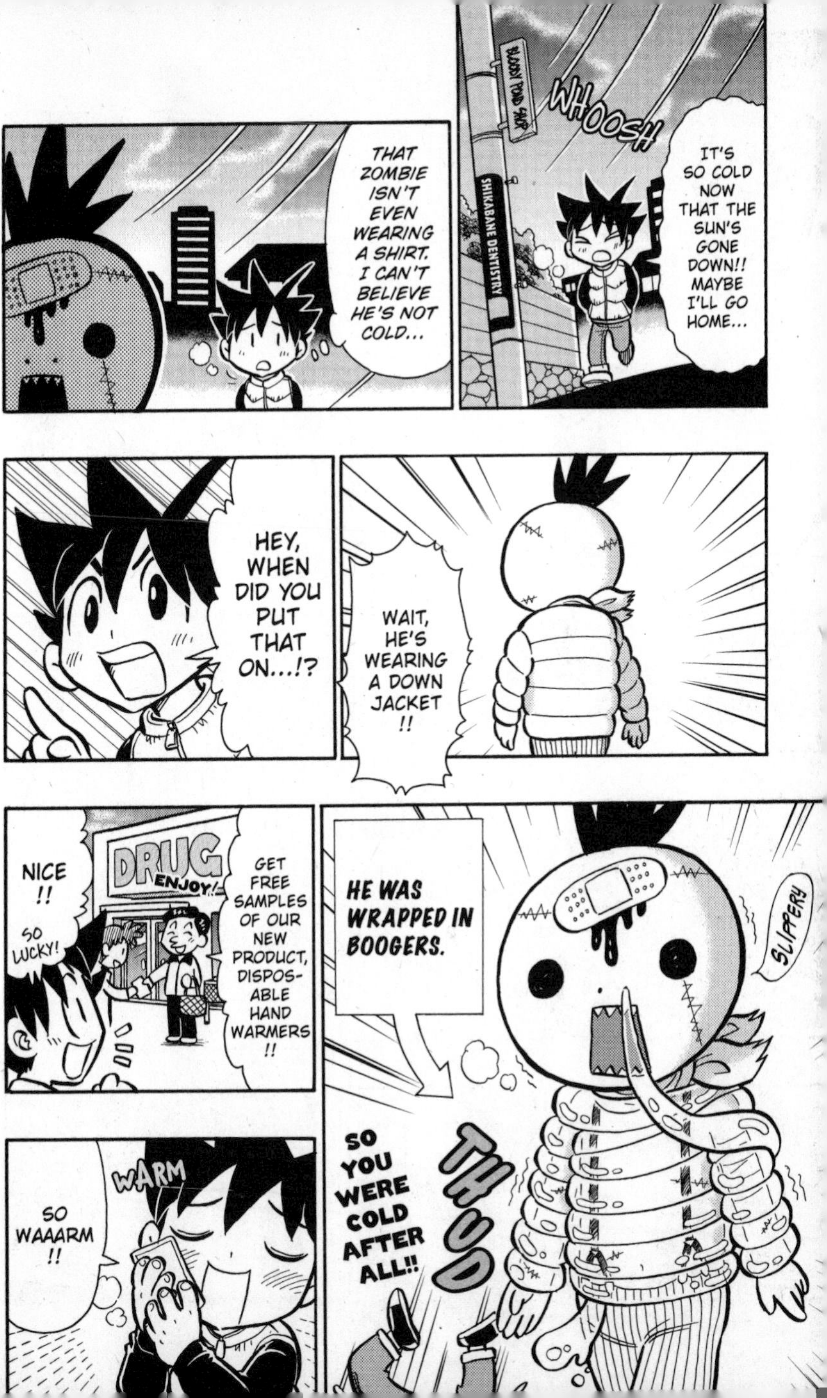
BLOODY POND SHOP
SHIKABANE DENTISTRY
WHOOSH
IT'S SO COLD NOW THAT THE SUN'S GONE DOWN!! MAYBE I'LL GO HOME...
THAT ZOMBIE ISN'T EVEN WEARING A SHIRT. I CAN'T BELIEVE HE'S NOT COLD...
WAIT, HE'S WEARING A DOWN JACKET !!
HEY, WHEN DID YOU PUT THAT ON...!?
HE WAS WRAPPED IN BOOGERS.
SLIPPERY
THUD
SO YOU WERE COLD AFTER ALL!!
DRUG
ENJOY!
GET FREE SAMPLES OF OUR NEW PRODUCT, DISPOSABLE HAND WARMERS !!
NICE !!
SO LUCKY!
WARM
SO WAAARM !!

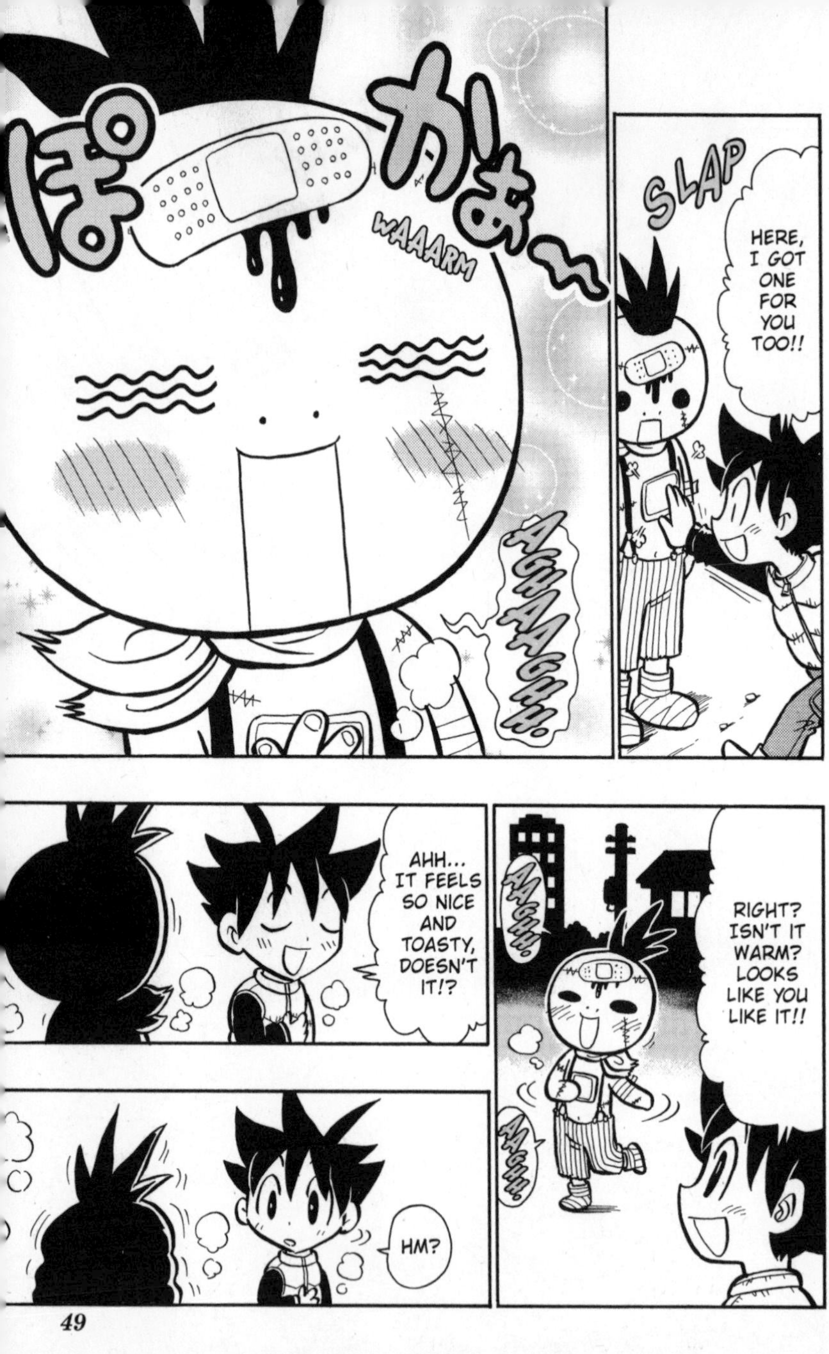
SLAP
HERE, I GOT ONE FOR YOU TOO!!
ぽかぁ~
WAAARM
AGHAAAAGHH.
RIGHT? ISN'T IT WARM? LOOKS LIKE YOU LIKE IT!!
AAGHH.
AAGHH.
AHH... IT FEELS SO NICE AND TOASTY, DOESN'T IT!?
HM?

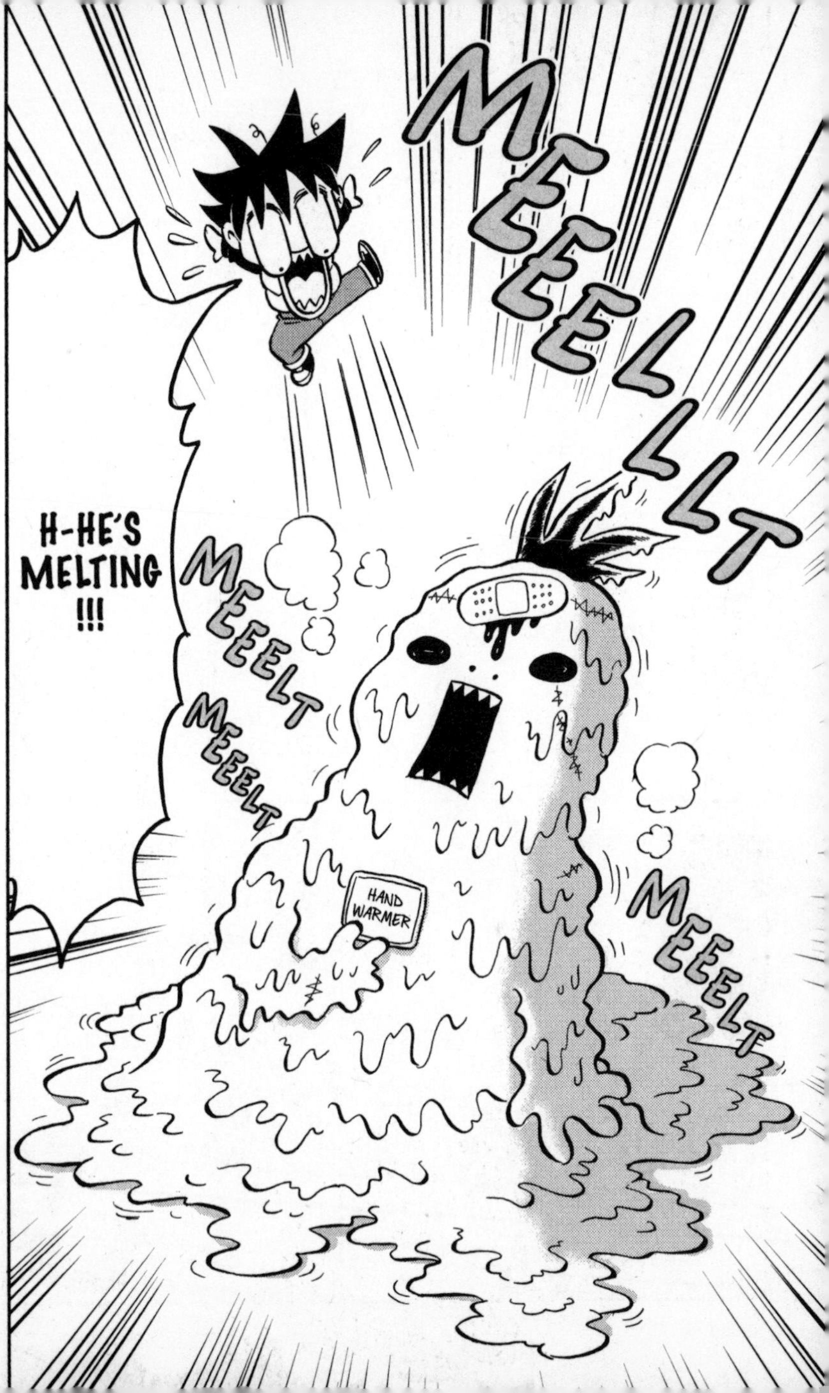
MÊÊELLLT
H-HE'S MELTING!!!
MEEELT MEEELT
HAND WARMER
MEEELT

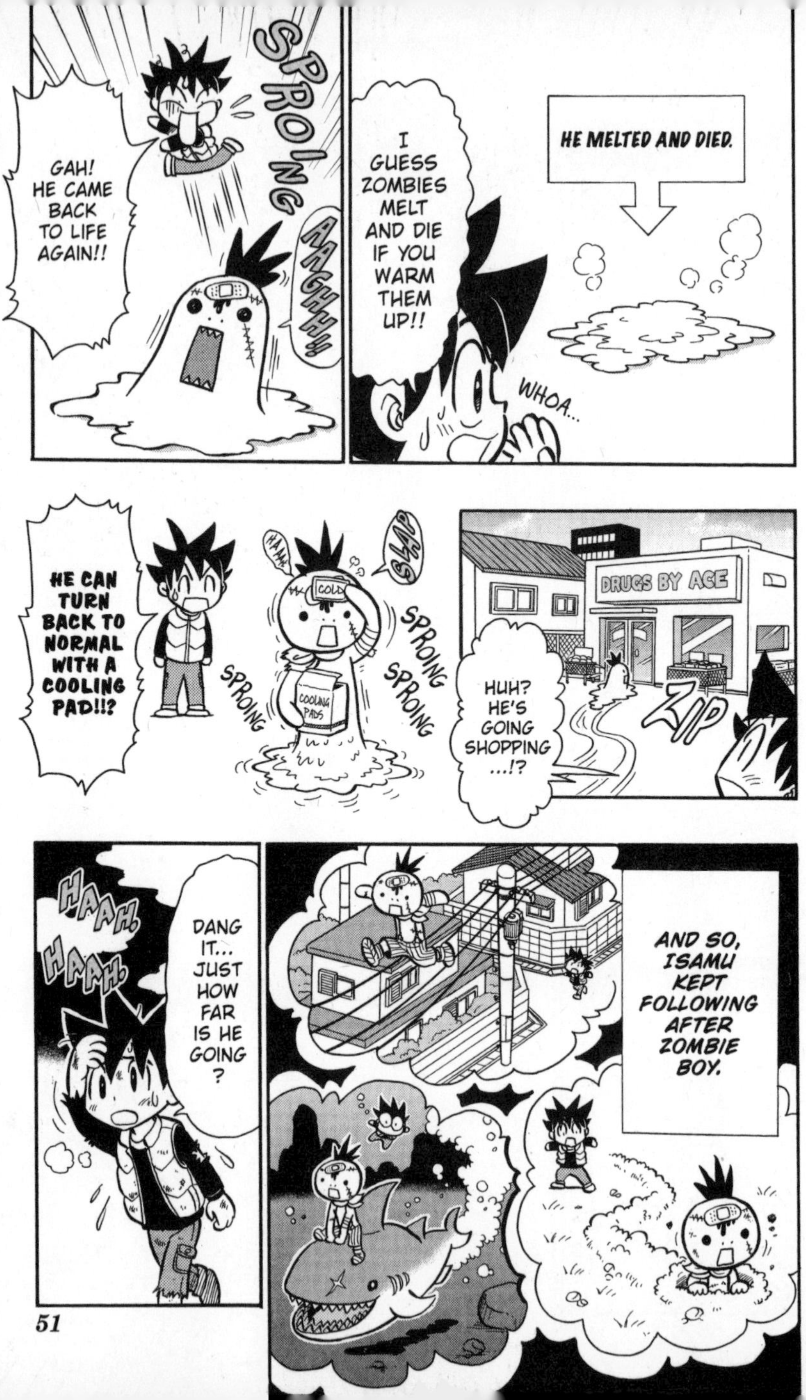
HE MELTED AND DIED.
WHOA...
I GUESS ZOMBIES MELT AND DIE IF YOU WARM THEM UP!!
SPRO'ING
AAAGHHH!!
GAH! HE CAME BACK TO LIFE AGAIN!!
DRUGS BY ACE
ZIP
HUH? HE'S GOING SHOPPING ...!?
SLAP
COLD
COOLING PADS
SPROING
SPROING
SPROING
HE CAN TURN BACK TO NORMAL WITH A COOLING PAD!!?
AND SO, ISAMU KEPT FOLLOWING AFTER ZOMBIE BOY.
HAAAH. HAAAH.
DANG IT... JUST HOW FAR IS HE GOING?

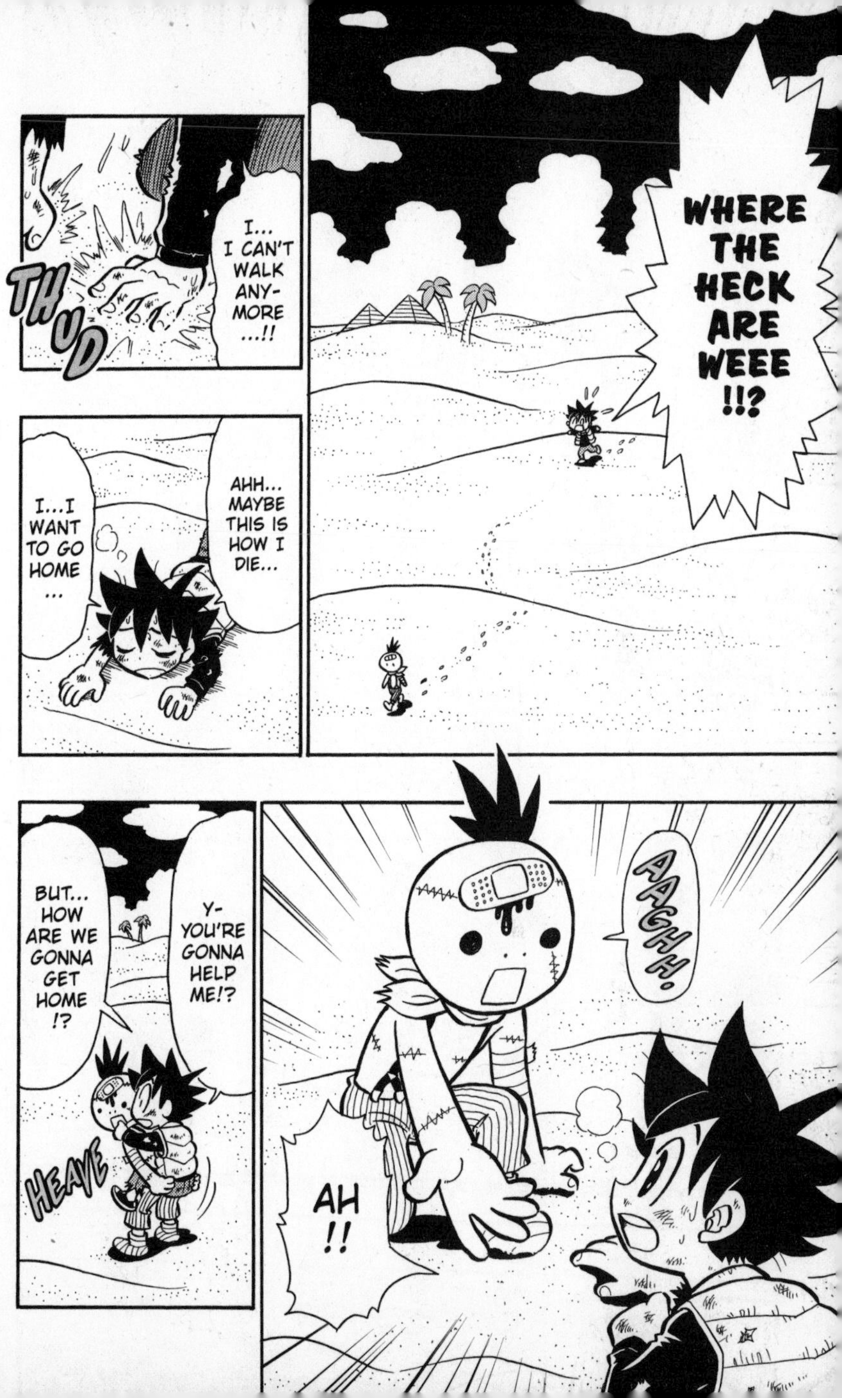
WHERE THE HECK ARE WEEE !!?
I... I CAN'T WALK ANYMORE ...!!
THUD
AHH... MAYBE THIS IS HOW I DIE...
I...I WANT TO GO HOME ...
AAGHH.
AH !!
Y- YOU'RE GONNA HELP ME!?
BUT... HOW ARE WE GONNA GET HOME !?
HEAVE

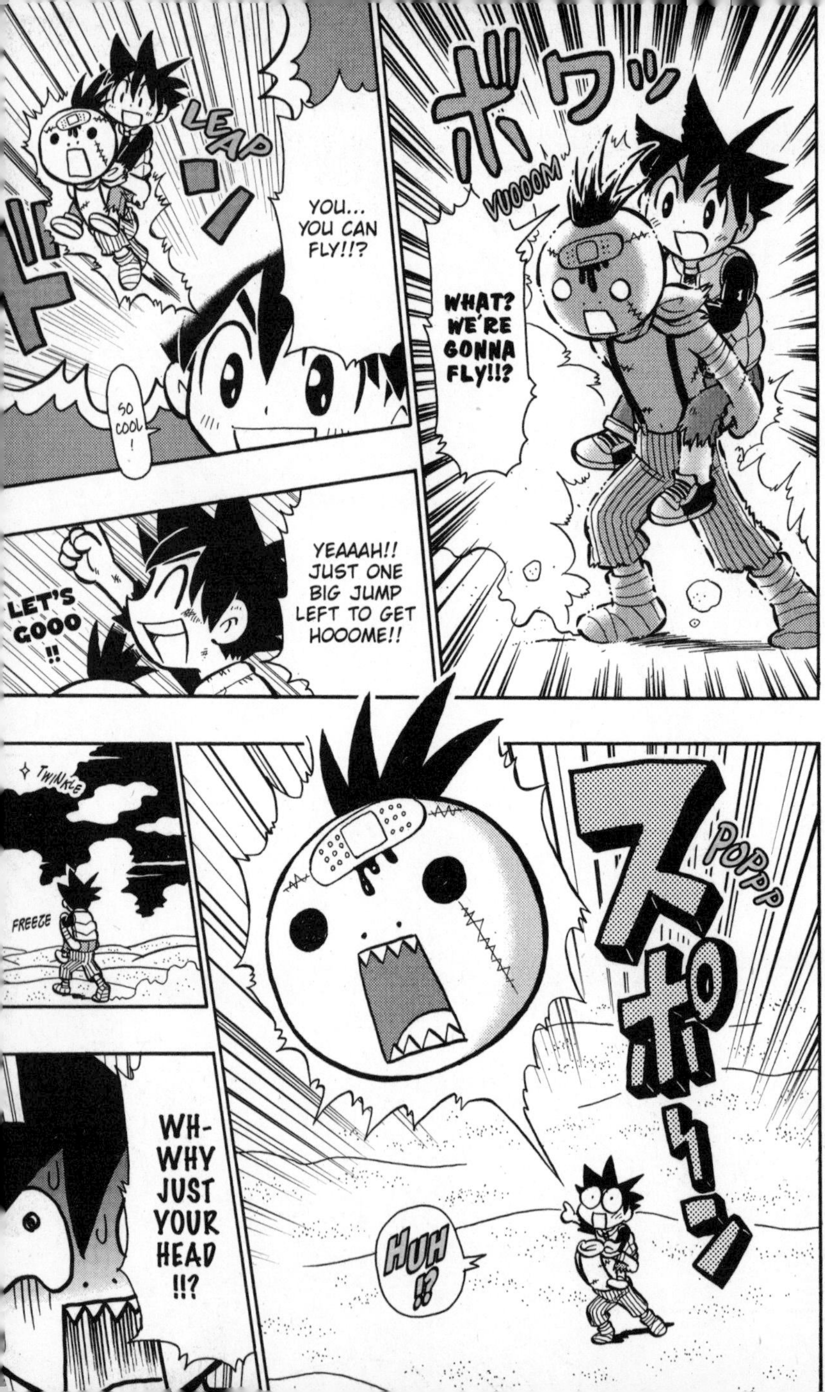
ボワッ
VUOOOM
WHAT? WE'RE GONNA FLY!!?
LEAP
YOU... YOU CAN FLY!!?
SO COOL!
YEAAAH!! JUST ONE BIG JUMP LEFT TO GET HOOOME!!
LET'S GOOO!!
スポーン
POPPP
HUH!?
TWINKLE
FREEZE
WH-WHY JUST YOUR HEAD!!?

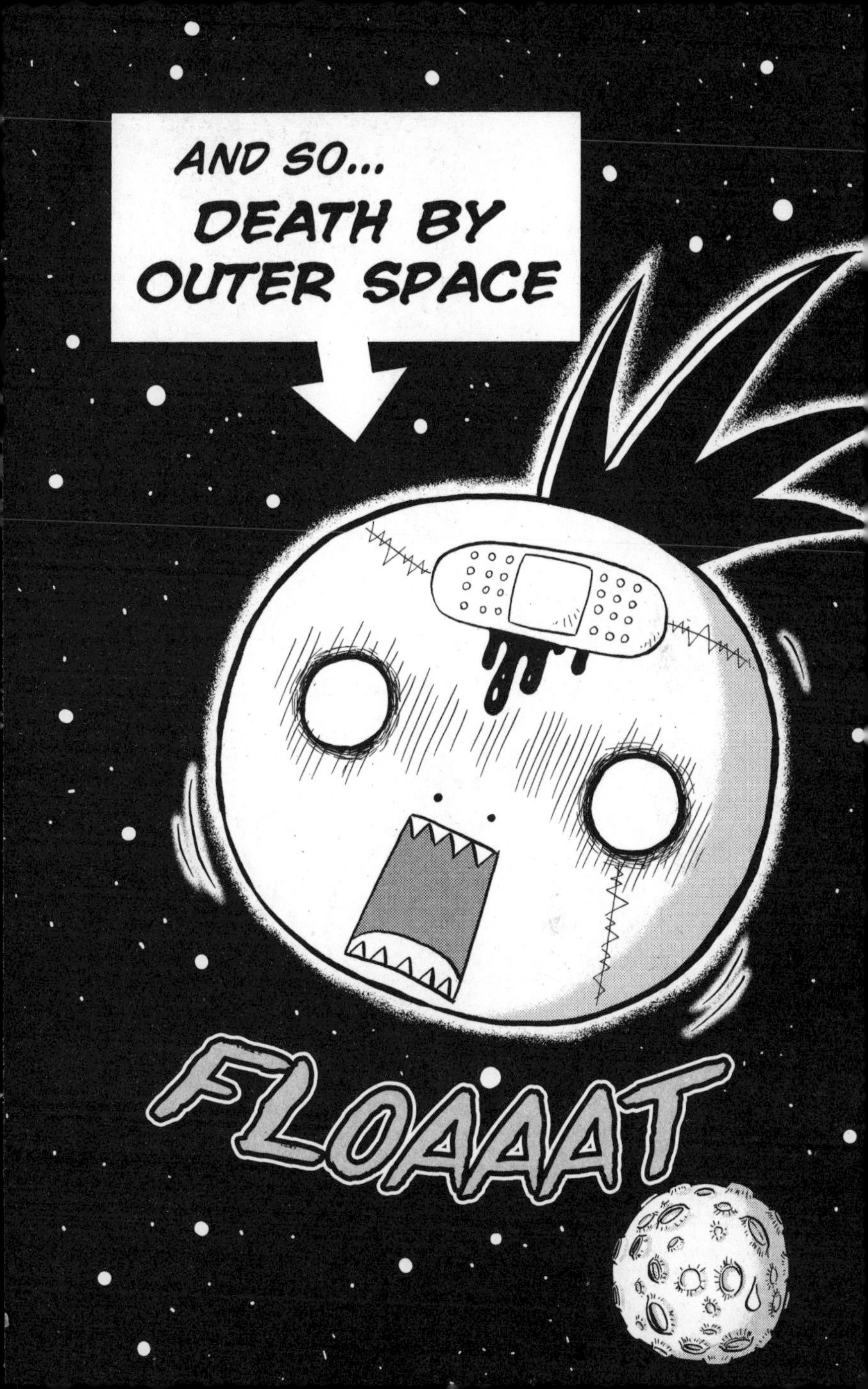
AND SO... DEATH BY OUTER SPACE
FLOAAAT

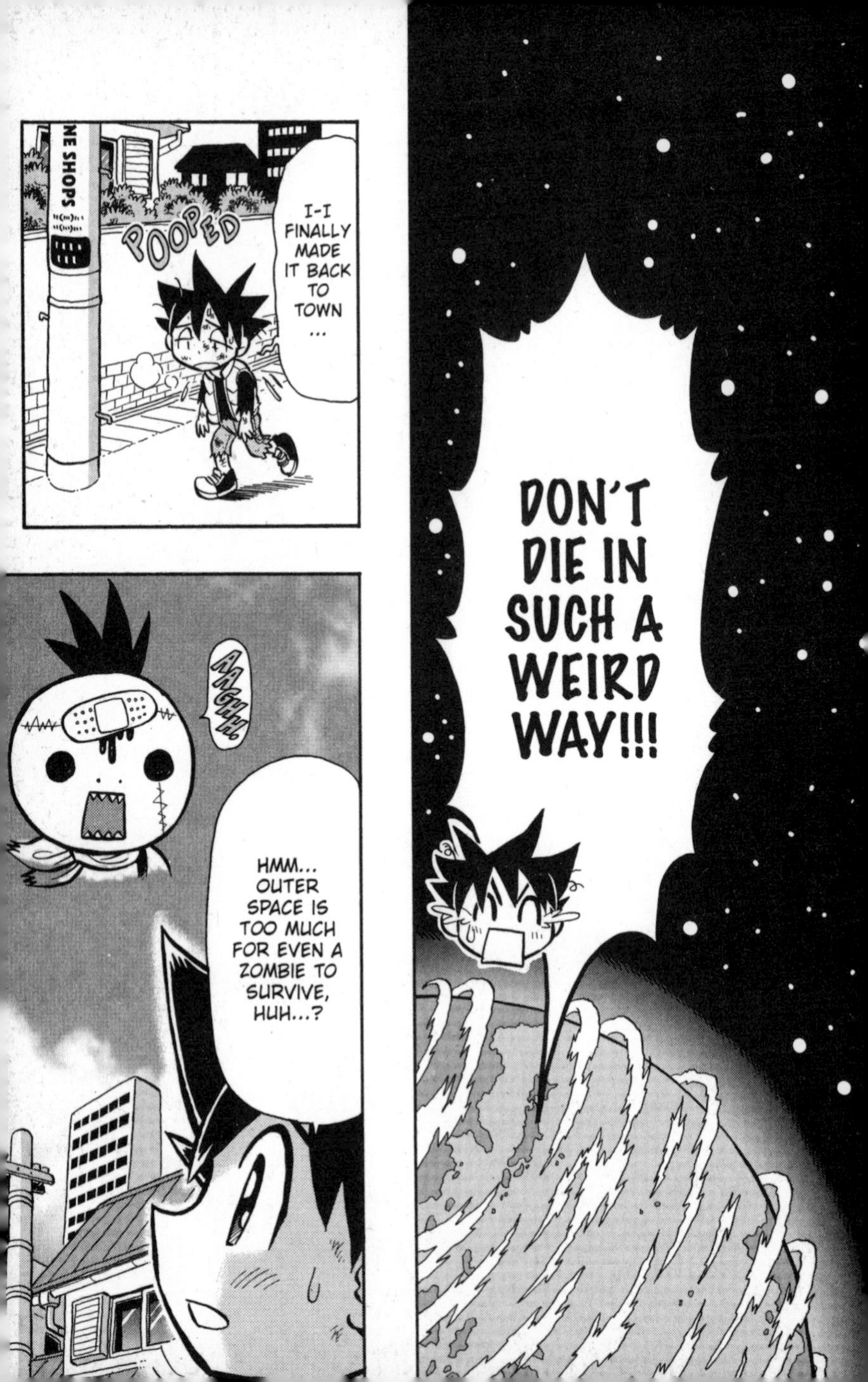
DON'T DIE IN SUCH A WEIRD WAY!!!
NE SHOPS
POOPED
I-I FINALLY MADE IT BACK TO TOWN ...
HMM... OUTER SPACE IS TOO MUCH FOR EVEN A ZOMBIE TO SURVIVE, HUH...?

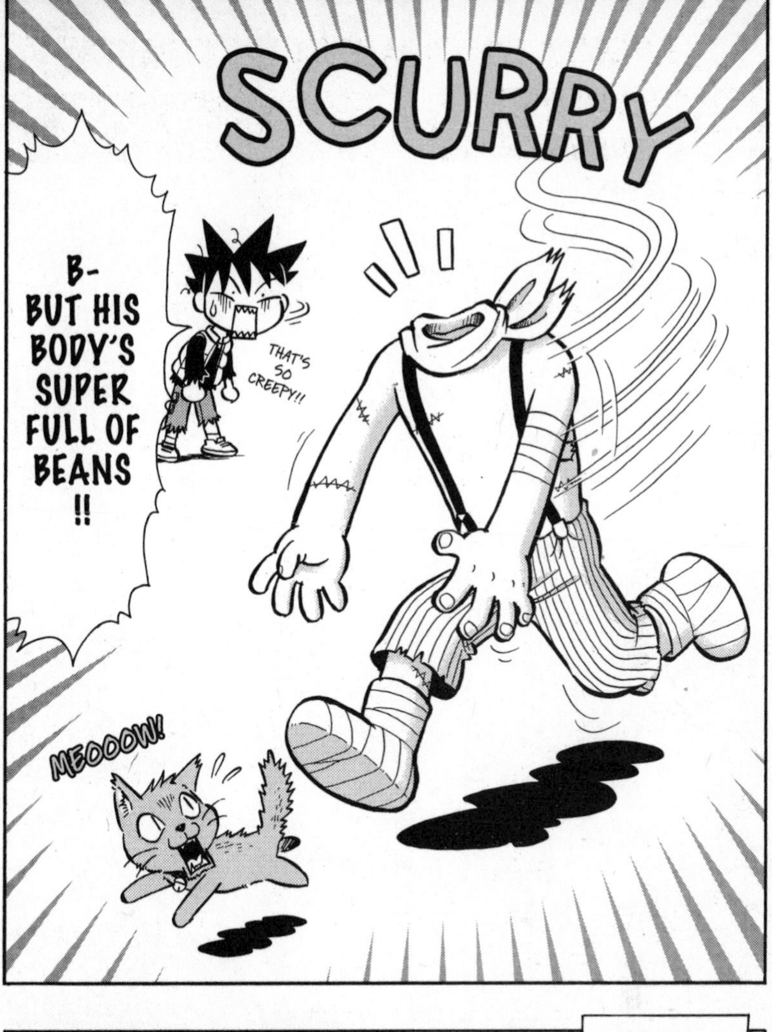
SCURRY
B-
BUT HIS BODY'S SUPER FULL OF BEANS!!
THAT'S SO CREEPY!!
MEOOOW!

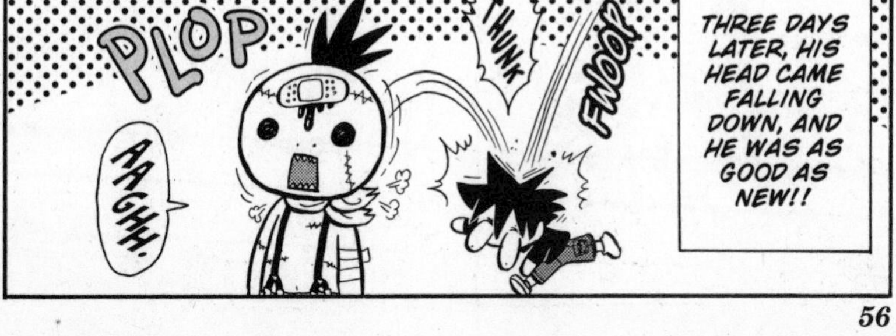
THREE DAYS LATER, HIS HEAD CAME FALLING DOWN, AND HE WAS AS GOOD AS NEW!!
FWOOP
THUNK
PLOP
AAGHH.

SPECIAL FOUR-PANEL COMIC PART 2

STRONGHEARTED
AH, IT'S A ZOMBIE! GROSS—GO AWAY !!
STUUUPID.
HEY, STITCHES !!
IGNORE
STAYING CALM LIKE THAT EVEN THOUGH THEY'RE BEING MEAN...YOU MUST HAVE A REALLY STRONG HEART !!
TAKE THIS !!!
ORANGE JUICE
CHUCK
SMASH
SPROING
HEART
IT ACTUALLY WAS STRONG.

CHARMERS
TOOT TOOT
WORLD STREET PERFORMANCES SHOW!!
THAT SNAKE CHARMER IS SO COOOL !!
SPROING
AAAGHXX.
HUH? YOU CAN DO IT TOO !?
TWEET TWEET
SPROING
Y-YOU REALLY CAN! THAT'S CRAZY !!
TWEET
SPROING
INTESTINES
AAARGH.

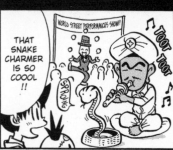

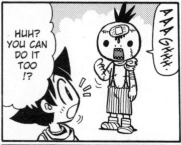

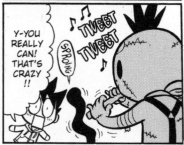

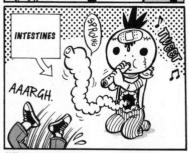

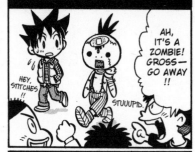

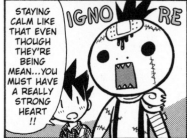

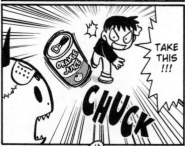

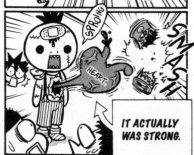

AFTER IT, ZTAT!

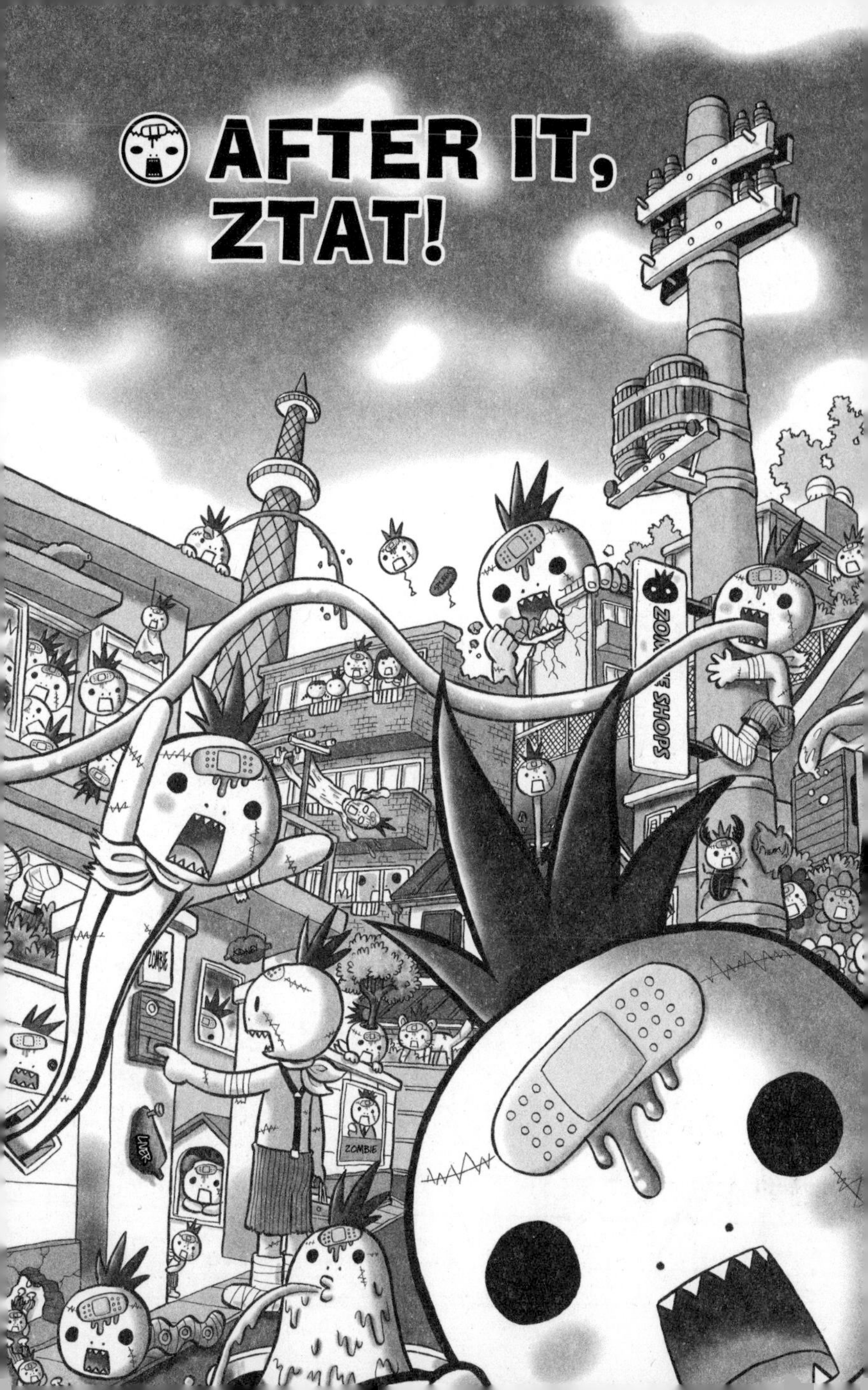
ZOMBIE
KIDNEY
LIVER
ZOMBIE

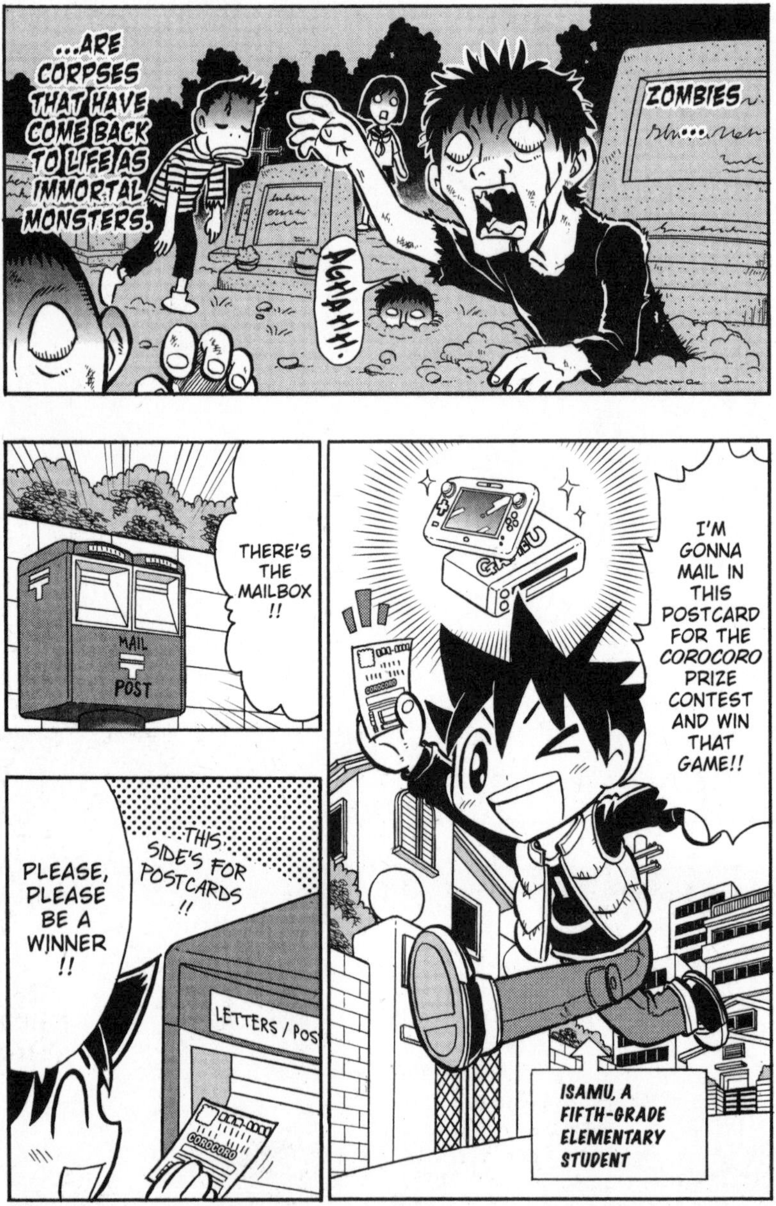

ZOMBIES...
AGHAHH.
...ARE CORPSES THAT HAVE COME BACK TO LIFE AS IMMORTAL MONSTERS.
I'M GONNA MAIL IN THIS POSTCARD FOR THE *COROCORO* PRIZE CONTEST AND WIN THAT GAME!!
COROCORO
ISAMU, A FIFTH-GRADE ELEMENTARY STUDENT
THERE'S THE MAILBOX!!
MAIL
POST
THIS SIDE'S FOR POSTCARDS!!
PLEASE, PLEASE BE A WINNER!!
LETTERS / POS
COROCORO

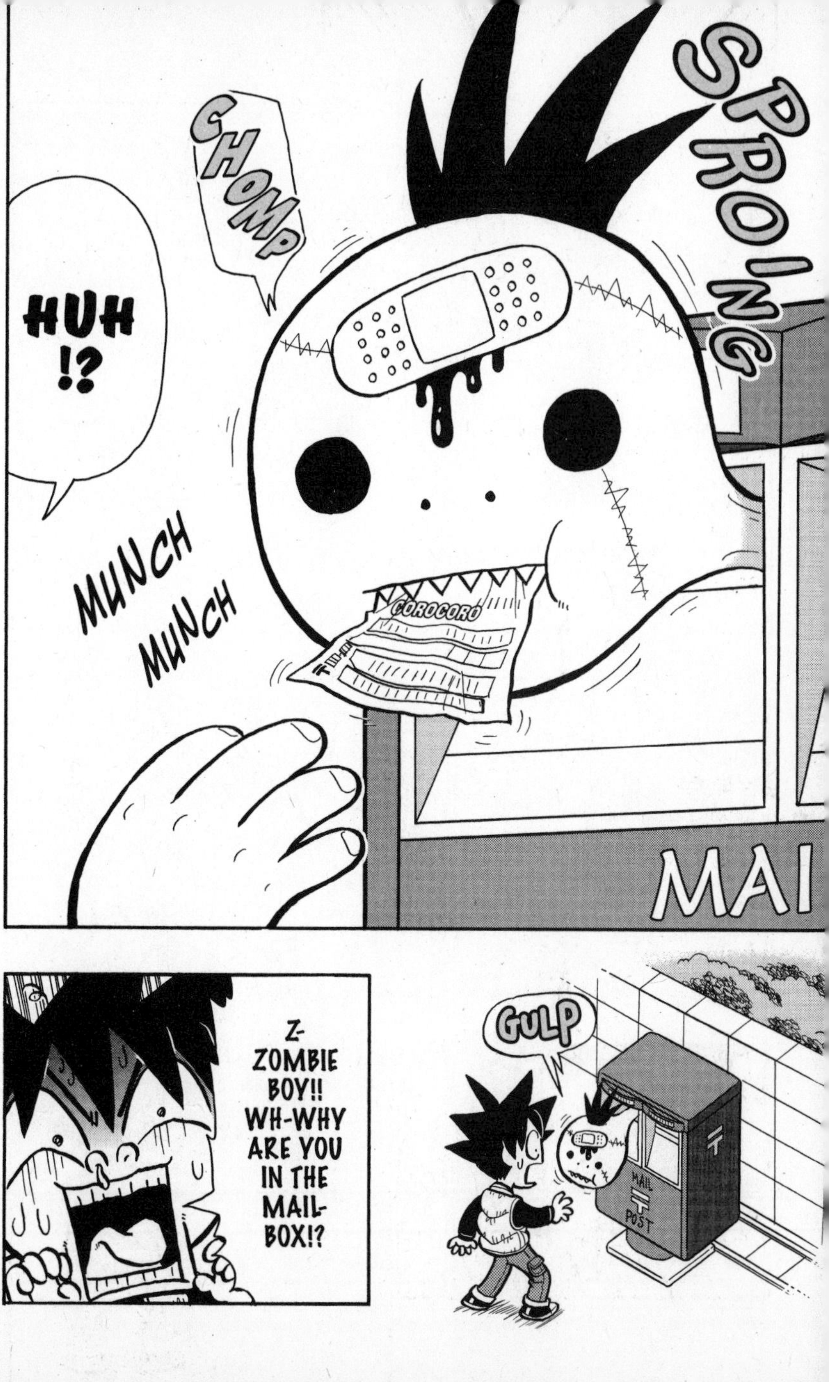
SPROING
CHOMP
HUH !?
MUNCH MUNCH
COROCORO
MAI
GULP
MAIL
POST
Z- ZOMBIE BOY!! WH-WHY ARE YOU IN THE MAIL-BOX!?

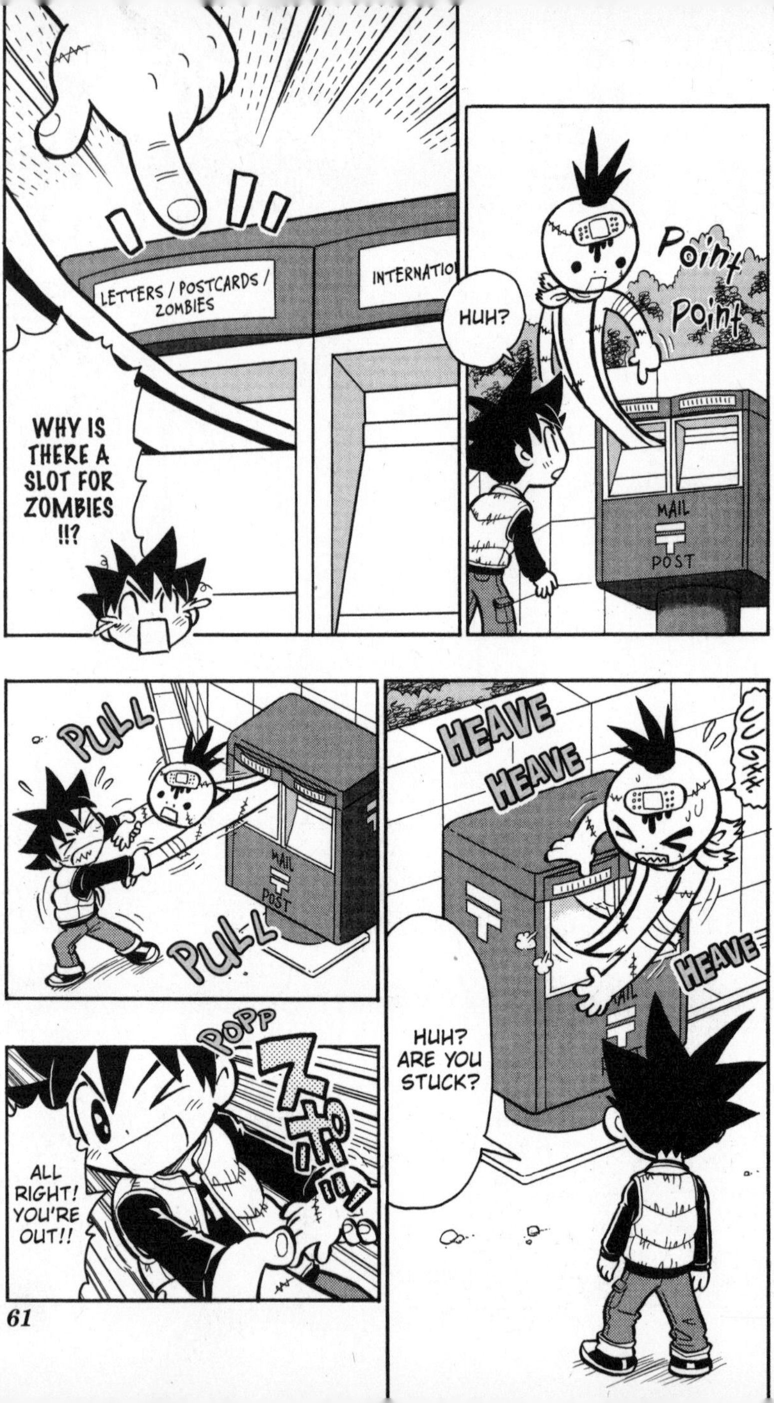
HUH?
Point
Point
MAIL
POST
LETTERS / POSTCARDS / ZOMBIES
INTERNATIO
WHY IS THERE A SLOT FOR ZOMBIES!!?
HEAVE
HEAVE
UUGHH.
HEAVE
HUH? ARE YOU STUCK?
PULL
MAIL
POST
PULL
POPP
ALL RIGHT! YOU'RE OUT!!

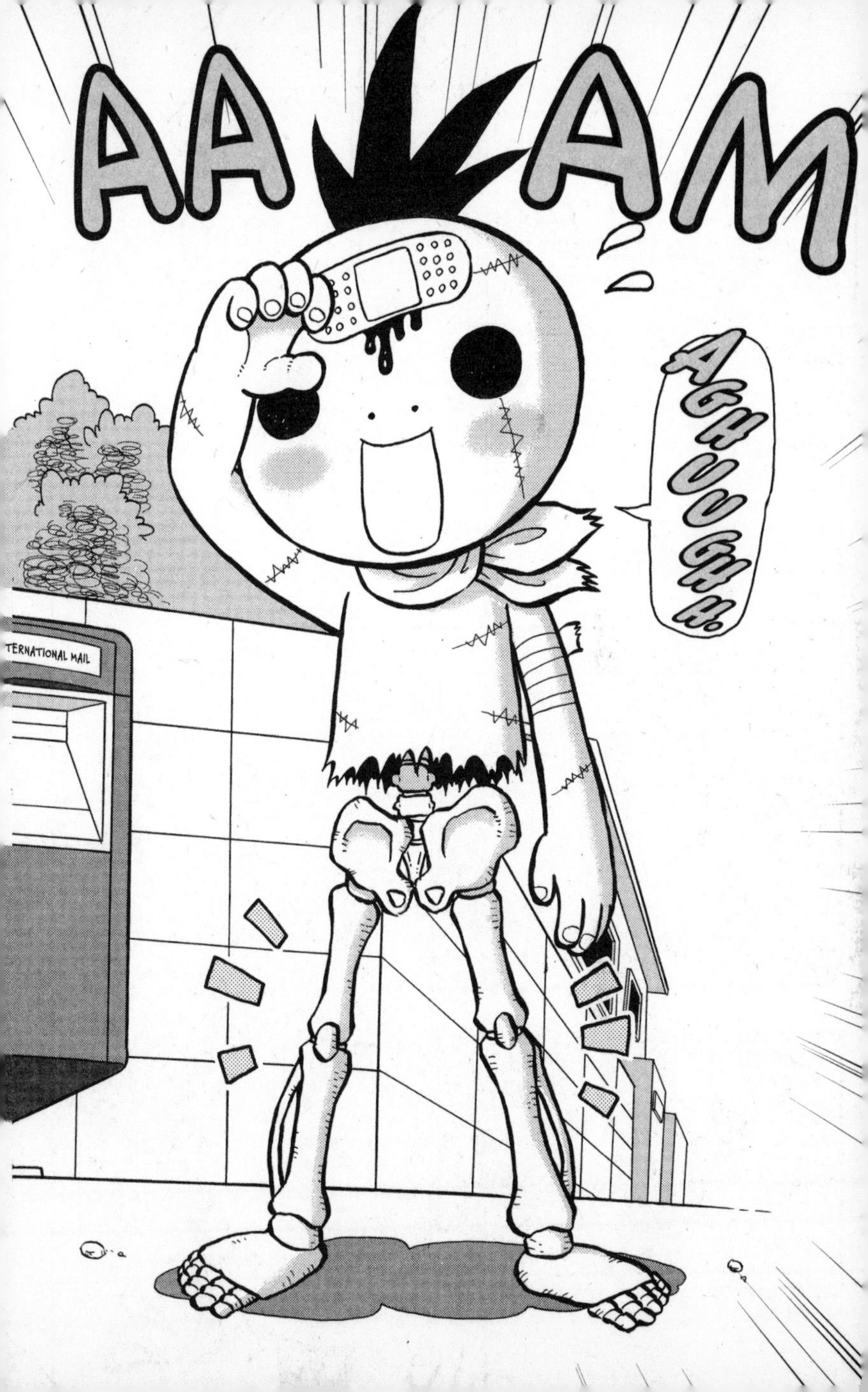
AAAAM
AGHUUGHH.
TERNATIONAL MAIL

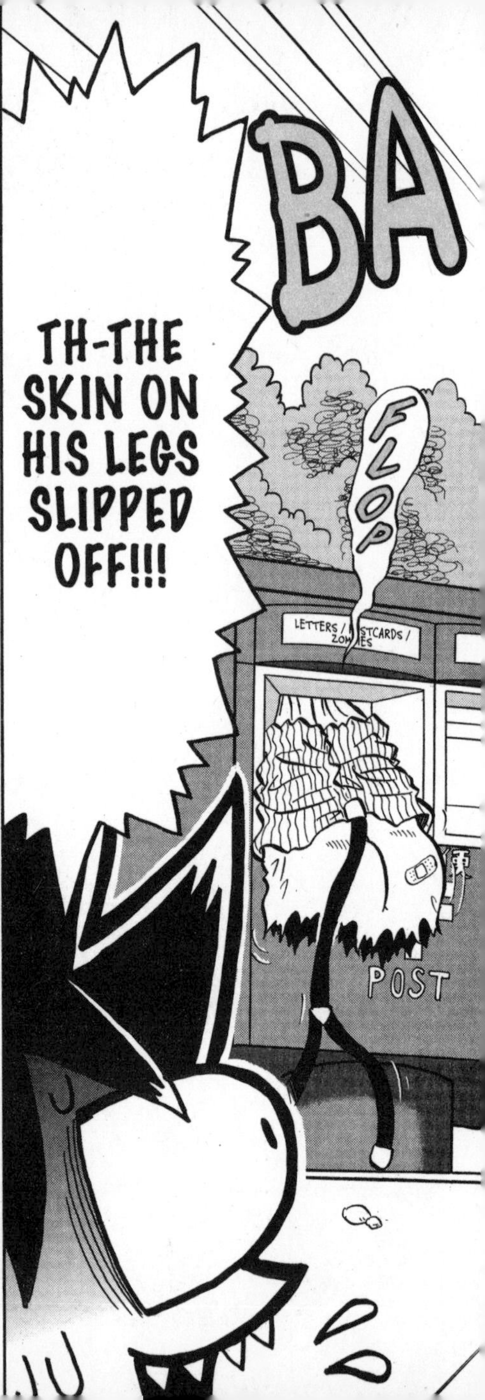
BA
TH-THE SKIN ON HIS LEGS SLIPPED OFF!!!
FLOP
POST

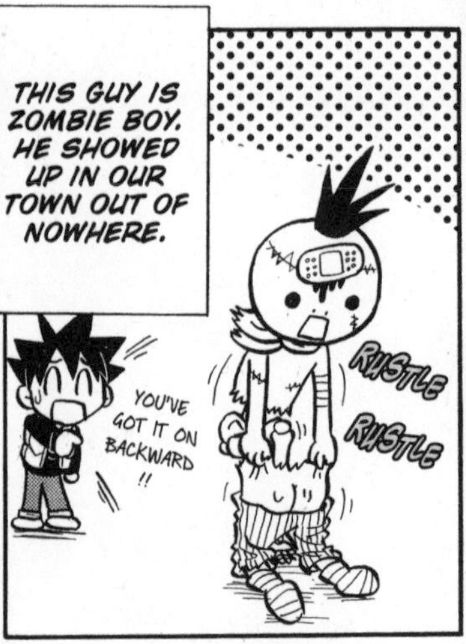
THIS GUY IS ZOMBIE BOY. HE SHOWED UP IN OUR TOWN OUT OF NOWHERE.
RUSTLE
RUSTLE
YOU'VE GOT IT ON BACKWARD!!

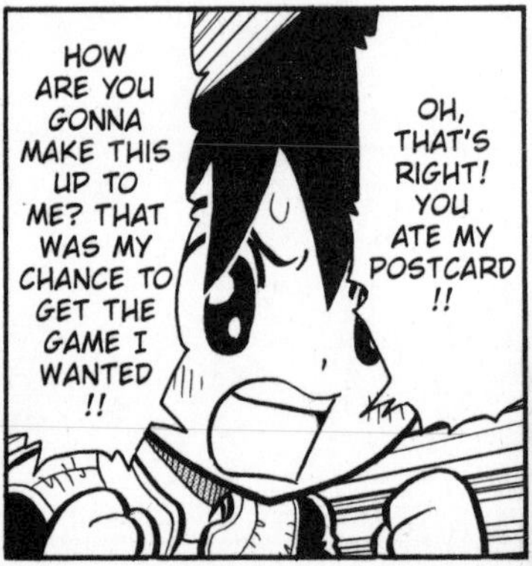
OH, THAT'S RIGHT! YOU ATE MY POSTCARD!!
HOW ARE YOU GONNA MAKE THIS UP TO ME? THAT WAS MY CHANCE TO GET THE GAME I WANTED!!

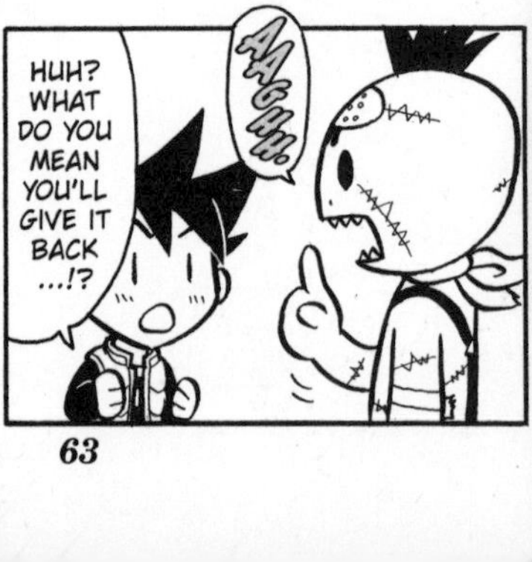
AAGHH.
HUH? WHAT DO YOU MEAN YOU'LL GIVE IT BACK...!?

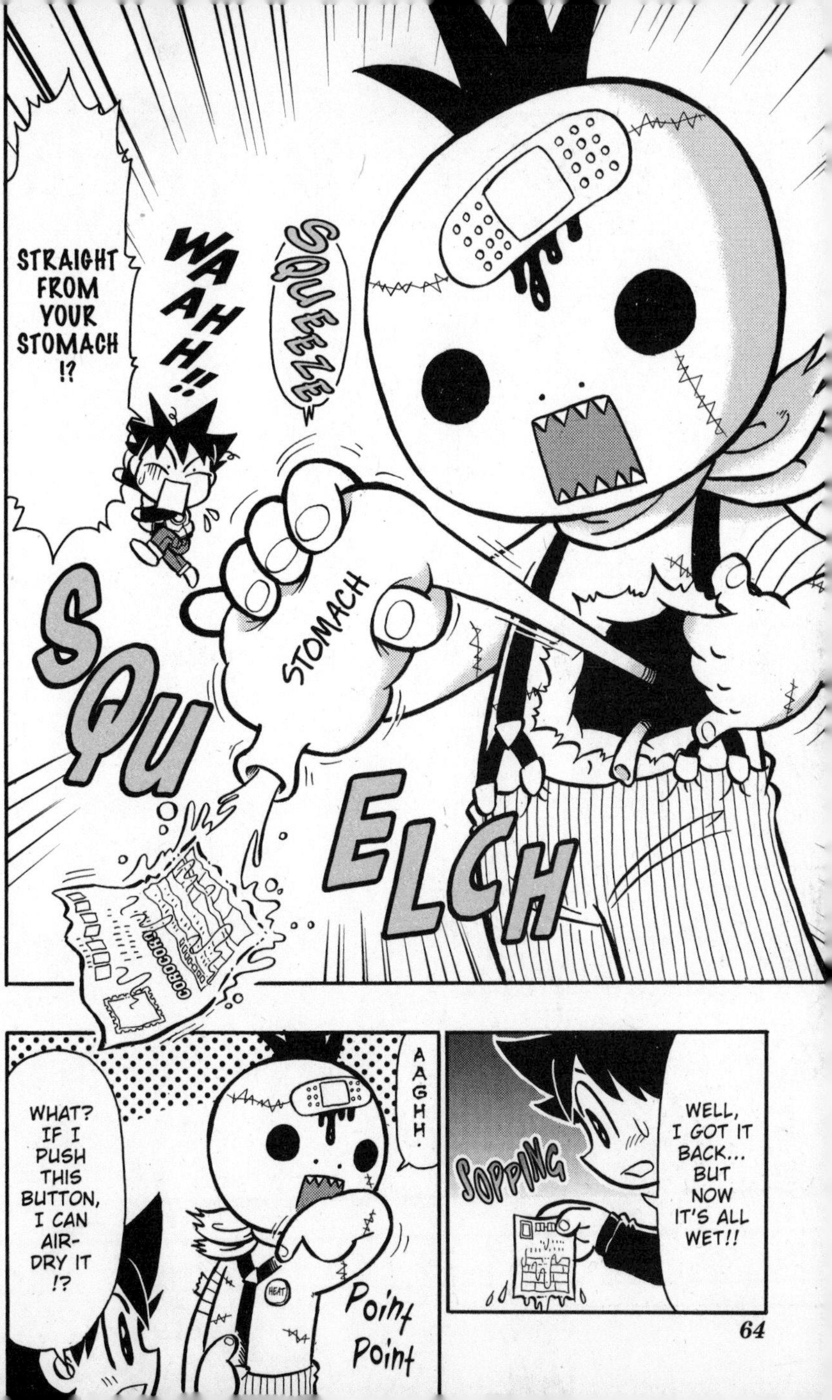
SQUEEZE
WAAHH!!
STRAIGHT FROM YOUR STOMACH !?
STOMACH
SQUELCH
WELL, I GOT IT BACK... BUT NOW IT'S ALL WET!!
SOPPING
AAGHH.
WHAT? IF I PUSH THIS BUTTON, I CAN AIR-DRY IT !?
HEAT
Point Point

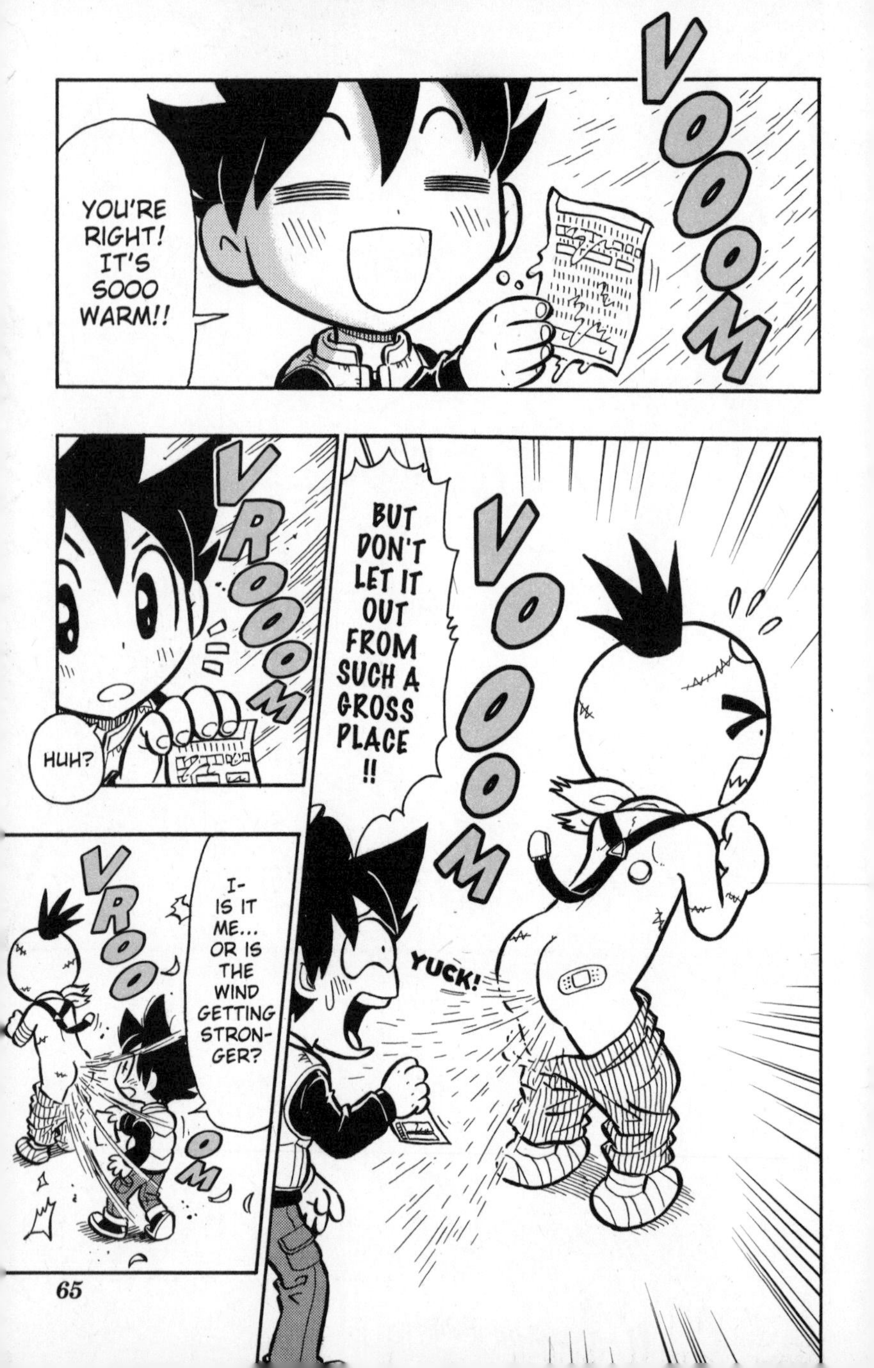
VOOOOM
YOU'RE RIGHT! IT'S SOOO WARM!!
VOOOOM
BUT DON'T LET IT OUT FROM SUCH A GROSS PLACE !!
YUCK!
VROOOOM
HUH?
VROO
OM
I- IS IT ME... OR IS THE WIND GETTING STRONGER?

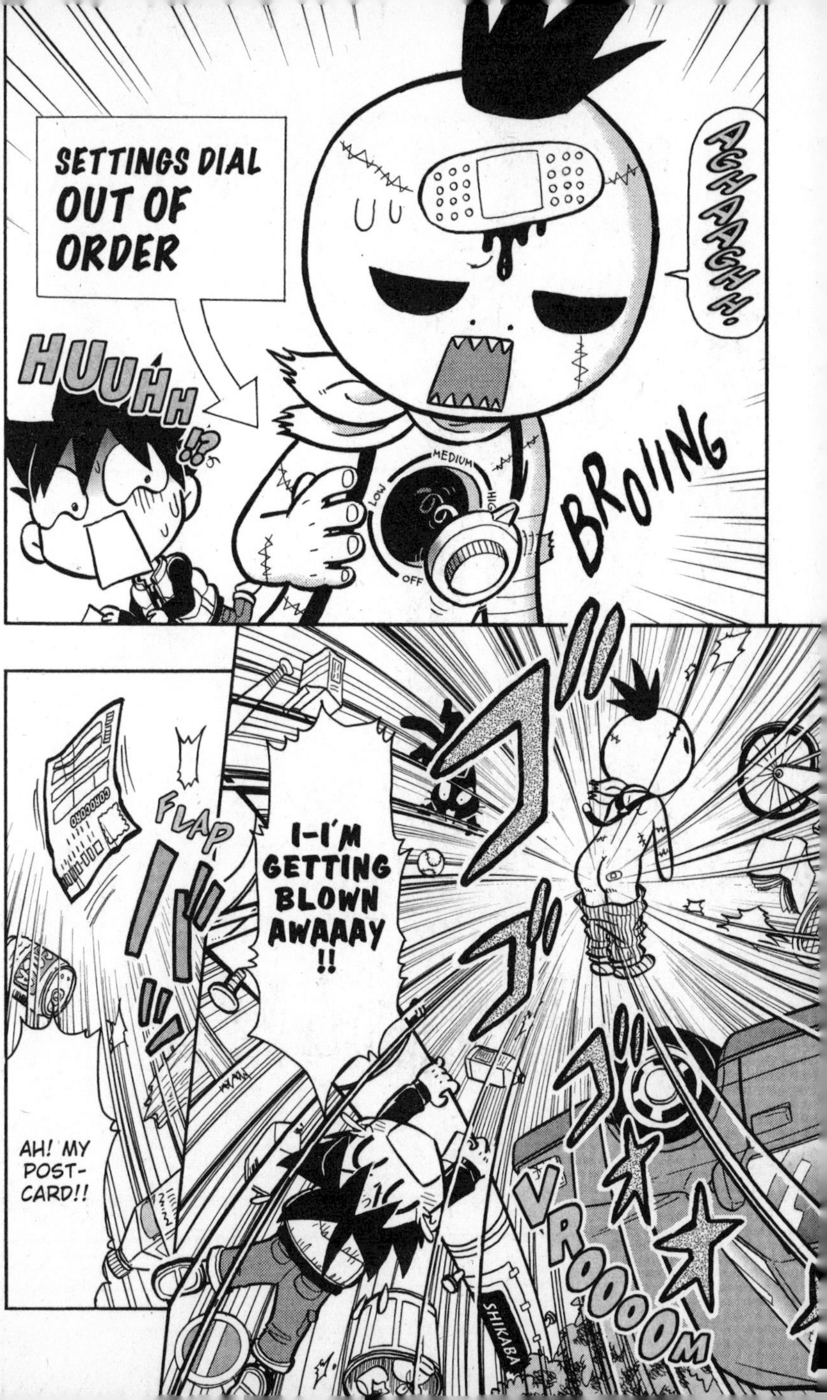
AGHAAAGHH!
SETTINGS DIAL OUT OF ORDER
HUUHH!!?
MEDIUM
LOW
HIGH
OFF
BROIING
I-I'M GETTING BLOWN AWAAAY!!
FLAP
COROCORO
AH! MY POST-CARD!!
VROOOOOM
SHIKABA

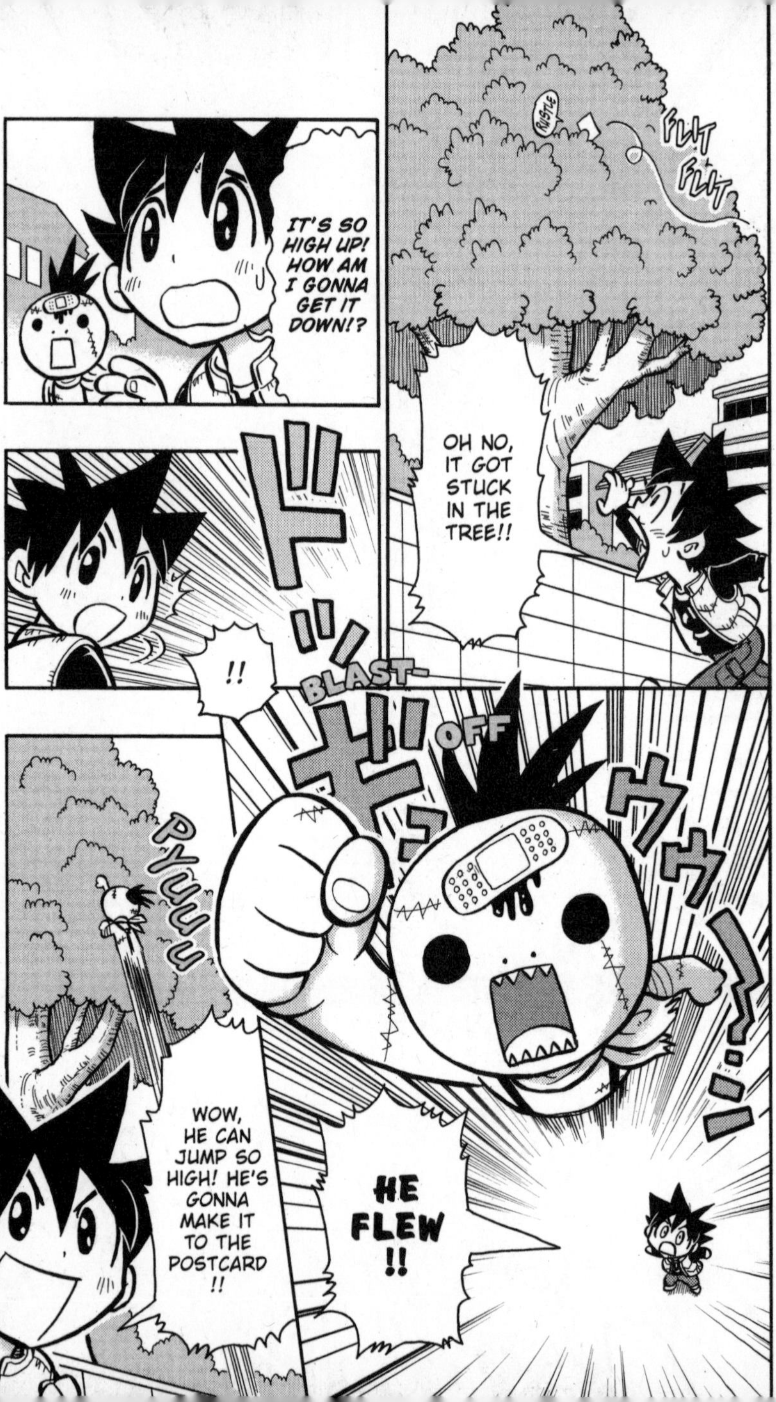
RUSTLE
FLIT FLIT
OH NO, IT GOT STUCK IN THE TREE!!
IT'S SO HIGH UP! HOW AM I GONNA GET IT DOWN!?
!!
BLAST-OFF
HE FLEW!!
PYUUU
WOW, HE CAN JUMP SO HIGH! HE'S GONNA MAKE IT TO THE POSTCARD!!

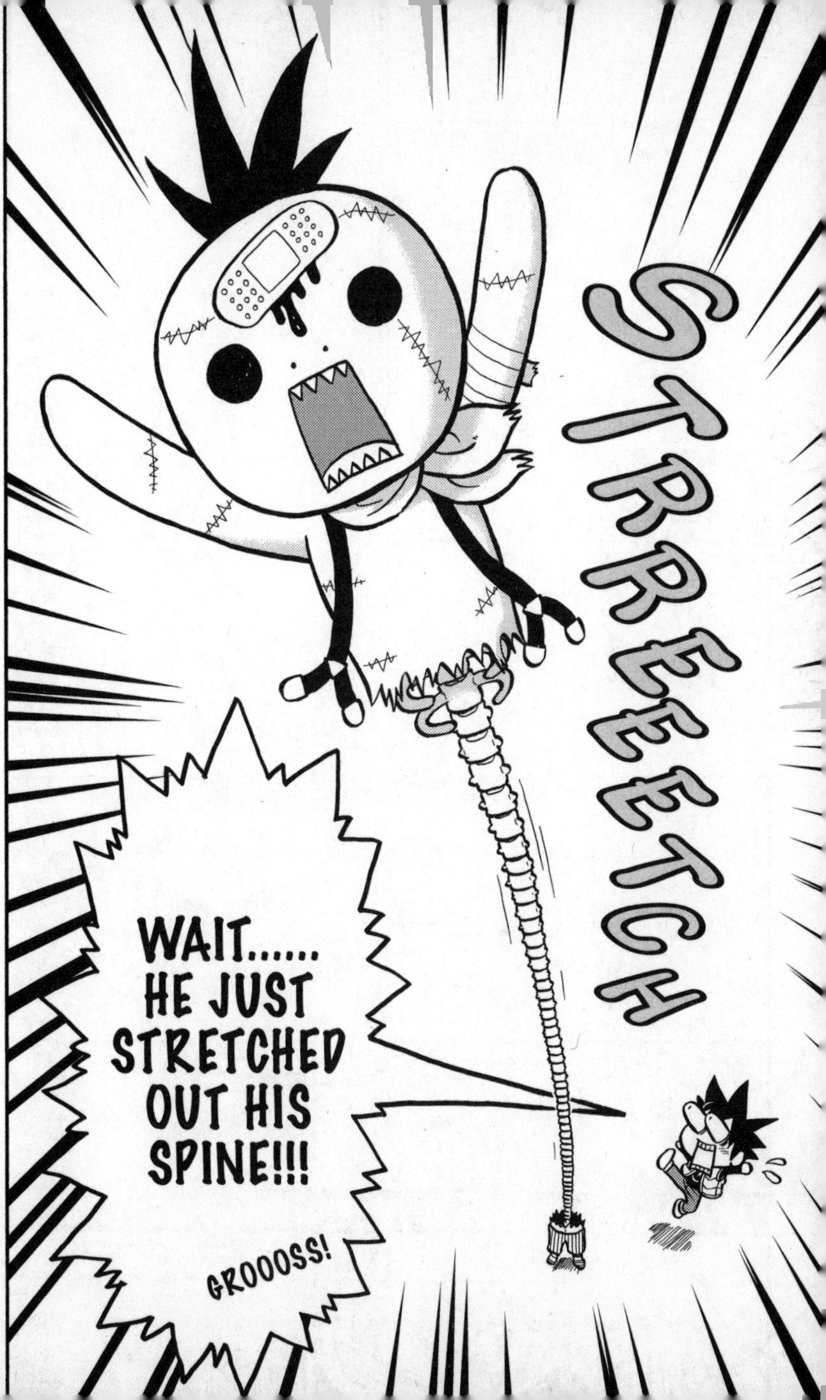
STRETCH
WAIT...... HE JUST STRETCHED OUT HIS SPINE!!!
GROOOSS!

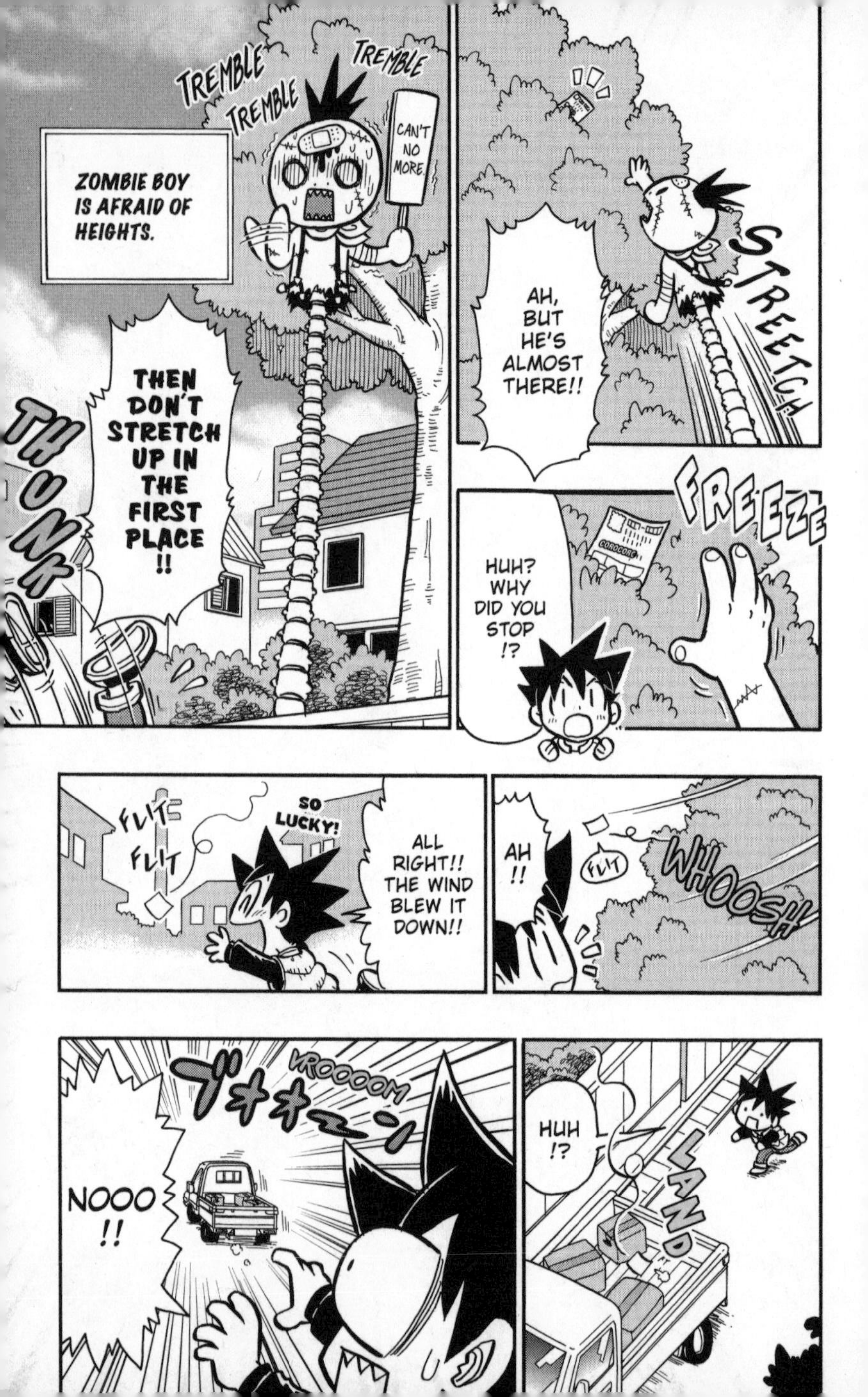
STRETCH
AH, BUT HE'S ALMOST THERE!!
FREEZE
HUH? WHY DID YOU STOP !?
TREMBLE
TREMBLE
TREMBLE
CAN'T NO MORE.
ZOMBIE BOY IS AFRAID OF HEIGHTS.
THEN DON'T STRETCH UP IN THE FIRST PLACE !!
THUNK
WHOOSH
FLIT
AH !!
ALL RIGHT!! THE WIND BLEW IT DOWN!!
SO LUCKY!
FLIT FLIT
HUH !?
LAND
VROOOOM
NOOO !!

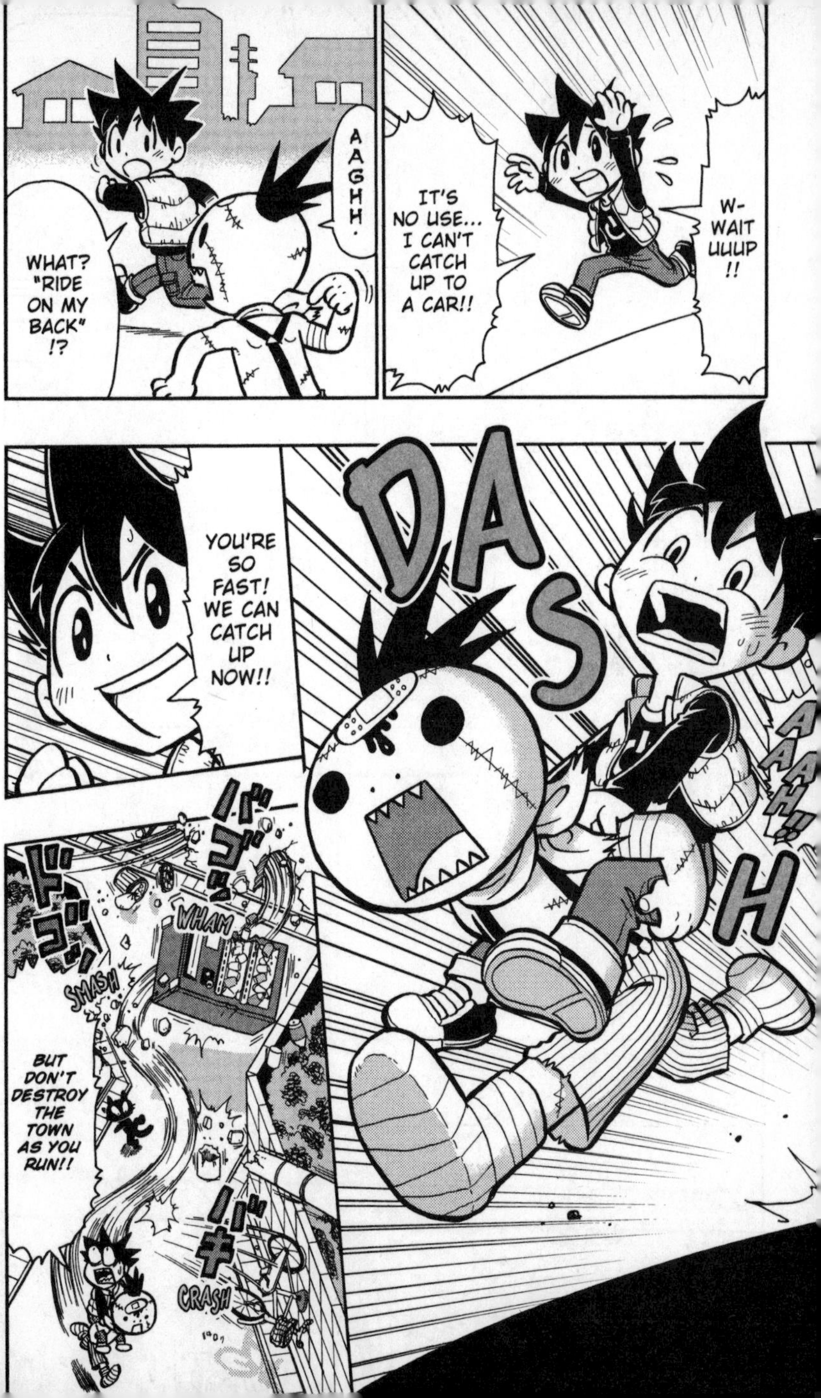
W- WAIT UUUP!!
IT'S NO USE... I CAN'T CATCH UP TO A CAR!!
AAGHH.
WHAT? "RIDE ON MY BACK" !?
DASH
AAAAH!!
YOU'RE SO FAST! WE CAN CATCH UP NOW!!
WHAM
SMASH
BUT DON'T DESTROY THE TOWN AS YOU RUN!!
CRASH

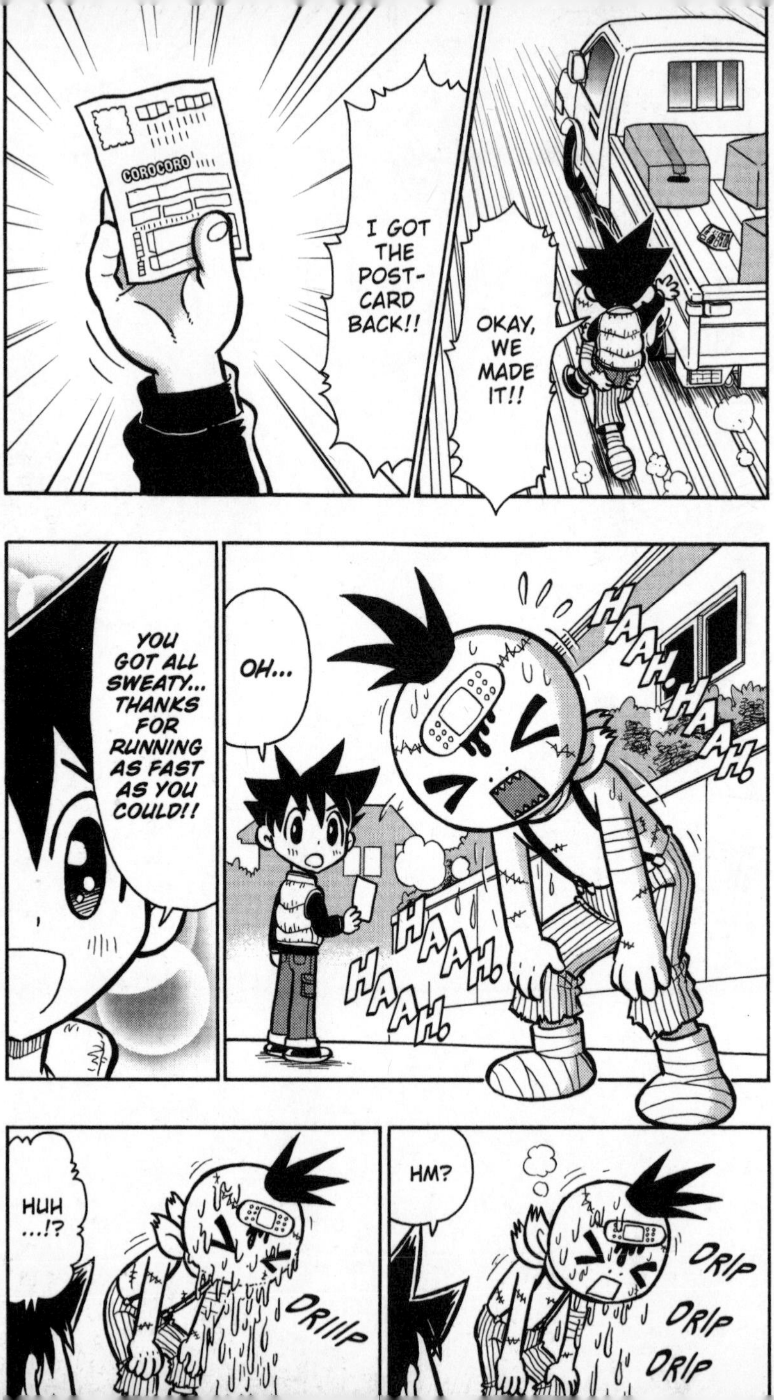
OKAY, WE MADE IT!!
I GOT THE POST-CARD BACK!!
HAAH HAAH HAAH
OH...
HAAH HAAH
YOU GOT ALL SWEATY... THANKS FOR RUNNING AS FAST AS YOU COULD!!
HM?
DRIP DRIP DRIP
HUH ...!?
DRIIIP

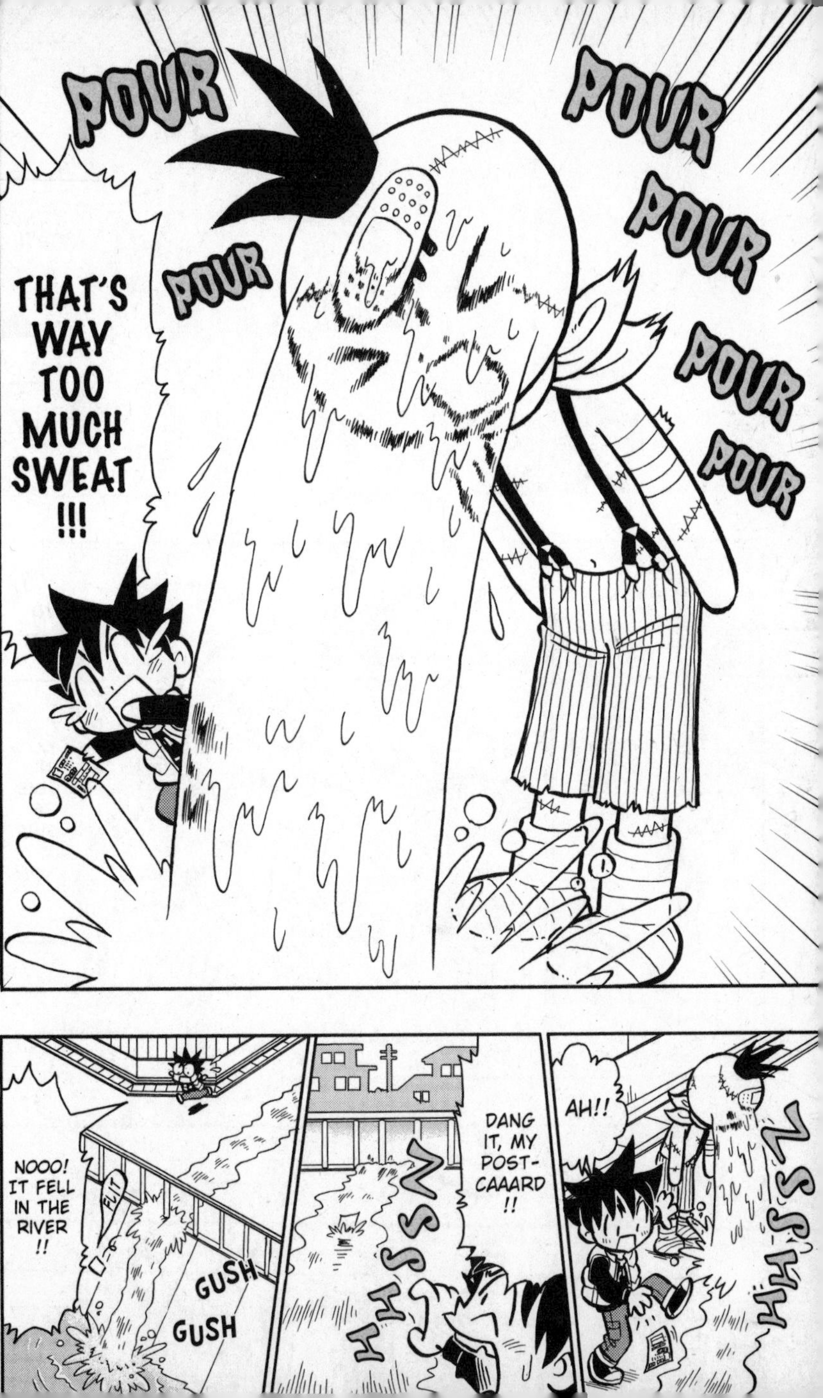
POUR
POUR
POUR
POUR
POUR
POUR
THAT'S WAY TOO MUCH SWEAT!!!
AH!!
DANG IT, MY POST-CAAARD!!
NOOO! IT FELL IN THE RIVER!!
FLIT
GUSH
GUSH

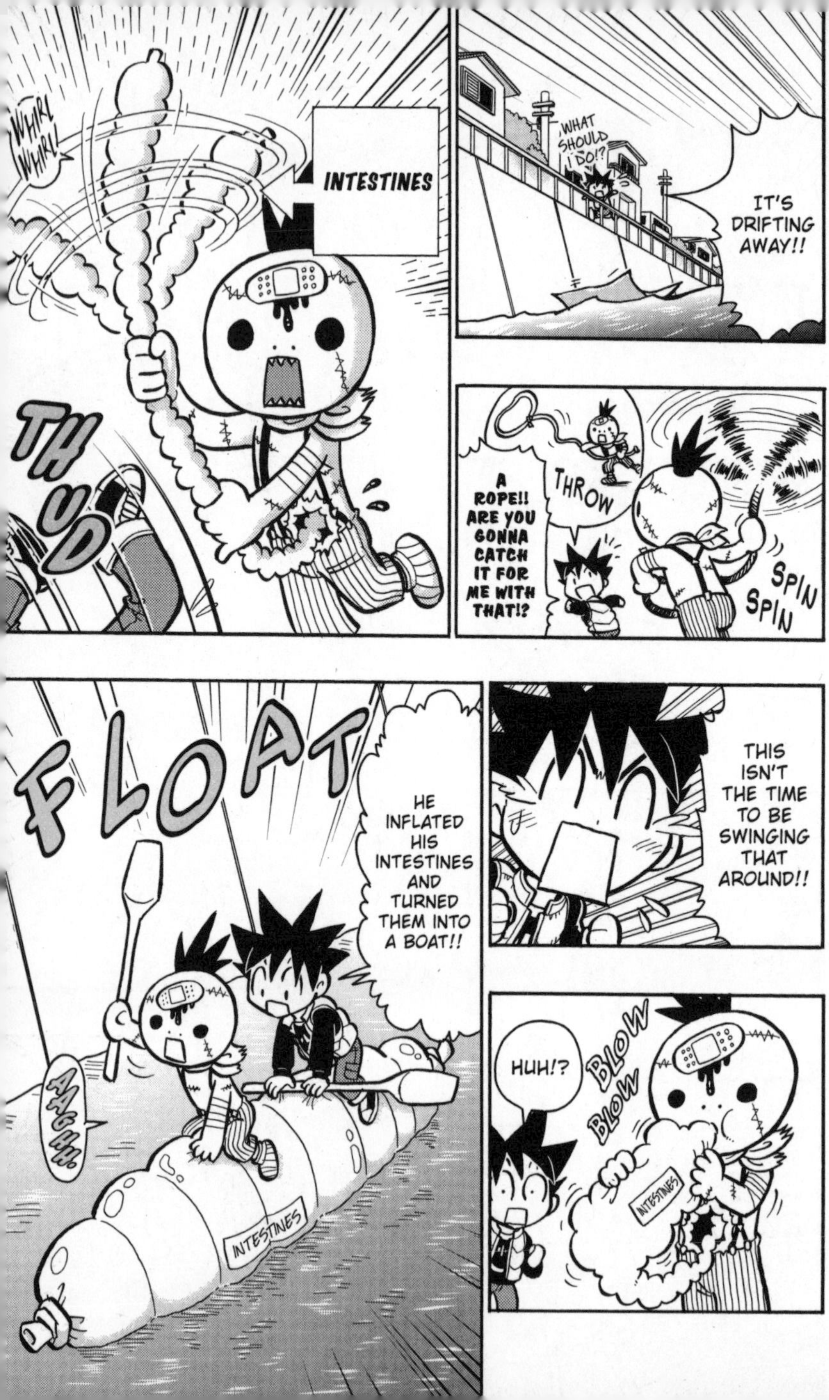
WHAT SHOULD I DO!?
IT'S DRIFTING AWAY!!
THROW
A ROPE!! ARE YOU GONNA CATCH IT FOR ME WITH THAT!?
SPIN SPIN
INTESTINES
WHIRL WHIRL
THUD
THIS ISN'T THE TIME TO BE SWINGING THAT AROUND!!
BLOW BLOW
HUH!?
INTESTINES
FLOAT
HE INFLATED HIS INTESTINES AND TURNED THEM INTO A BOAT!!
AAGH
INTESTINES

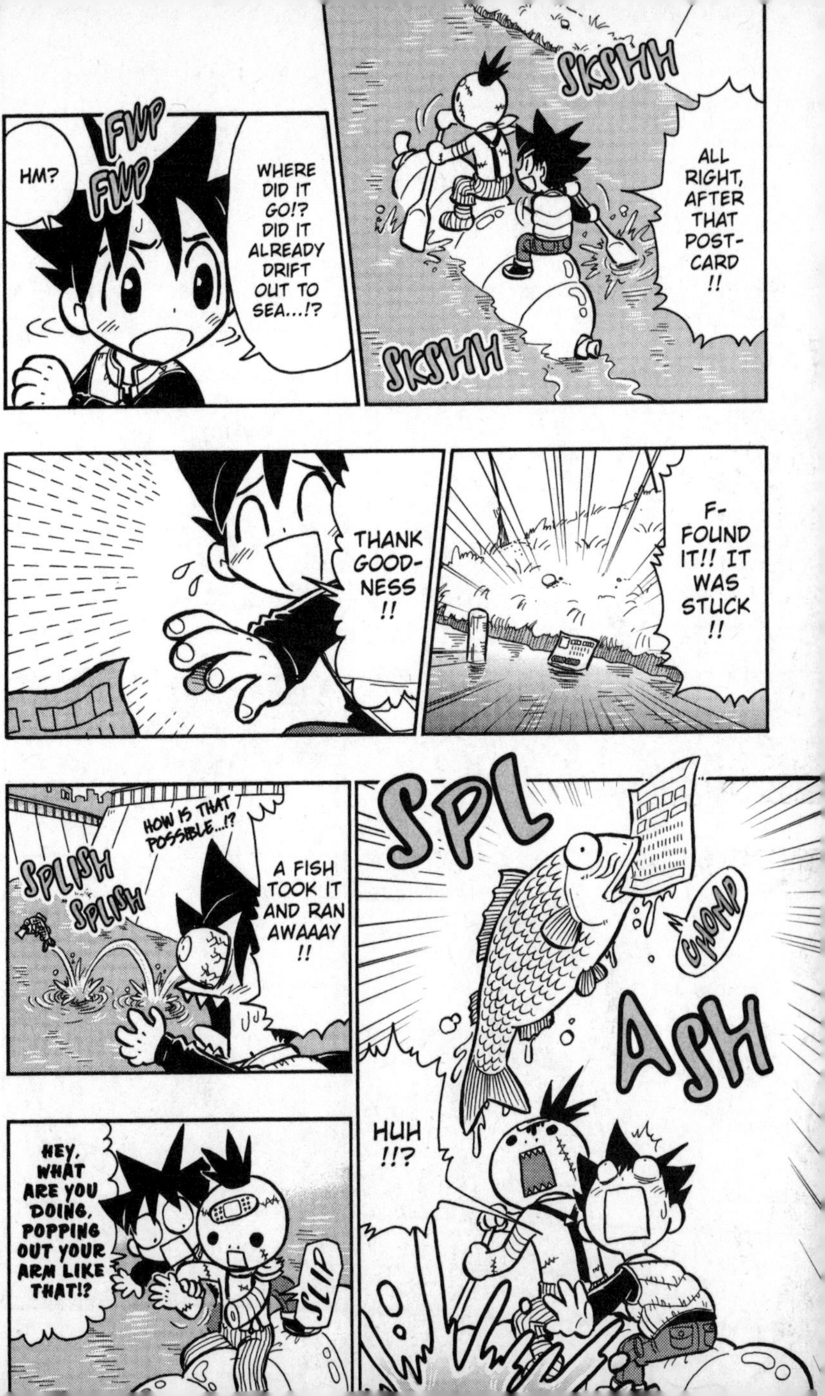
SKSHH
ALL RIGHT, AFTER THAT POST-CARD!!
SKSHH
FWP FWP
HM?
WHERE DID IT GO!? DID IT ALREADY DRIFT OUT TO SEA...!?
F-FOUND IT!! IT WAS STUCK!!
THANK GOODNESS!!
SPLASH
CHOMP
HUH!!?
HOW IS THAT POSSIBLE...!?
A FISH TOOK IT AND RAN AWAAAY!!
SPLISH
SPLISH
HEY, WHAT ARE YOU DOING, POPPING OUT YOUR ARM LIKE THAT!?
SLIP

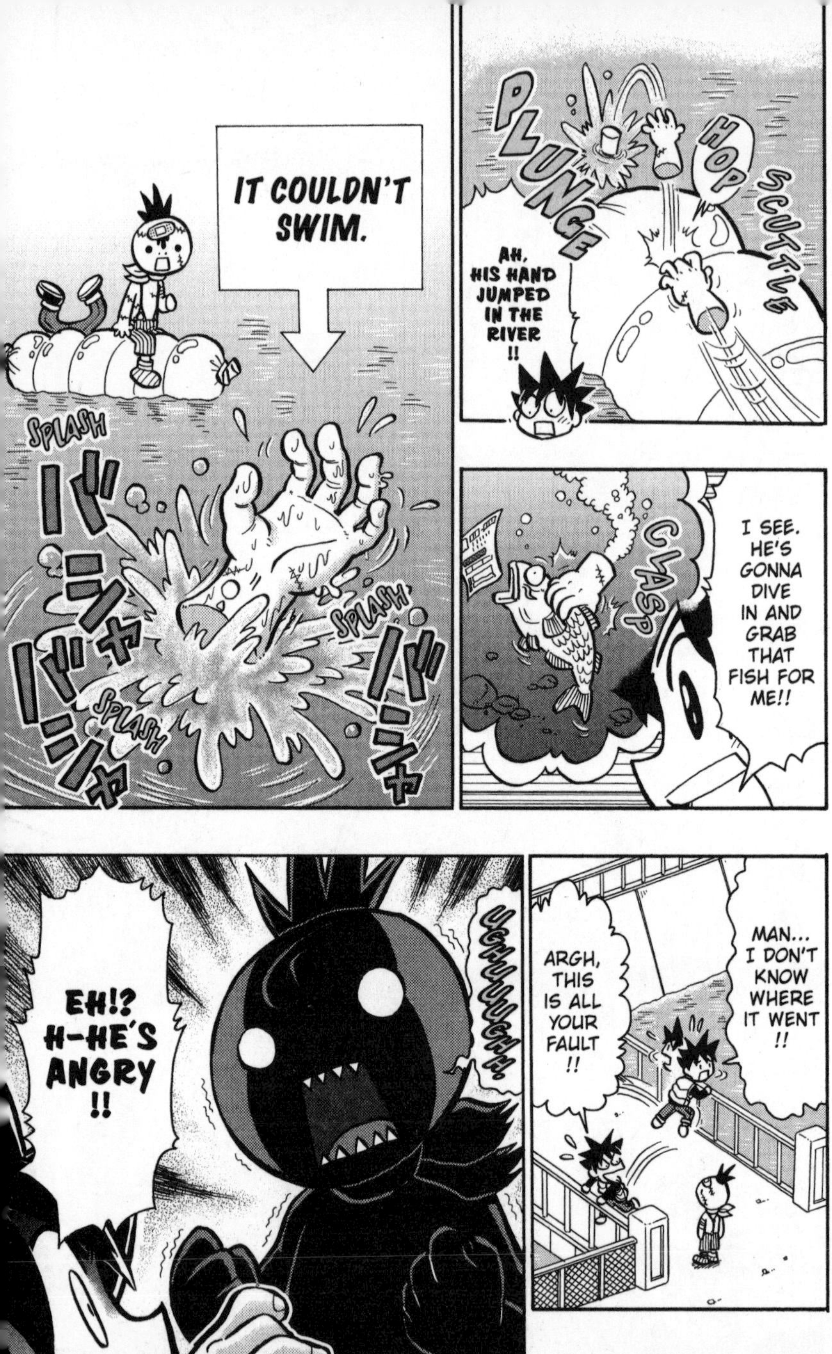
SCUTTLE
HOP
PLUNGE
AH, HIS HAND JUMPED IN THE RIVER !!
I SEE. HE'S GONNA DIVE IN AND GRAB THAT FISH FOR ME!!
CLASP
IT COULDN'T SWIM.
SPLASH
バシャ
SPLASH
バシャ
SPLASH
バシャ
MAN... I DON'T KNOW WHERE IT WENT !!
ARGH, THIS IS ALL YOUR FAULT !!
UGHUUUGHH!
EH!? H-HE'S ANGRY !!

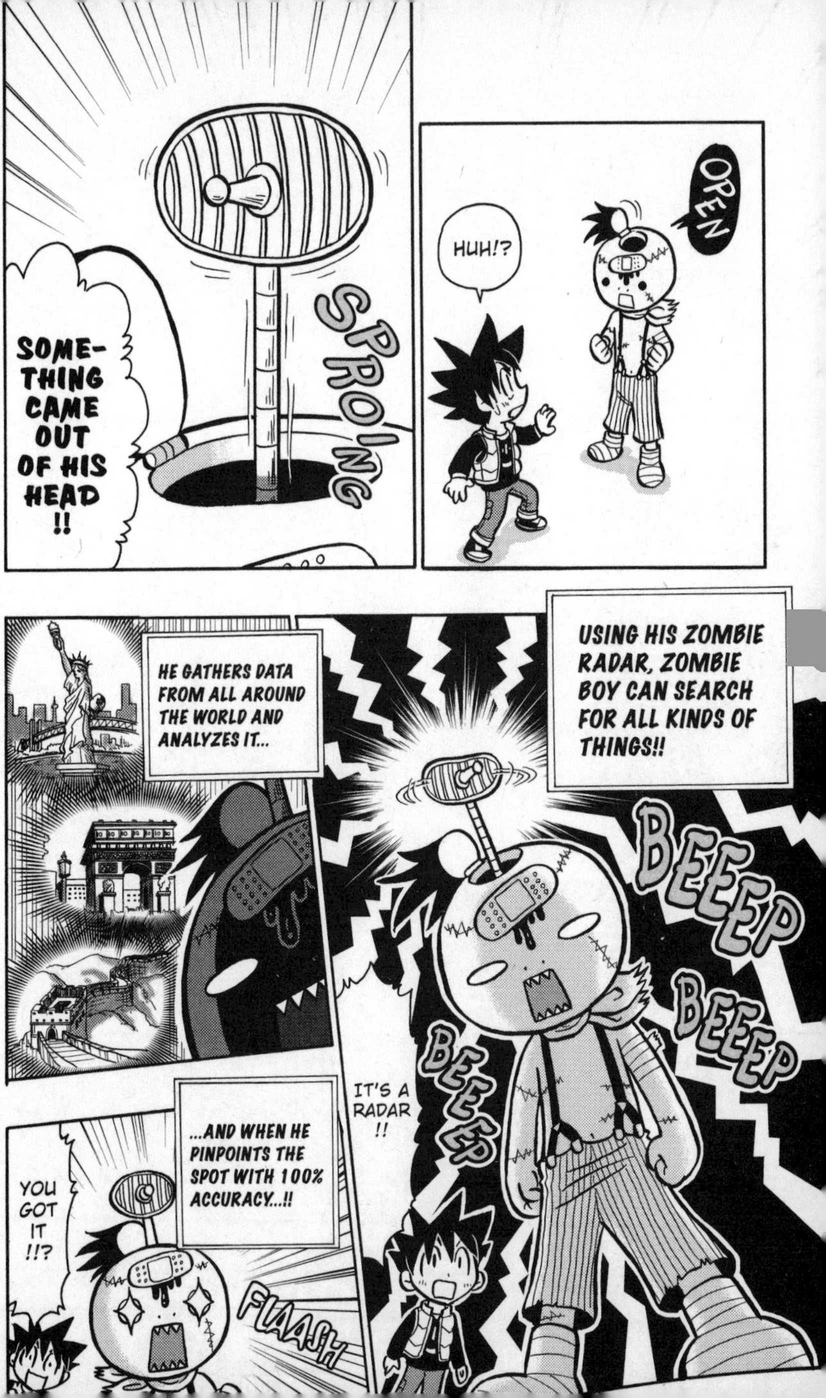
OPEN
HUH!?
SPROING
SOME-THING CAME OUT OF HIS HEAD!!
USING HIS ZOMBIE RADAR, ZOMBIE BOY CAN SEARCH FOR ALL KINDS OF THINGS!!
BEEEP
BEEEP
BEEEP
IT'S A RADAR!!
HE GATHERS DATA FROM ALL AROUND THE WORLD AND ANALYZES IT...
...AND WHEN HE PINPOINTS THE SPOT WITH 100% ACCURACY...!!
YOU GOT IT!!?
FLAASH

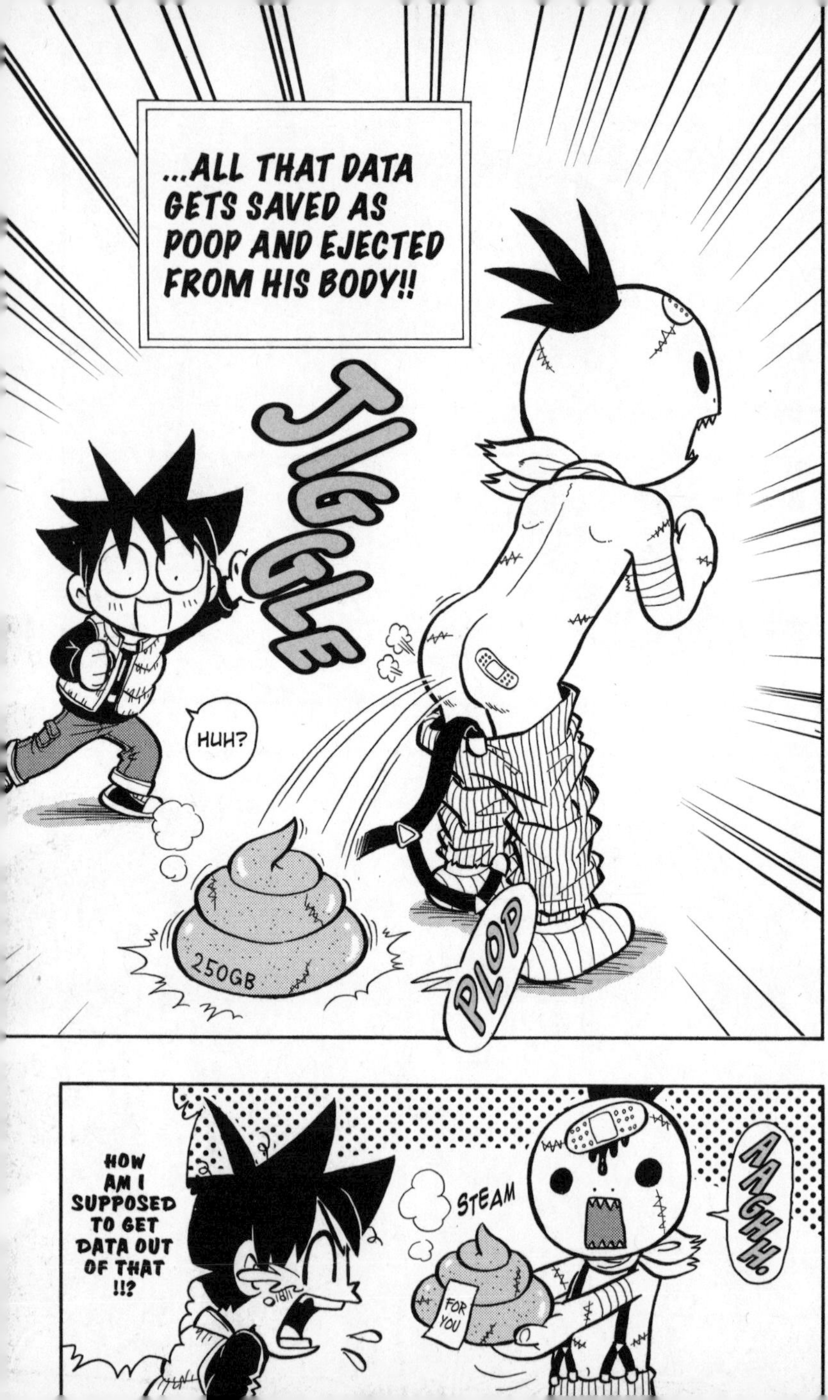
...ALL THAT DATA GETS SAVED AS POOP AND EJECTED FROM HIS BODY!!
JIGGLE
HUH?
250GB
PLOP
AAGHH.
STEAM
FOR YOU
HOW AM I SUPPOSED TO GET DATA OUT OF THAT !!?

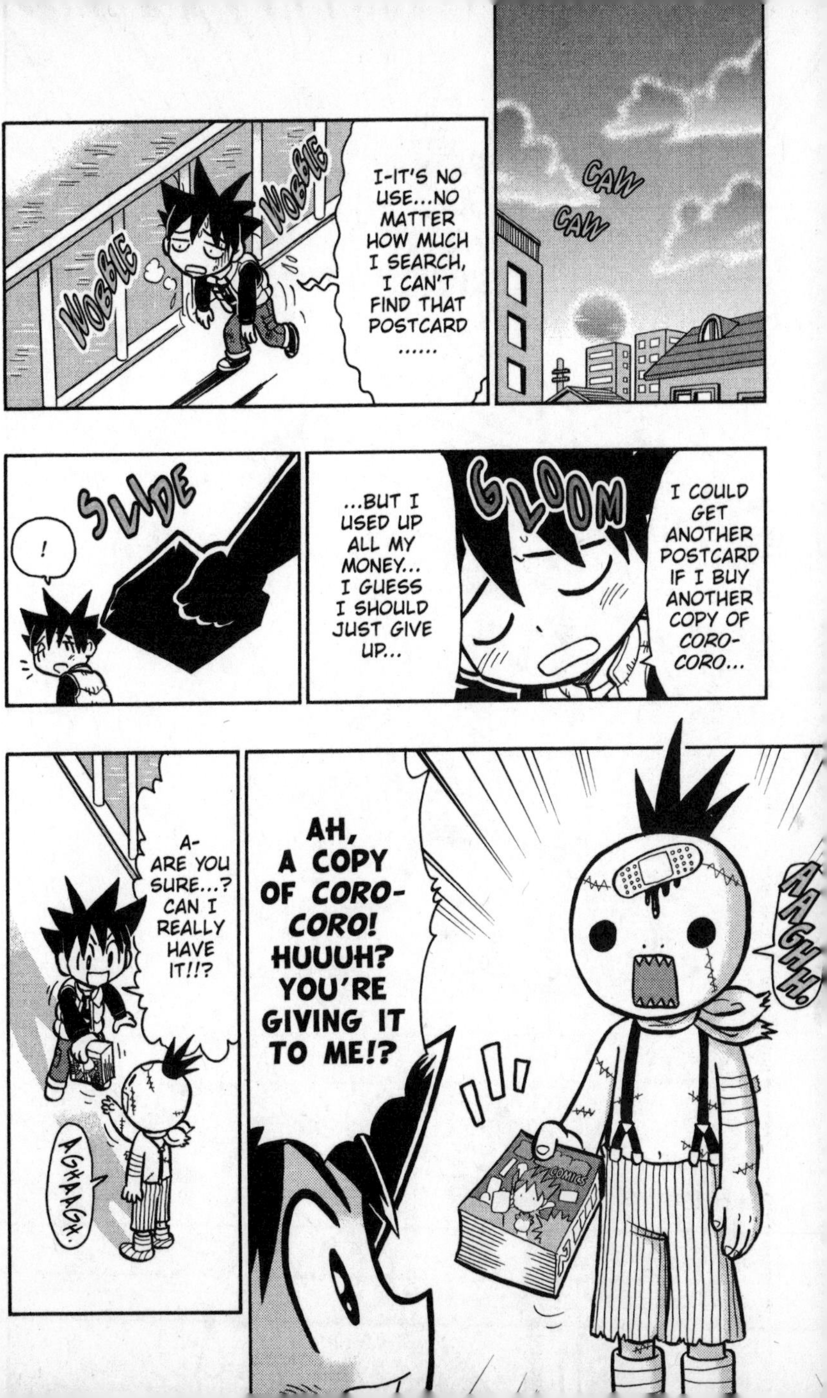
CAW
CAW
WOBBLE
WOBBLE
I-IT'S NO USE...NO MATTER HOW MUCH I SEARCH, I CAN'T FIND THAT POSTCARD ......
I COULD GET ANOTHER POSTCARD IF I BUY ANOTHER COPY OF CORO-CORO...
GLOOM
...BUT I USED UP ALL MY MONEY... I GUESS I SHOULD JUST GIVE UP...
SLIDE
!
AAAGHH.
AH, A COPY OF *CORO-CORO*! HUUUH? YOU'RE GIVING IT TO ME!?
A- ARE YOU SURE...? CAN I REALLY HAVE IT!!?
AGHAAGH.

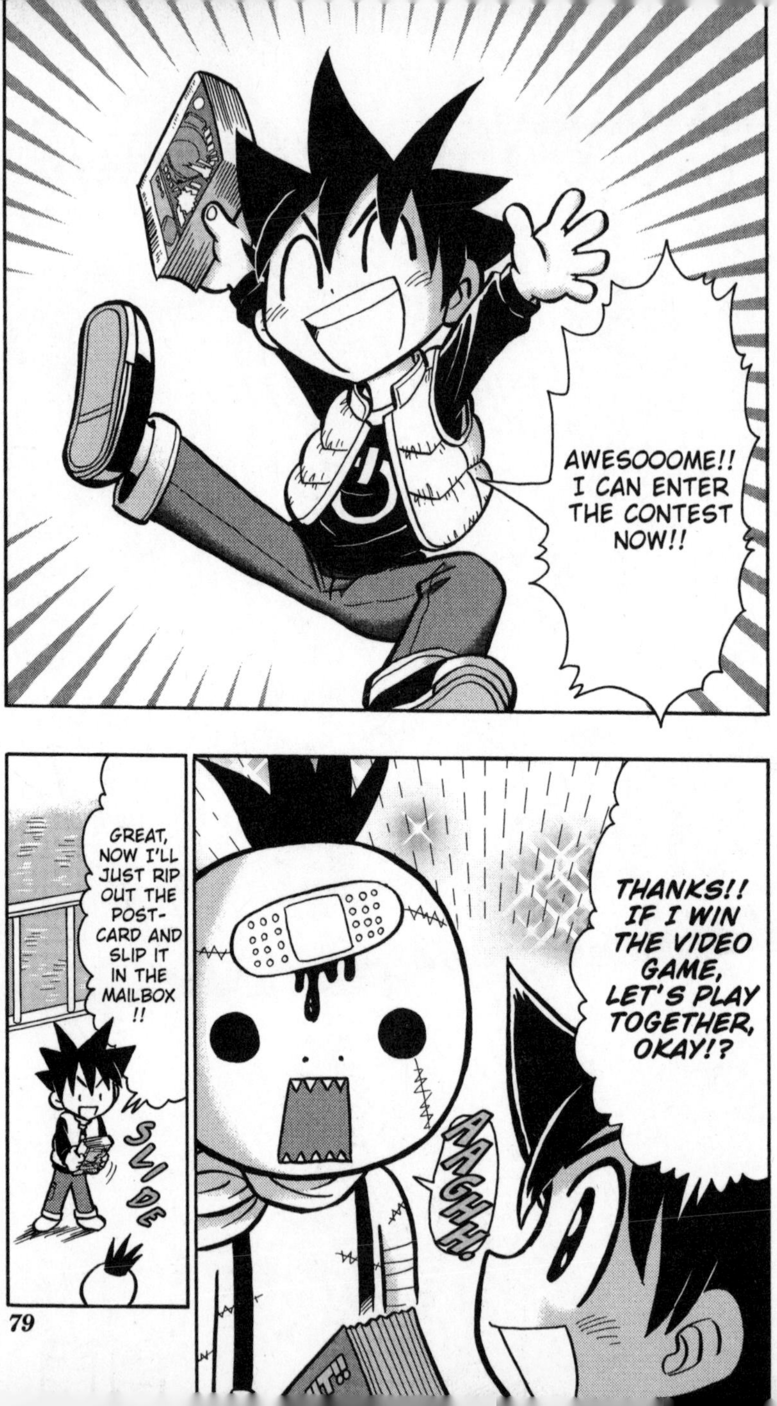
AWESOOOME!! I CAN ENTER THE CONTEST NOW!!
THANKS!! IF I WIN THE VIDEO GAME, LET'S PLAY TOGETHER, OKAY!?
AAAGHH!
GREAT, NOW I'LL JUST RIP OUT THE POST-CARD AND SLIP IT IN THE MAILBOX!!
SLIDE

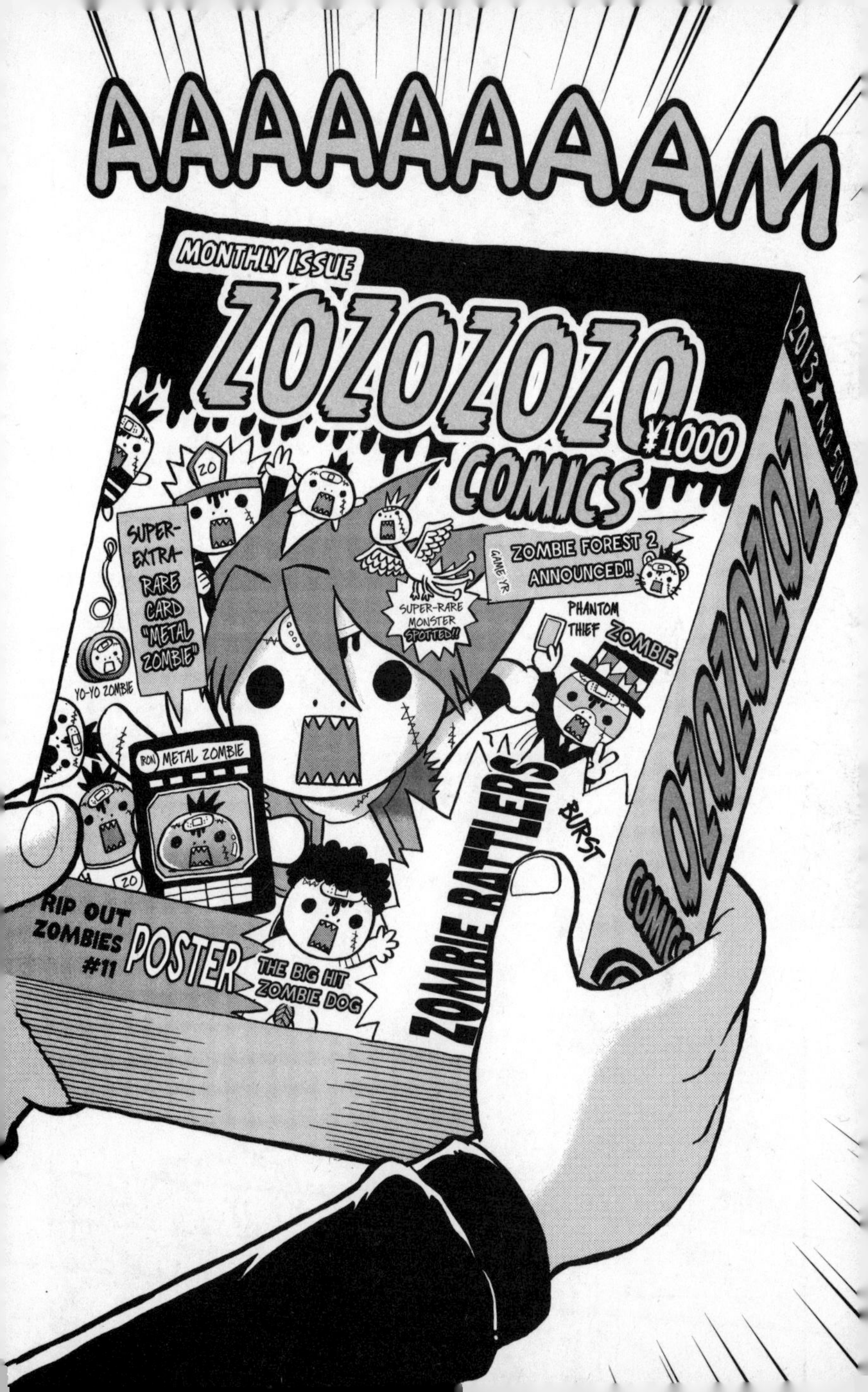
AAAAAAAAAM
MONTHLY ISSUE
ZOZOZOZO
¥1000
COMICS
2013★No.500
SUPER-EXTRA-RARE CARD "METAL ZOMBIE"
ZO
GAME YR
ZOMBIE FOREST 2 ANNOUNCED!!
SUPER-RARE MONSTER SPOTTED!!
PHANTOM THIEF ZOMBIE
YO-YO ZOMBIE
IRON METAL ZOMBIE
ZO
ZOMBIE RATTLERS
BURST
RIP OUT ZOMBIES #11 POSTER
THE BIG HIT ZOMBIE DOG
ZOZOZOZO COMICS

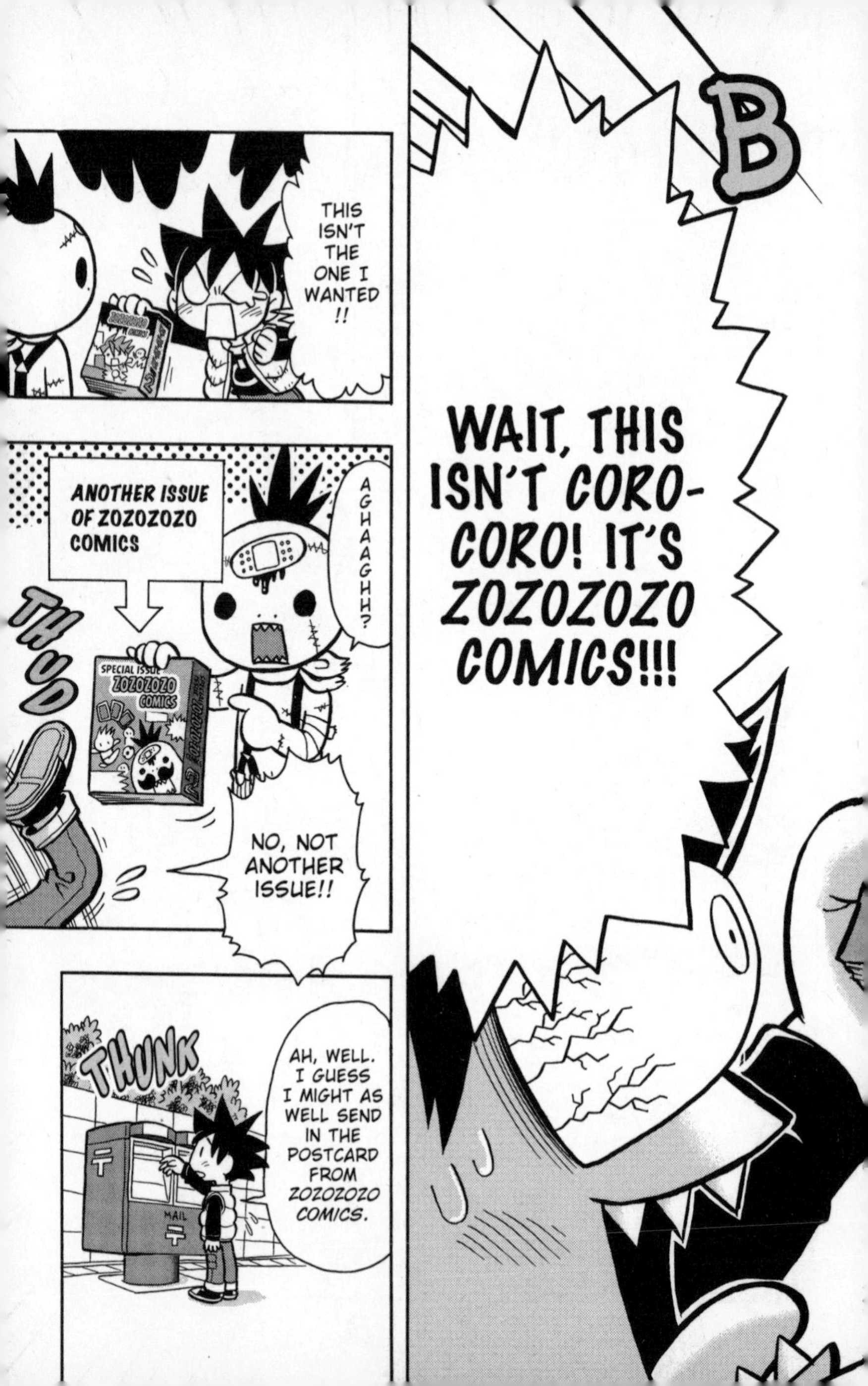
B
WAIT, THIS ISN'T *CORO-CORO*! IT'S *ZOZOZOZO COMICS*!!!
THIS ISN'T THE ONE I WANTED!!
ZOZOZOZO COMICS
ANOTHER ISSUE OF ZOZOZOZO COMICS
AGHAAGH?
THUD
SPECIAL ISSUE ZOZOZOZO COMICS
NO, NOT ANOTHER ISSUE!!
THUNK
AH, WELL. I GUESS I MIGHT AS WELL SEND IN THE POSTCARD FROM *ZOZOZOZO COMICS*.
MAIL

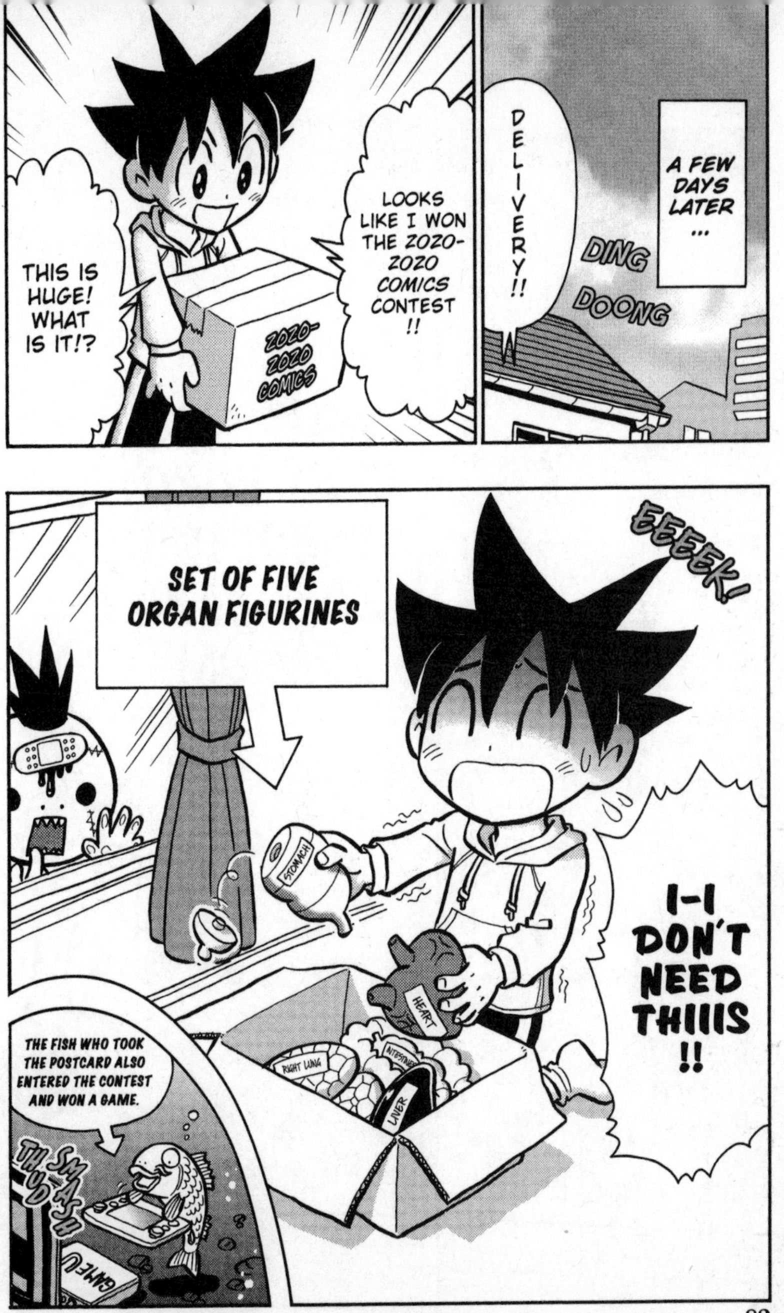
A FEW DAYS LATER ...
DING DOONG
DELIVERY!!
LOOKS LIKE I WON THE ZOZO-ZOZO COMICS CONTEST !!
ZOZO-ZOZO COMICS
THIS IS HUGE! WHAT IS IT!?
EEEEK!
SET OF FIVE ORGAN FIGURINES
I-I DON'T NEED THIIIS !!
STOMACH
HEART
RIGHT LUNG
INTESTINES
LIVER
THE FISH WHO TOOK THE POSTCARD ALSO ENTERED THE CONTEST AND WON A GAME.
SMASH
THUD

A ZOMBIE HOME INVAZION!

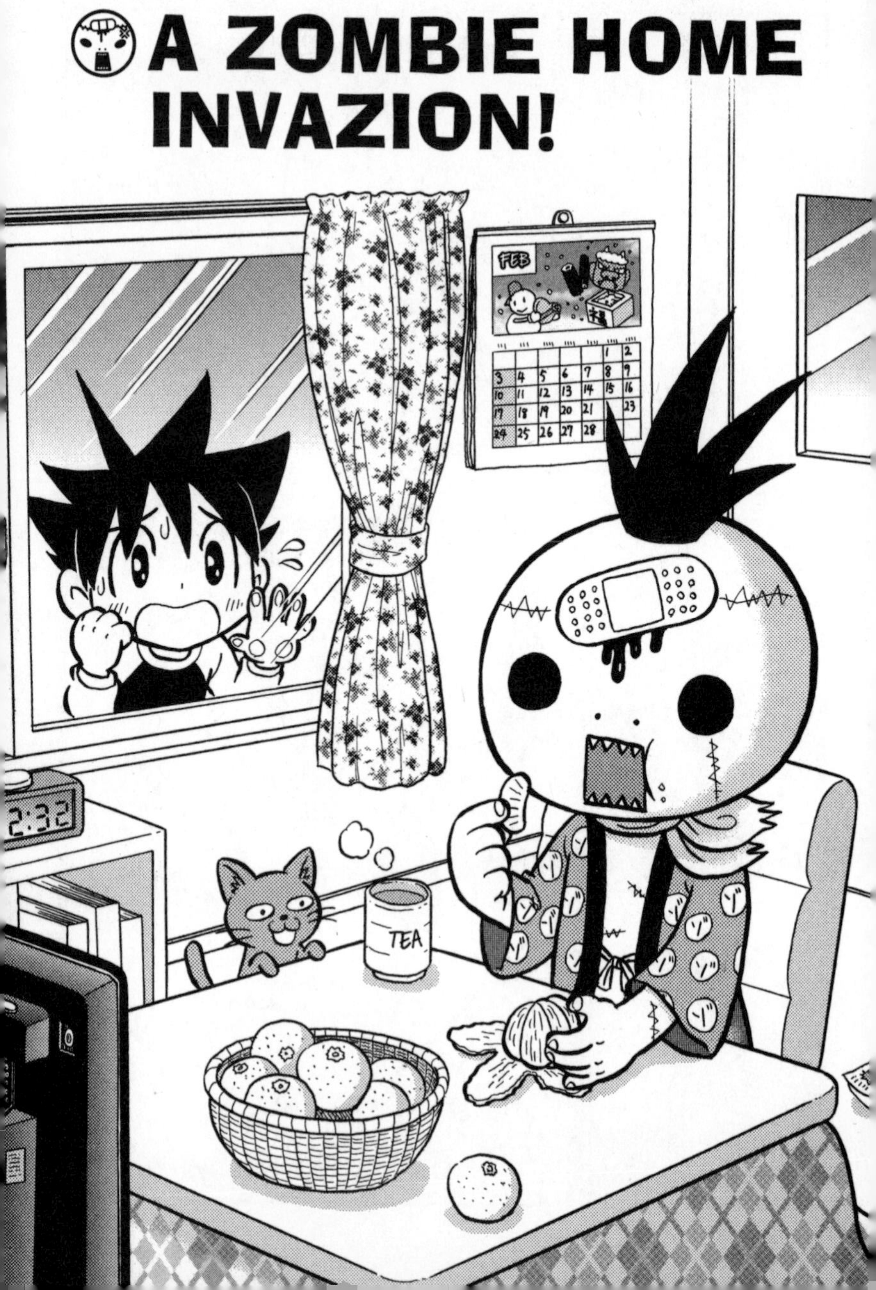
FEB
1 2
3 4 5 6 7 8 9
10 11 12 13 14 15 16
17 18 19 20 21 23
24 25 26 27 28
2:32
TEA

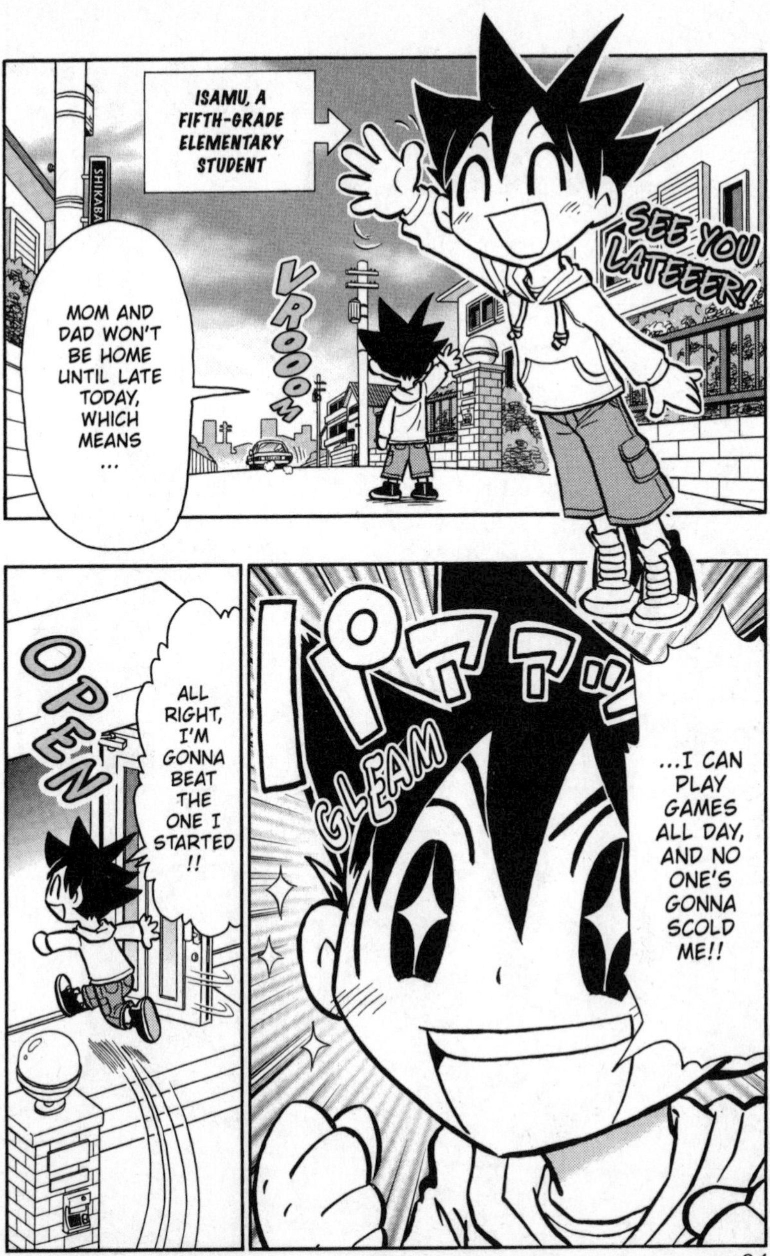
SEE YOU LATEEEER!
ISAMU, A FIFTH-GRADE ELEMENTARY STUDENT
VROOOM
MOM AND DAD WON'T BE HOME UNTIL LATE TODAY, WHICH MEANS ...
パァァッ
GLEAM
...I CAN PLAY GAMES ALL DAY, AND NO ONE'S GONNA SCOLD ME!!
OPEN
ALL RIGHT, I'M GONNA BEAT THE ONE I STARTED!!

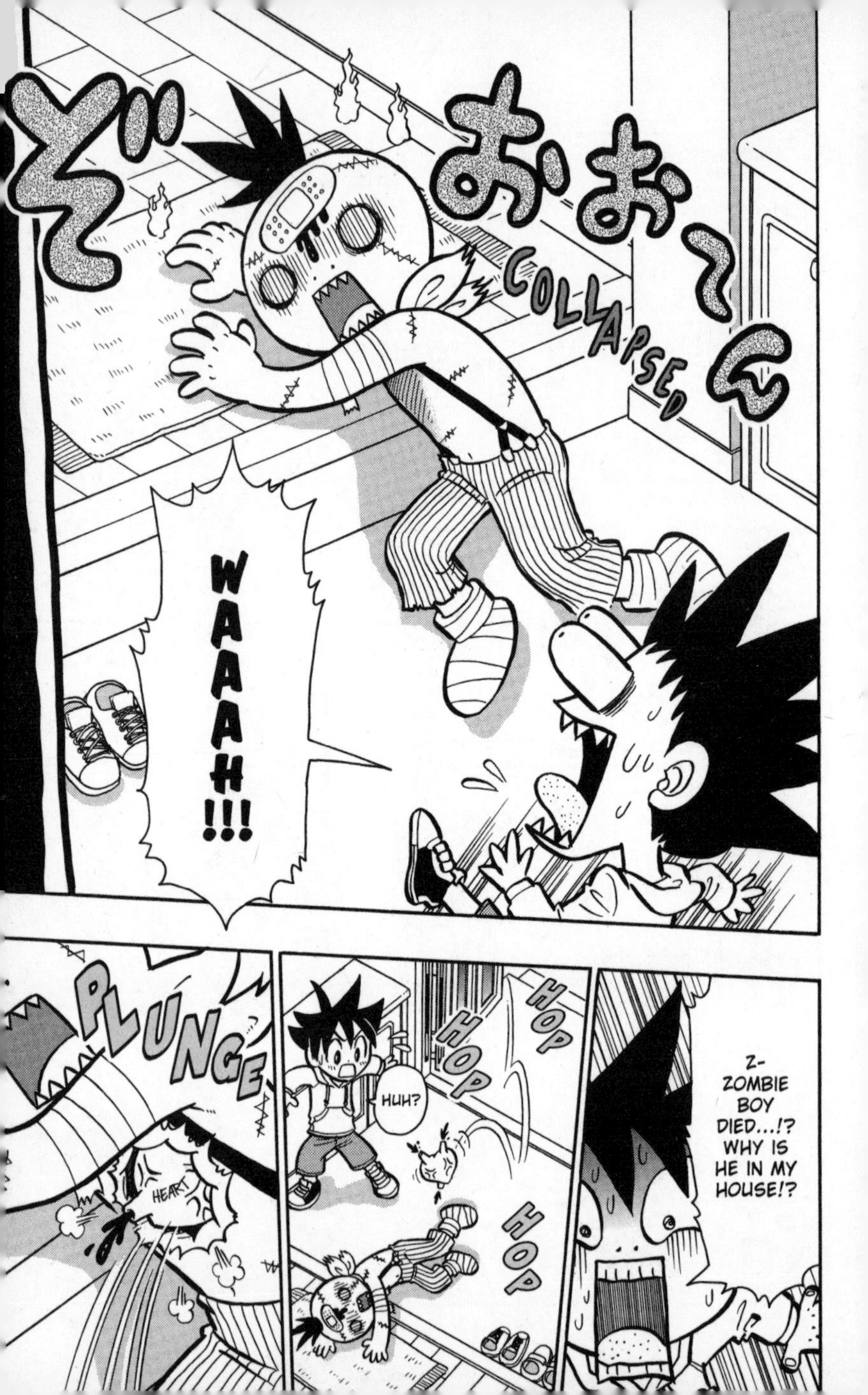
COLLAPSED
WAAAAH!!!
Z-ZOMBIE BOY DIED...!? WHY IS HE IN MY HOUSE!?
HOP HOP
HUH?
HOP HOP
PLUNGE
HEART

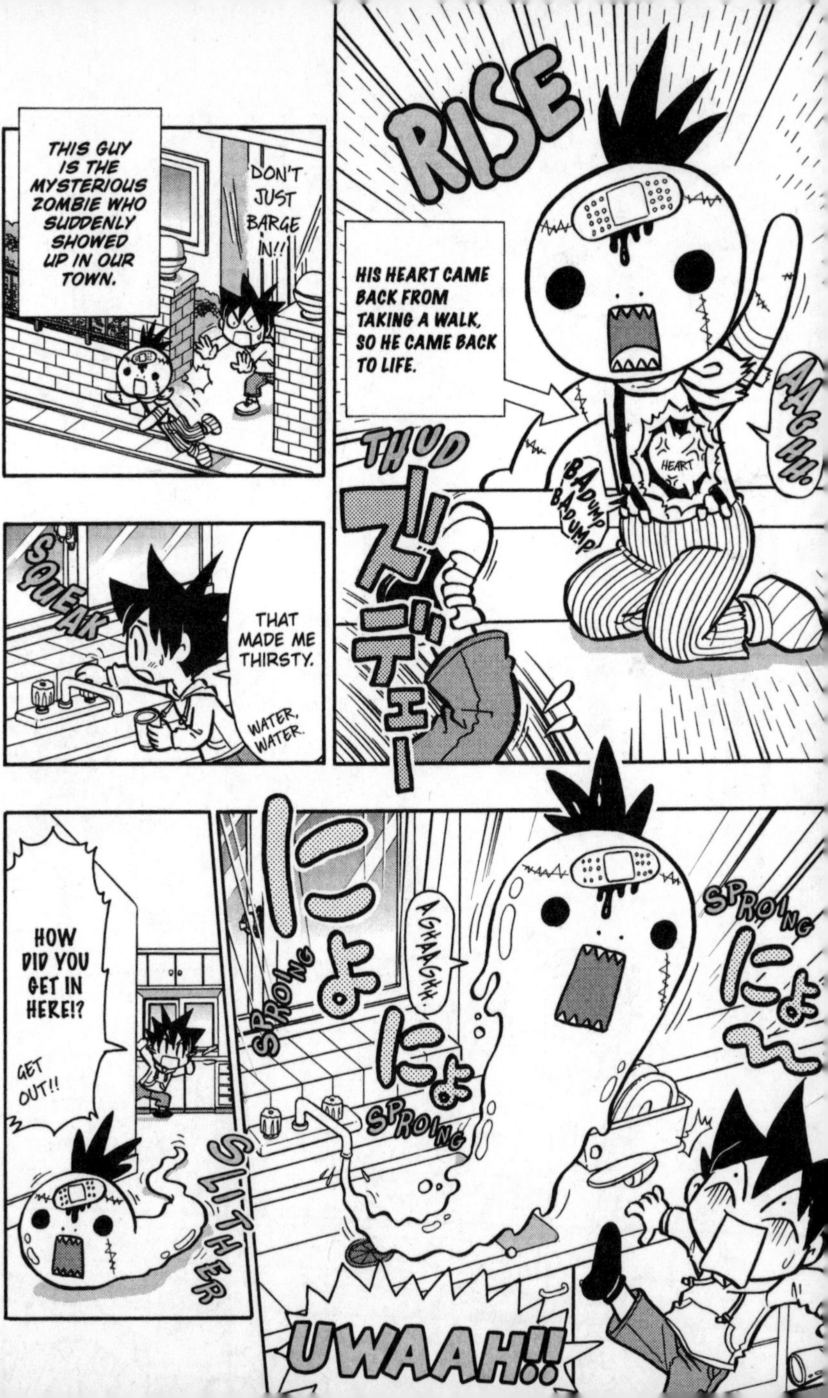
RISE
HIS HEART CAME BACK FROM TAKING A WALK, SO HE CAME BACK TO LIFE.
AAGHH.
THUD
BADUMP BADUMP
HEART
THIS GUY IS THE MYSTERIOUS ZOMBIE WHO SUDDENLY SHOWED UP IN OUR TOWN.
DON'T JUST BARGE IN!!
SQUEAK
THAT MADE ME THIRSTY.
WATER, WATER.
SPROING
にょ~
AGHAAGHH.
にょ
SPROING
にょ
SPROING
SLITHER
UWAAH!!
HOW DID YOU GET IN HERE!?
GET OUT!!

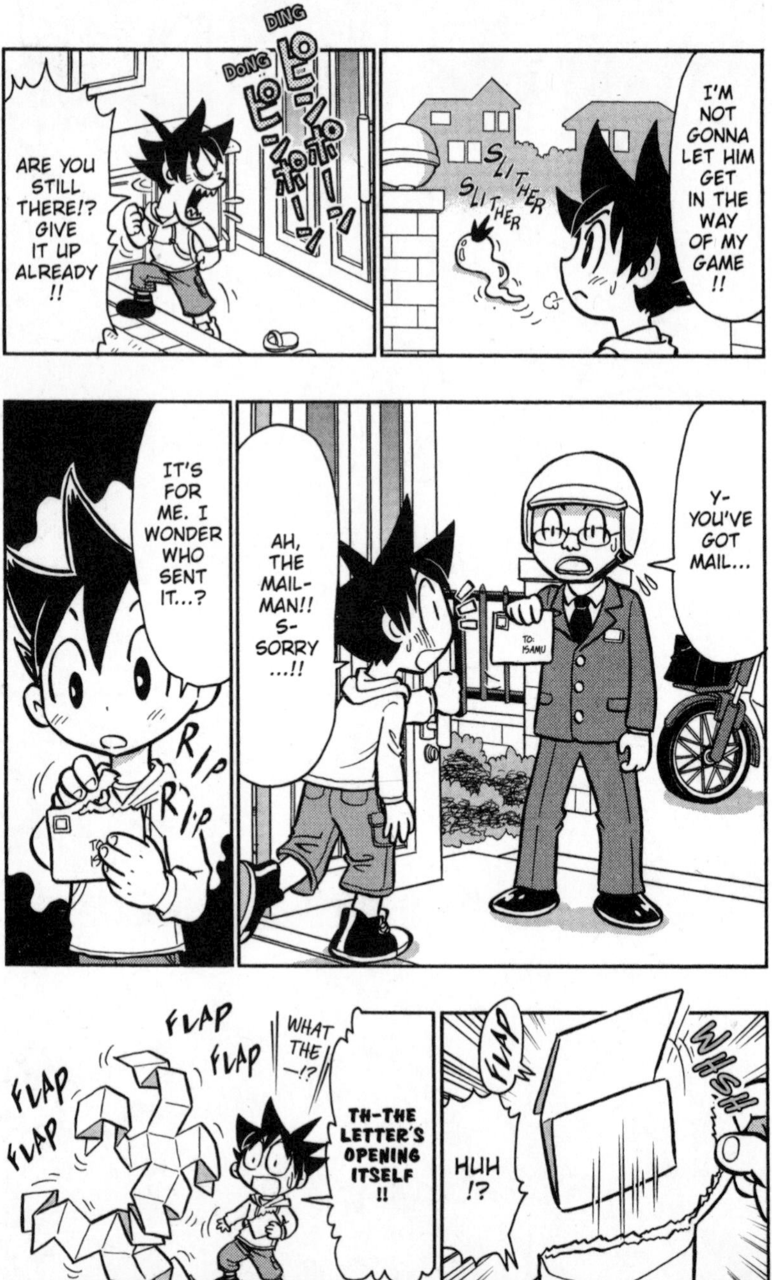
I'M NOT GONNA LET HIM GET IN THE WAY OF MY GAME !!
SLITHER
SLITHER
DING
DONG
ARE YOU STILL THERE!? GIVE IT UP ALREADY !!
Y-YOU'VE GOT MAIL...
TO: ISAMU
AH, THE MAIL-MAN!! S-SORRY ...!!
IT'S FOR ME. I WONDER WHO SENT IT...?
RIP
RIP
FLAP
WHSH
HUH !?
WHAT THE—!?
TH-THE LETTER'S OPENING ITSELF !!
FLAP
FLAP
FLAP
FLAP

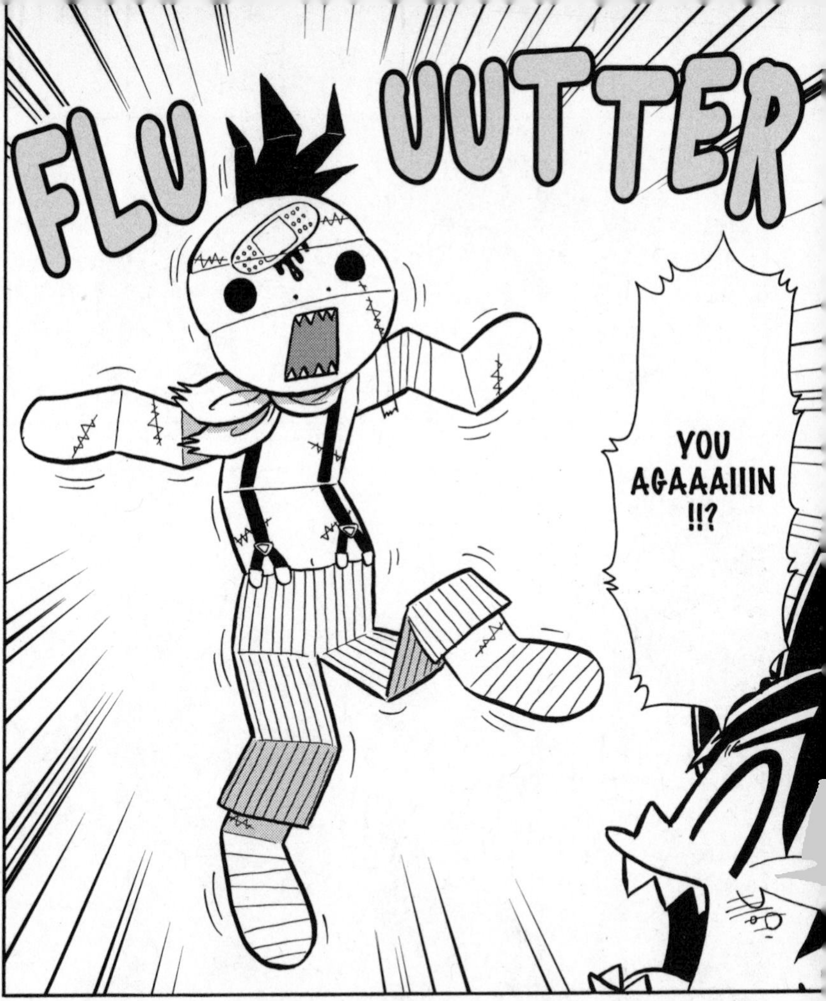
FLUUUTTER
YOU AGAAAIIIN!!?

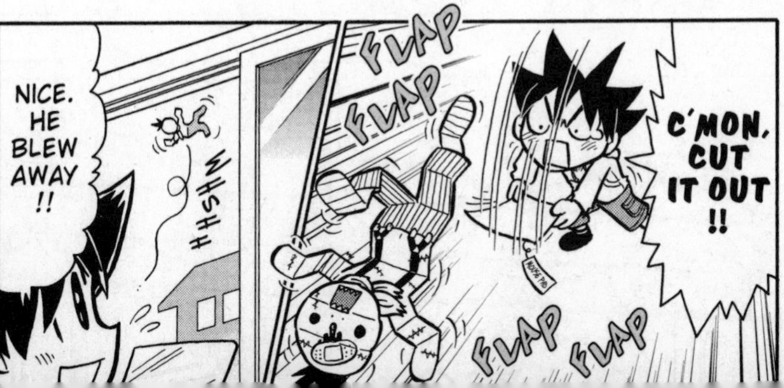
C'MON, CUT IT OUT!!
FLAP
FLAP
FLAP
FLAP
WHSH
NICE. HE BLEW AWAY!!

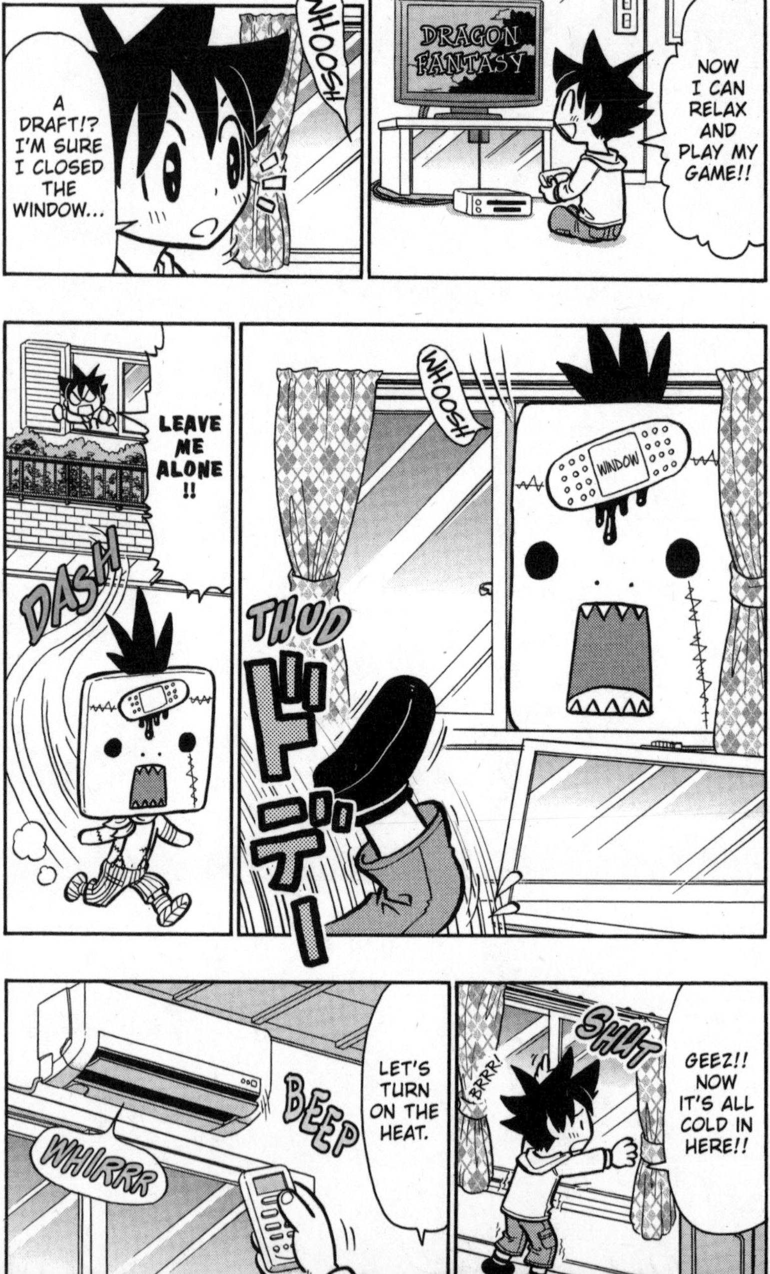
TA-DAA
DRAGON FANTASY
NOW I CAN RELAX AND PLAY MY GAME!!
WHOOSH
A DRAFT!? I'M SURE I CLOSED THE WINDOW...
WHOOSH
WINDOW
THUD
LEAVE ME ALONE!!
DASH
SHUT
BRRR!
GEEZ!! NOW IT'S ALL COLD IN HERE!!
LET'S TURN ON THE HEAT.
BEEP
WHIRRR

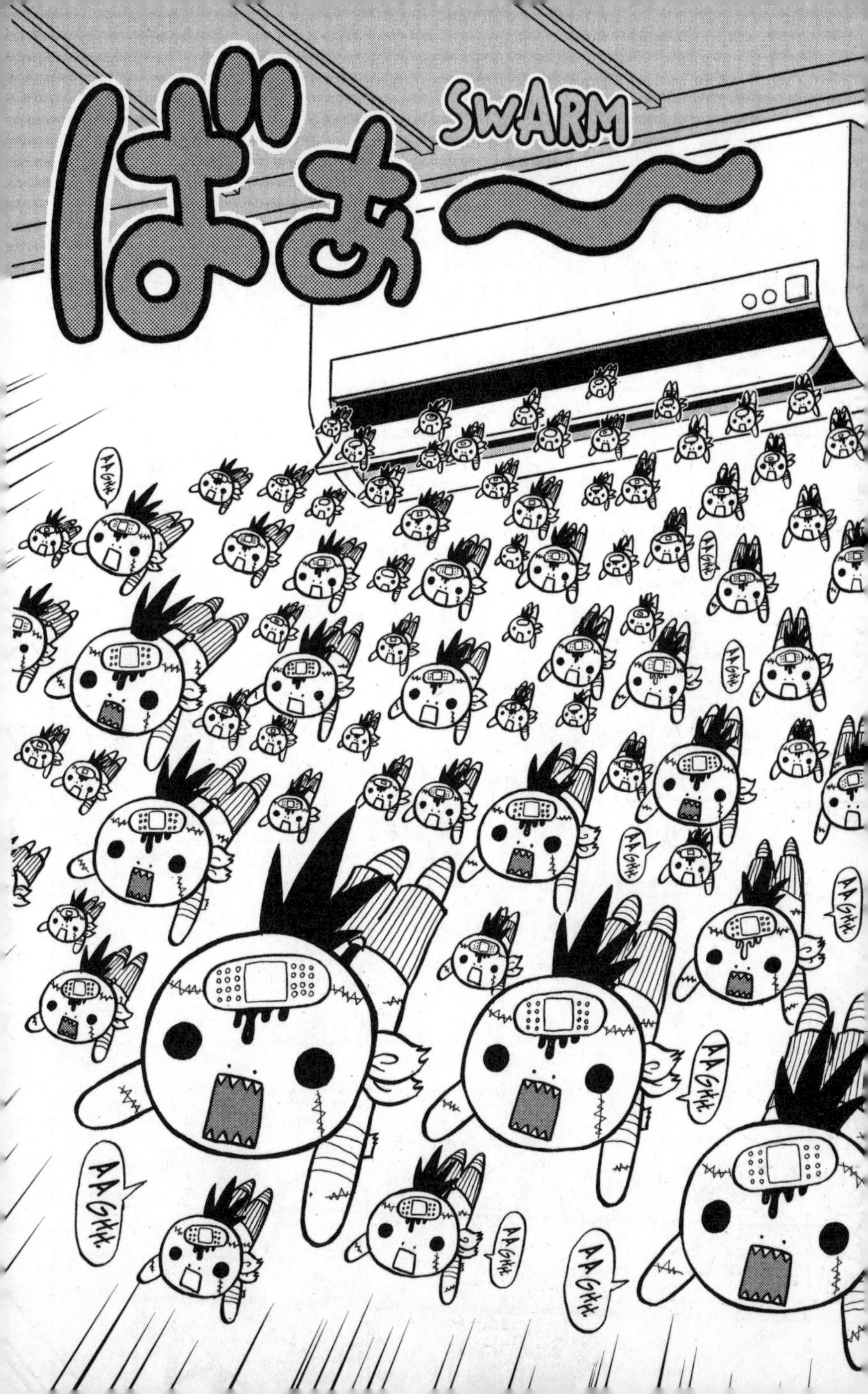
ばぁ〜
SWARM
AAGHK
AAGHK
AAGHK
AAGHK
AAGHK
AAGHK
AAGHK
AAGHK
AAGHK
AAGHK

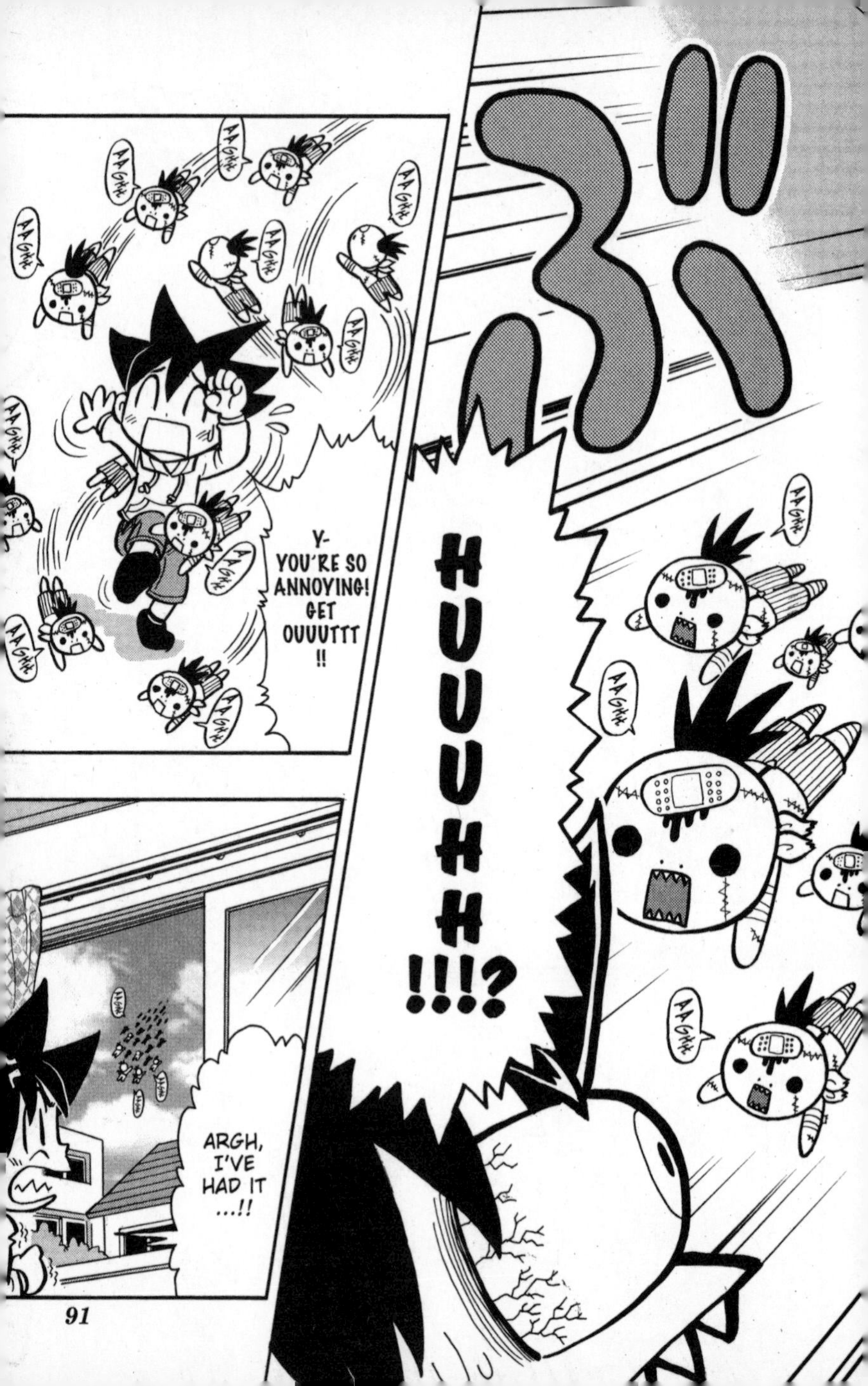
ぶ゛
HUUUUHHH!!!?
AAGHH
AAGHH
AAGHH
AAGHH
AAGHH
AAGHH
AAGHH
AAGHH
AAGHH
AAGHH
AAGHH
AAGHH
AAGHH
AAGHH
Y- YOU'RE SO ANNOYING! GET OUUUTTT!!
ARGH, I'VE HAD IT ...!!

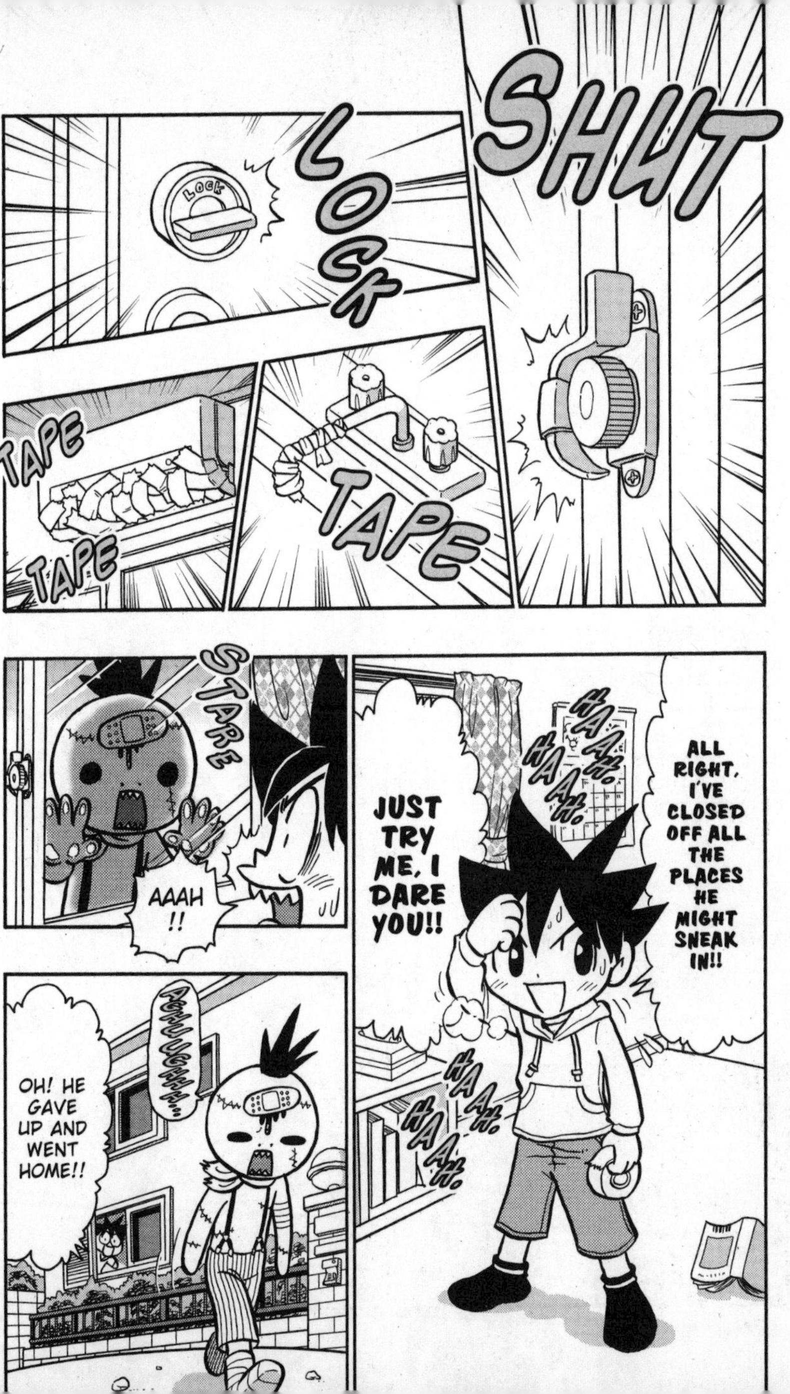
SHUT
LOCK
LOCK
TAPE
TAPE
TAPE
HAAH. HAAH.
ALL RIGHT, I'VE CLOSED OFF ALL THE PLACES HE MIGHT SNEAK IN!!
JUST TRY ME, I DARE YOU!!
HAAH. HAAH.
STARE
AAAH!!
ACHUUGHH...
OH! HE GAVE UP AND WENT HOME!!

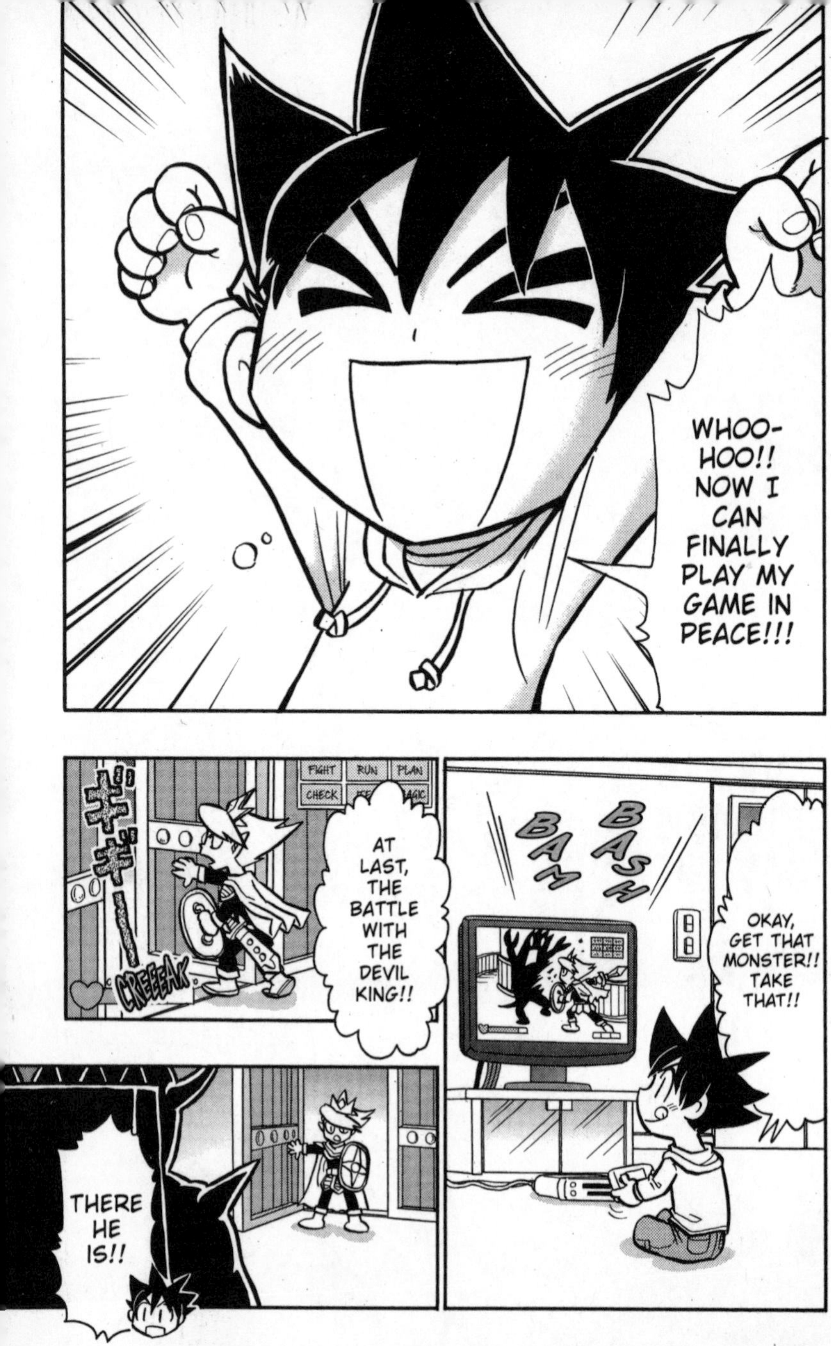
WHOO-HOO!! NOW I CAN FINALLY PLAY MY GAME IN PEACE!!!
BAM
BASH
OKAY, GET THAT MONSTER!! TAKE THAT!!
FIGHT
RUN
PLAN
CHECK
AT LAST, THE BATTLE WITH THE DEVIL KING!!
CREEEAK
THERE HE IS!!

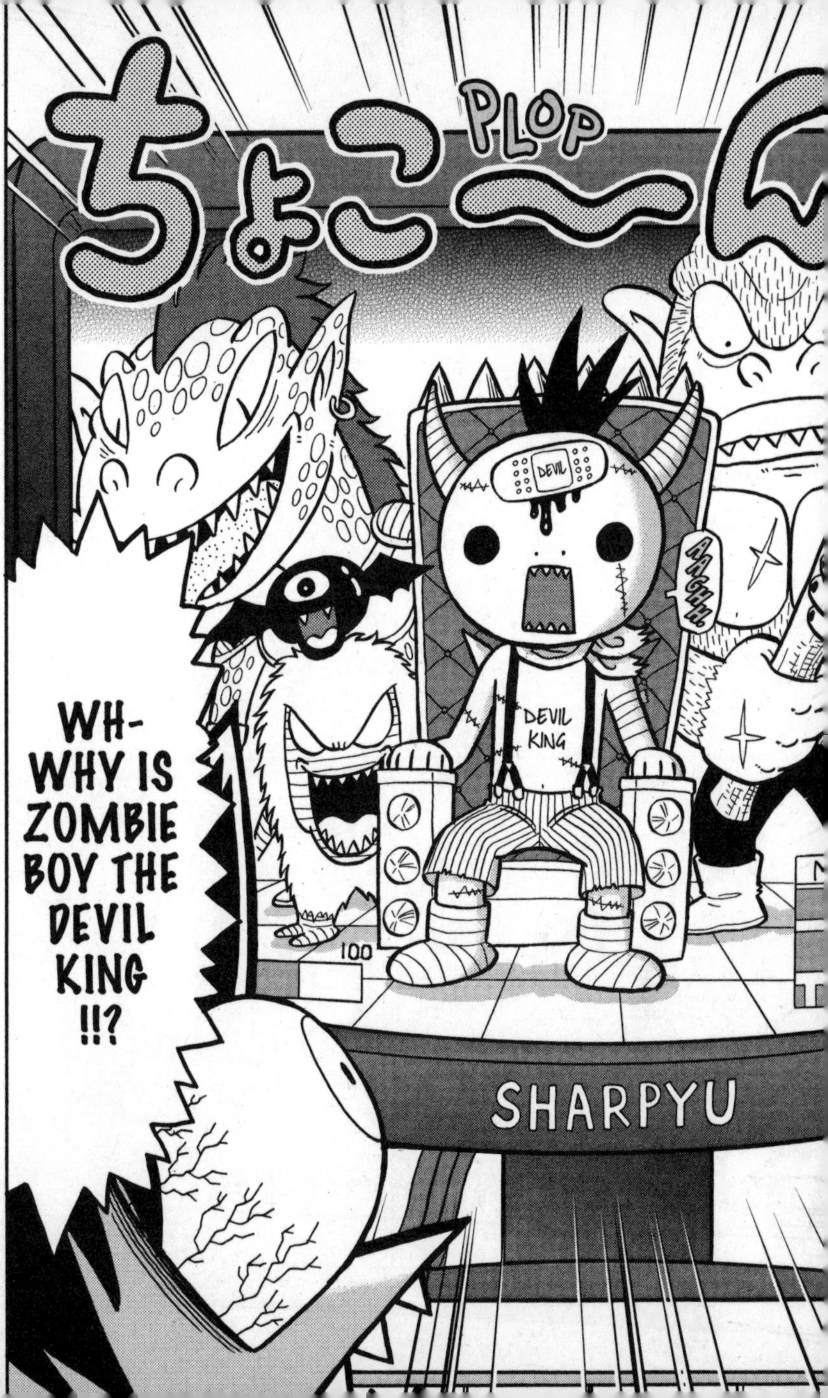
ちょこ〜ん
PLOP
DEVIL
DEVIL KING
AAGHH
100
WH- WHY IS ZOMBIE BOY THE DEVIL KING !!?
SHARPYU

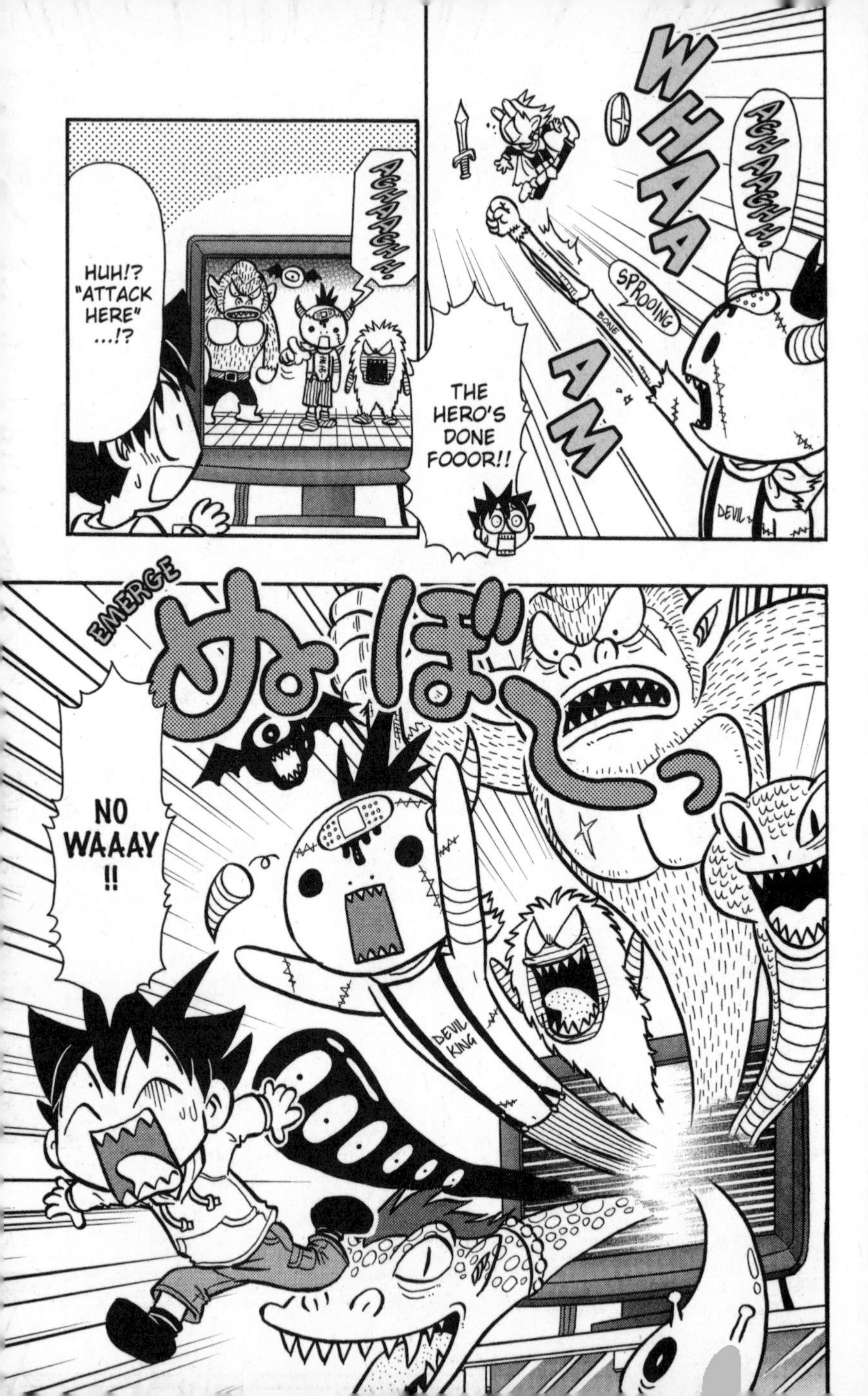
WHAAAM
ACHAAAGHH.
SPROOING
BONE
THE HERO'S DONE FOOOR!!
DEVIL
ACHAAAGHH.
HUH!? "ATTACK HERE" ...!?
EMERGE
NO WAAAY !!
DEVIL KING

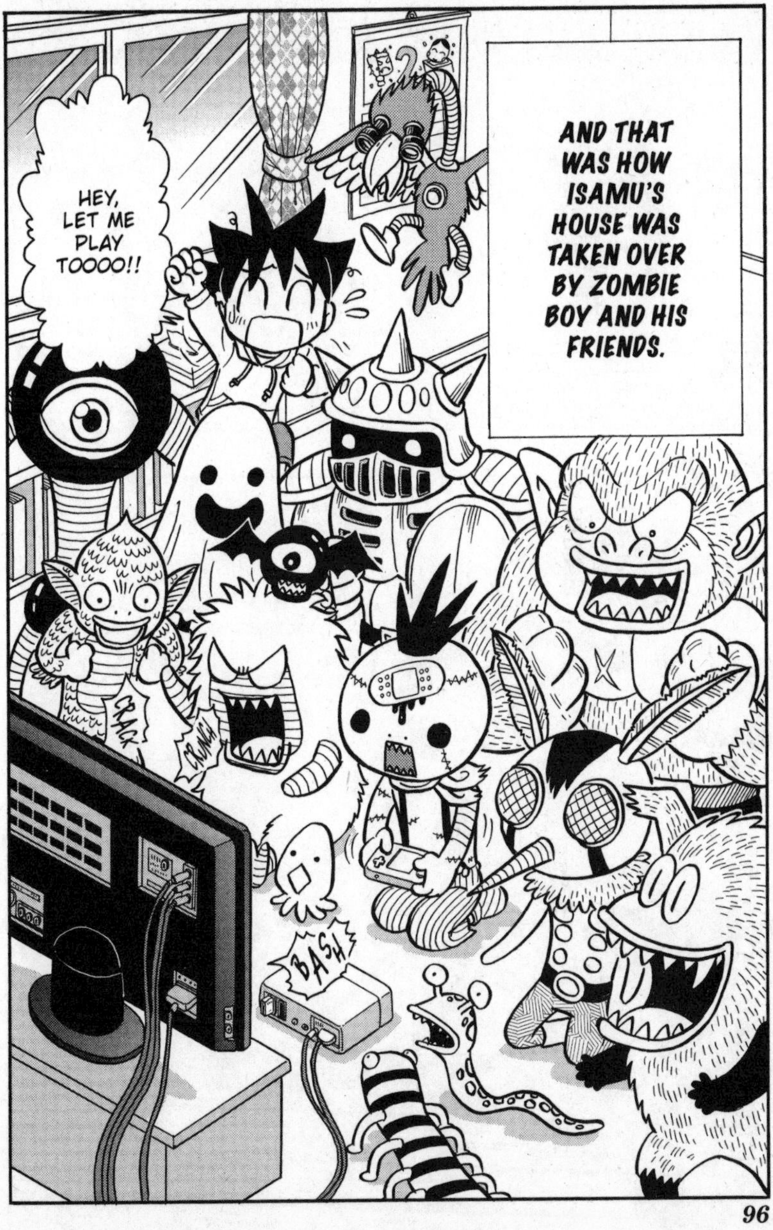
AND THAT WAS HOW ISAMU'S HOUSE WAS TAKEN OVER BY ZOMBIE BOY AND HIS FRIENDS.
HEY, LET ME PLAY TOOOO!!
CRACK
CRUNCH
BASH

SPECIAL FOUR-PANEL COMIC PART 3

KEY

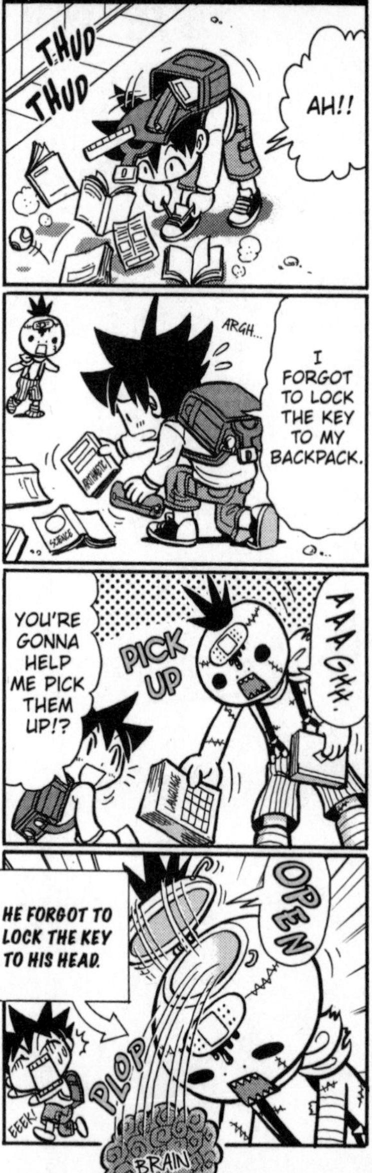

THUD
THUD
AH!!
ARGH...
I FORGOT TO LOCK THE KEY TO MY BACKPACK.
ARITHMETIC
SCIENCE
AAAGHH.
PICK UP
YOU'RE GONNA HELP ME PICK THEM UP!?
LANGUAGE
OPEN
HE FORGOT TO LOCK THE KEY TO HIS HEAD.
PLOP
EEEK!
BRAIN

THE SPEECH

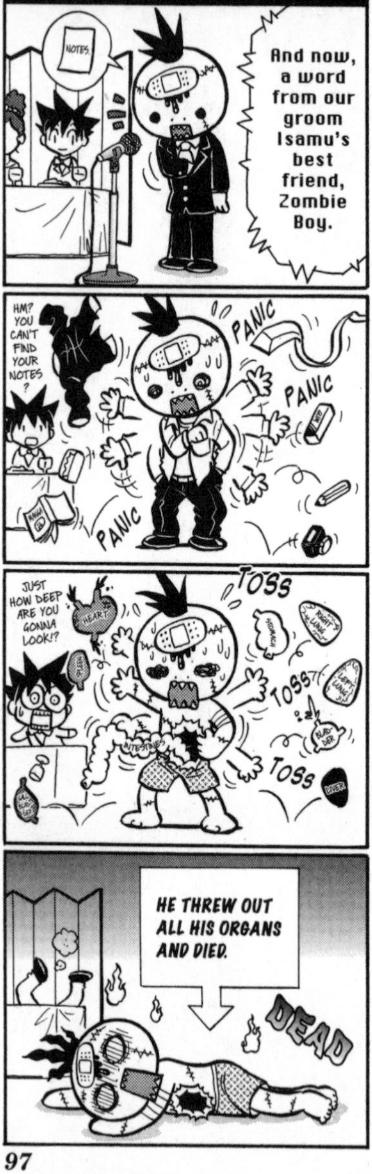

And now, a word from our groom Isamu's best friend, Zombie Boy.
NOTES
PANIC
PANIC
HM? YOU CAN'T FIND YOUR NOTES?
PANIC
TOSS
RIGHT LUNG
STOMACH
JUST HOW DEEP ARE YOU GONNA LOOK!?
HEART
TOSS
LEFT LUNG
BLADDER
INTESTINES
TOSS
LIVER
HE THREW OUT ALL HIS ORGANS AND DIED.
DEAD

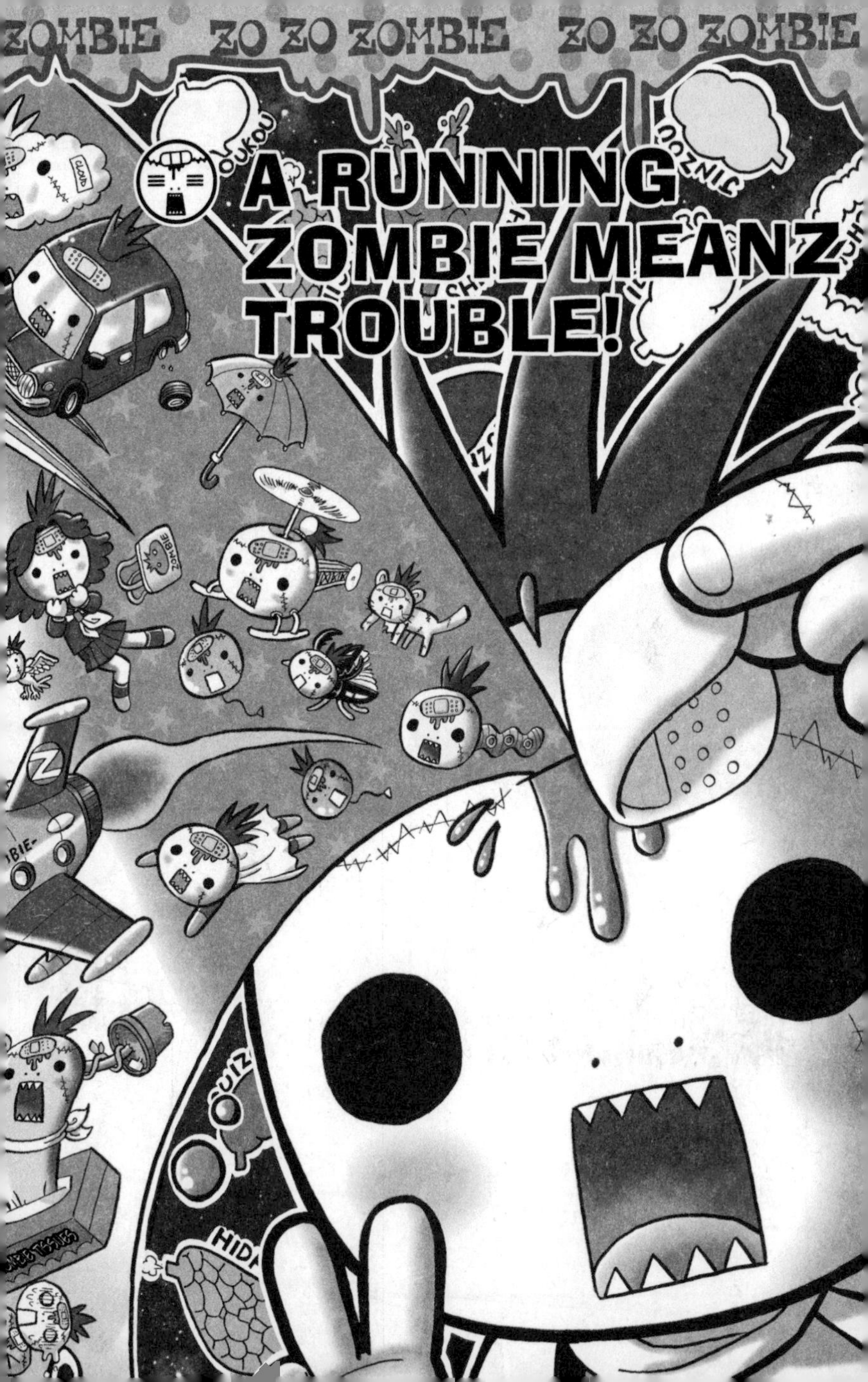
ZOMBIE ZO ZO ZOMBIE ZO ZO ZOMBIE
A RUNNING ZOMBIE MEANZ TROUBLE!

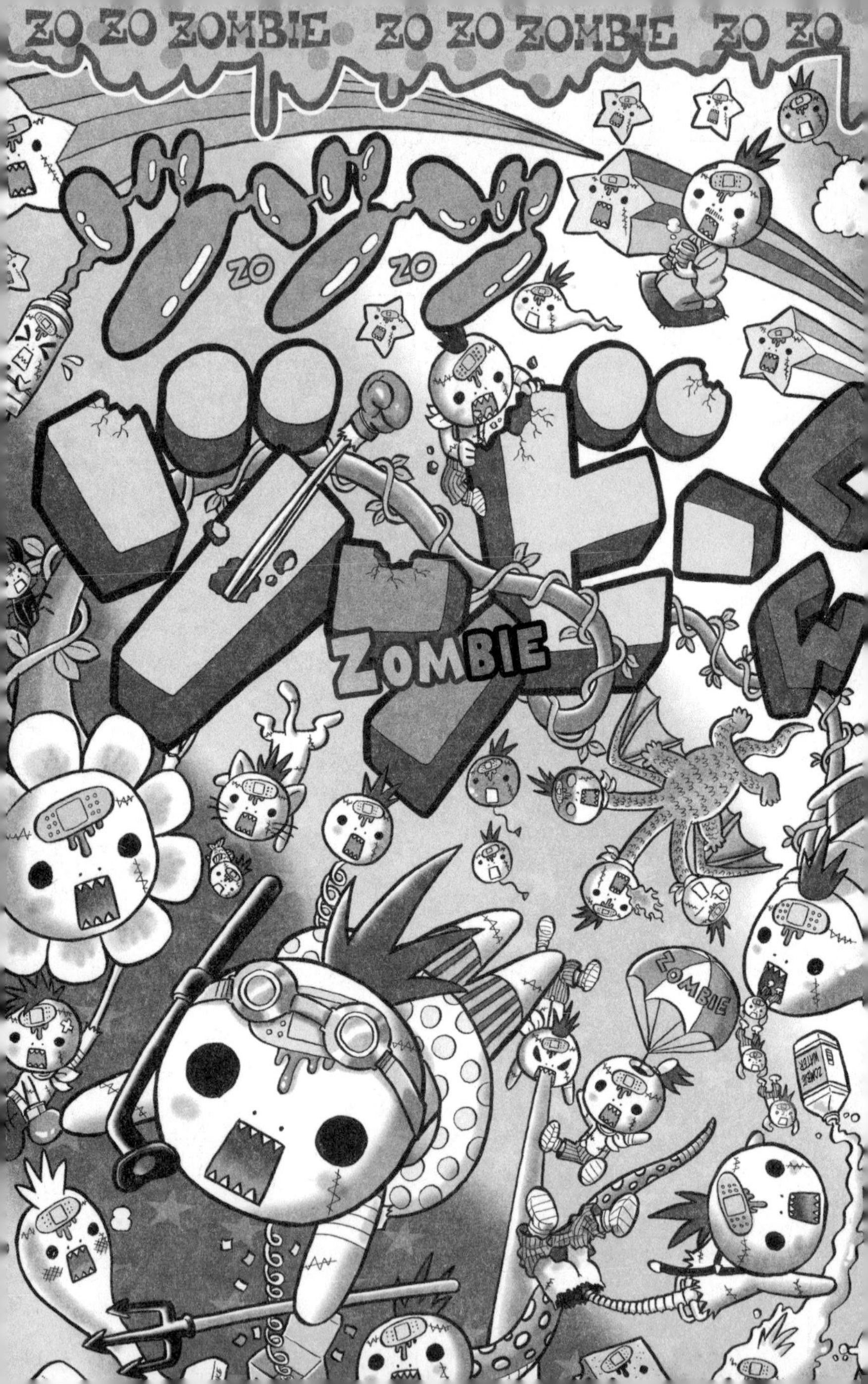
ZO ZO ZOMBIE ZO ZO ZOMBIE ZO ZO
ZO
ZO
ZOMBIE
ZOMBIE
ZOMBIE WATER

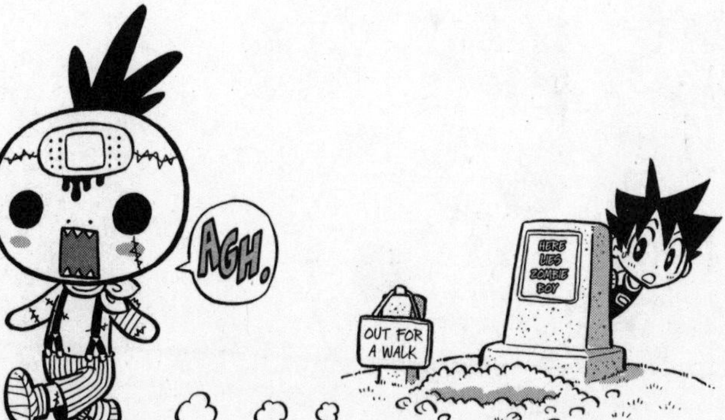
AGH.
OUT FOR A WALK
HERE LIES ZOMBIE BOY

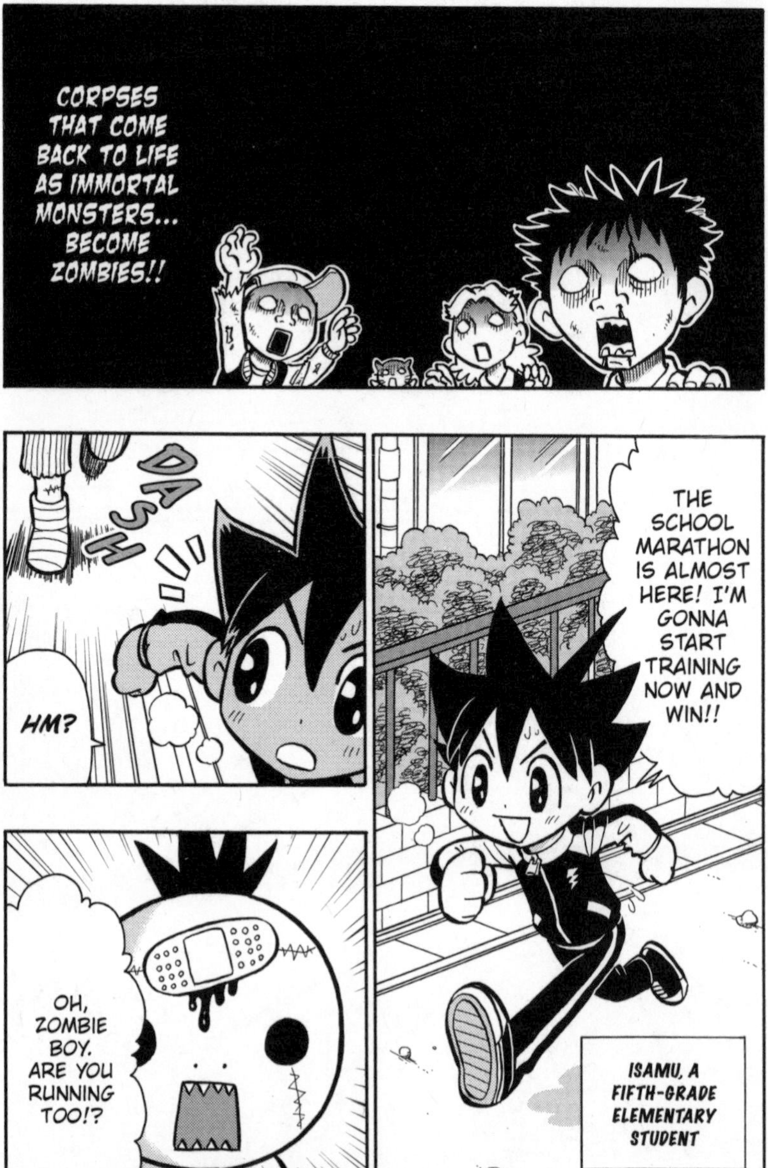
CORPSES THAT COME BACK TO LIFE AS IMMORTAL MONSTERS... BECOME ZOMBIES!!
THE SCHOOL MARATHON IS ALMOST HERE! I'M GONNA START TRAINING NOW AND WIN!!
ISAMU, A FIFTH-GRADE ELEMENTARY STUDENT
DASH
HM?
OH, ZOMBIE BOY. ARE YOU RUNNING TOO!?

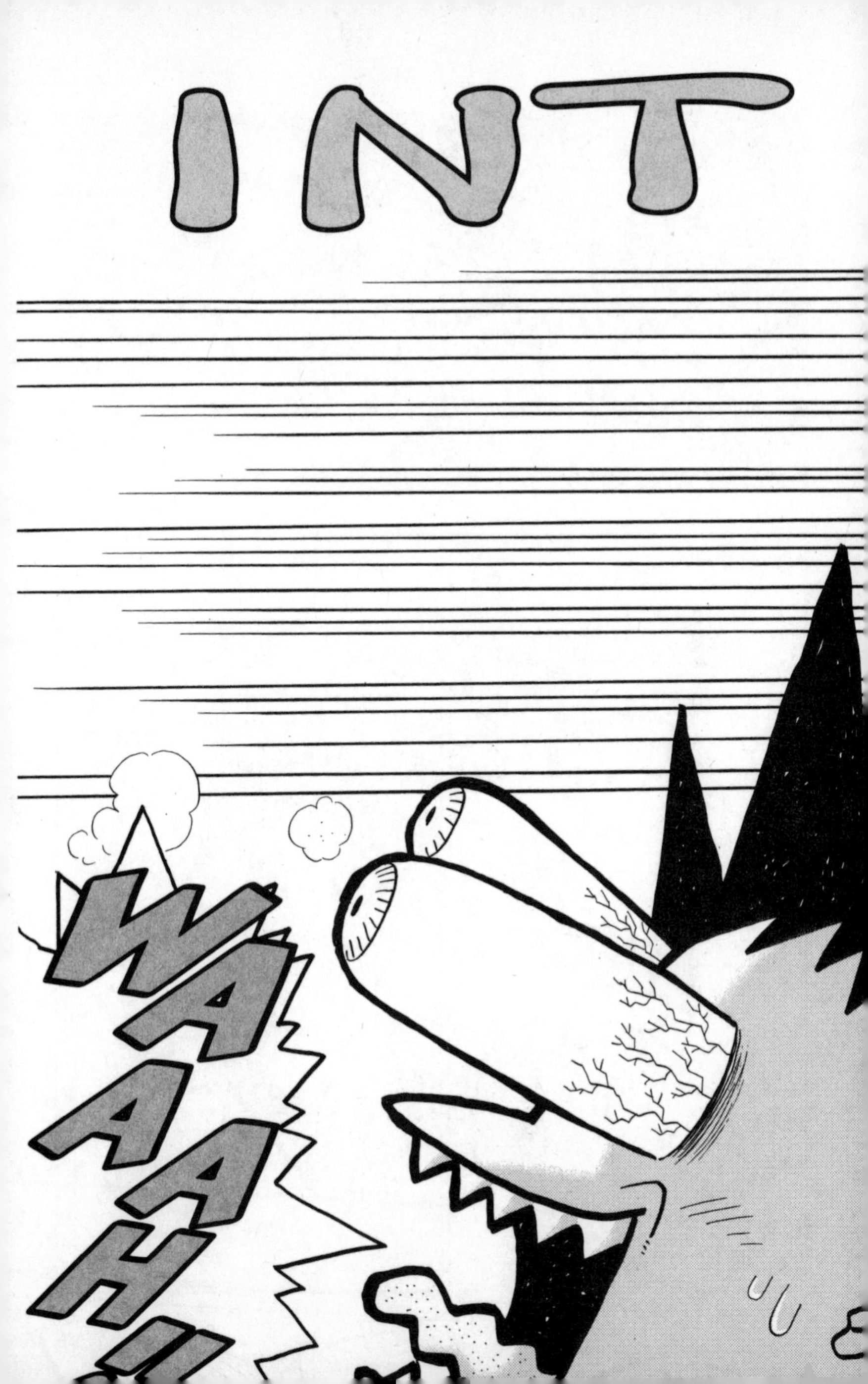
INT
WAAAHH!!

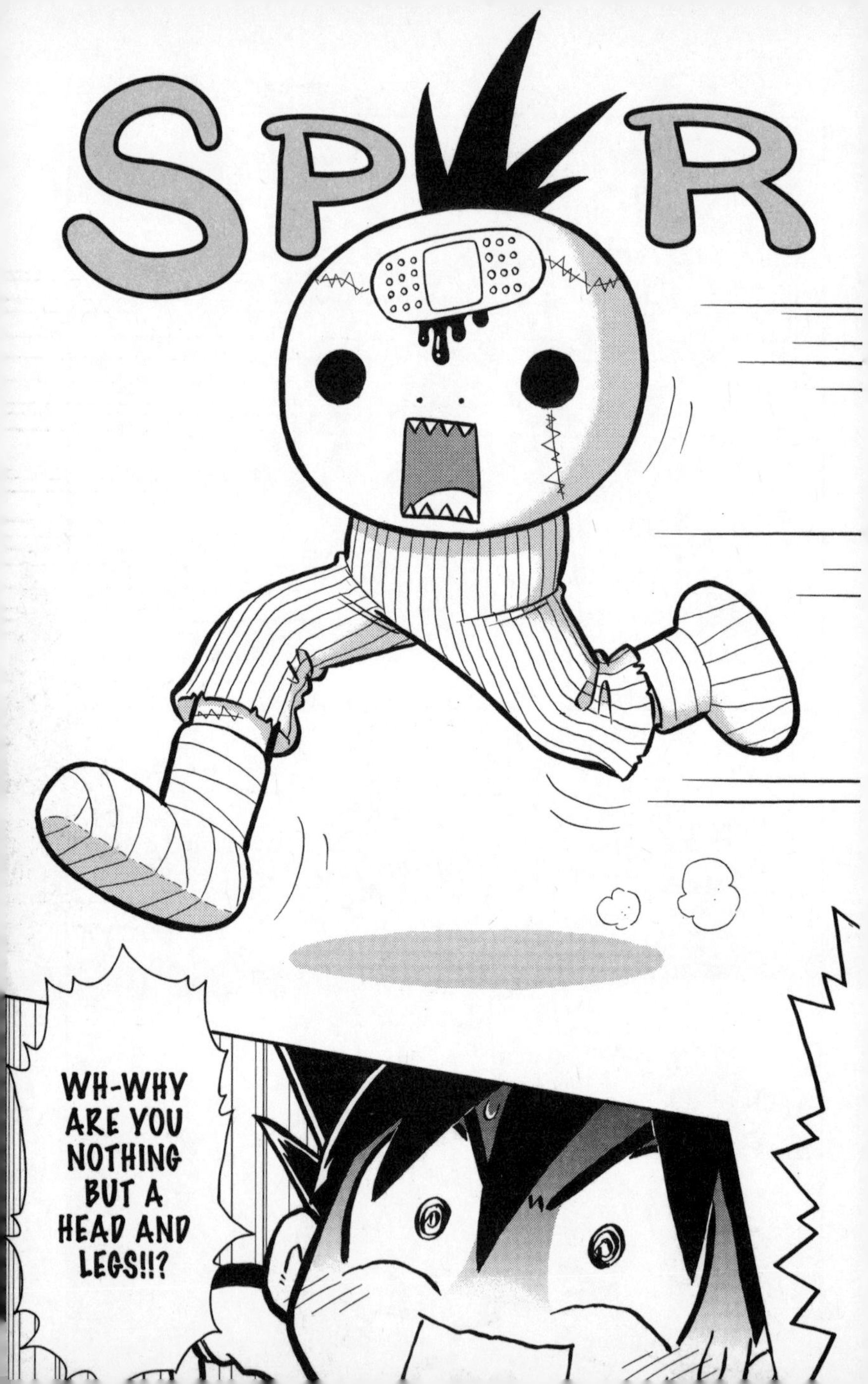

SP R
WH-WHY ARE YOU NOTHING BUT A HEAD AND LEGS!!?

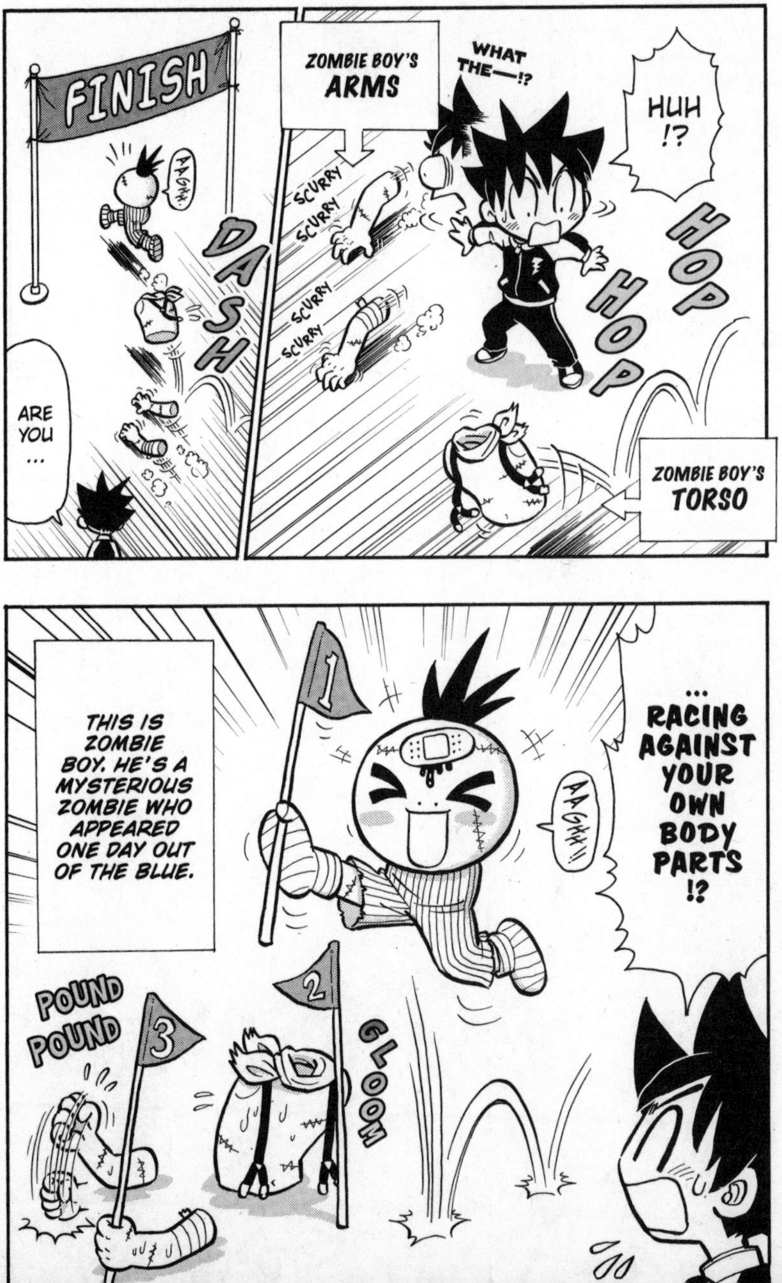
HUH !?
WHAT THE—!?
ZOMBIE BOY'S ARMS
HOP HOP HOP
SCURRY SCURRY
SCURRY SCURRY
ZOMBIE BOY'S TORSO
FINISH
AAGHH.
DASH
ARE YOU ...
... RACING AGAINST YOUR OWN BODY PARTS !?
AAGHH!!
THIS IS ZOMBIE BOY. HE'S A MYSTERIOUS ZOMBIE WHO APPEARED ONE DAY OUT OF THE BLUE.
GLOOM
POUND POUND

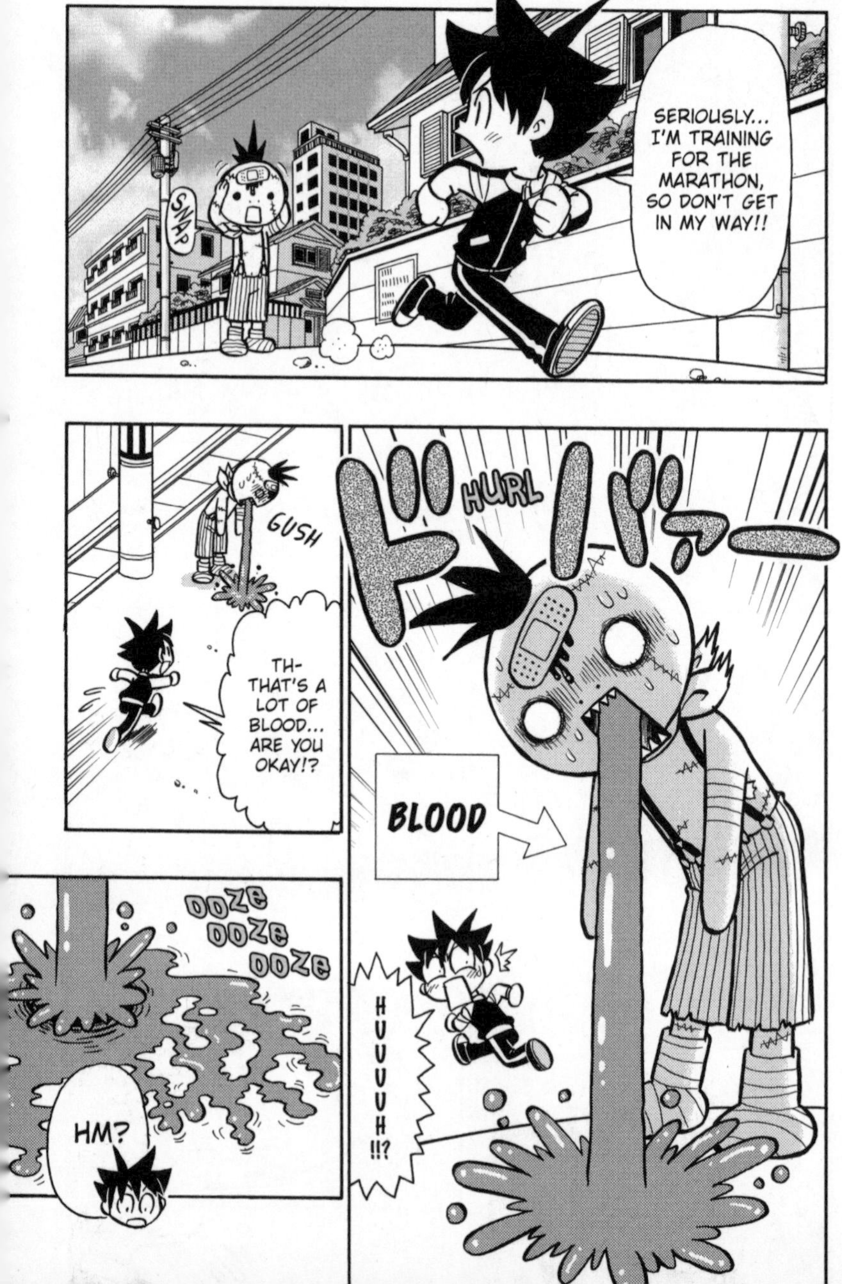
SERIOUSLY... I'M TRAINING FOR THE MARATHON, SO DON'T GET IN MY WAY!!
SNAP
ドバァー
HURL
BLOOD
HUUUUUH!!?
GUSH
TH- THAT'S A LOT OF BLOOD... ARE YOU OKAY!?
OOZE OOZE OOZE
HM?

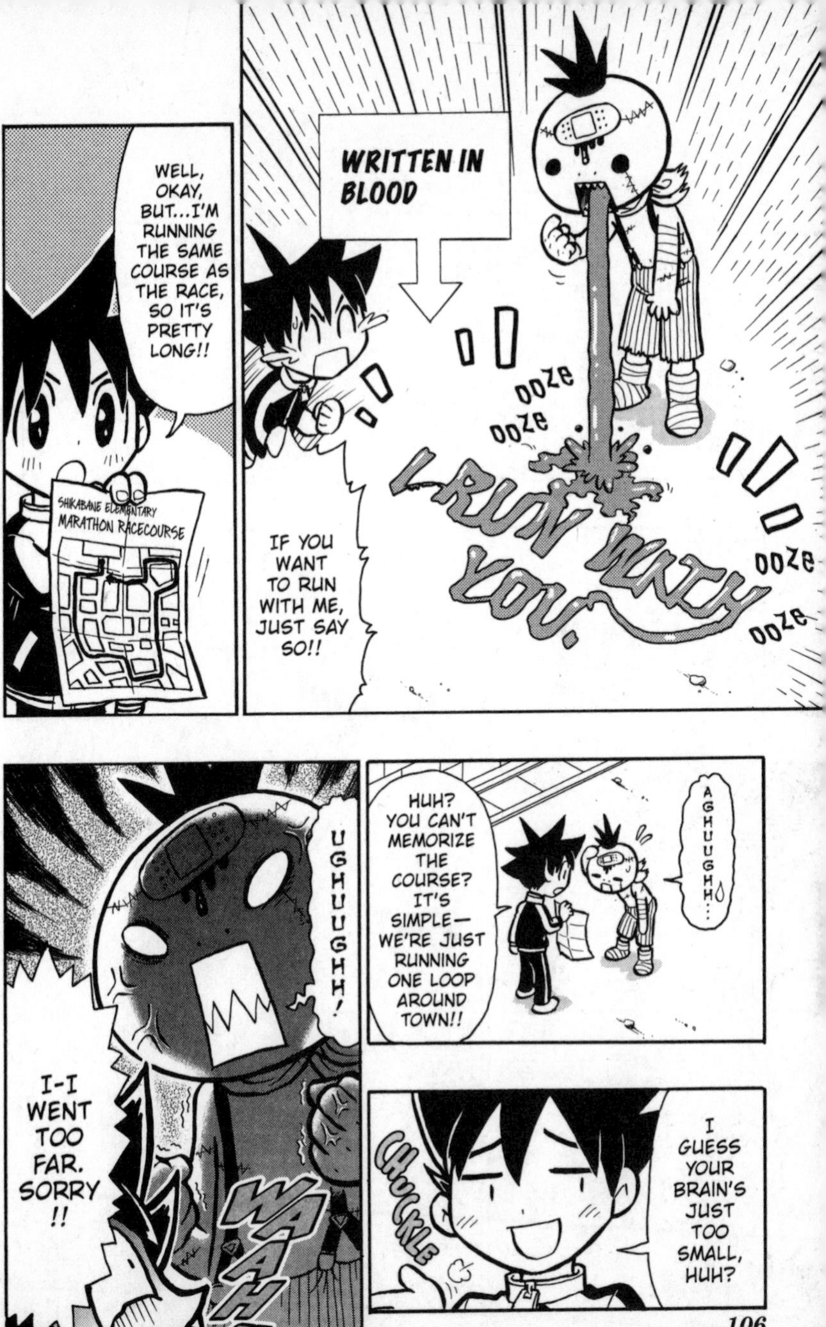
WRITTEN IN BLOOD
OOZE
OOZE
I RUN WITH YOU.
OOZE
OOZE
IF YOU WANT TO RUN WITH ME, JUST SAY SO!!
WELL, OKAY, BUT...I'M RUNNING THE SAME COURSE AS THE RACE, SO IT'S PRETTY LONG!!
SHIKABANE ELEMENTARY
MARATHON RACECOURSE
AGHUUGHH...
HUH? YOU CAN'T MEMORIZE THE COURSE? IT'S SIMPLE— WE'RE JUST RUNNING ONE LOOP AROUND TOWN!!
I GUESS YOUR BRAIN'S JUST TOO SMALL, HUH?
CHUCKLE
UGHUUGHH!
I-I WENT TOO FAR. SORRY!!
WAAAH!!

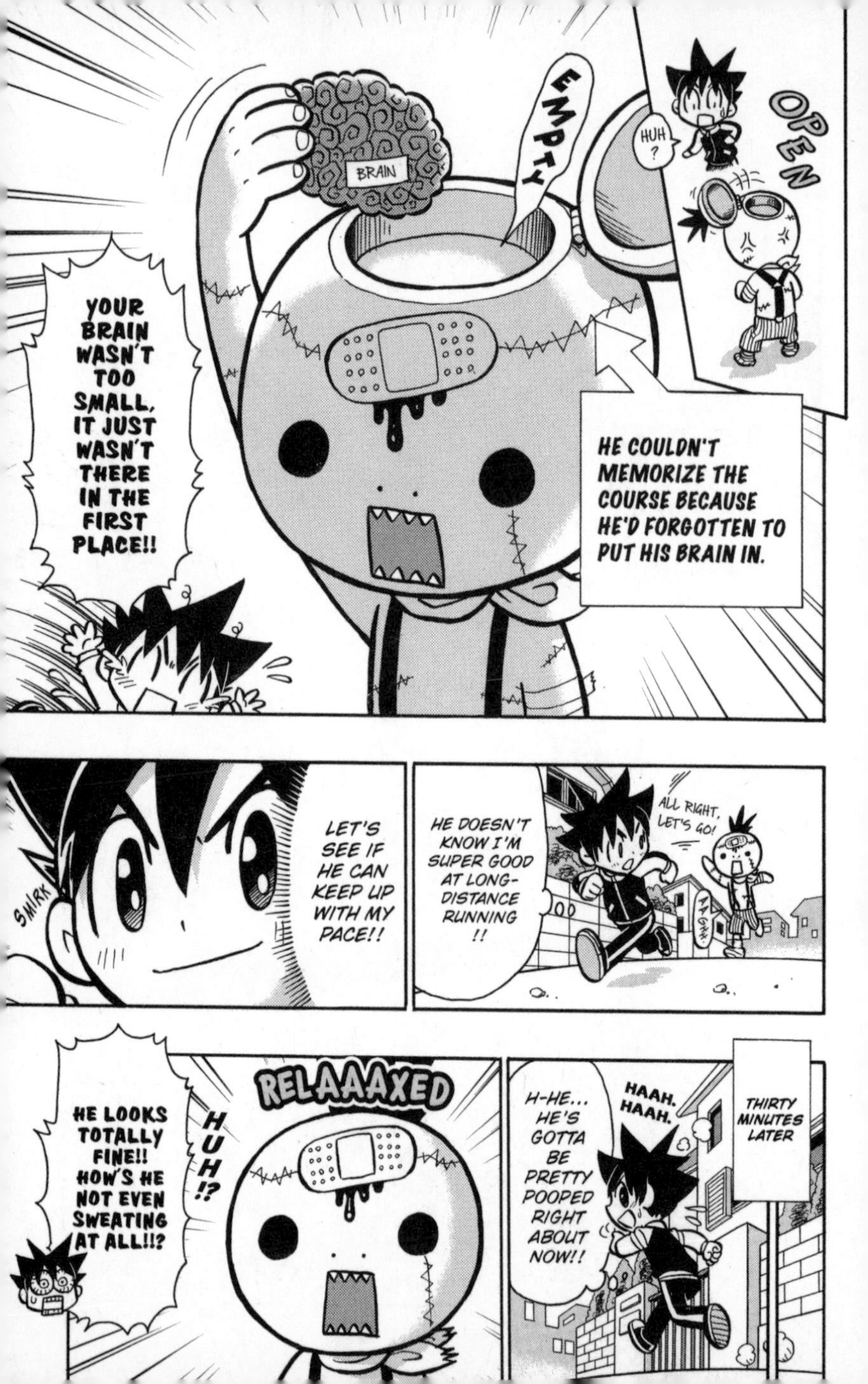
OPEN
HUH ?
EMPTY
BRAIN
HE COULDN'T MEMORIZE THE COURSE BECAUSE HE'D FORGOTTEN TO PUT HIS BRAIN IN.
YOUR BRAIN WASN'T TOO SMALL, IT JUST WASN'T THERE IN THE FIRST PLACE!!
ALL RIGHT, LET'S GO!
HE DOESN'T KNOW I'M SUPER GOOD AT LONG-DISTANCE RUNNING !!
LET'S SEE IF HE CAN KEEP UP WITH MY PACE!!
SMIRK
THIRTY MINUTES LATER
HAAH. HAAH.
H-HE... HE'S GOTTA BE PRETTY POOPED RIGHT ABOUT NOW!!
RELAAAXED
HUH!?
HE LOOKS TOTALLY FINE!! HOW'S HE NOT EVEN SWEATING AT ALL!!?

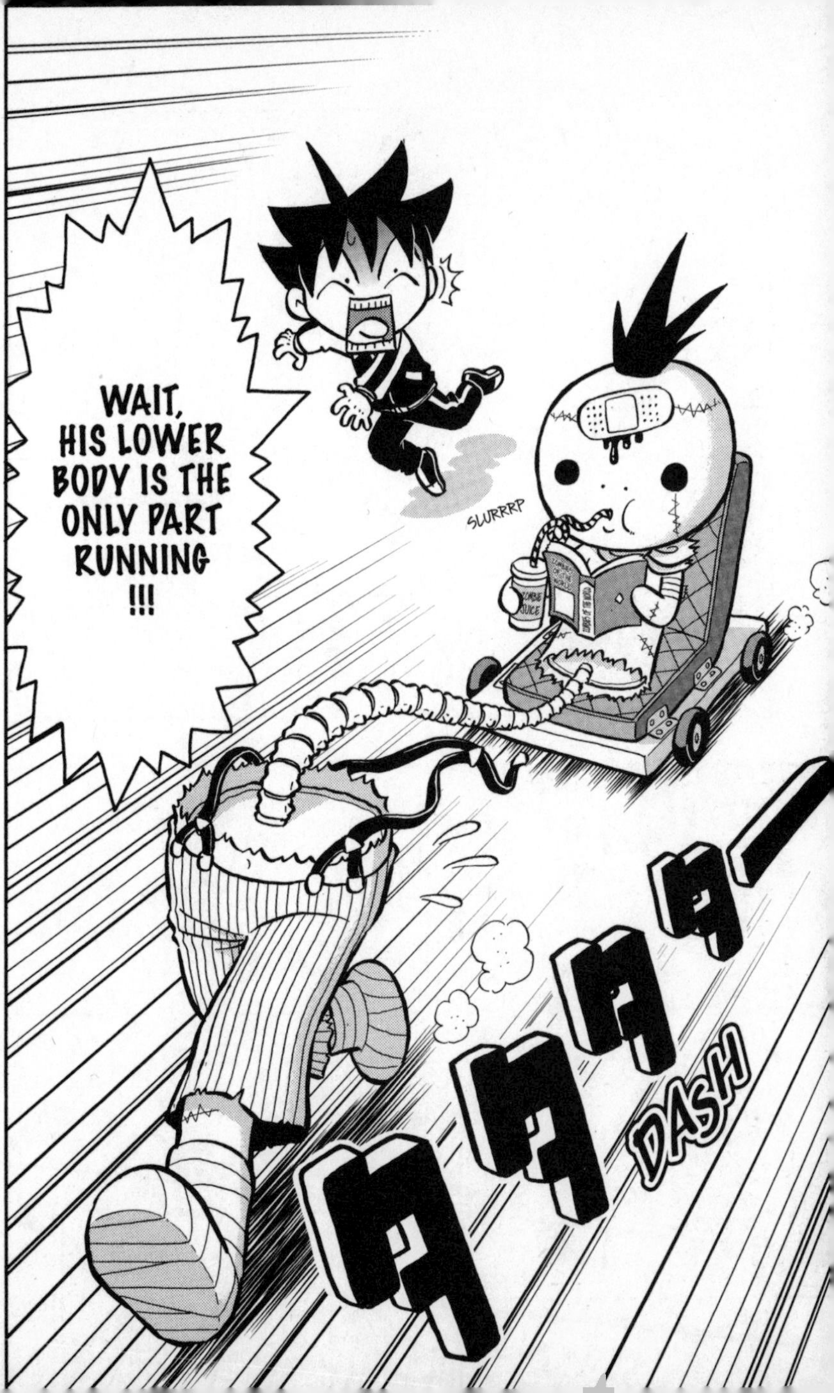
WAIT, HIS LOWER BODY IS THE ONLY PART RUNNING !!!
SLURRRP
DASH

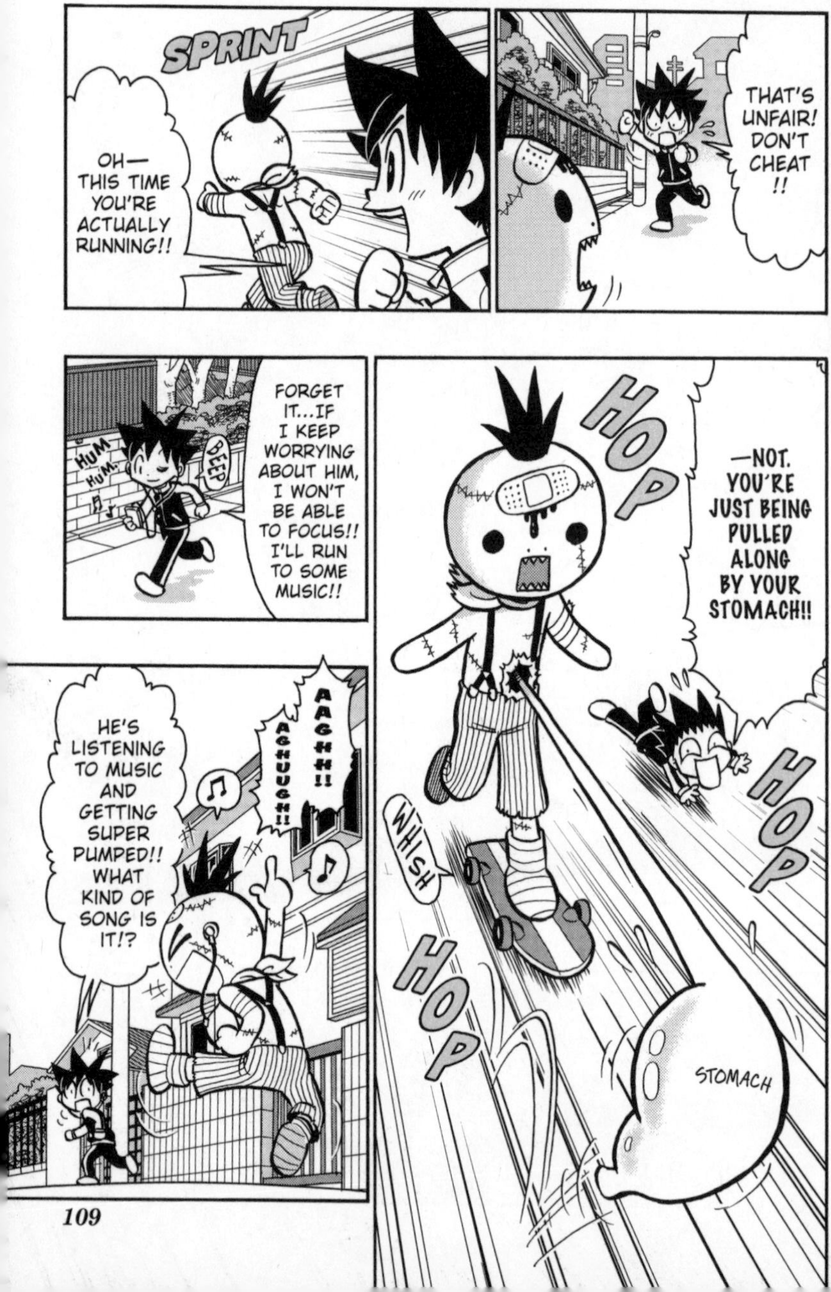
THAT'S UNFAIR! DON'T CHEAT!!
SPRINT
OH— THIS TIME YOU'RE ACTUALLY RUNNING!!
HOP
—NOT. YOU'RE JUST BEING PULLED ALONG BY YOUR STOMACH!!
HOP
WHISH
HOP HOP
STOMACH
FORGET IT...IF I KEEP WORRYING ABOUT HIM, I WON'T BE ABLE TO FOCUS!! I'LL RUN TO SOME MUSIC!!
BEEP
HUM HUM
AAGHH!!
AGHUUGH!!
HE'S LISTENING TO MUSIC AND GETTING SUPER PUMPED!! WHAT KIND OF SONG IS IT!?

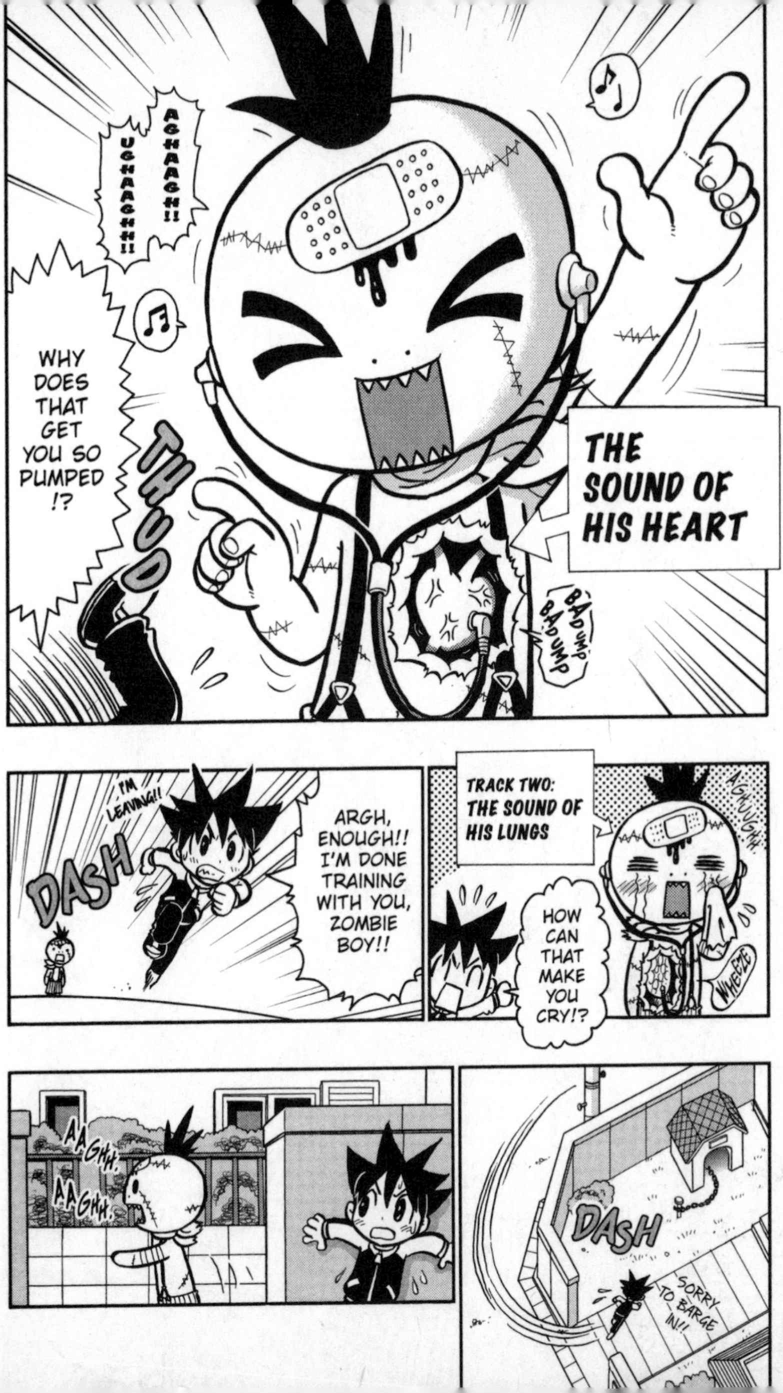
AGHAAGH!!
UGHAAGH!!
THE SOUND OF HIS HEART
BADUMP BADUMP
WHY DOES THAT GET YOU SO PUMPED!?
THUD
TRACK TWO: THE SOUND OF HIS LUNGS
AGHUUGHH.
HOW CAN THAT MAKE YOU CRY!?
WHEEZE
ARGH, ENOUGH!! I'M DONE TRAINING WITH YOU, ZOMBIE BOY!!
I'M LEAVING!!
DASH
DASH
SORRY TO BARGE IN!!
AAGHH.
AAGHH.

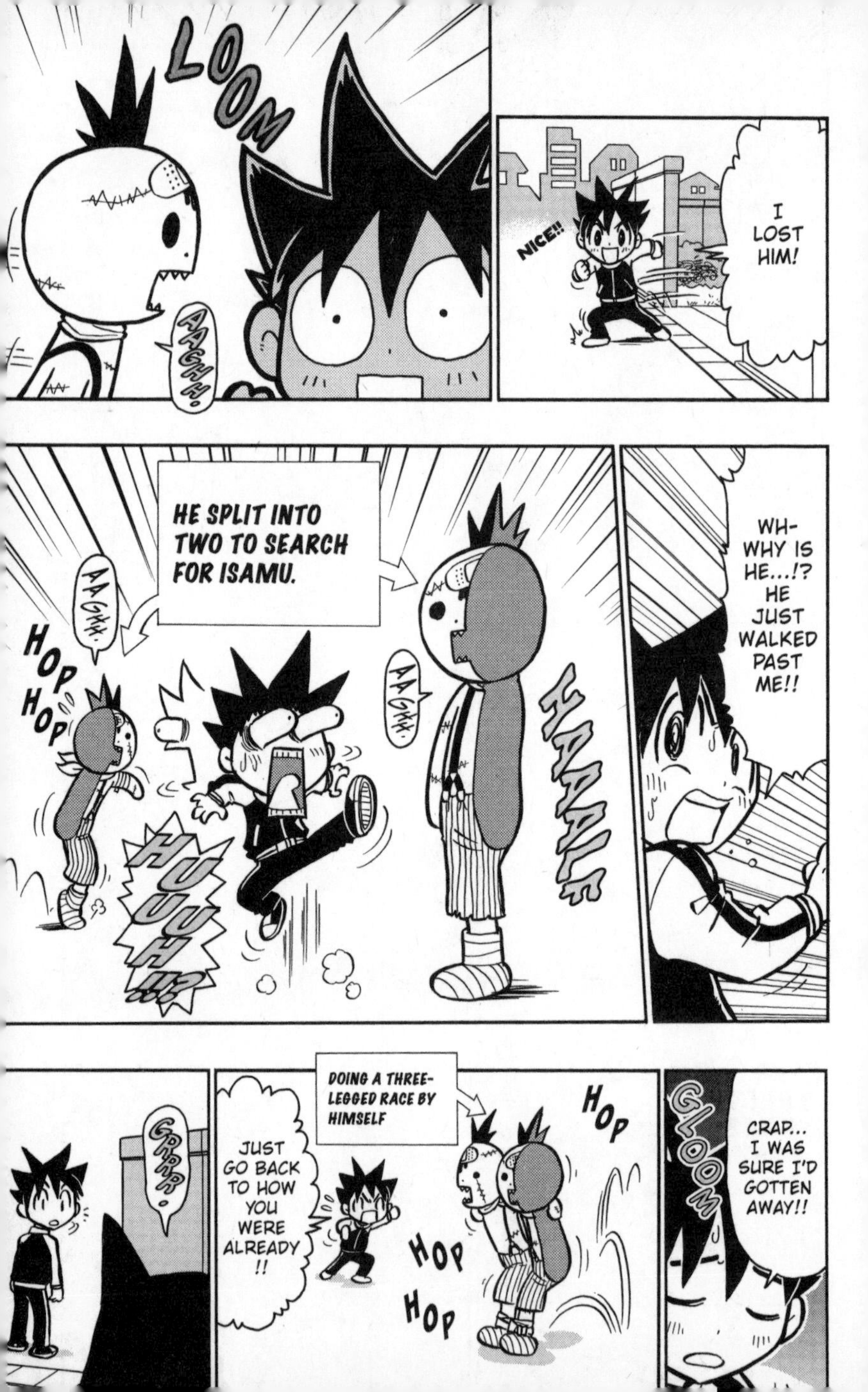
NICE!!
I LOST HIM!
LOOM
AAGHH.
WH- WHY IS HE...!? HE JUST WALKED PAST ME!!
HE SPLIT INTO TWO TO SEARCH FOR ISAMU.
HAAAH
AAGHH.
HUUUH!!?
AAGHH.
HOP HOP
GLOOM
CRAP... I WAS SURE I'D GOTTEN AWAY!!
DOING A THREE-LEGGED RACE BY HIMSELF
HOP
HOP HOP
JUST GO BACK TO HOW YOU WERE ALREADY!!
GRRR.

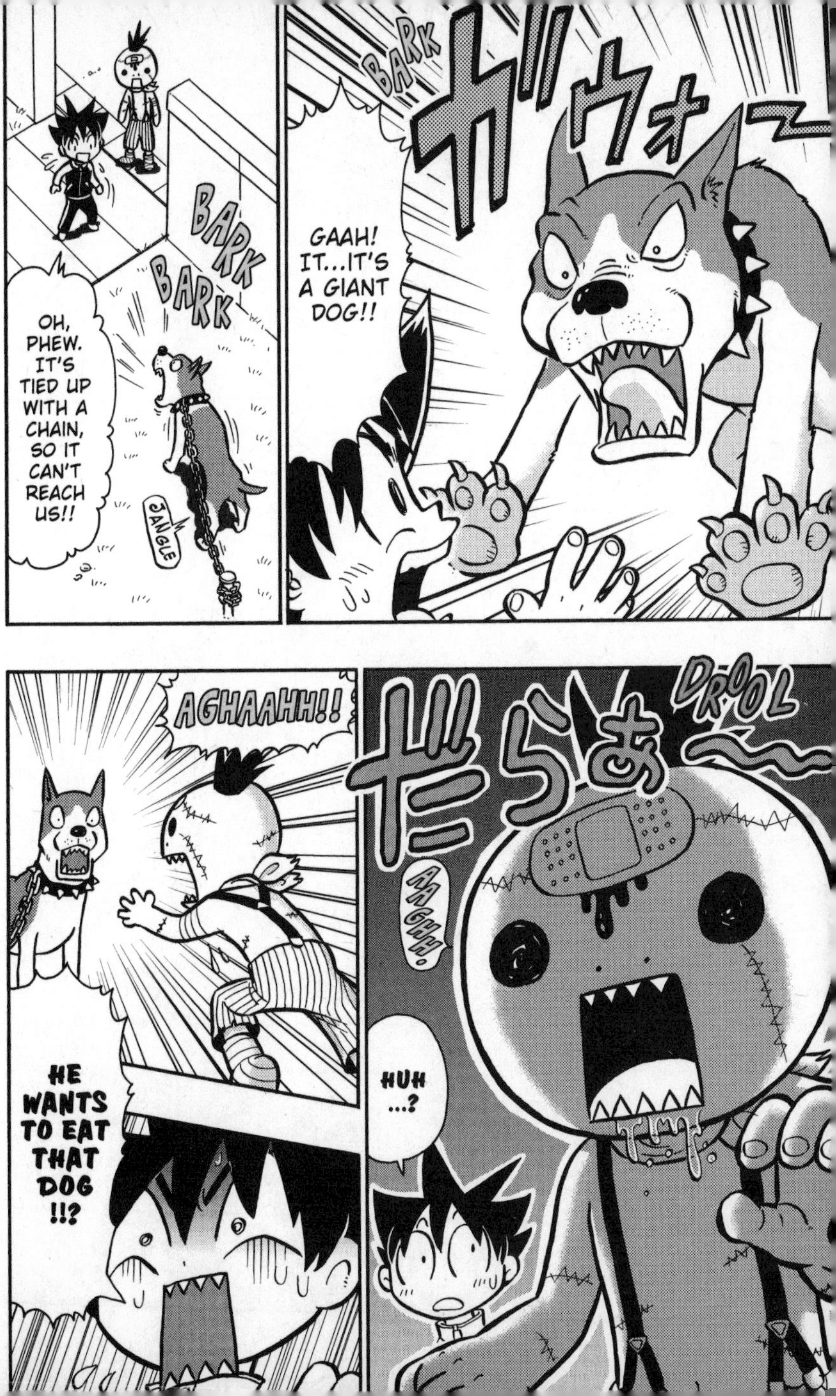

BARK
GAAH! IT...IT'S A GIANT DOG!!
BARK
BARK
BARK
OH, PHEW. IT'S TIED UP WITH A CHAIN, SO IT CAN'T REACH US!!
JANGLE
DROOL
AAGHH.
HUH ...?
AGHAAHH!!
HE WANTS TO EAT THAT DOG !!?

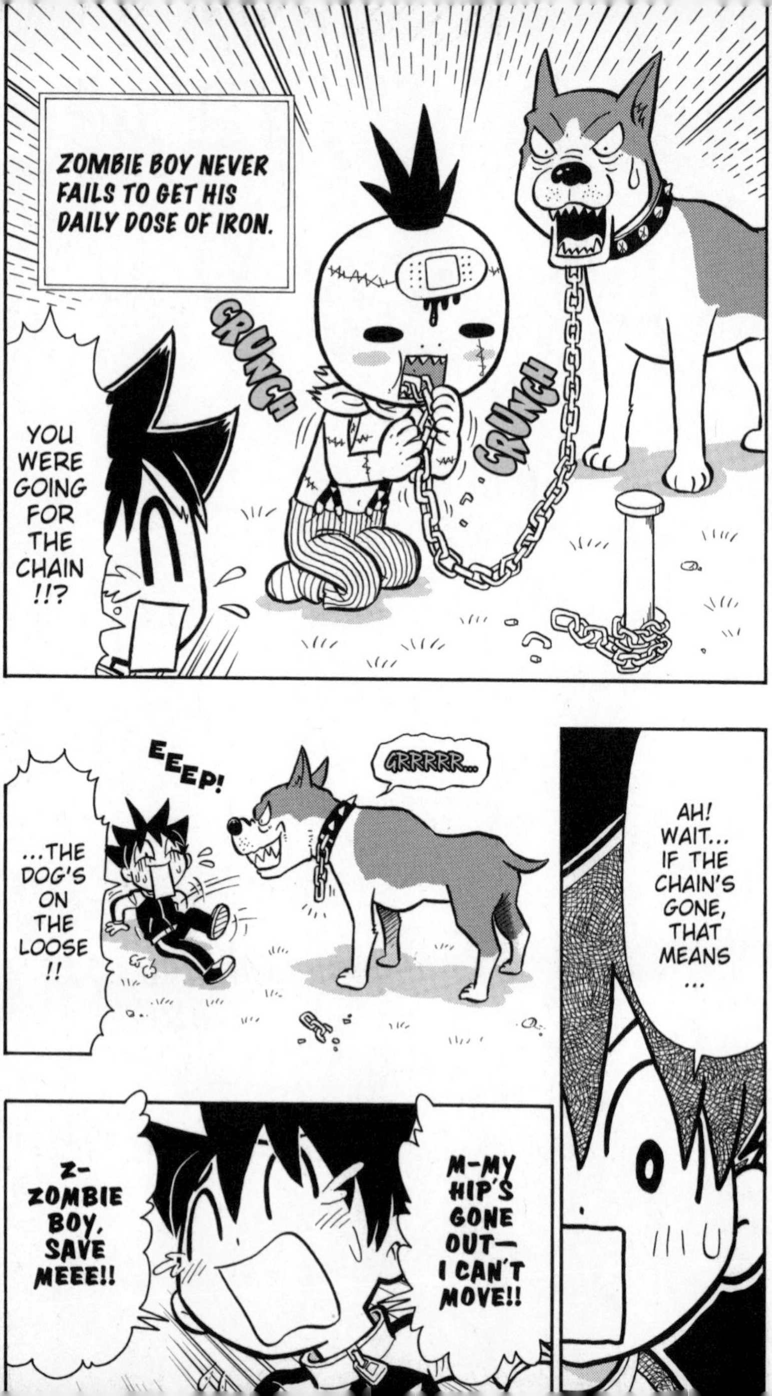

ZOMBIE BOY NEVER FAILS TO GET HIS DAILY DOSE OF IRON.
CRUNCH
CRUNCH
YOU WERE GOING FOR THE CHAIN!!?
AH! WAIT... IF THE CHAIN'S GONE, THAT MEANS...
GRRRRR...
EEEEP!
...THE DOG'S ON THE LOOSE!!
M-MY HIP'S GONE OUT— I CAN'T MOVE!!
Z-ZOMBIE BOY, SAVE MEEE!!

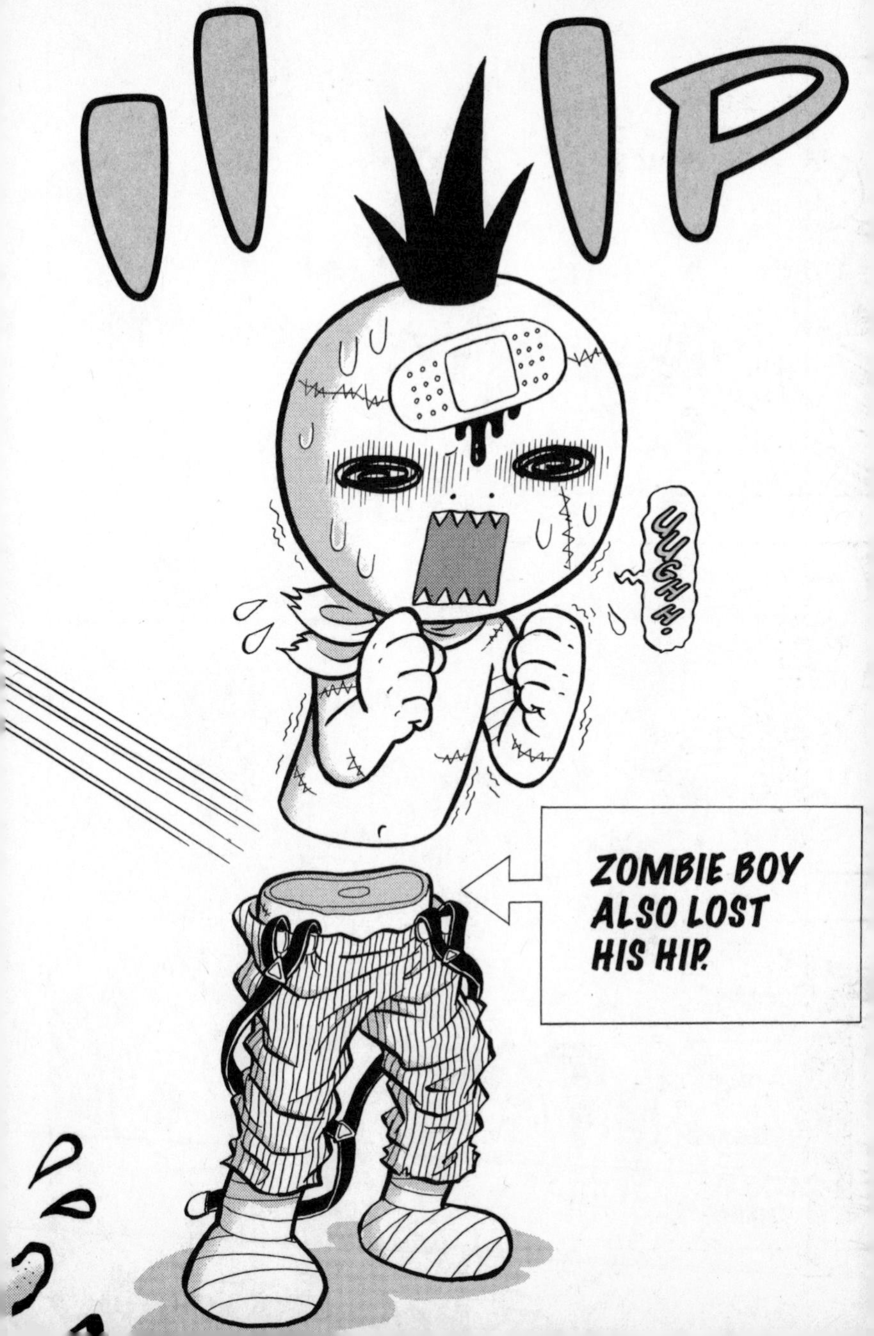
HIP
UUGHH.
ZOMBIE BOY ALSO LOST HIS HIP.

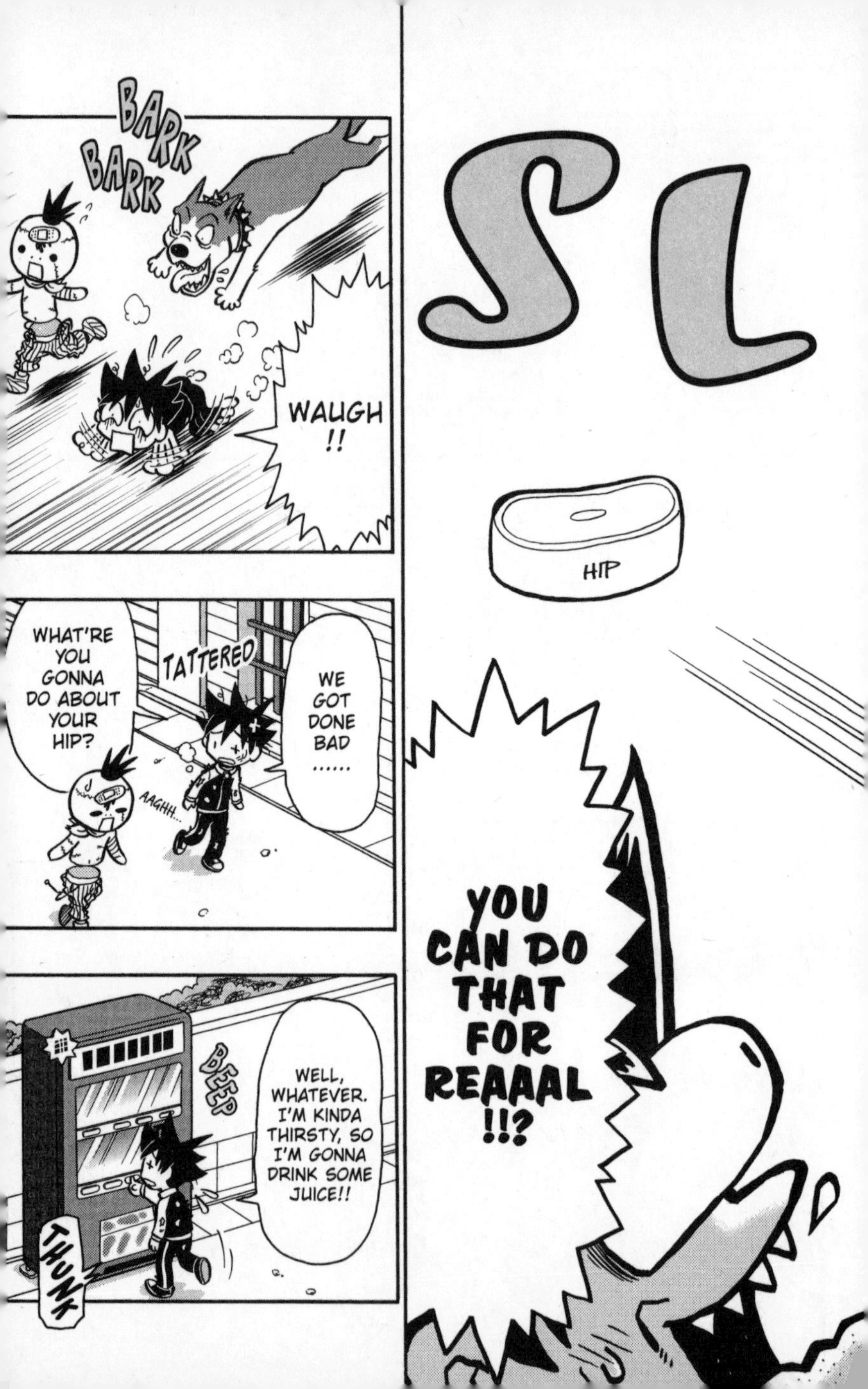
SL
HIP
YOU CAN DO THAT FOR REAAAL!!?
BARK BARK
WAUGH!!
WE GOT DONE BAD……
TATTERED
WHAT'RE YOU GONNA DO ABOUT YOUR HIP?
AAGHH…
WELL, WHATEVER. I'M KINDA THIRSTY, SO I'M GONNA DRINK SOME JUICE!!
BEEP
THUNK

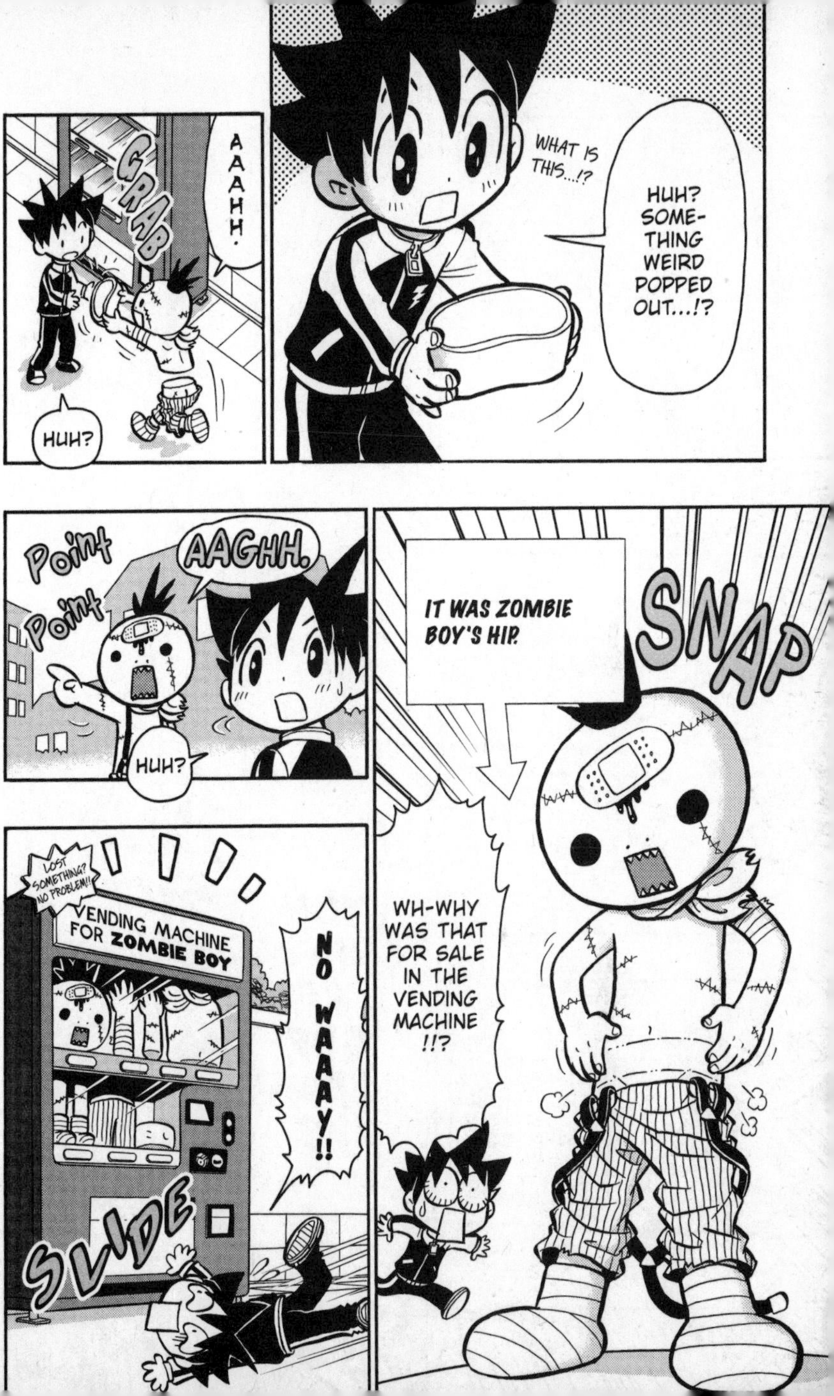
WHAT IS THIS...!?
HUH? SOME-THING WEIRD POPPED OUT...!?
AAAHH.
GRAB
HUH?
SNAP
IT WAS ZOMBIE BOY'S HIP.
WH-WHY WAS THAT FOR SALE IN THE VENDING MACHINE!!?
AAGHH.
Point
Point
HUH?
LOST SOMETHING? NO PROBLEM!!
VENDING MACHINE FOR ZOMBIE BOY
NO WAAAAY!!
SLIDE

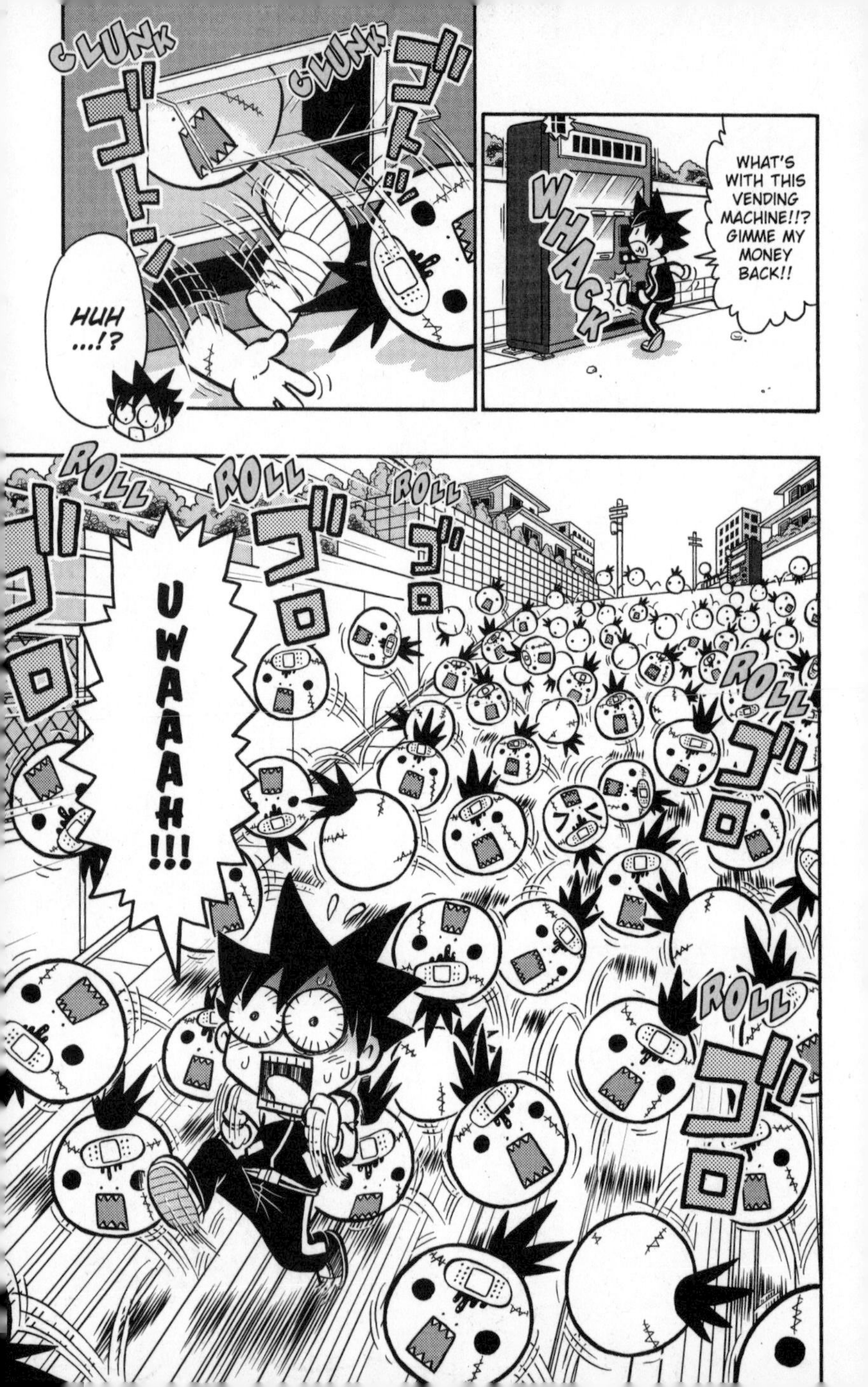
WHAT'S WITH THIS VENDING MACHINE!!? GIMME MY MONEY BACK!!
WHACK
CLUNK
CLUNK
HUH ...!?
ROLL
ROLL
ROLL
UWAAAAH!!!
ROLL
ROLL

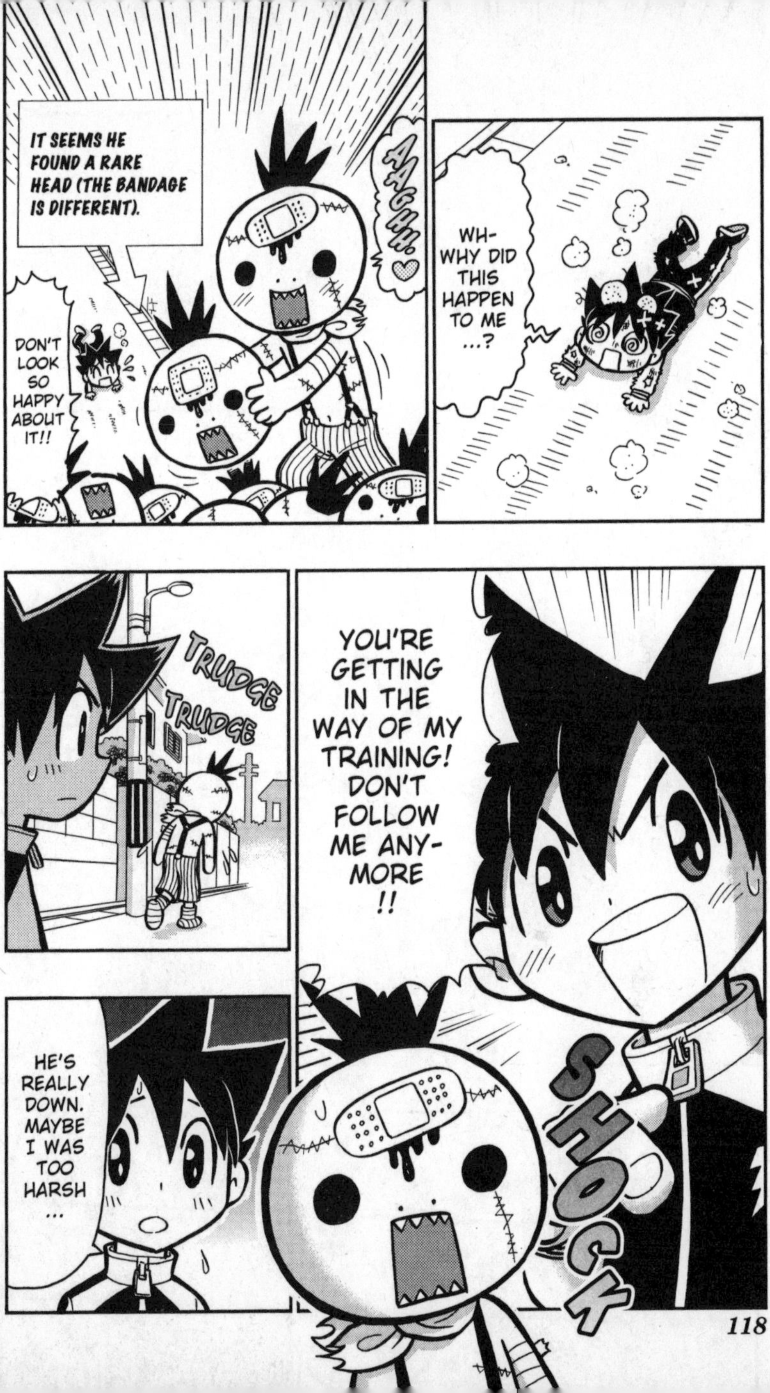
WH- WHY DID THIS HAPPEN TO ME ...?
AAGHH! ♥
IT SEEMS HE FOUND A RARE HEAD (THE BANDAGE IS DIFFERENT).
DON'T LOOK SO HAPPY ABOUT IT!!
YOU'RE GETTING IN THE WAY OF MY TRAINING! DON'T FOLLOW ME ANY-MORE !!
SHOCK
TRUDGE
TRUDGE
HE'S REALLY DOWN. MAYBE I WAS TOO HARSH ...

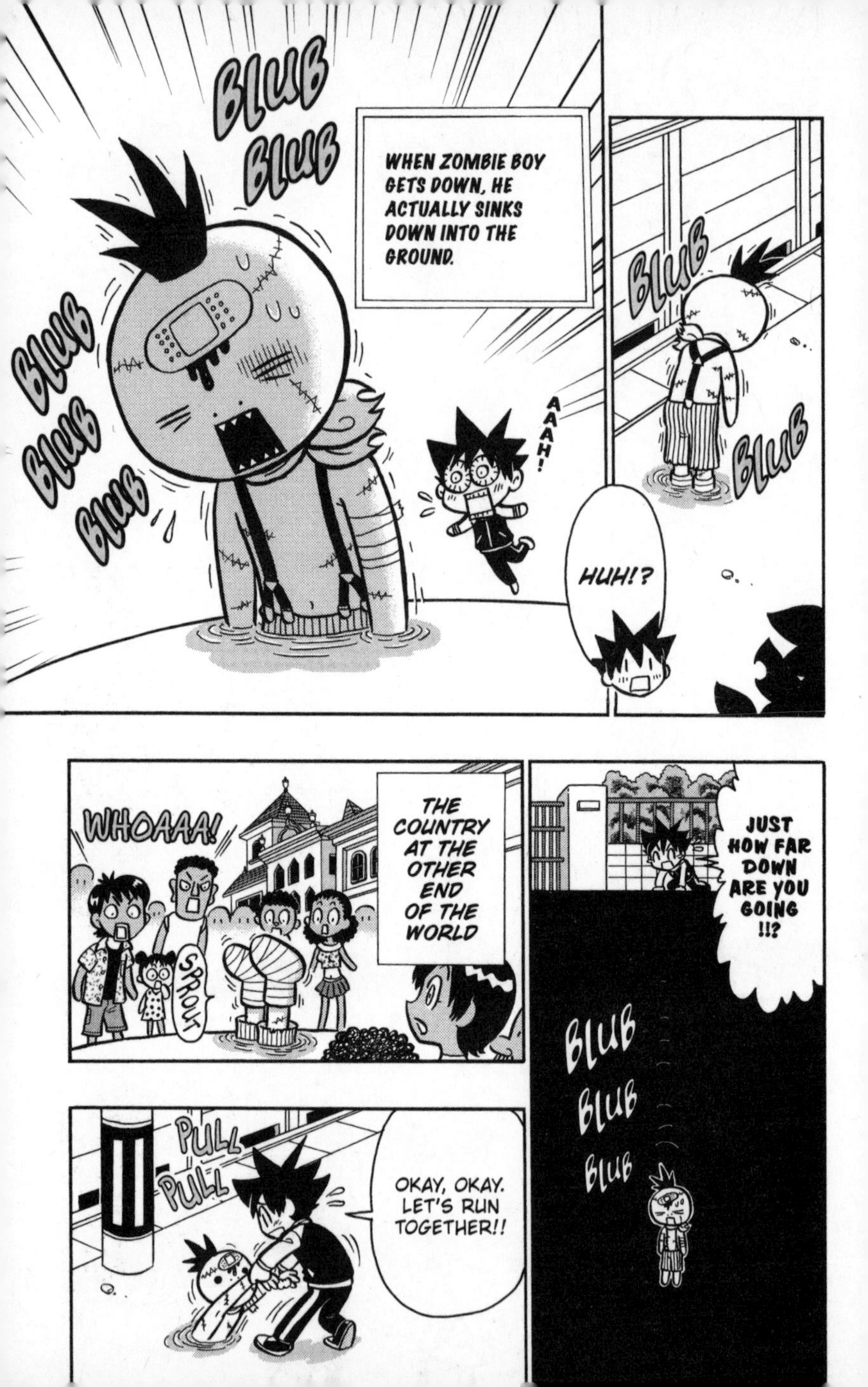
BLUB
BLUB
HUH!?
WHEN ZOMBIE BOY GETS DOWN, HE ACTUALLY SINKS DOWN INTO THE GROUND.
BLUB BLUB
AAAH!
BLUB BLUB BLUB
JUST HOW FAR DOWN ARE YOU GOING !!?
BLUB BLUB BLUB
THE COUNTRY AT THE OTHER END OF THE WORLD
WHOAAA!
SPROUT
OKAY, OKAY. LET'S RUN TOGETHER!!
PULL PULL

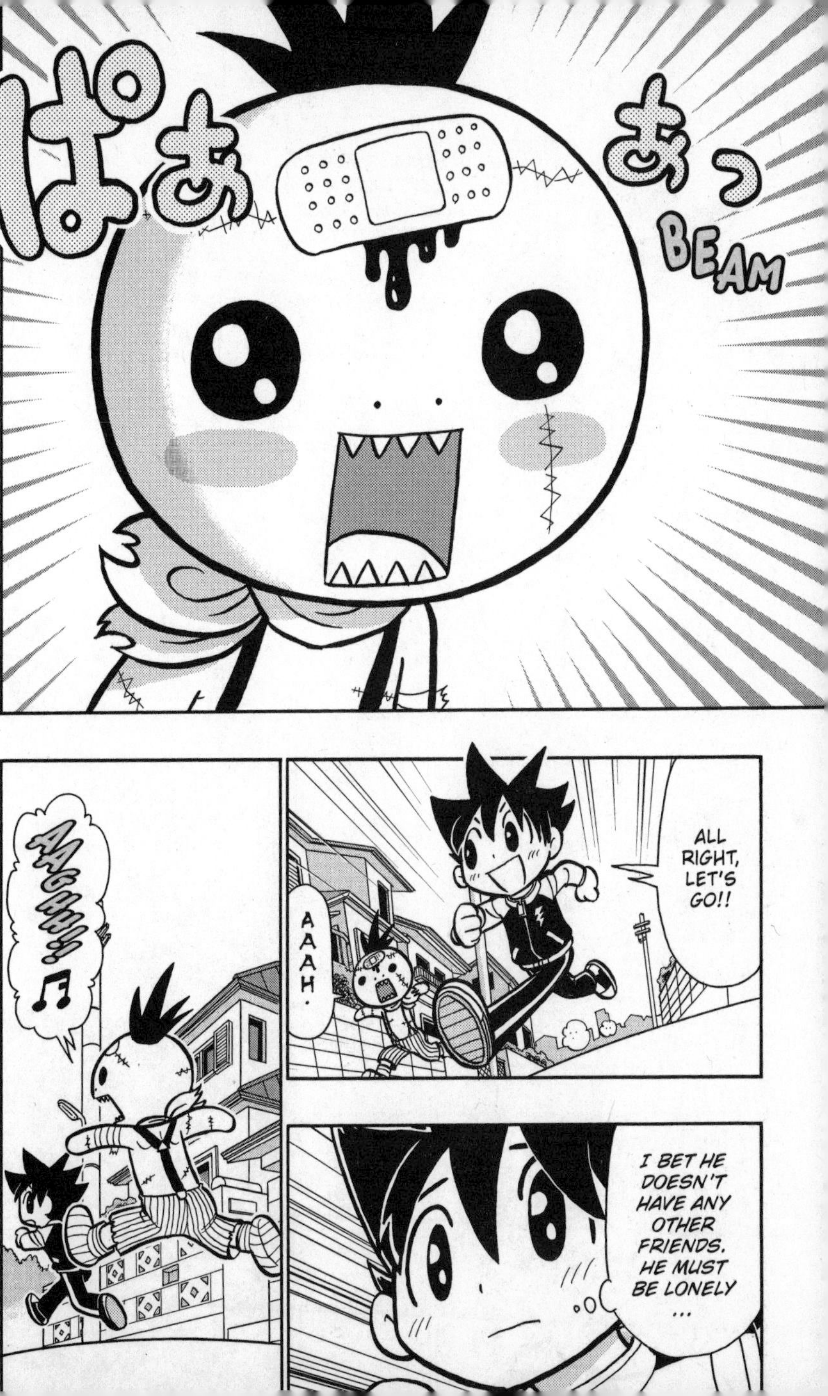
ぱあ
あっ
BEAM
ALL RIGHT, LET'S GO!!
AAAH.
I BET HE DOESN'T HAVE ANY OTHER FRIENDS. HE MUST BE LONELY ...
AAGHH!! ♫

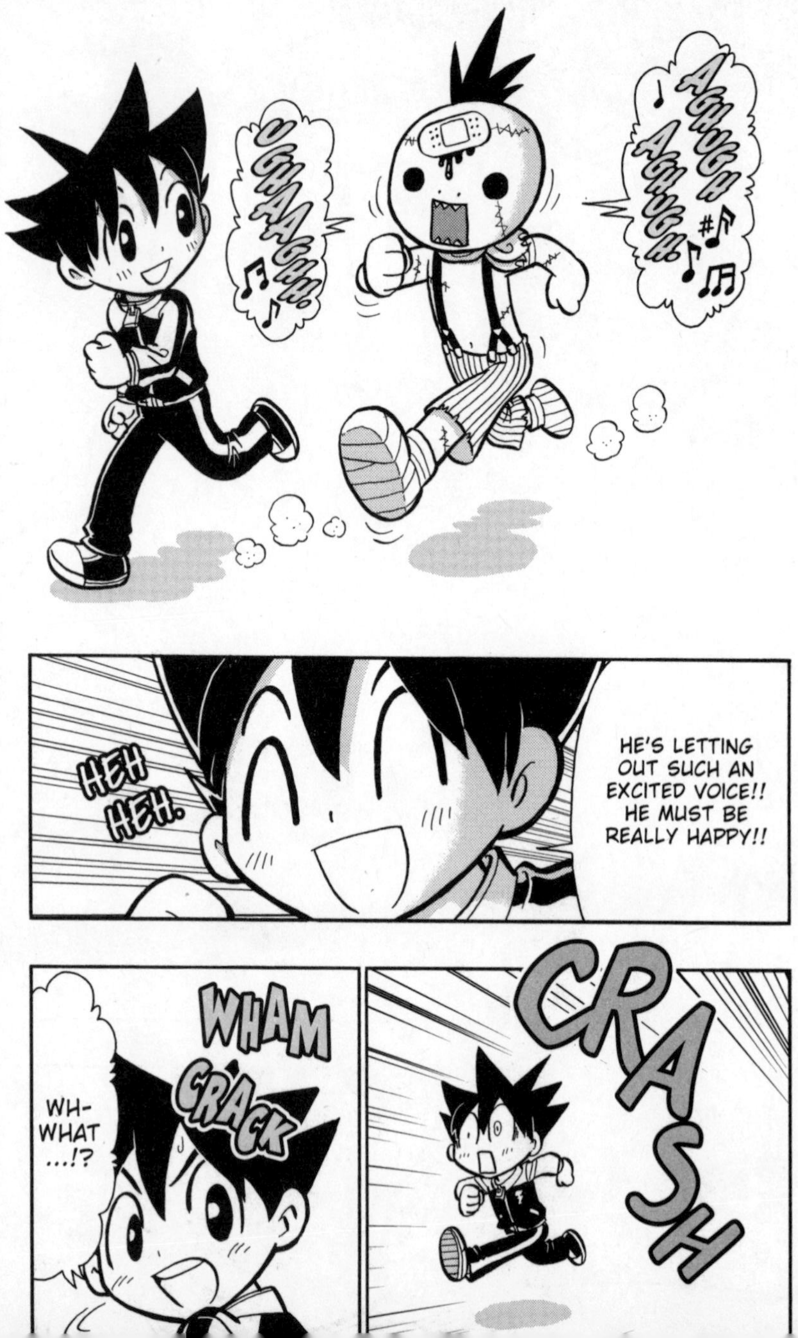
AGHUGH AGHUGH.
UGHAAAGHH.
HE'S LETTING OUT SUCH AN EXCITED VOICE!! HE MUST BE REALLY HAPPY!!
HEH HEH.
CRASH
WHAM
CRACK
WH-WHAT ...!?

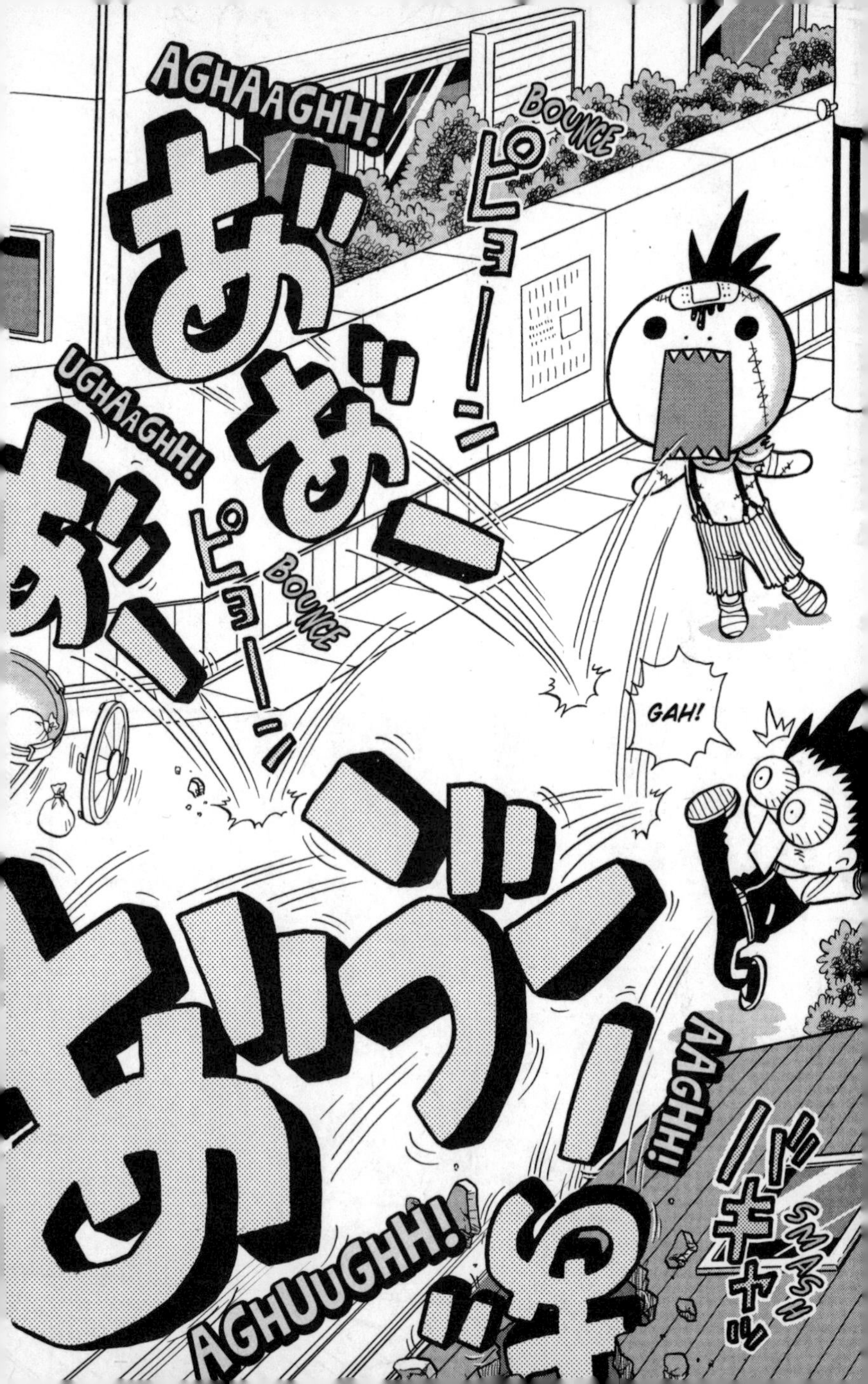
AGHAAGHH!
BOUNCE
UGHAAGHH!
BOUNCE
GAH!
AAGHH!
SMASH
AGHUUGHH!

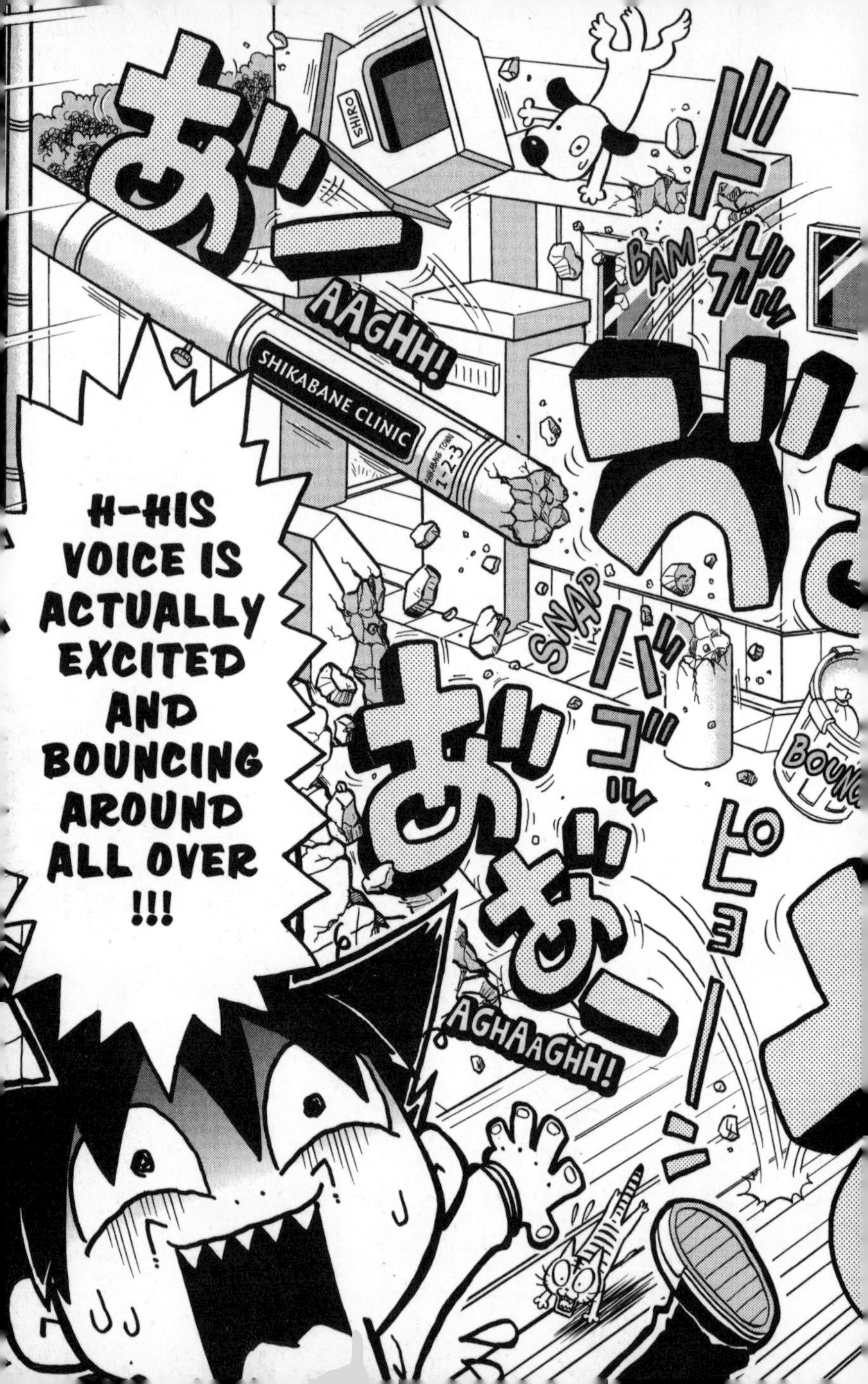
BAM
SHIRO
AAGHH!
SHIKABANE CLINIC
1-2-3
SNAP
AGHAaGHH!
H-HIS VOICE IS ACTUALLY EXCITED AND BOUNCING AROUND ALL OVER!!!

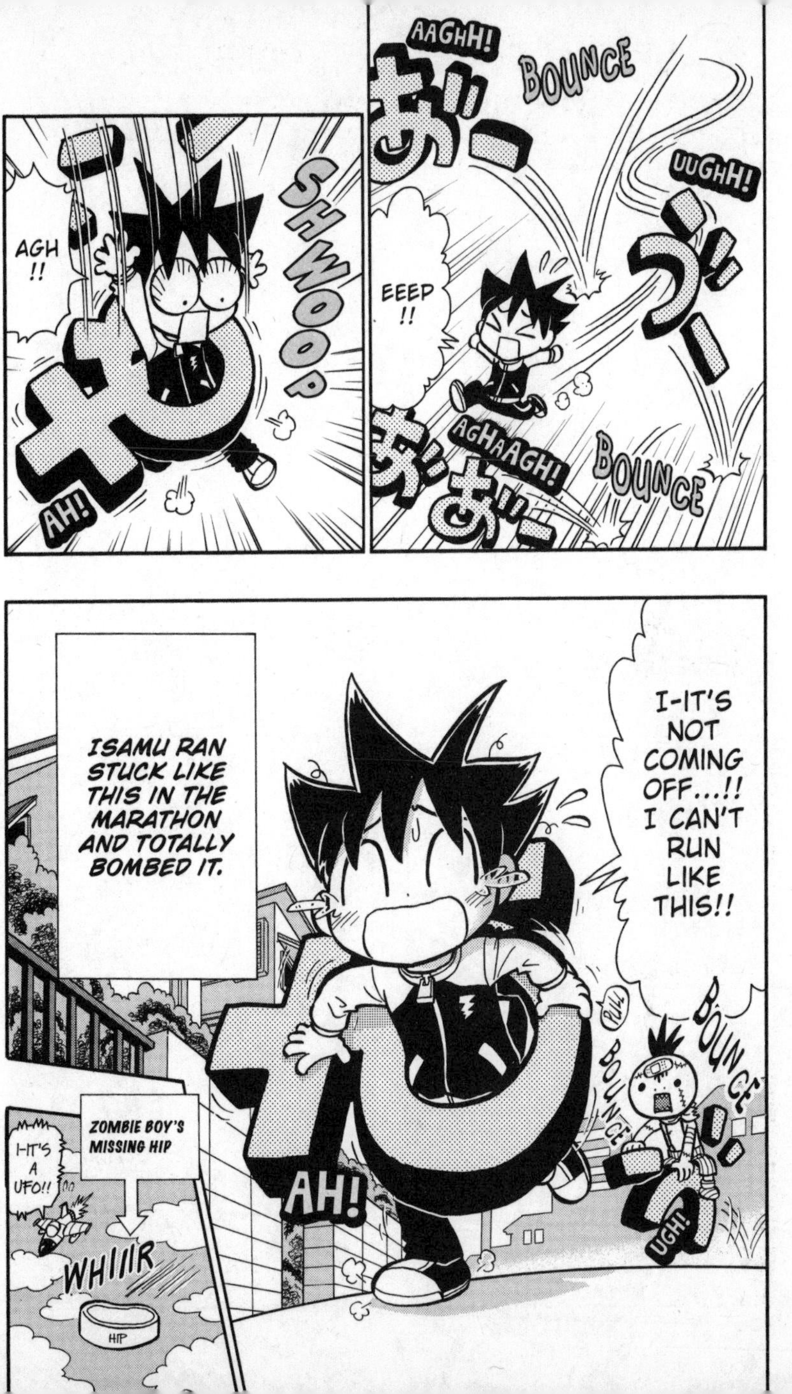
AAGHH!
BOUNCE
UUGHH!
EEEP!!
AGHAAGH!
BOUNCE
SHWOOP
AGH!!
AH!
I-IT'S NOT COMING OFF...!! I CAN'T RUN LIKE THIS!!
ISAMU RAN STUCK LIKE THIS IN THE MARATHON AND TOTALLY BOMBED IT.
PULL
BOUNCE
BOUNCE
UGH!
AH!
ZOMBIE BOY'S MISSING HIP
I-IT'S A UFO!!
WHIIIR
HIP

SPECIAL FOUR-PANEL COMIC PART 4

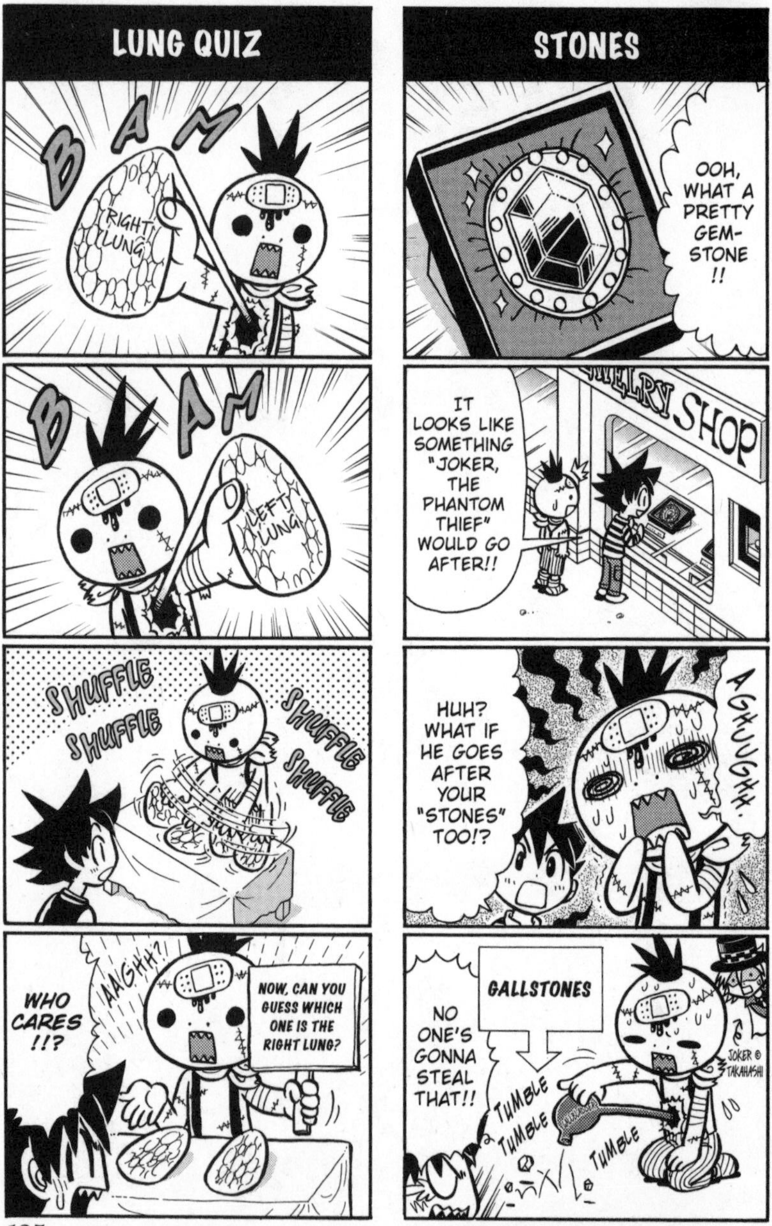
STONES
OOH, WHAT A PRETTY GEM-STONE !!
SHOP
IT LOOKS LIKE SOMETHING "JOKER, THE PHANTOM THIEF" WOULD GO AFTER!!
HUH? WHAT IF HE GOES AFTER YOUR "STONES" TOO!?
AGHUUGHH.
GALLSTONES
NO ONE'S GONNA STEAL THAT!!
TUMBLE
TUMBLE
TUMBLE
TUMBLE
JOKER © TAKAHASHI
LUNG QUIZ
BAM
RIGHT LUNG
BAM
LEFT LUNG
SHUFFLE
SHUFFLE
SHUFFLE
SHUFFLE
NOW, CAN YOU GUESS WHICH ONE IS THE RIGHT LUNG?
AAGHH?
WHO CARES !!?

TAKAHASHI, CONGRATULATIONS ON WINNING THE SHOGAKUKAN MANGA AWARD!!

HE'Z IMMORTAL, AZLEEP OR AWAKE!

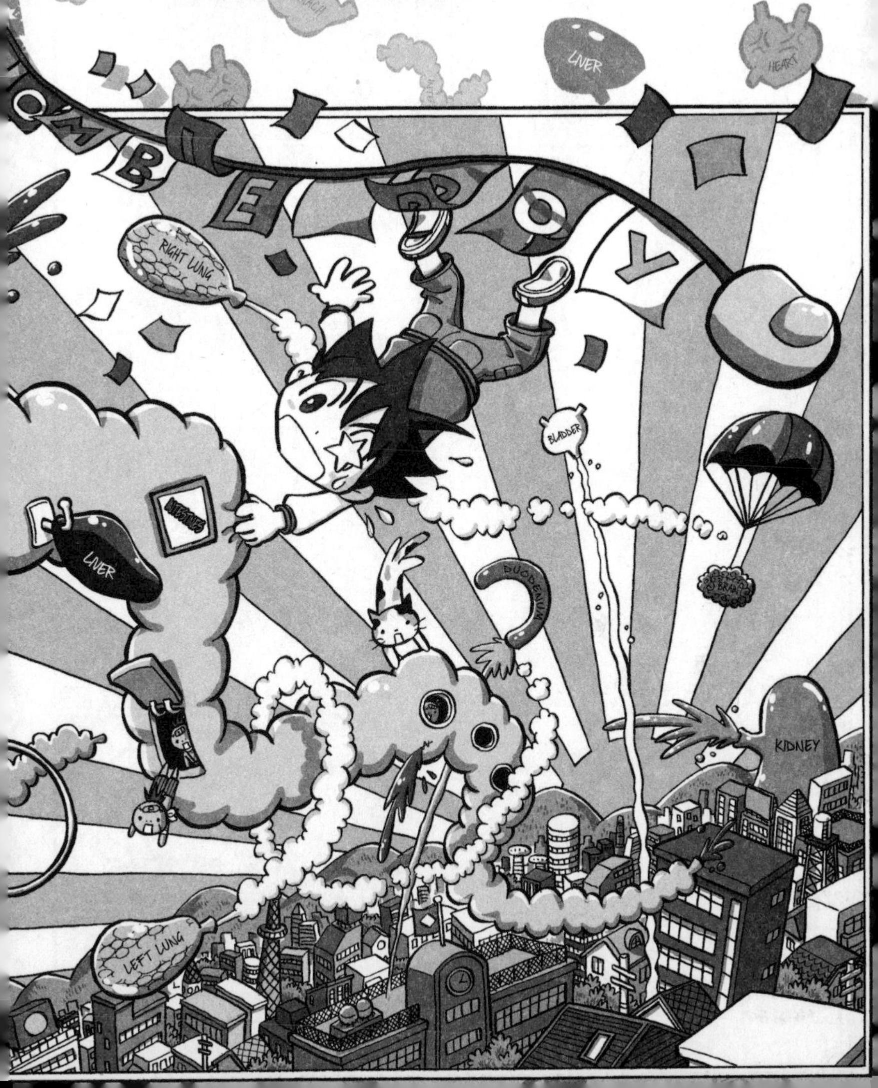
LIVER
HEART
RIGHT LUNG
BLADDER
LIVER
DUODENUM
BRAIN
KIDNEY
LEFT LUNG

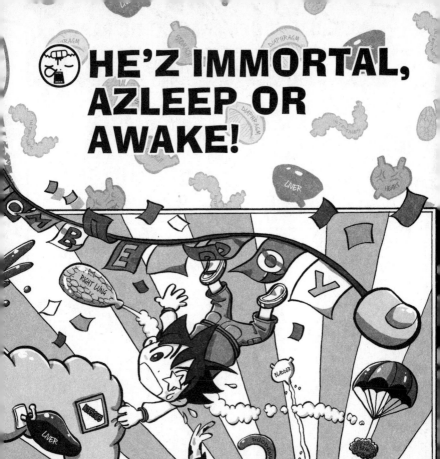

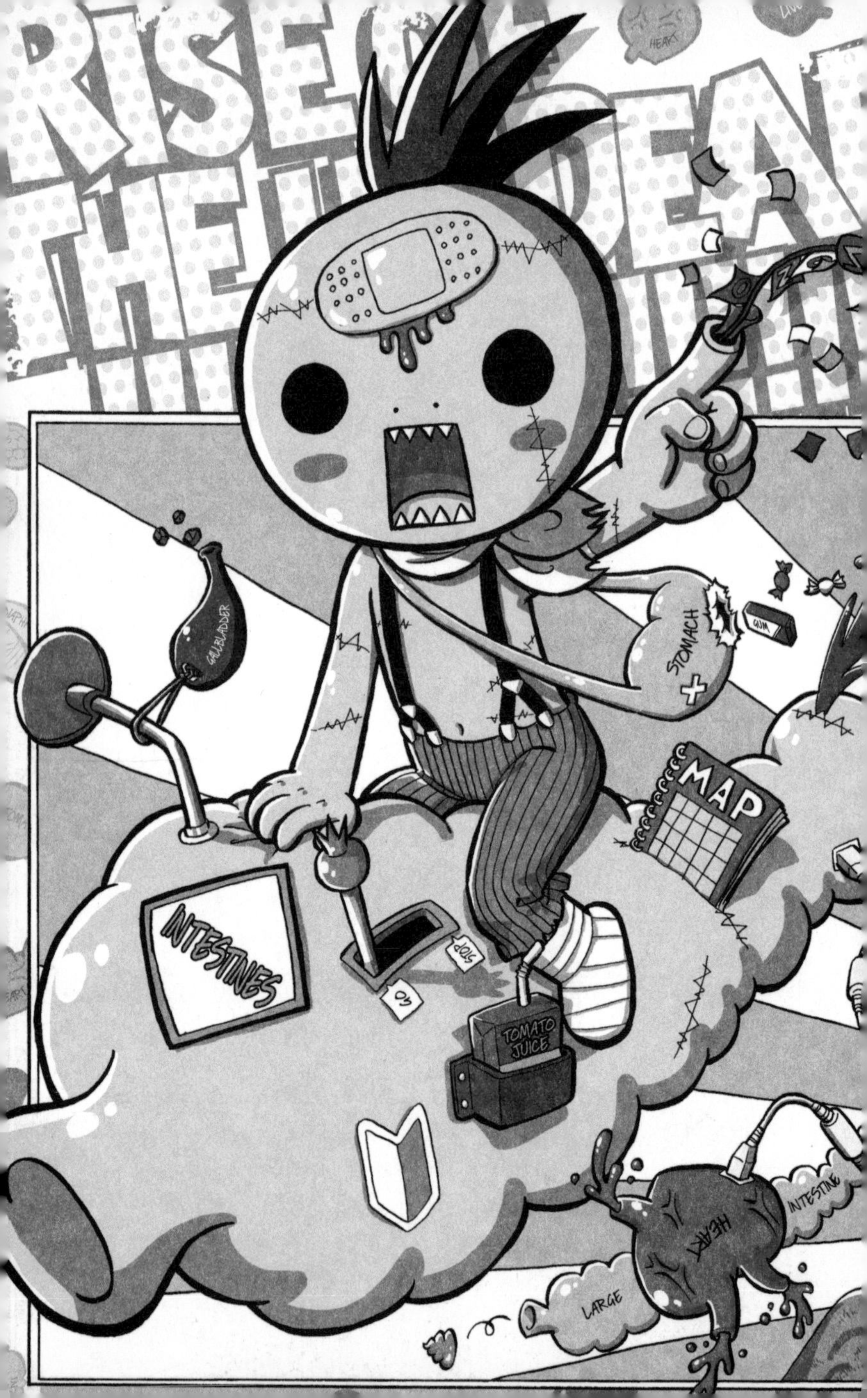
GALLBLADDER
STOMACH
GUM
MAP
INTESTINES
STOP
GO
TOMATO JUICE
HEART
INTESTINE
LARGE

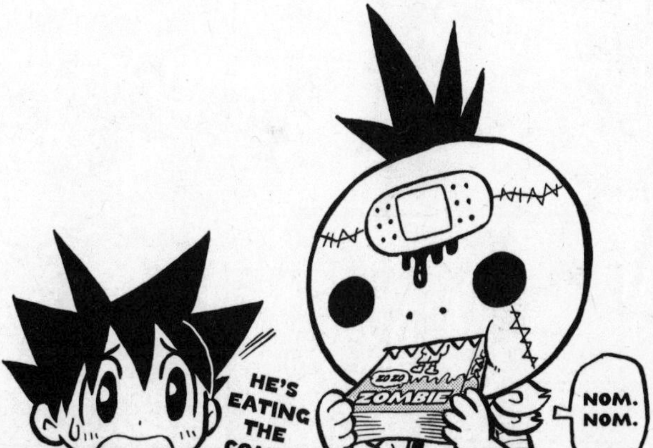
NOM. NOM.
ZO ZO ZOMBIE
HE'S EATING THE COMIC ...!

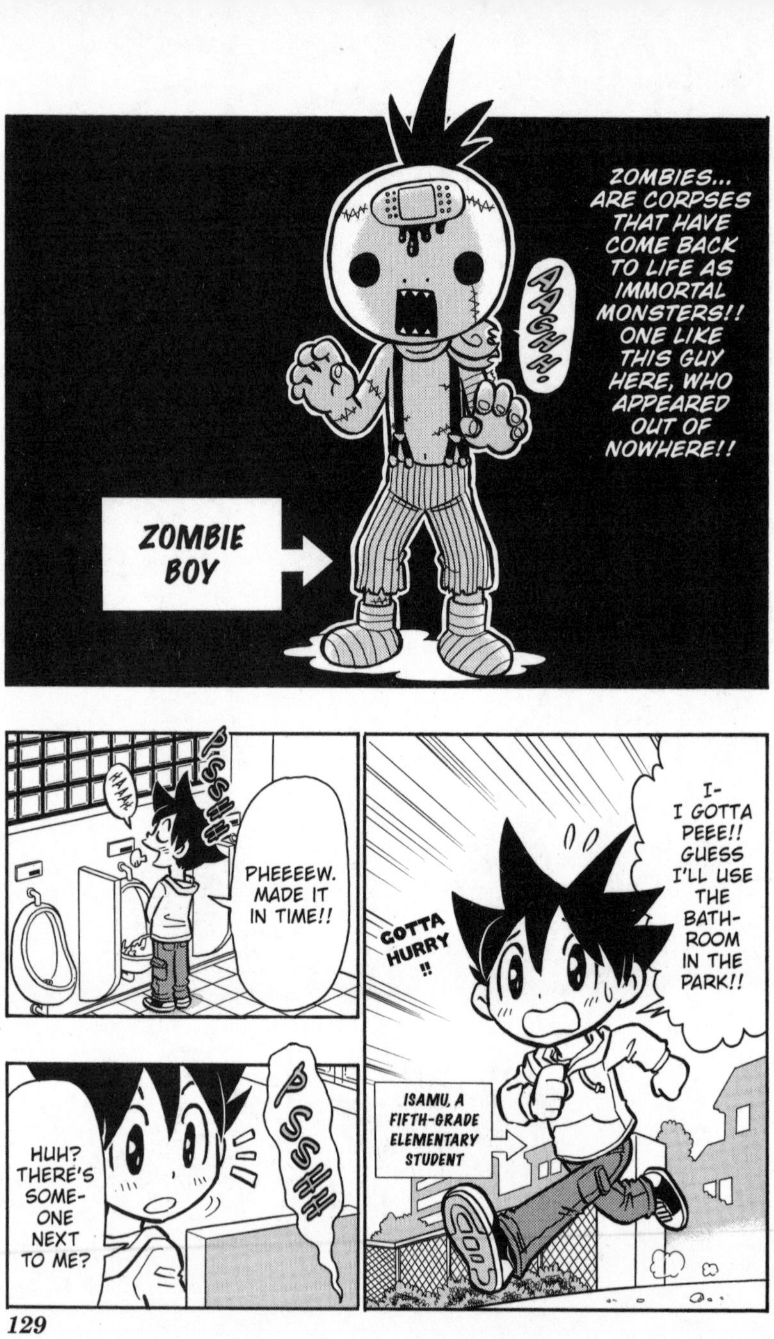
ZOMBIES... ARE CORPSES THAT HAVE COME BACK TO LIFE AS IMMORTAL MONSTERS!! ONE LIKE THIS GUY HERE, WHO APPEARED OUT OF NOWHERE!!
AAGHH.
ZOMBIE BOY
I- I GOTTA PEEE!! GUESS I'LL USE THE BATH-ROOM IN THE PARK!!
GOTTA HURRY!!
ISAMU, A FIFTH-GRADE ELEMENTARY STUDENT
PSSHH
PHEEEEW. MADE IT IN TIME!!
PSSHH
HUH? THERE'S SOME-ONE NEXT TO ME?

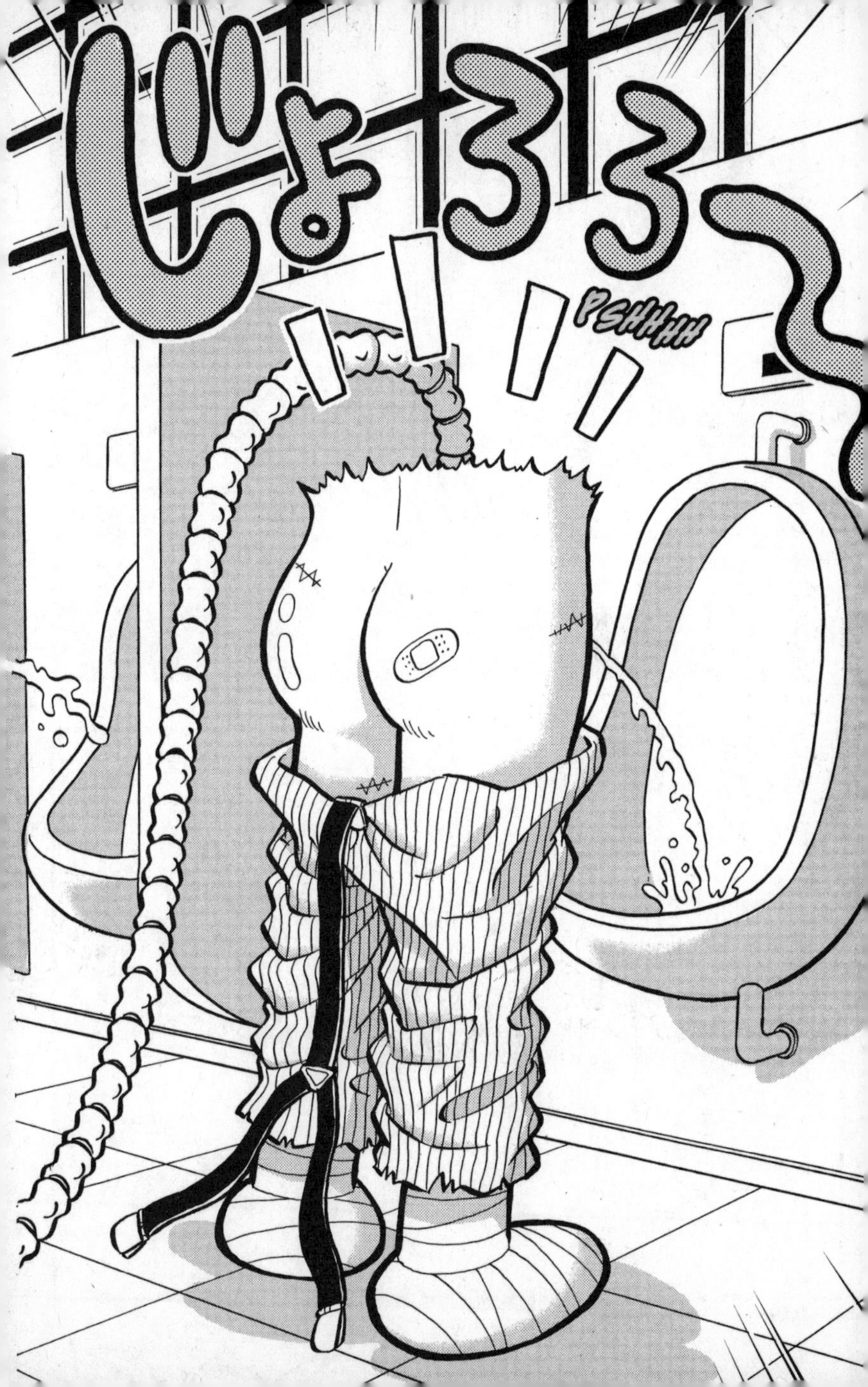
じょろろ〜
PSHHHH

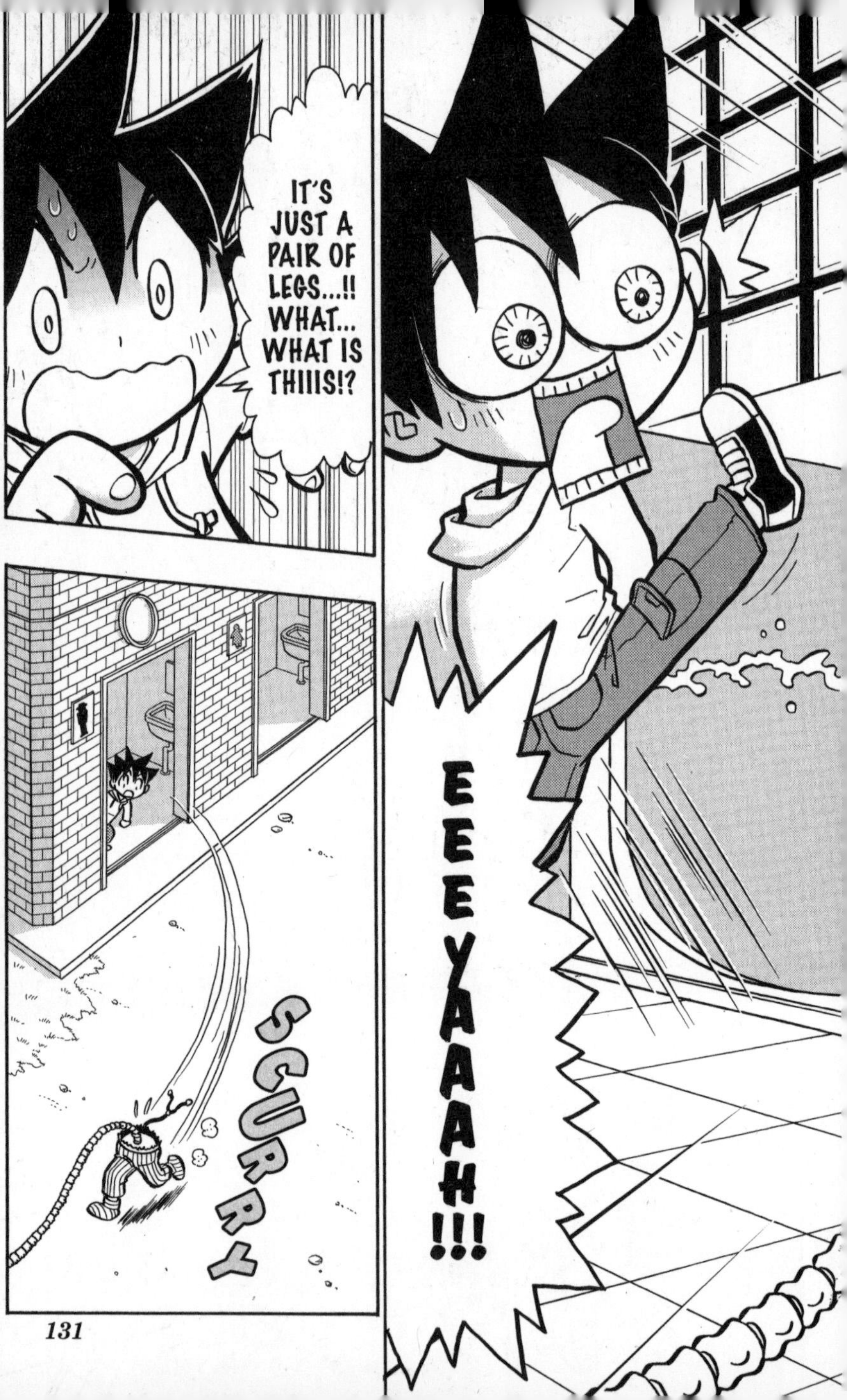
EEEYAAAAH!!!
IT'S JUST A PAIR OF LEGS...!! WHAT... WHAT IS THIIIS!?
SCURRY

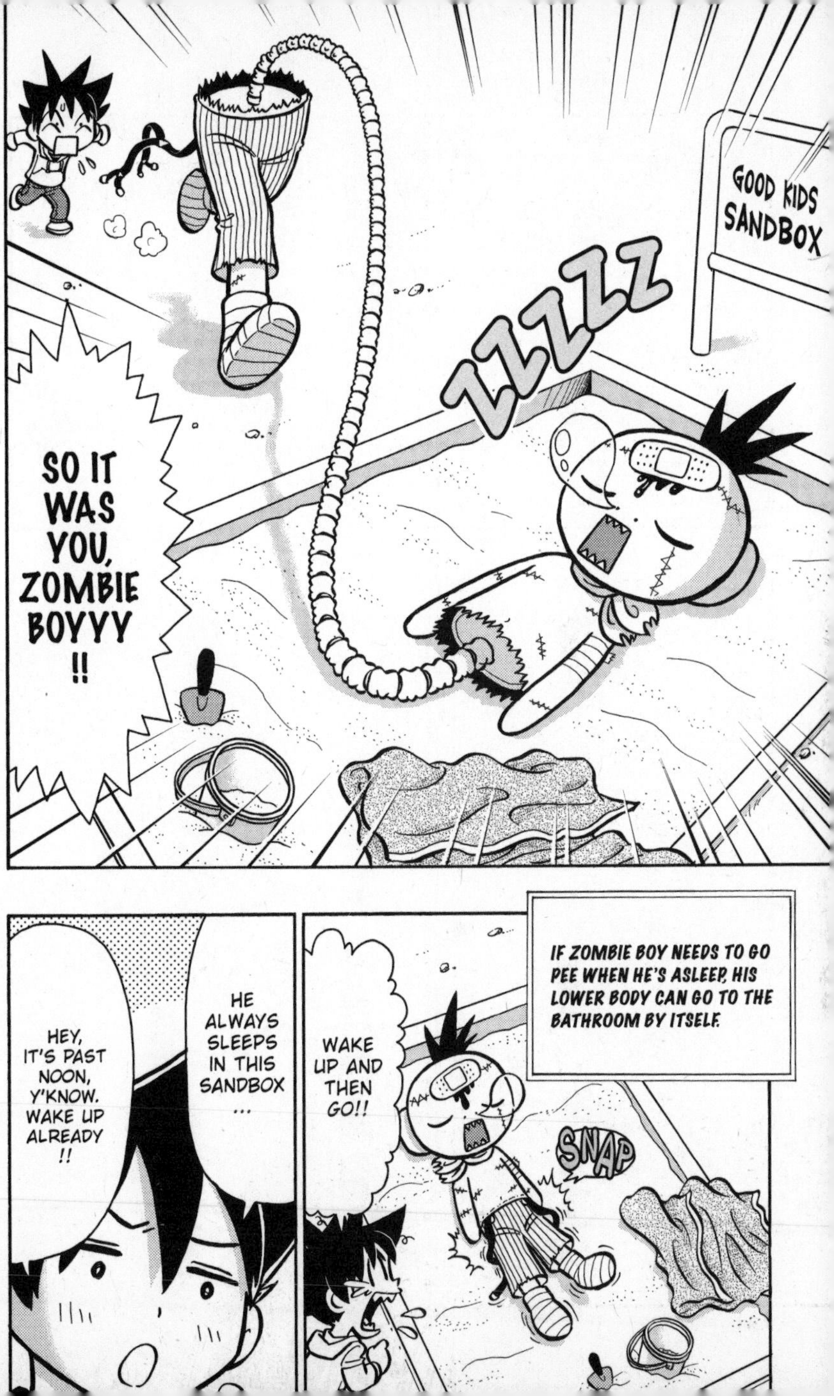
GOOD KIDS SANDBOX
ZZZZZZ
SO IT WAS YOU, ZOMBIE BOYYY!!
IF ZOMBIE BOY NEEDS TO GO PEE WHEN HE'S ASLEEP, HIS LOWER BODY CAN GO TO THE BATHROOM BY ITSELF.
WAKE UP AND THEN GO!!
SNAP
HE ALWAYS SLEEPS IN THIS SANDBOX ...
HEY, IT'S PAST NOON, Y'KNOW. WAKE UP ALREADY!!

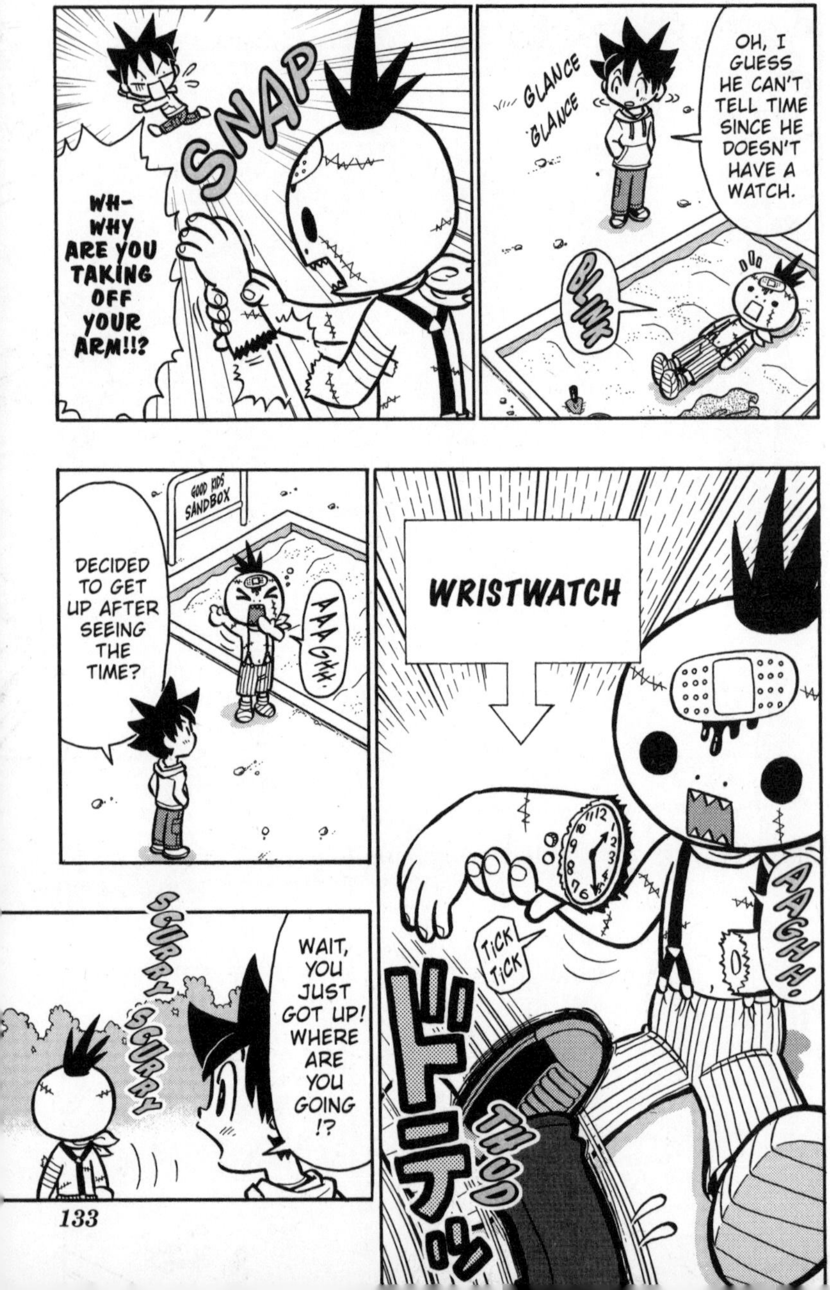
GLANCE GLANCE
OH, I GUESS HE CAN'T TELL TIME SINCE HE DOESN'T HAVE A WATCH.
BLINK
SNAP
WH-WHY ARE YOU TAKING OFF YOUR ARM!!?
WRISTWATCH
TICK TICK
AAGHH.
ドテッ
THUD
GOOD KIDS SANDBOX
DECIDED TO GET UP AFTER SEEING THE TIME?
AAAGHH.
WAIT, YOU JUST GOT UP! WHERE ARE YOU GOING !?
SCURRY SCURRY

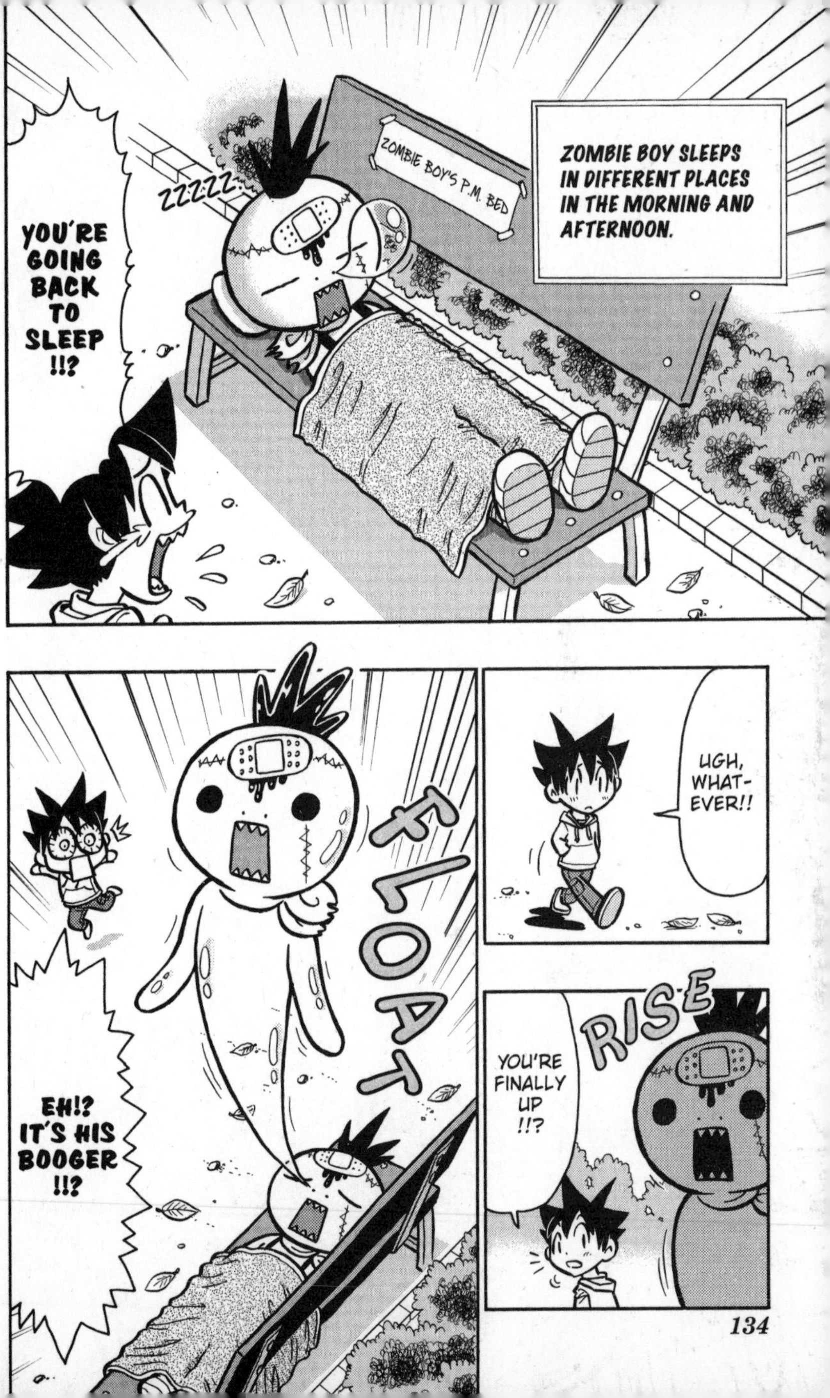
ZOMBIE BOY SLEEPS IN DIFFERENT PLACES IN THE MORNING AND AFTERNOON.
ZOMBIE BOY'S P.M. BED
ZZZZZ
YOU'RE GOING BACK TO SLEEP!!?
UGH, WHAT-EVER!!
RISE
YOU'RE FINALLY UP!!?
FLOAT
EH!? IT'S HIS BOOGER!!?

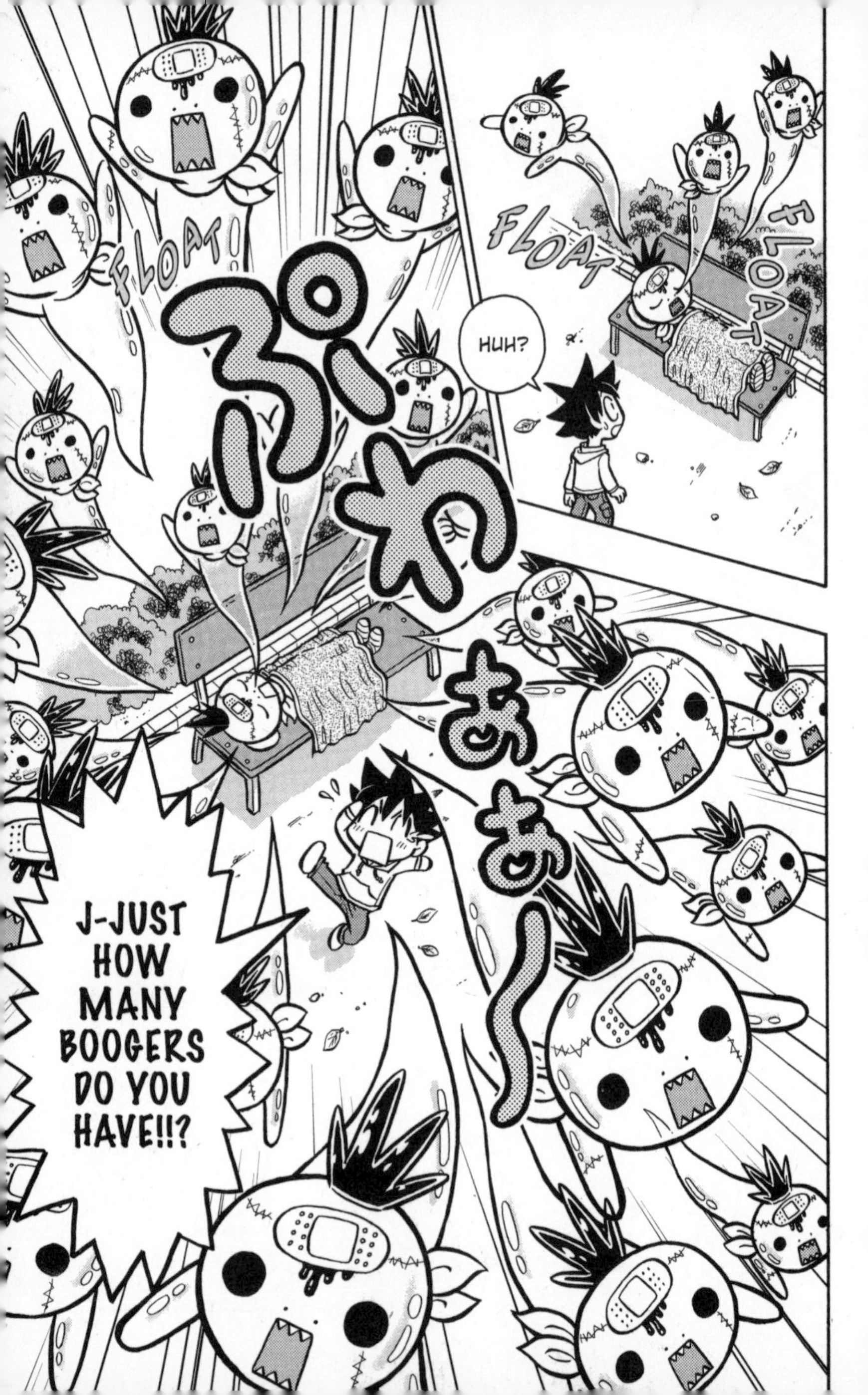
FLOAT
FLOAT
HUH?
FLOAT
ぷわぁぁ〜
J-JUST HOW MANY BOOGERS DO YOU HAVE!!?

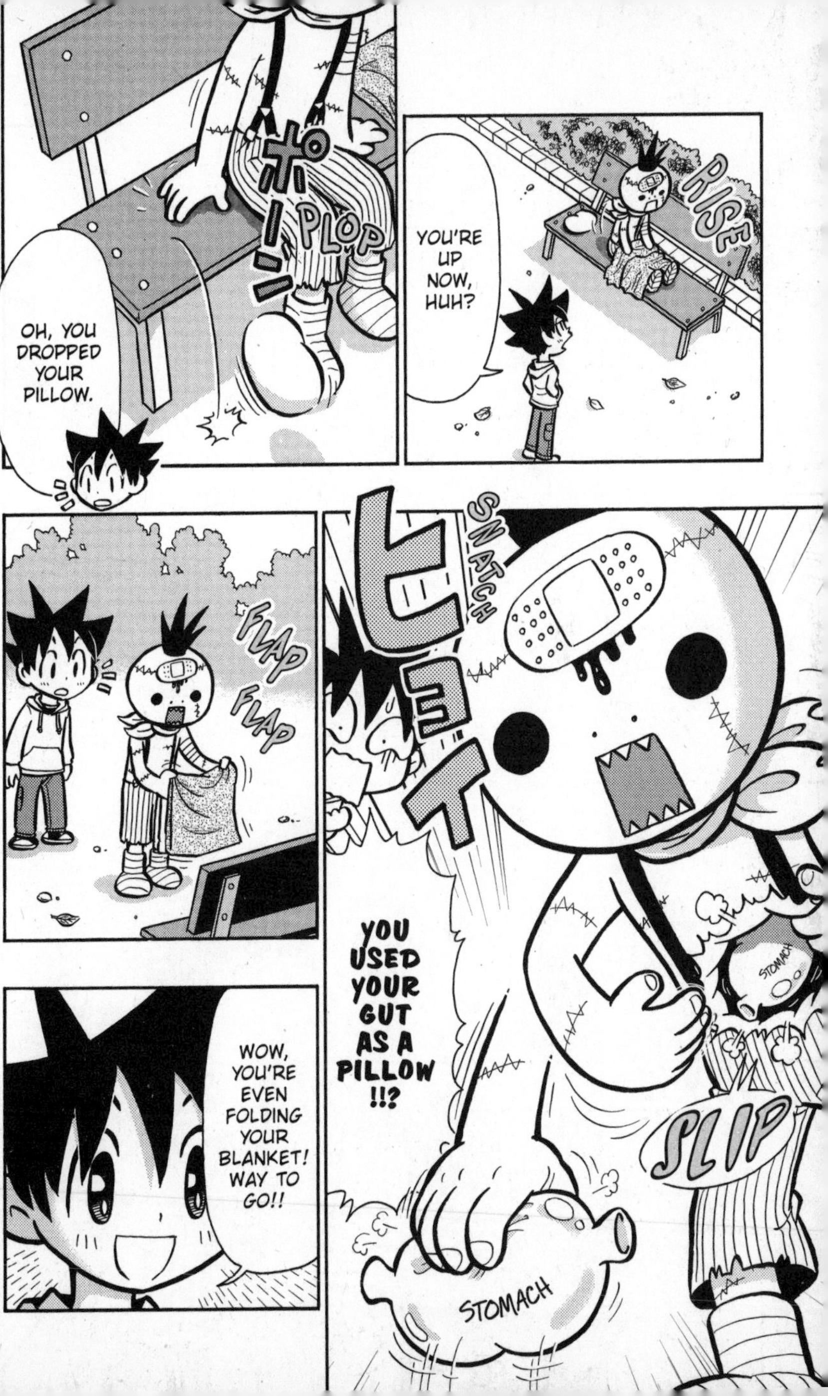
RISE
YOU'RE UP NOW, HUH?
ポー
PLOP
OH, YOU DROPPED YOUR PILLOW.
ヒョイ
SNATCH
YOU USED YOUR GUT AS A PILLOW!!?
STOMACH
SLIP
STOMACH
FLAP
FLAP
WOW, YOU'RE EVEN FOLDING YOUR BLANKET! WAY TO GO!!

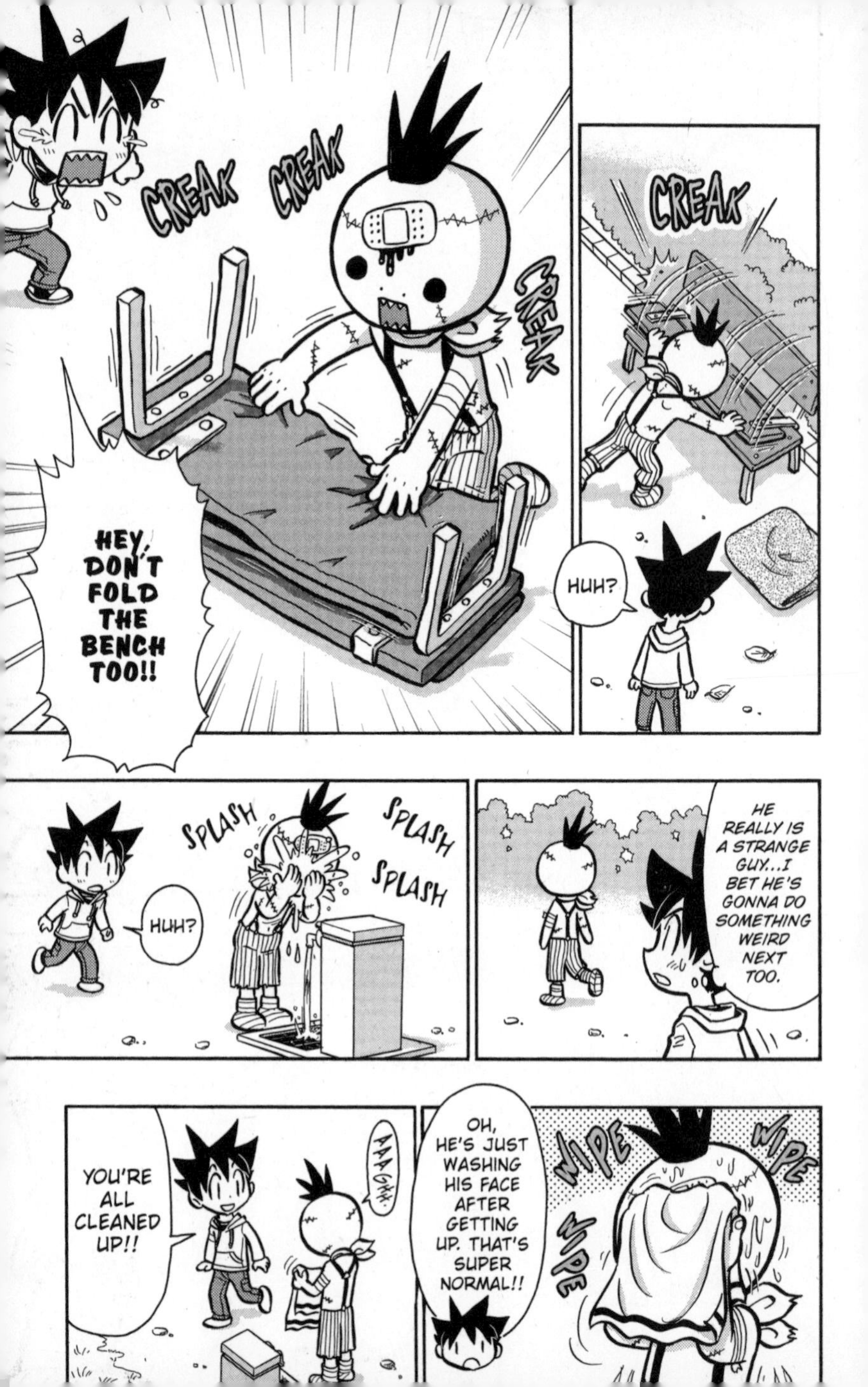

CREAK
HUH?
CREAK
CREAK
CREAK
HEY, DON'T FOLD THE BENCH TOO!!
HE REALLY IS A STRANGE GUY...I BET HE'S GONNA DO SOMETHING WEIRD NEXT TOO.
SPLASH
SPLASH
SPLASH
HUH?
WIPE
WIPE
WIPE
OH, HE'S JUST WASHING HIS FACE AFTER GETTING UP. THAT'S SUPER NORMAL!!
AAAGHH.
YOU'RE ALL CLEANED UP!!

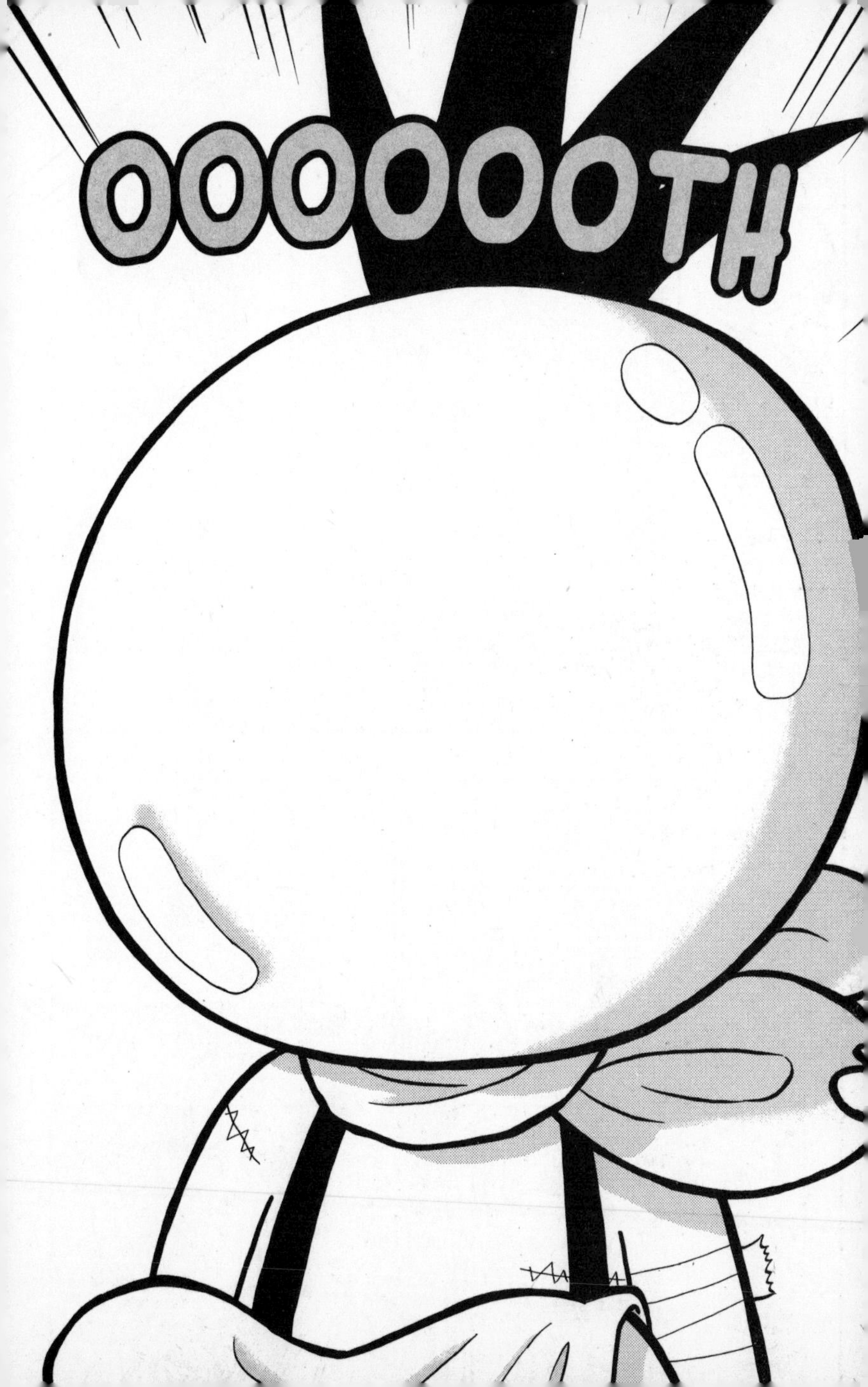
OOOOOOOTH

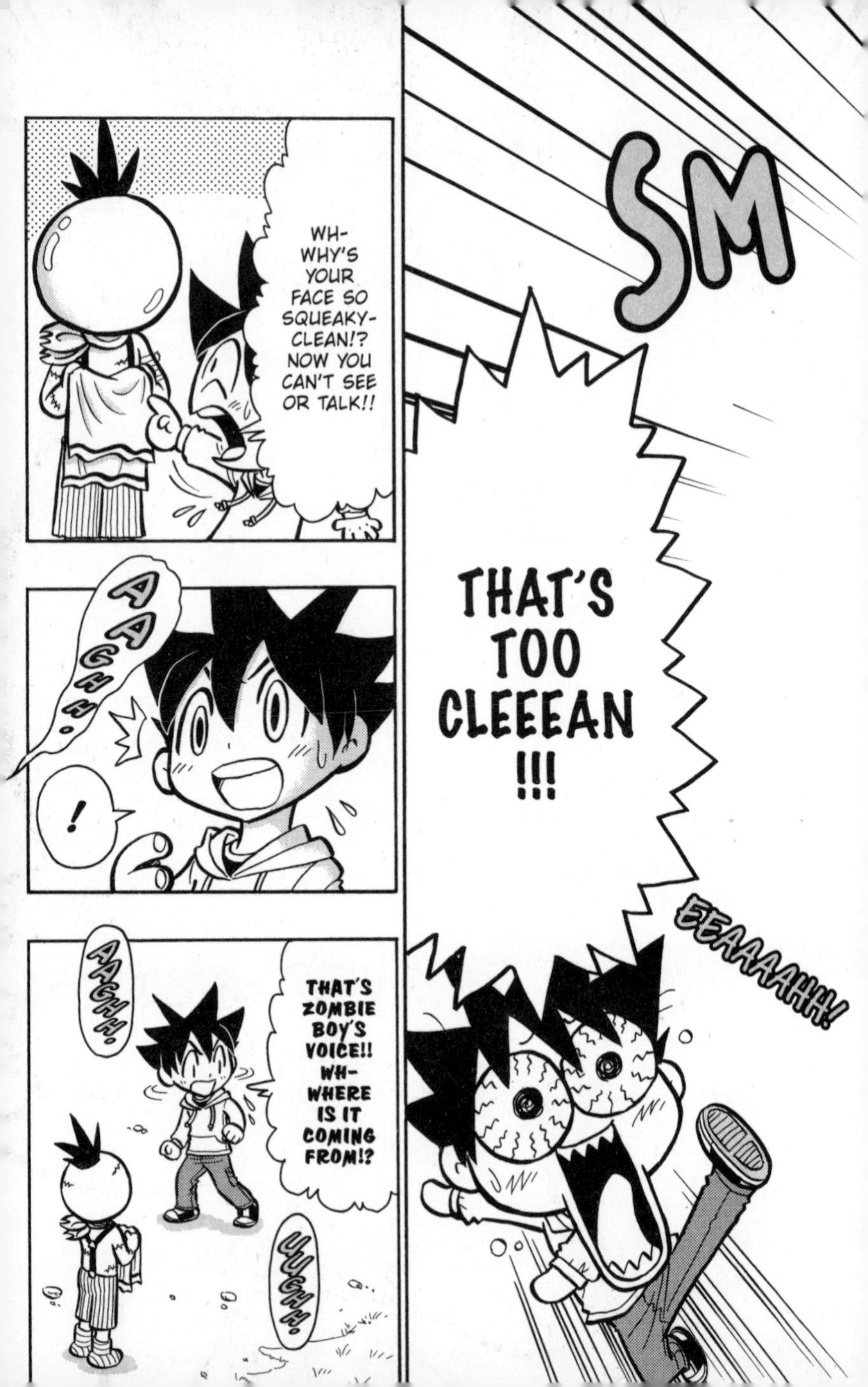
SM
THAT'S TOO CLEEEAN!!!
EEAAAAAHH!
WH-WHY'S YOUR FACE SO SQUEAKY-CLEAN!? NOW YOU CAN'T SEE OR TALK!!
AAGHH.
!
AAGHH.
THAT'S ZOMBIE BOY'S VOICE!! WH-WHERE IS IT COMING FROM!?
UUGHH.

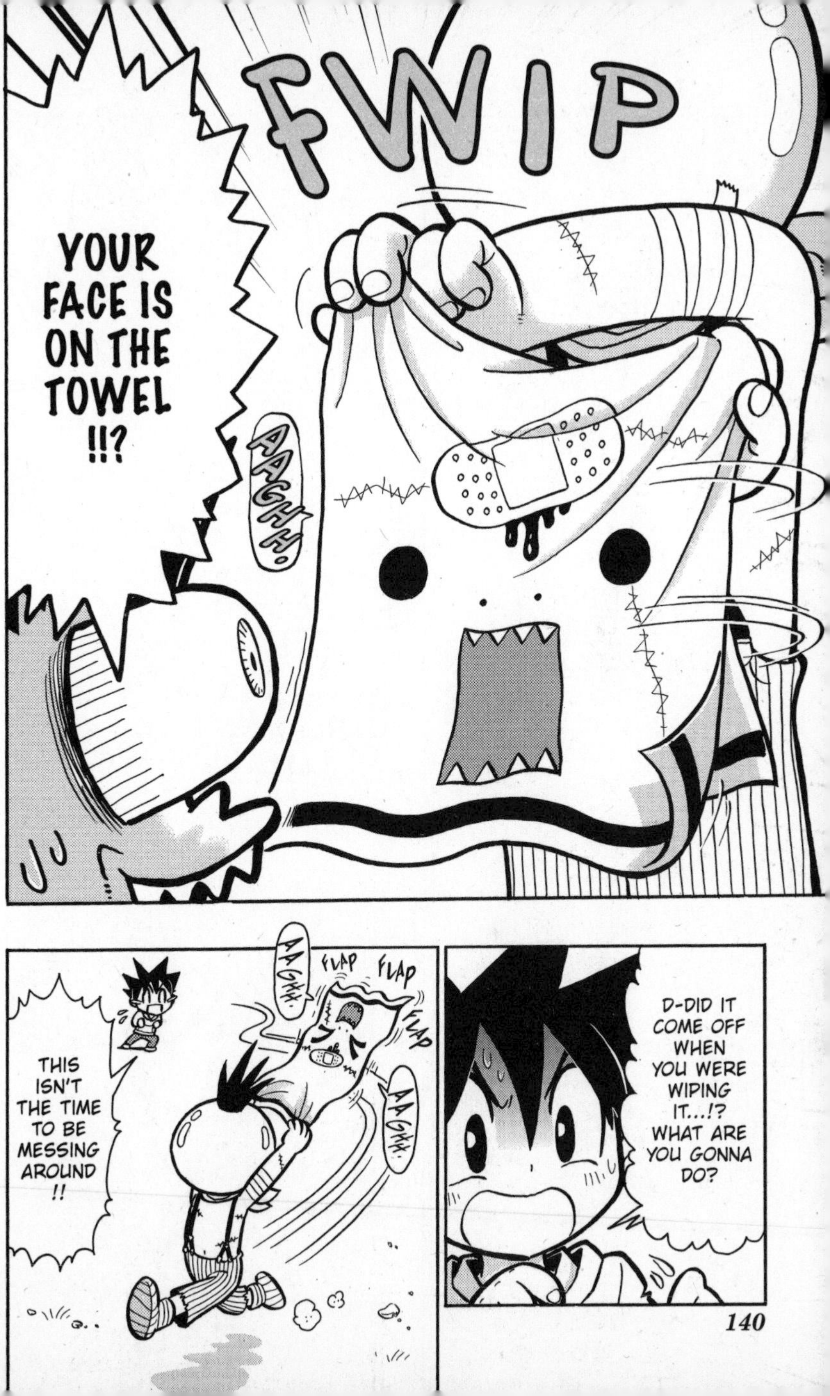
FWIP
YOUR FACE IS ON THE TOWEL !!?
AAGHH.
D-DID IT COME OFF WHEN YOU WERE WIPING IT...!? WHAT ARE YOU GONNA DO?
AAGHH.
FLAP FLAP
FLAP
AAGHH.
THIS ISN'T THE TIME TO BE MESSING AROUND !!

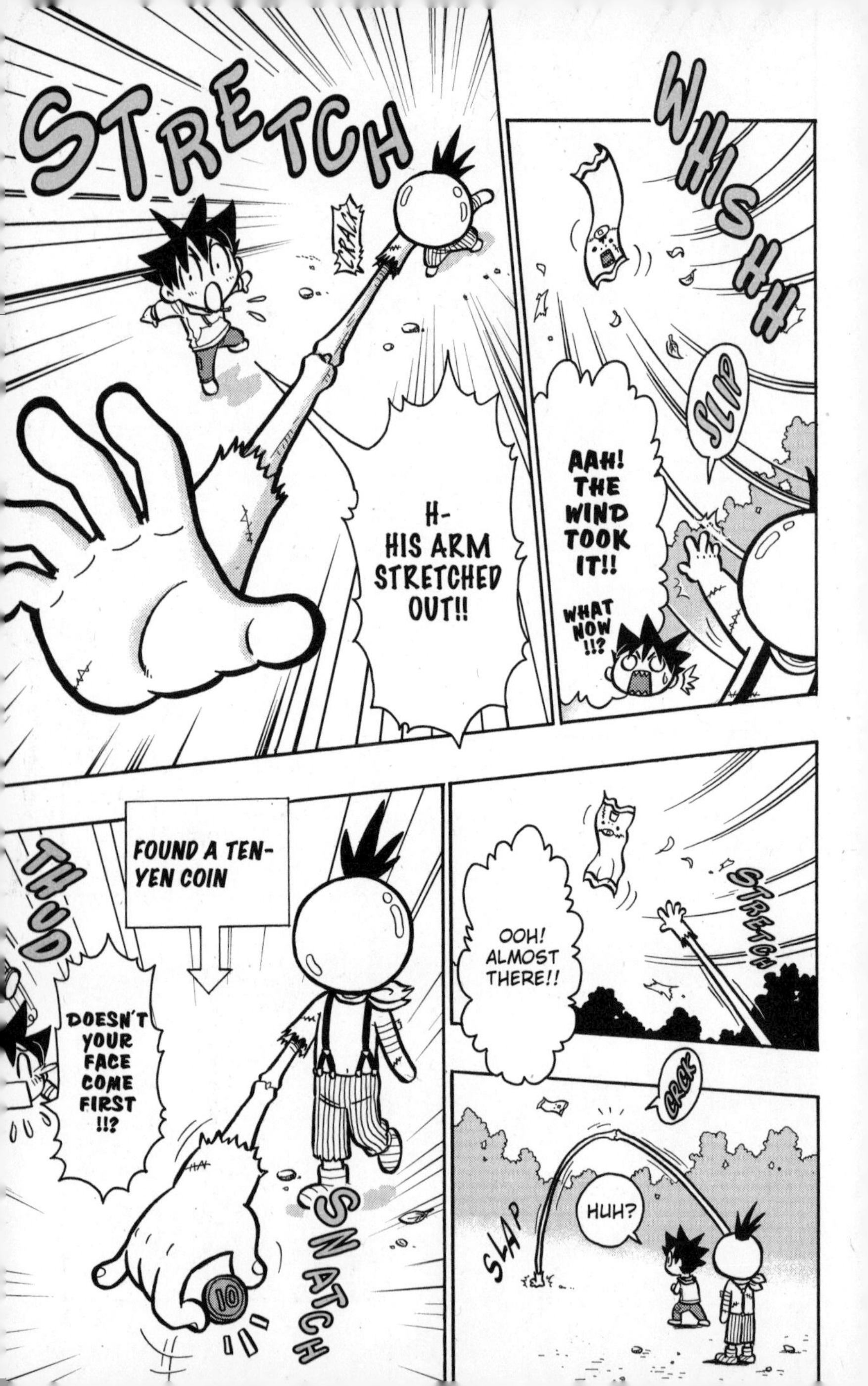
WHISHH
SLIP
AAH! THE WIND TOOK IT!!
WHAT NOW!!?
STRETCH
CRACK
H- HIS ARM STRETCHED OUT!!
STRETCH
OOH! ALMOST THERE!!
CRCK
HUH?
SLAP
FOUND A TEN-YEN COIN
DOESN'T YOUR FACE COME FIRST!!?
THUD
SNATCH
10

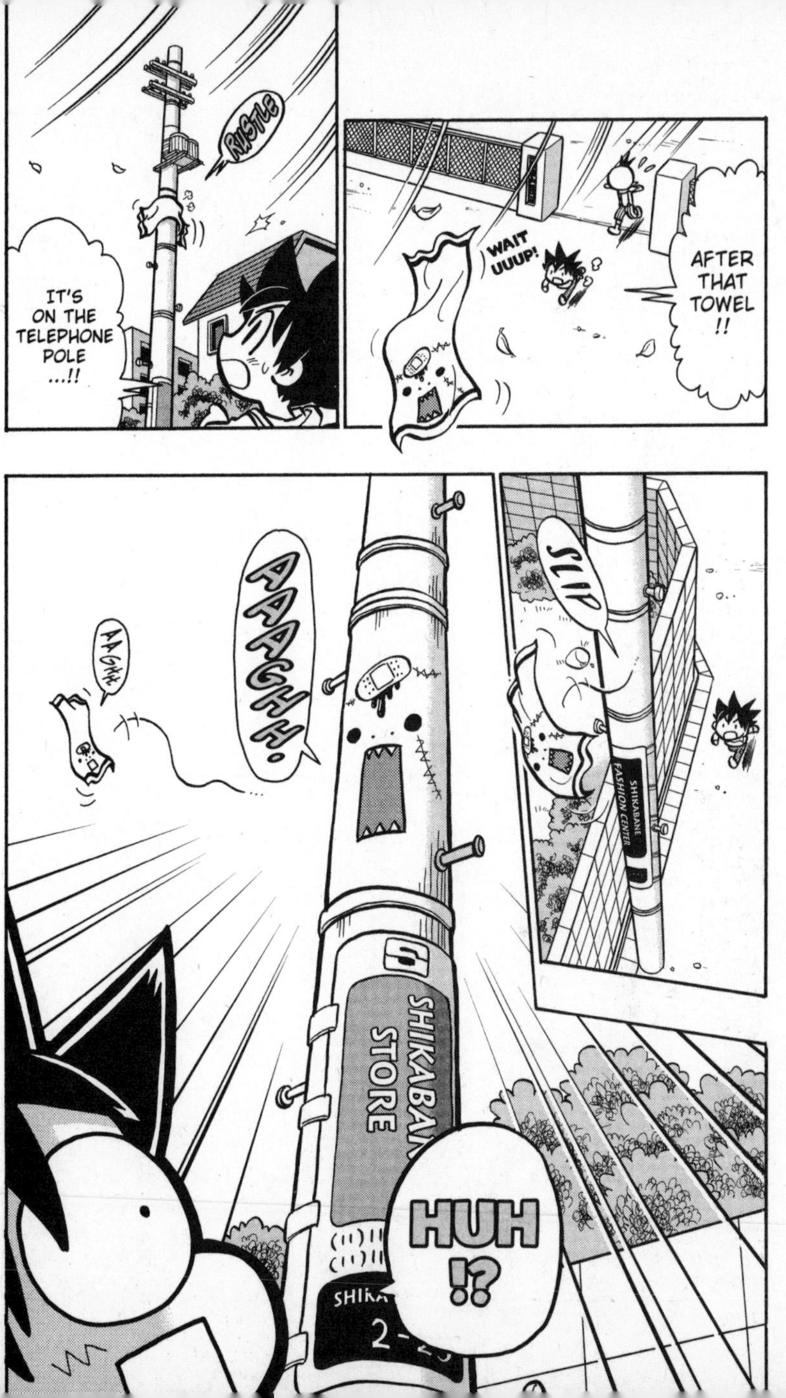
AFTER THAT TOWEL !!
WAIT UUUP!
RUSTLE
IT'S ON THE TELEPHONE POLE ...!!
SLIP
SHIKABANE FASHION CENTER
AAAAGHH.
AAGHH
HUH !?

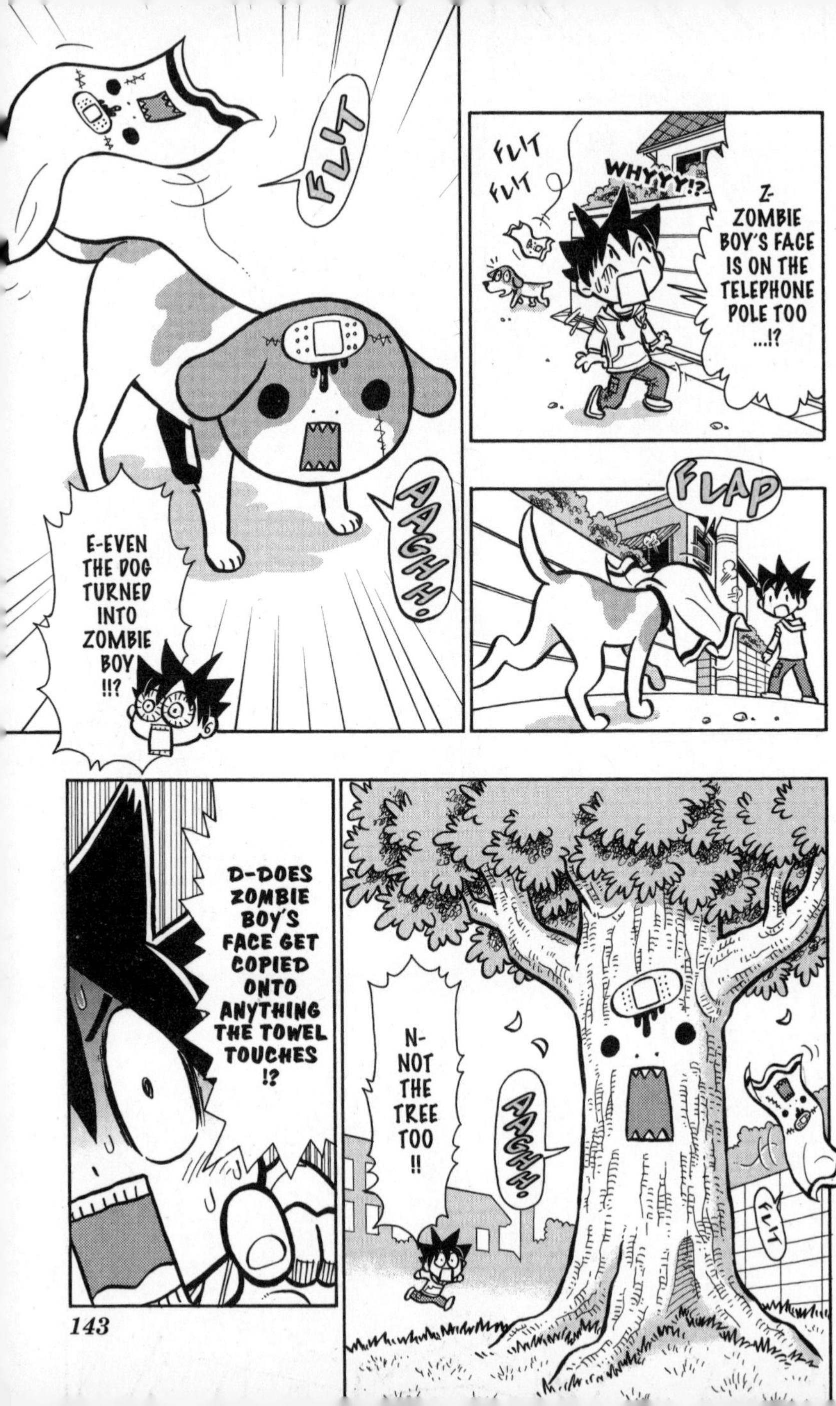
FLIT FLIT
WHYYY!?
Z-ZOMBIE BOY'S FACE IS ON THE TELEPHONE POLE TOO ...!?
FLAP
FLIT
AAGHH.
E-EVEN THE DOG TURNED INTO ZOMBIE BOY !!?
FLIT
AAGHH.
N-NOT THE TREE TOO !!
D-DOES ZOMBIE BOY'S FACE GET COPIED ONTO ANYTHING THE TOWEL TOUCHES !?

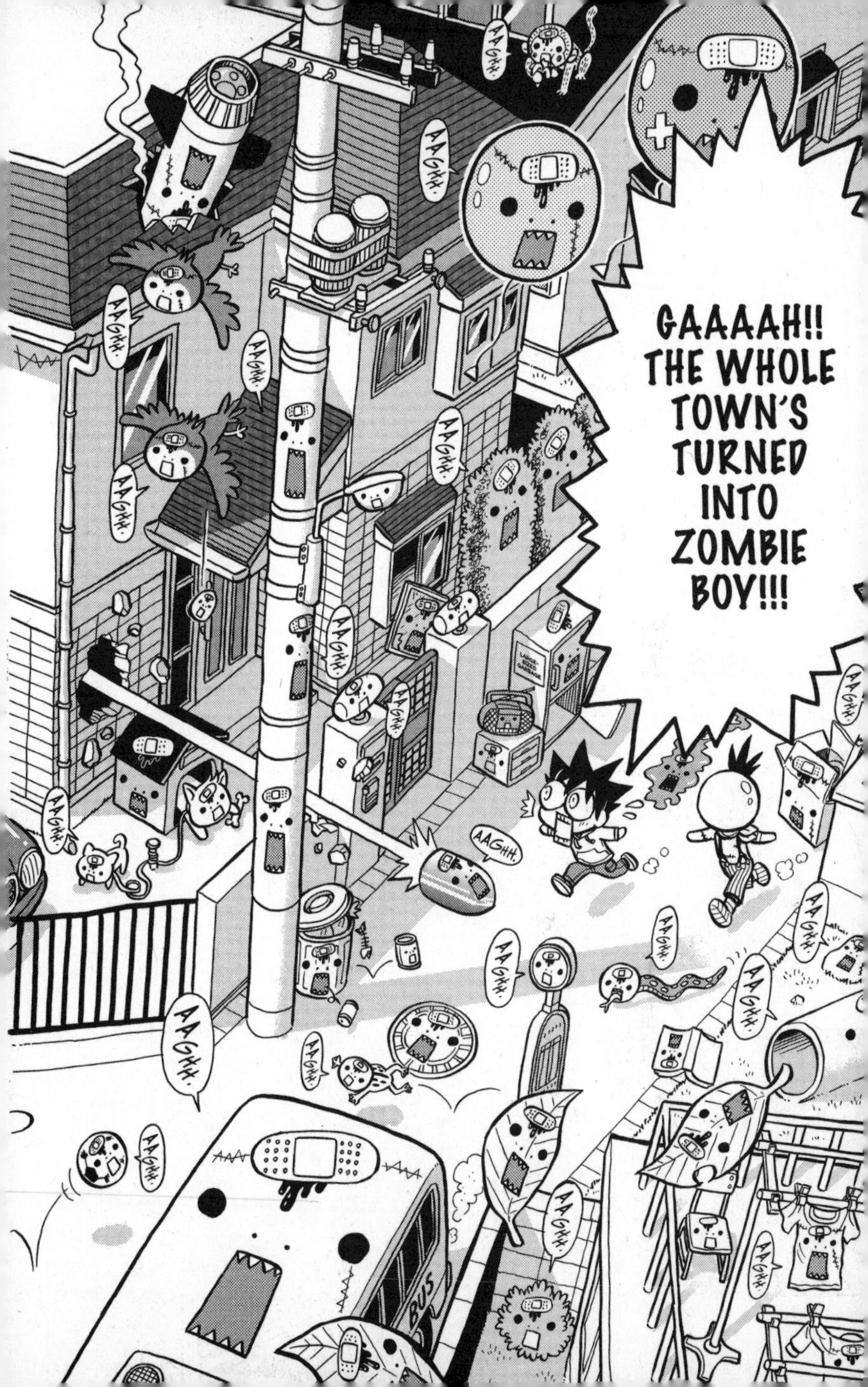
AAGHH.
AAGHH.
GAAAAH!! THE WHOLE TOWN'S TURNED INTO ZOMBIE BOY!!!
AAGHH.
AAGHH.
AAGHH.
AAGHH.
AAGHH.
AAGHH.
AAGHH.
AAGHH.
AAGHH.
AAGHH.
AAGHH.
AAGHH.
AAGHH.
AAGHH.
AAGHH.
AAGHH.
AAGHH.
AAGHH.
AAGHH.

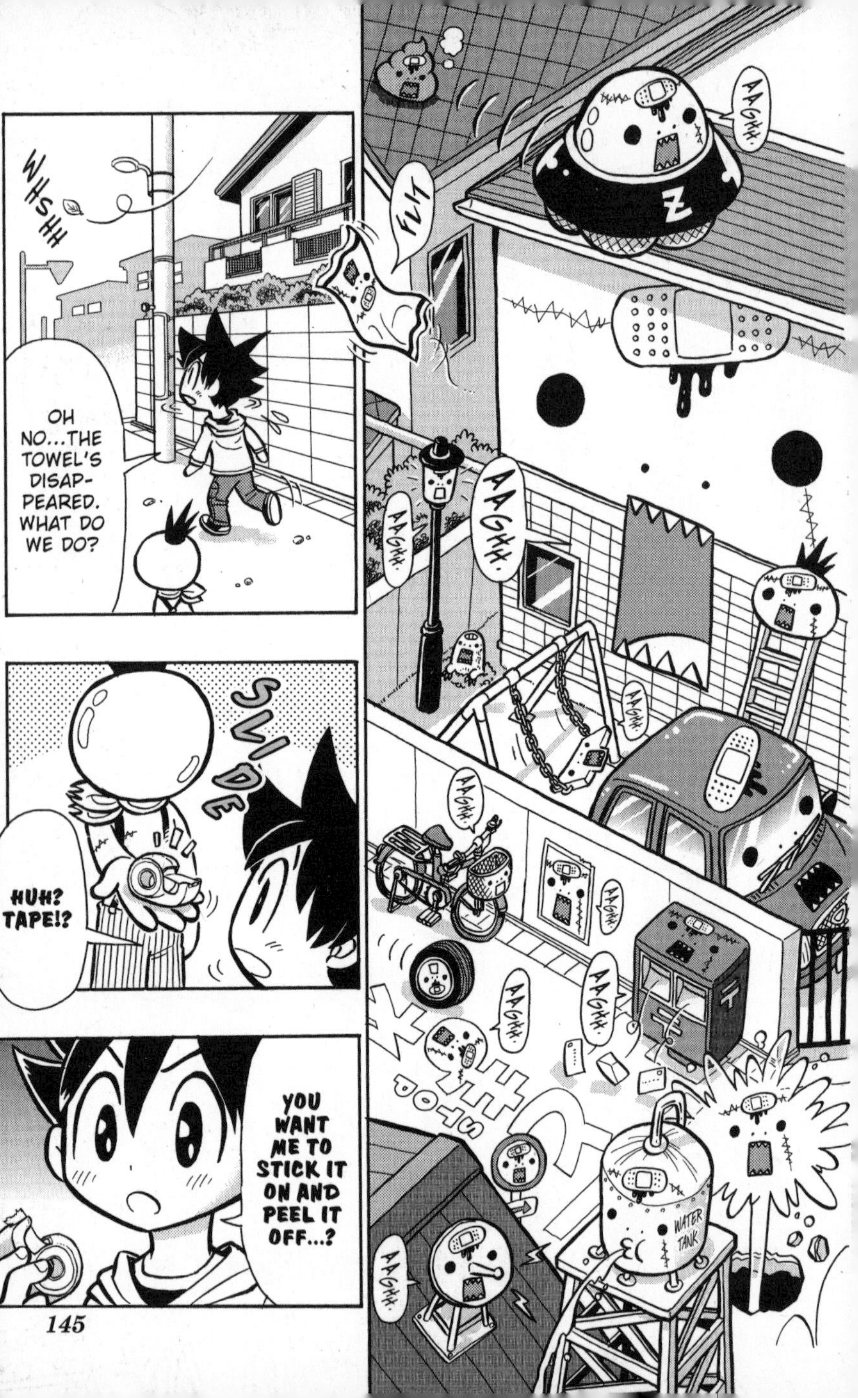
AAGHH.
FLIT
AAGHH.
AAGHH.
AAGHH.
AAGHH.
AAGHH.
AAGHH.
AAGHH.
AAGHH.
AAGHH.
WATER TANK
WHSHH
OH NO...THE TOWEL'S DISAPPEARED. WHAT DO WE DO?
SLIDE
HUH? TAPE!?
YOU WANT ME TO STICK IT ON AND PEEL IT OFF...?

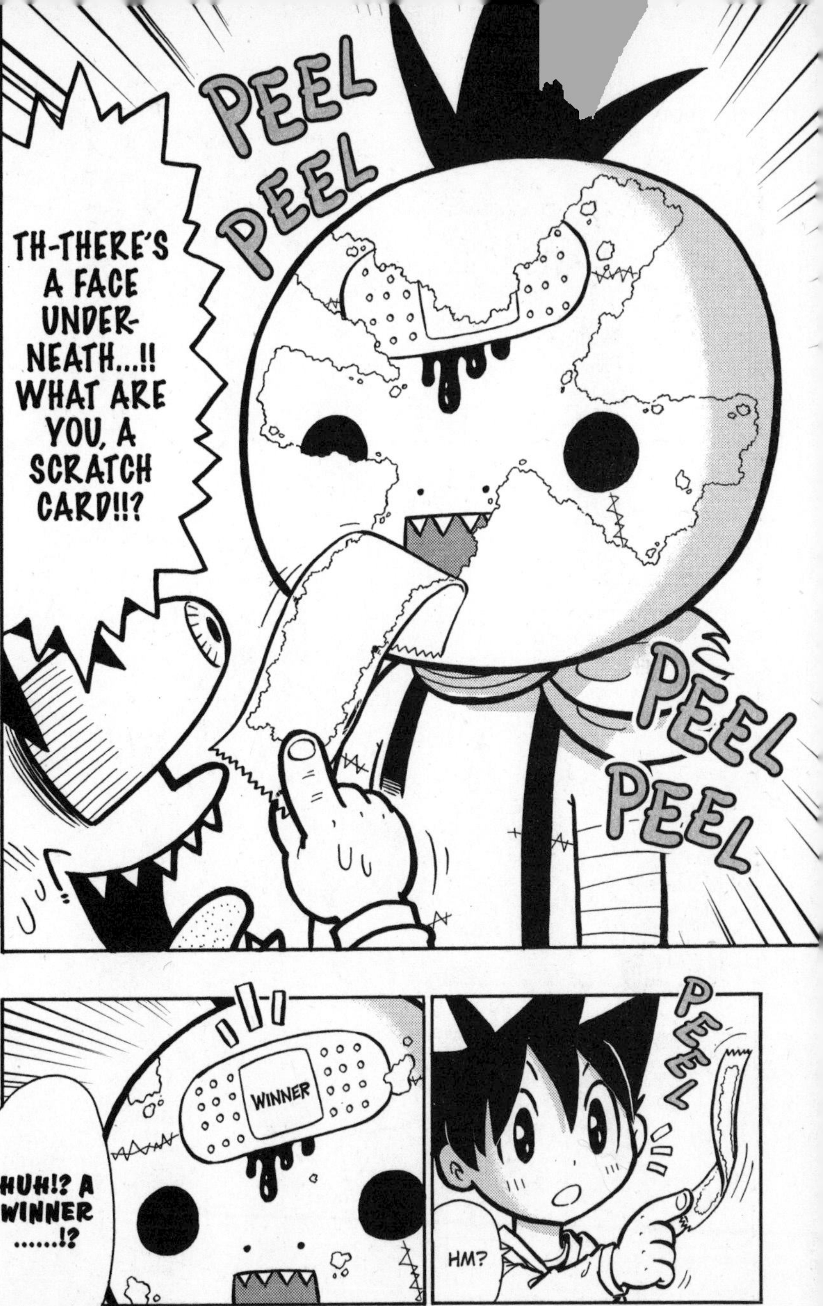
PEEL PEEL
TH-THERE'S A FACE UNDER-NEATH...!! WHAT ARE YOU, A SCRATCH CARD!!?
PEEL PEEL
PEEL
HM?
WINNER
HUH!? A WINNER ......!?

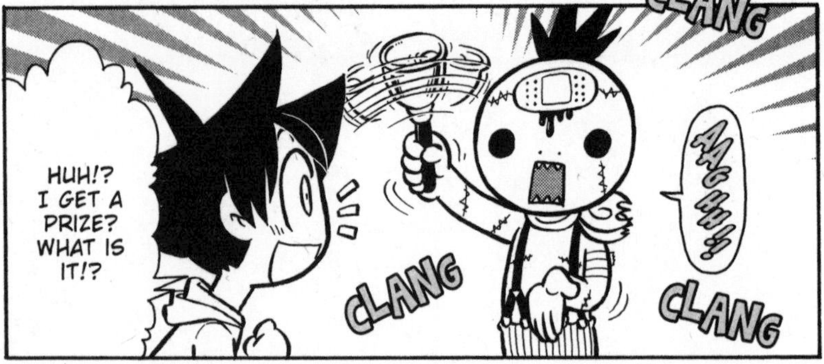
CLANG
AAGHHH!!
CLANG
CLANG
HUH!? I GET A PRIZE? WHAT IS IT!?

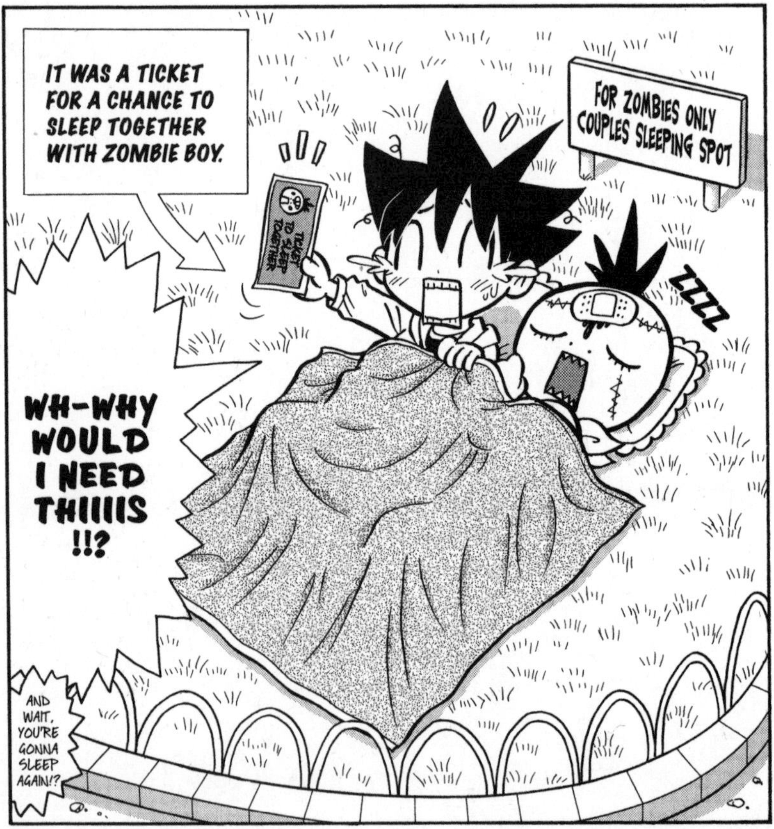
FOR ZOMBIES ONLY COUPLES SLEEPING SPOT
IT WAS A TICKET FOR A CHANCE TO SLEEP TOGETHER WITH ZOMBIE BOY.
ZZZZ
TICKET TO SLEEP TOGETHER
WH-WHY WOULD I NEED THIIIIS !!?
AND WAIT, YOU'RE GONNA SLEEP AGAIN!?

SPECIAL FOUR-PANEL COMIC PART 5

ZOMBIE BOY APPEARS

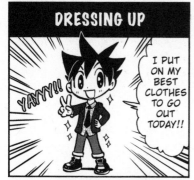

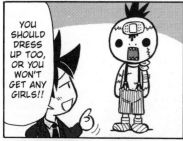

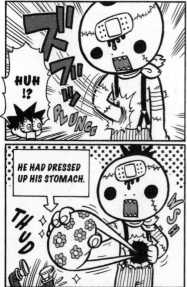

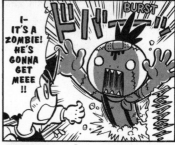

BURST
I- IT'S A ZOMBIE! HE'S GONNA GET MEEE !!
GRASP
HUH?
FWP
IT WASN'T TIME TO GET UP YET.
ZZZZ
YOU'RE NOT GONNA ATTACK !!?

DRESSING UP

I PUT ON MY BEST CLOTHES TO GO OUT TODAY!!
YAYYY!!
YOU SHOULD DRESS UP TOO, OR YOU WON'T GET ANY GIRLS!!
HUH !?
PLUNGE
HE HAD DRESSED UP HIS STOMACH.
WSH
THUD

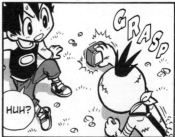

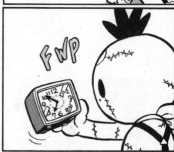

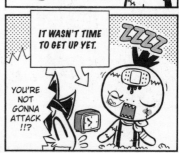

A NEW HERO IZ BORN!

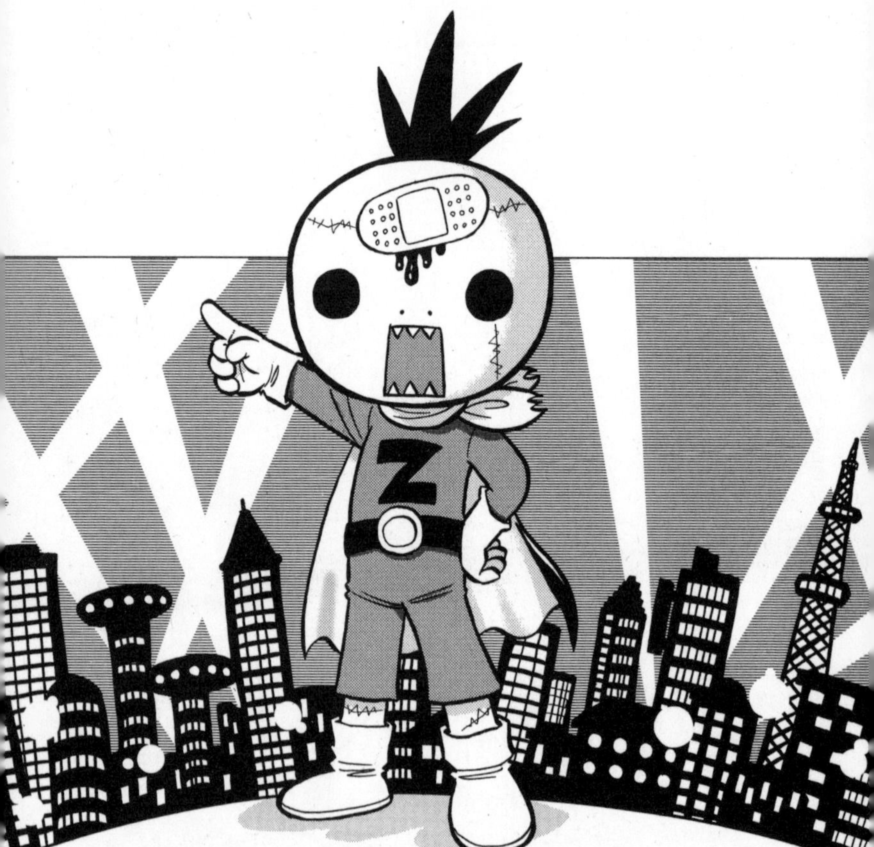

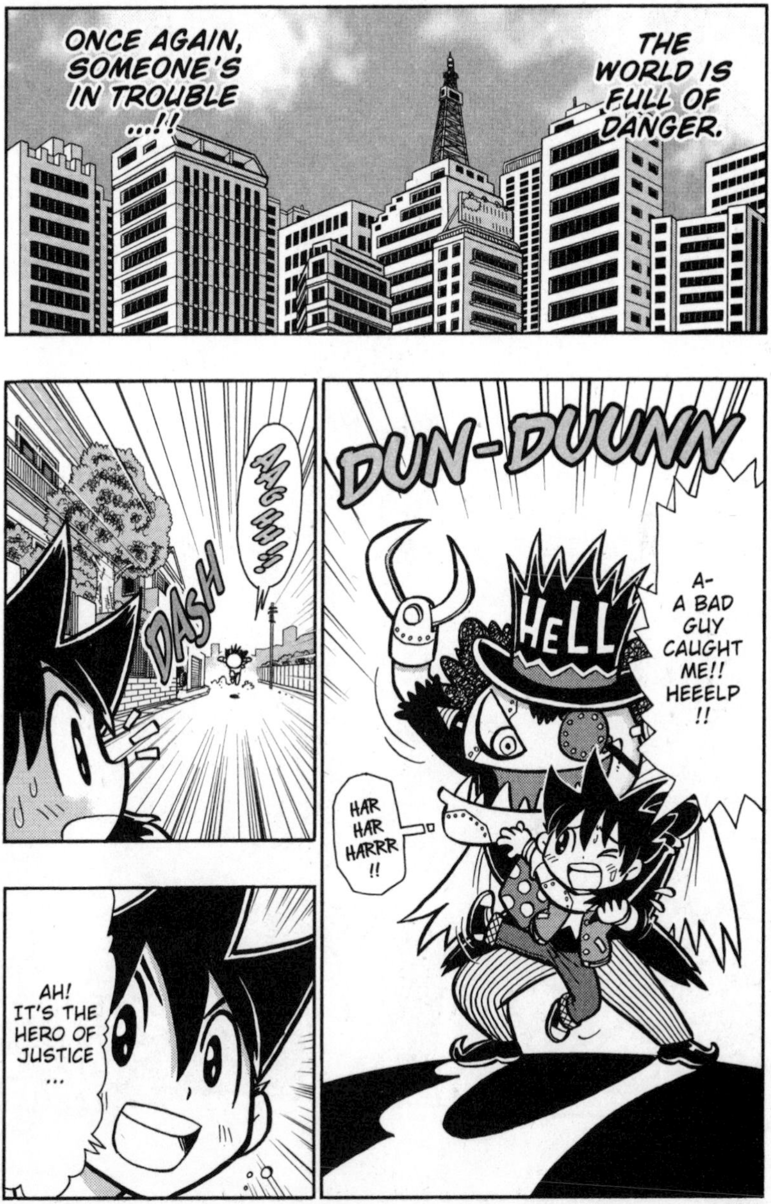
THE WORLD IS FULL OF DANGER.
ONCE AGAIN, SOMEONE'S IN TROUBLE ...!!
DUN-DUUNN
HELL
A- A BAD GUY CAUGHT ME!! HEEELP !!
HAR HAR HARRR !!
AAGHH!!
DASH
AH! IT'S THE HERO OF JUSTICE ...

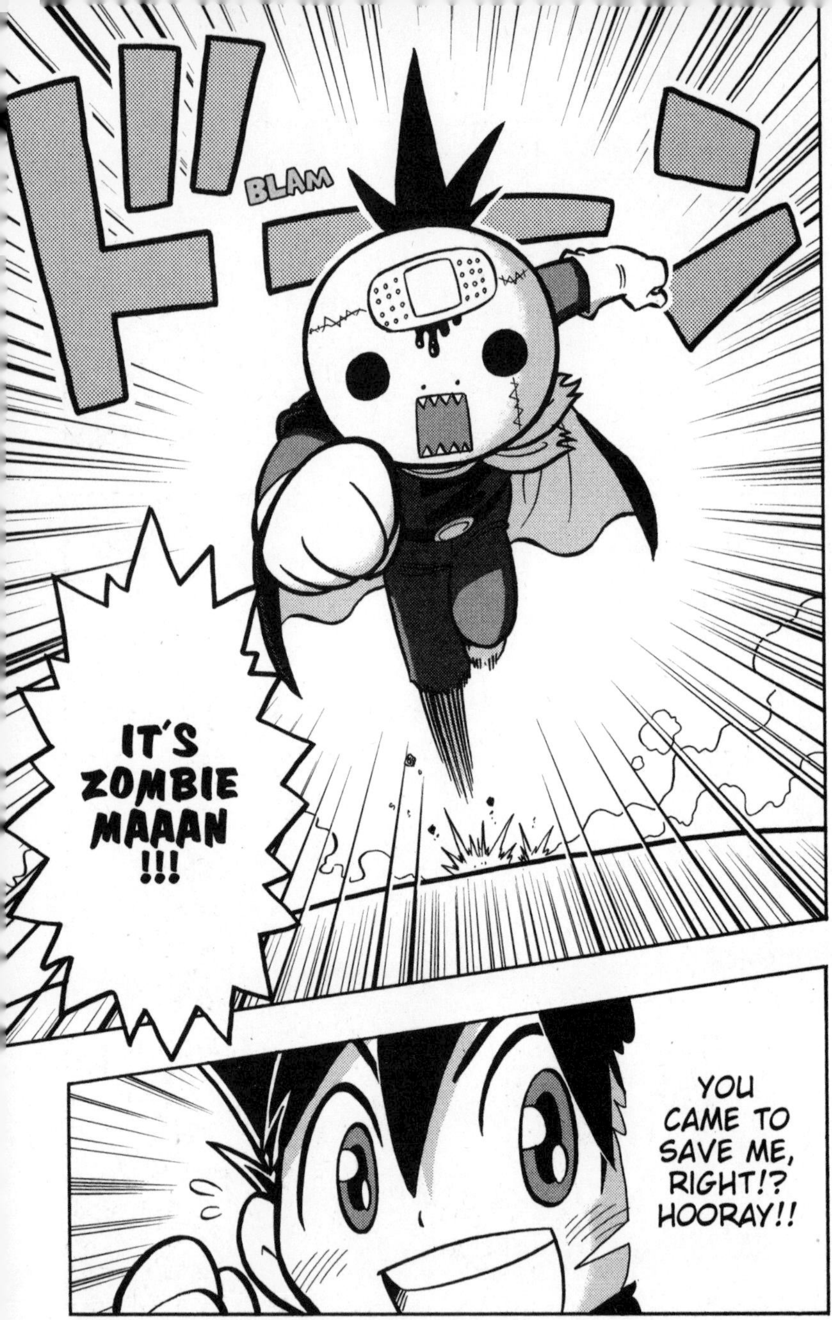
BLAM
IT'S ZOMBIE MAAAN!!!
YOU CAME TO SAVE ME, RIGHT!? HOORAY!!

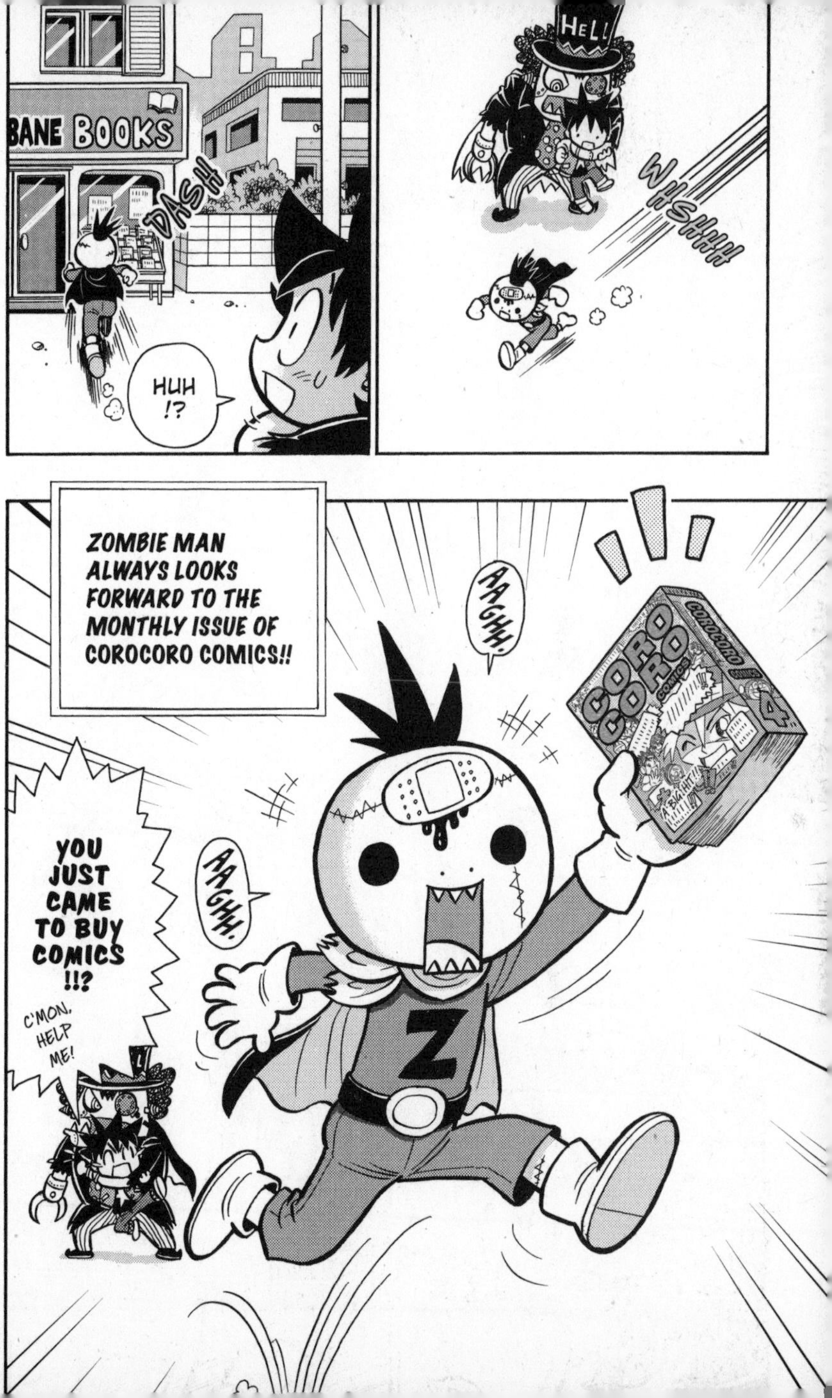
HELL
WHSHHHH
BANE BOOKS
DASH!!
HUH !?
ZOMBIE MAN ALWAYS LOOKS FORWARD TO THE MONTHLY ISSUE OF COROCORO COMICS!!
AAGHH.
COROCORO COMICS
A BIG HIT!!
AAGHH.
YOU JUST CAME TO BUY COMICS !!?
C'MON, HELP ME!

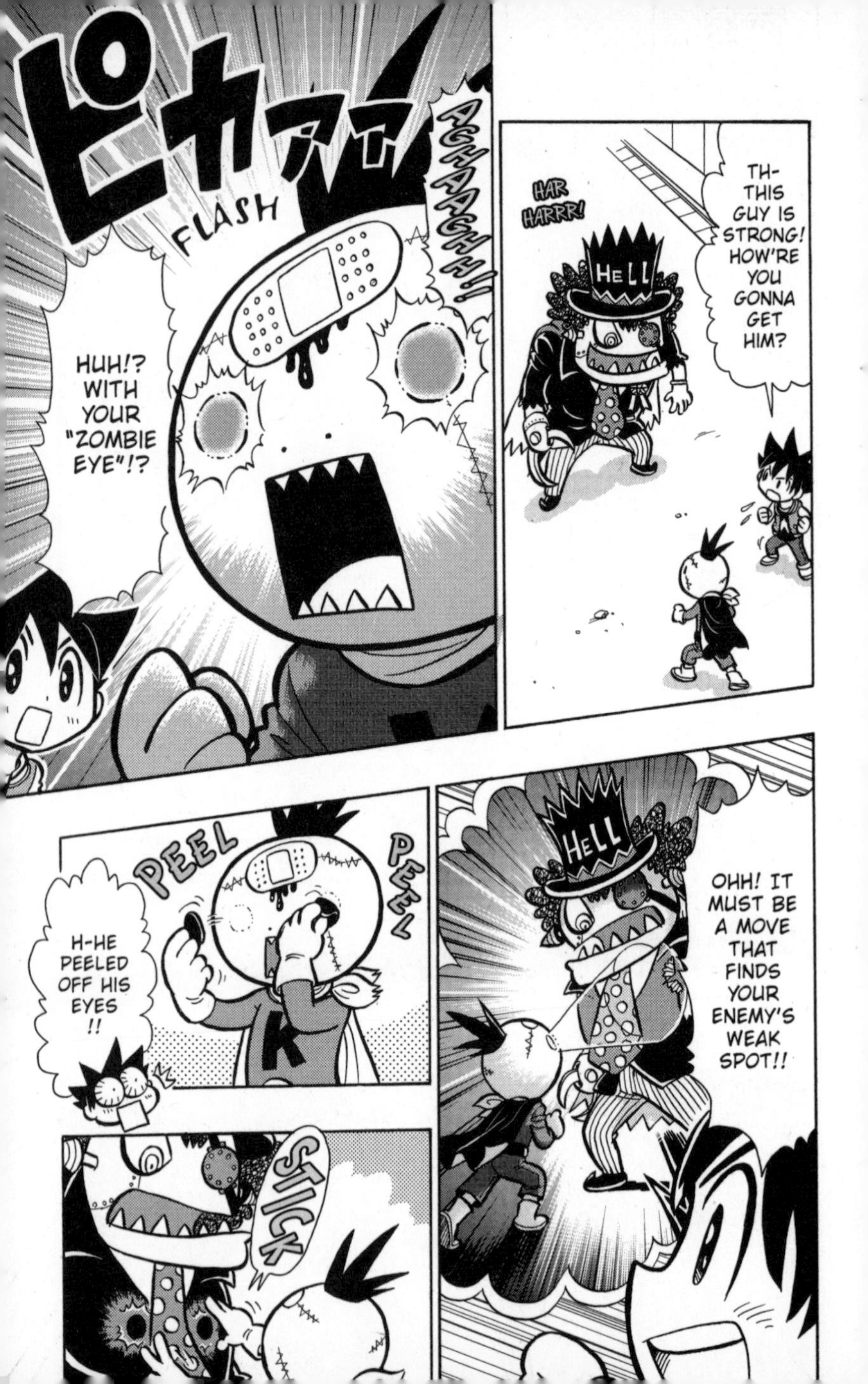
TH-THIS GUY IS STRONG! HOW'RE YOU GONNA GET HIM?
HAR HARRR!
ピカァァ
FLASH
AGHAAAGHH!!
HUH!? WITH YOUR "ZOMBIE EYE"!?
OHH! IT MUST BE A MOVE THAT FINDS YOUR ENEMY'S WEAK SPOT!!
PEEL
PEEL
H-HE PEELED OFF HIS EYES!!
STICK

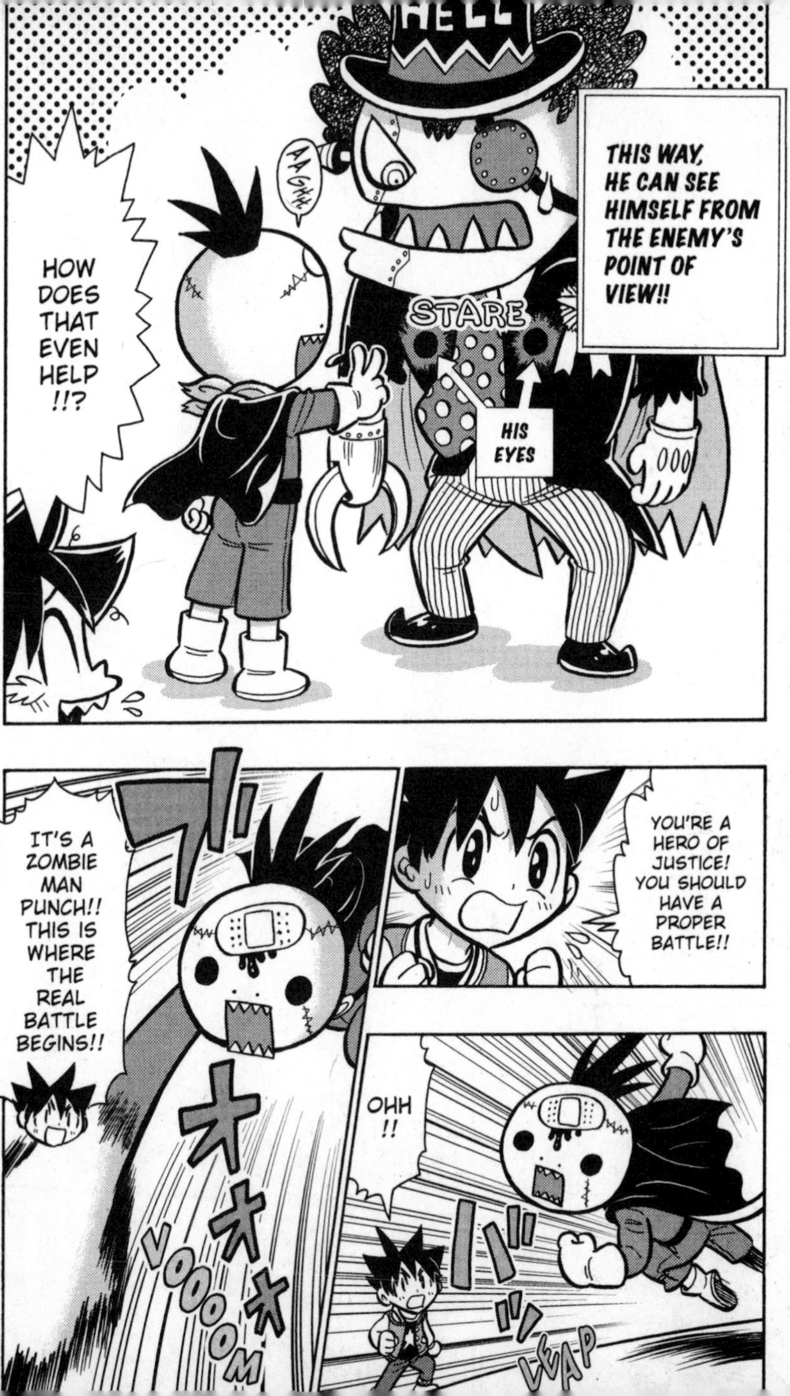
THIS WAY, HE CAN SEE HIMSELF FROM THE ENEMY'S POINT OF VIEW!!
AAGHH
STARE
HIS EYES
HOW DOES THAT EVEN HELP!!?
YOU'RE A HERO OF JUSTICE! YOU SHOULD HAVE A PROPER BATTLE!!
OHH!!
LEAP
IT'S A ZOMBIE MAN PUNCH!! THIS IS WHERE THE REAL BATTLE BEGINS!!
VOOOOM

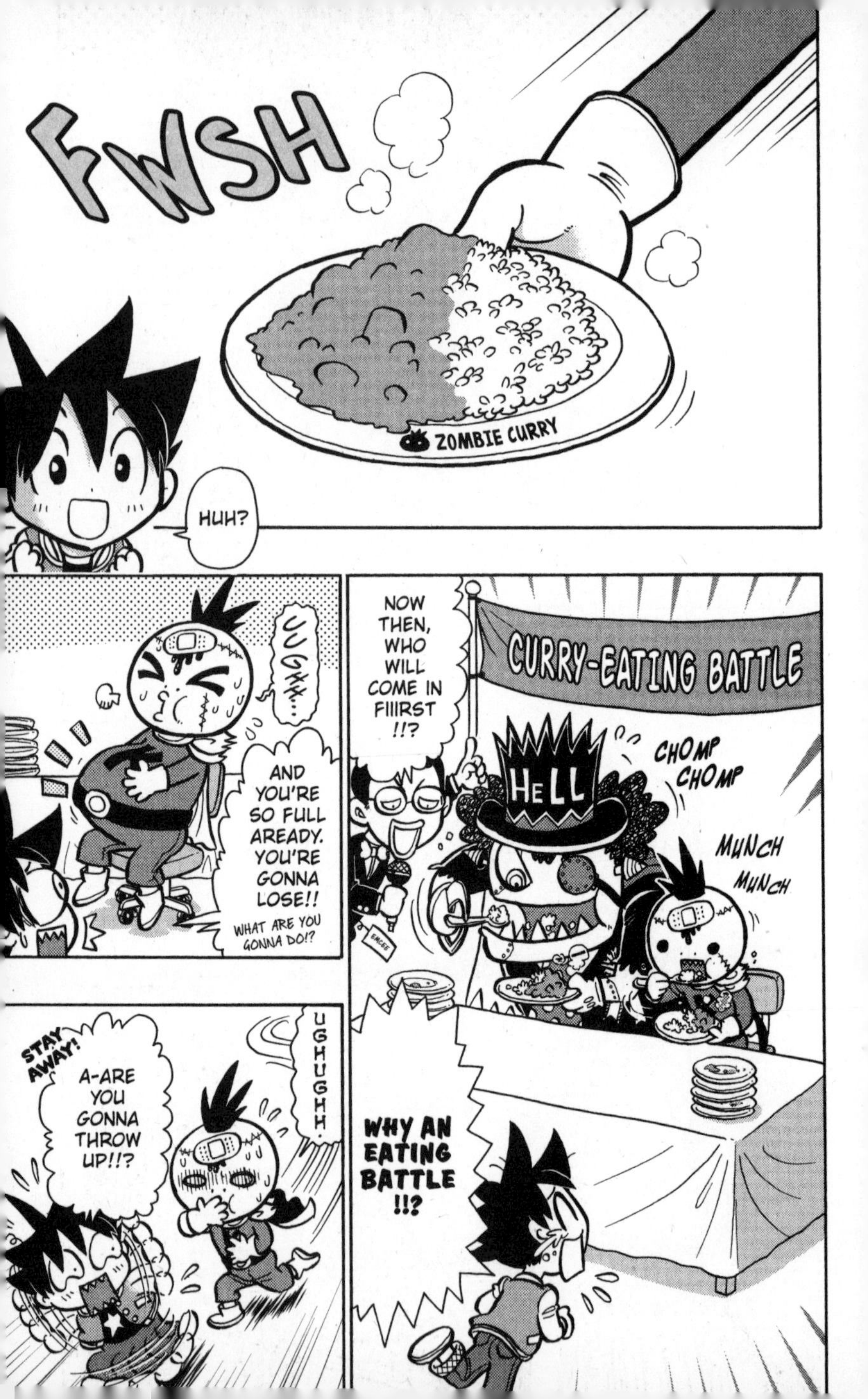
FWSH
ZOMBIE CURRY
HUH?
NOW THEN, WHO WILL COME IN FIIIRST!!?
CURRY-EATING BATTLE
HeLL
CHOMP CHOMP
MUNCH MUNCH
EMCEE
WHY AN EATING BATTLE!!?
UGHXX...
AND YOU'RE SO FULL AREADY. YOU'RE GONNA LOSE!!
WHAT ARE YOU GONNA DO!?
UGHUGHH.
STAY AWAY!
A-ARE YOU GONNA THROW UP!!?

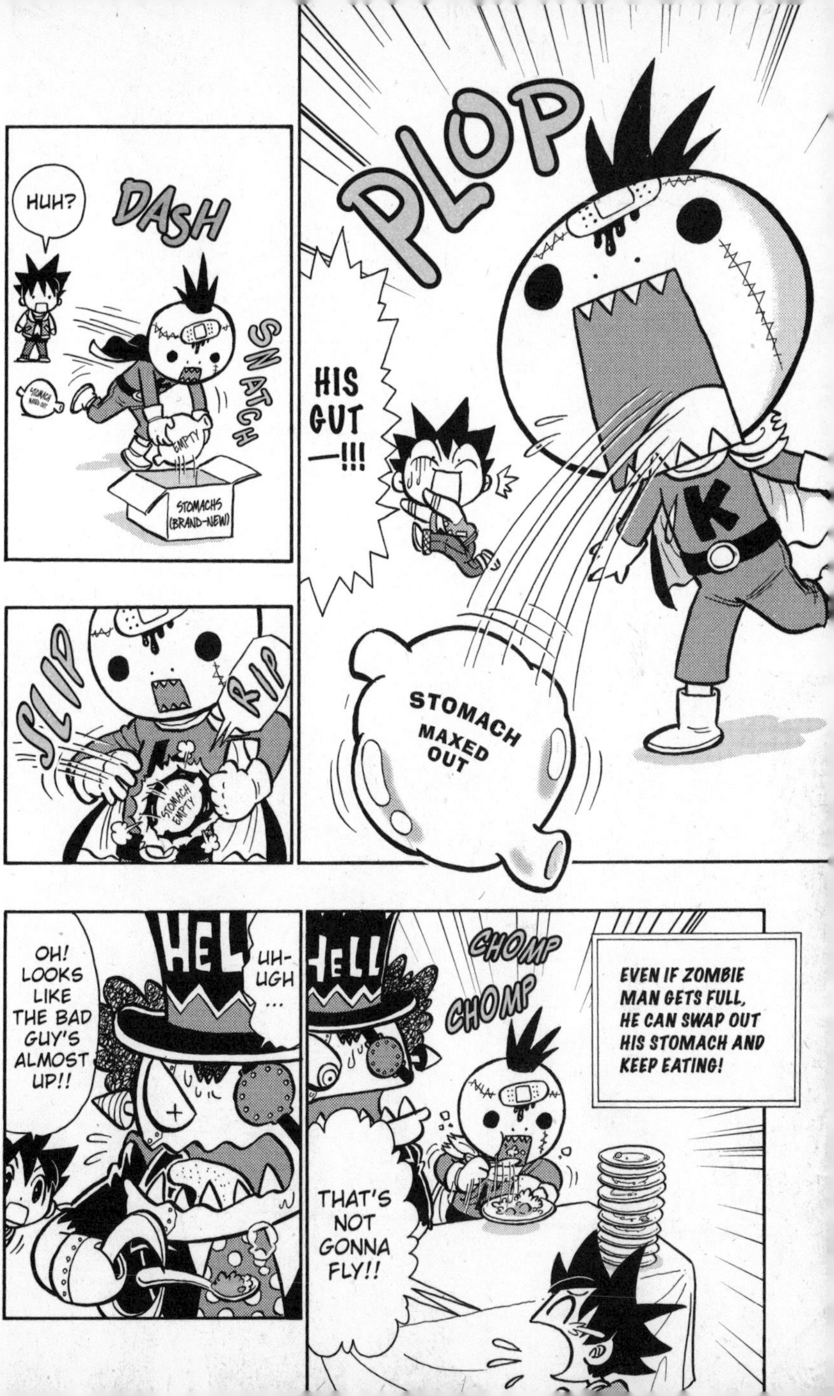
PLOP
HIS GUT—!!!
STOMACH MAXED OUT
DASH
HUH?
SNATCH
STOMACH MAXED OUT
EMPTY
STOMACHS (BRAND-NEW)
RIP
SLIP
STOMACH EMPTY
EVEN IF ZOMBIE MAN GETS FULL, HE CAN SWAP OUT HIS STOMACH AND KEEP EATING!
CHOMP
CHOMP
HELL
THAT'S NOT GONNA FLY!!
UH-UGH ...
HEL
OH! LOOKS LIKE THE BAD GUY'S ALMOST UP!!

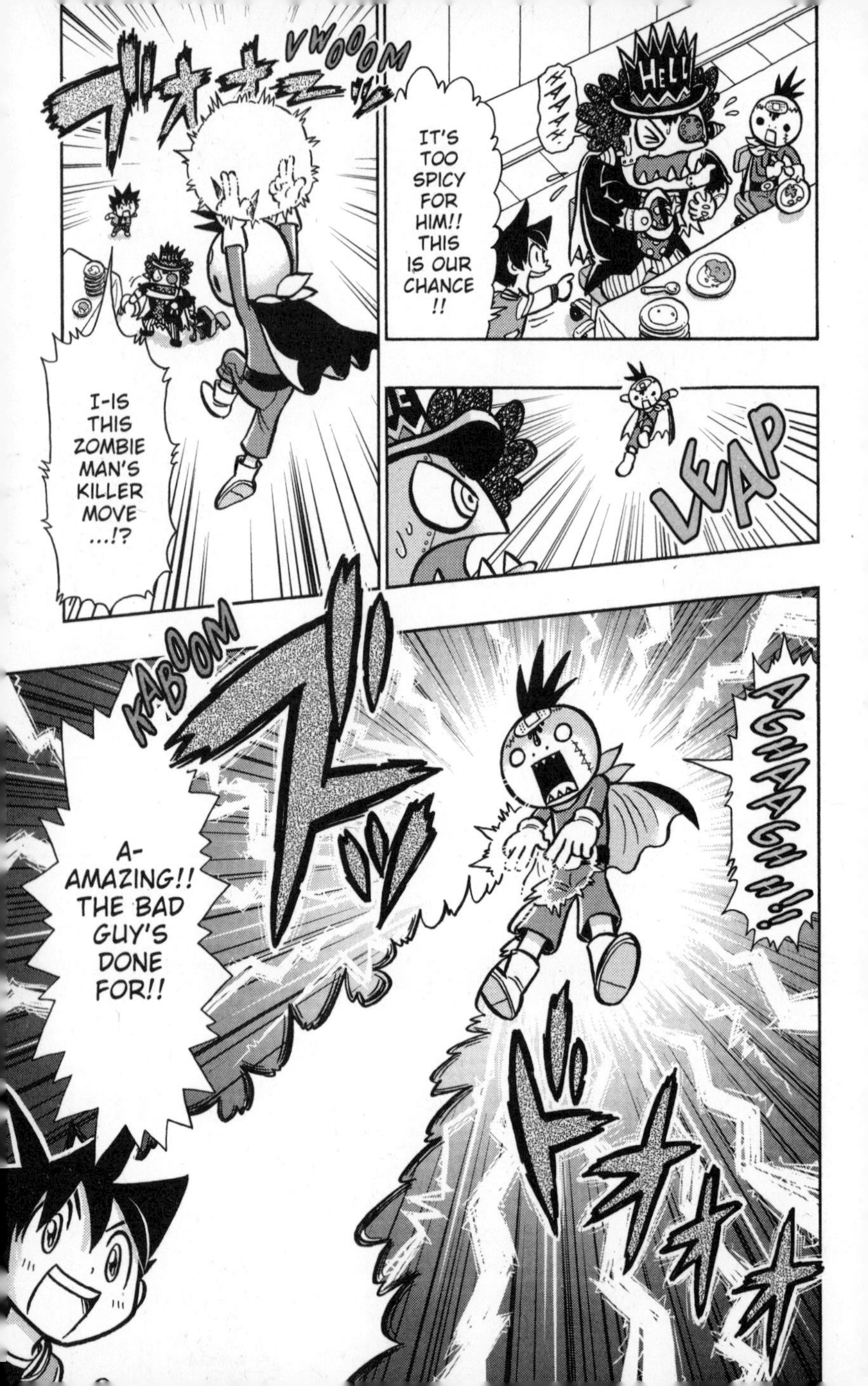
HAAAAH.
IT'S TOO SPICY FOR HIM!! THIS IS OUR CHANCE!!
LEAP
VWOOOM
I-IS THIS ZOMBIE MAN'S KILLER MOVE...!?
AGHAAAGH!!!
KABOOM
A-AMAZING!! THE BAD GUY'S DONE FOR!!

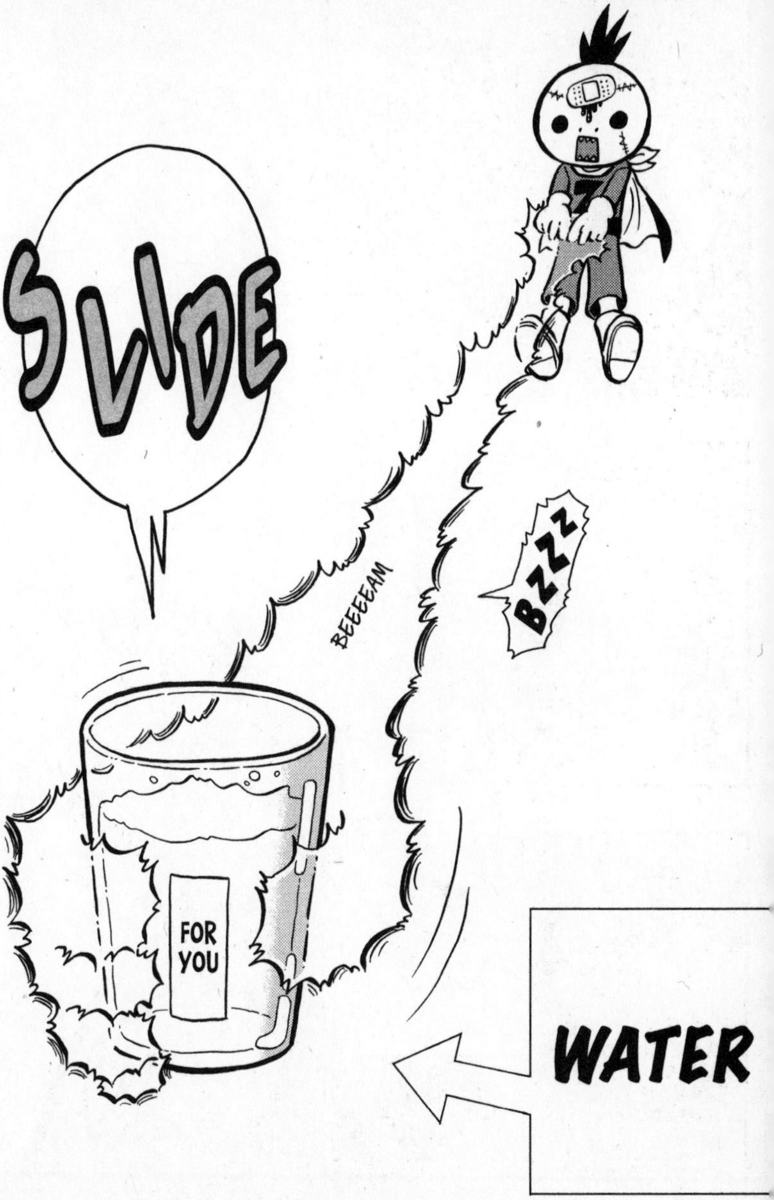
SLIDE
BZZZZ
BEEEEAM
FOR YOU
WATER

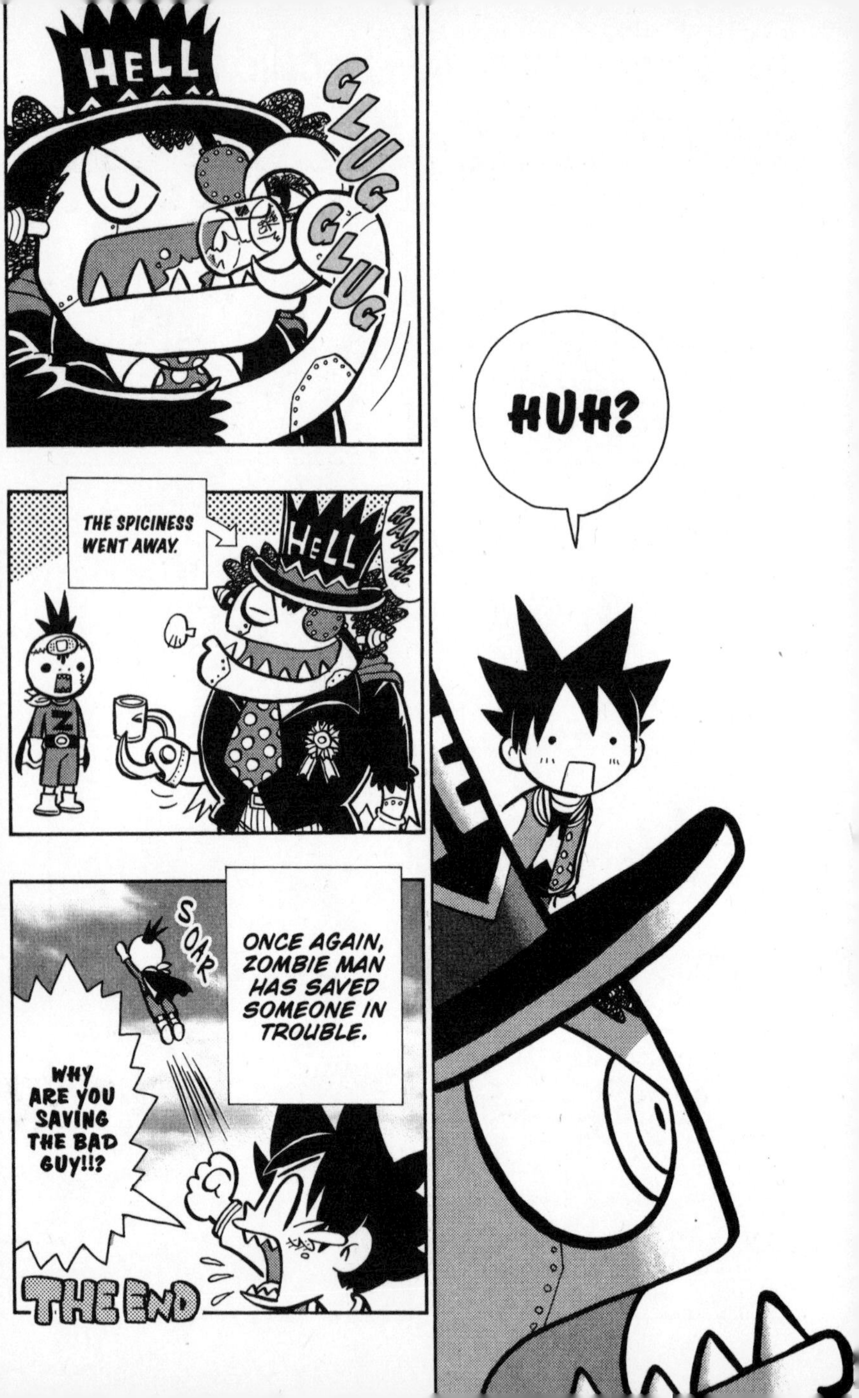
HUH?
HELL
GLUG GLUG
THE SPICINESS WENT AWAY.
HELL
HAAAA
ONCE AGAIN, ZOMBIE MAN HAS SAVED SOMEONE IN TROUBLE.
SOAR
WHY ARE YOU SAVING THE BAD GUY!!?
THE END

SPECIAL FOUR-PANEL COMIC PART 6

COULD THIS BE LOVE?

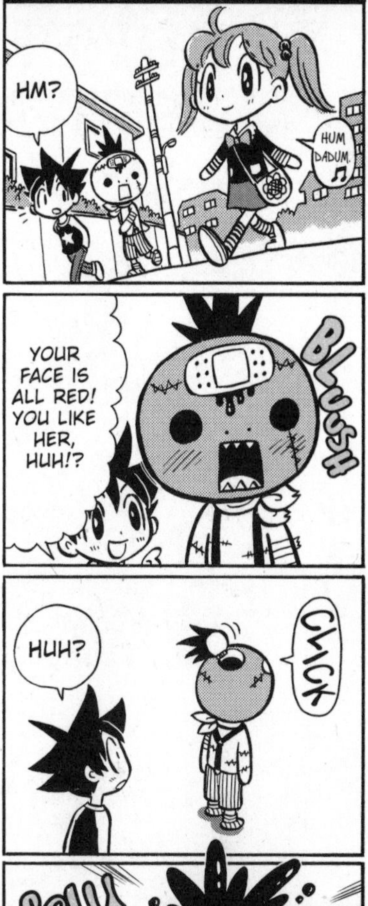
HUM DADUM. ♪
HM?
BLUSH
YOUR FACE IS ALL RED! YOU LIKE HER, HUH!?
CLICK
HUH?
SPLURT
ALL THE BLOOD RUSHED TO HIS HEAD.
AAAH!

SUDDEN FAREWELLS

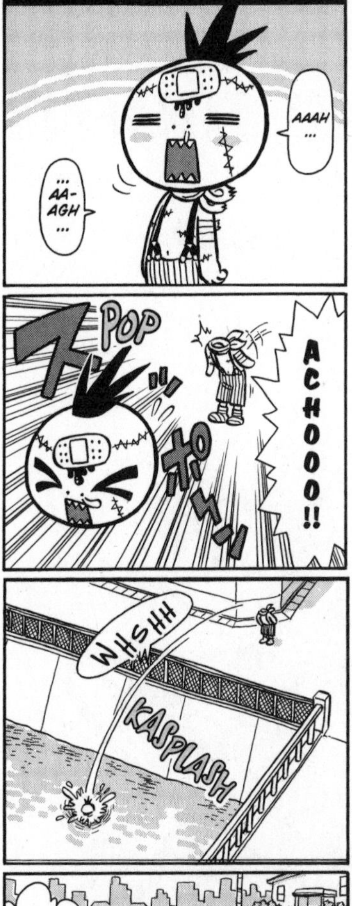
AAAH ...
... AA-AGH ...
ACHOOOO!!
POP
WHSHH
KASPLASH
YOU'RE NOT GONNA GO GET IT!!?

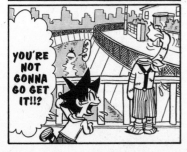

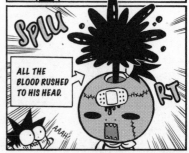

ZOMBIEZ POPPIN' OUT LEFT AND RIGHT!

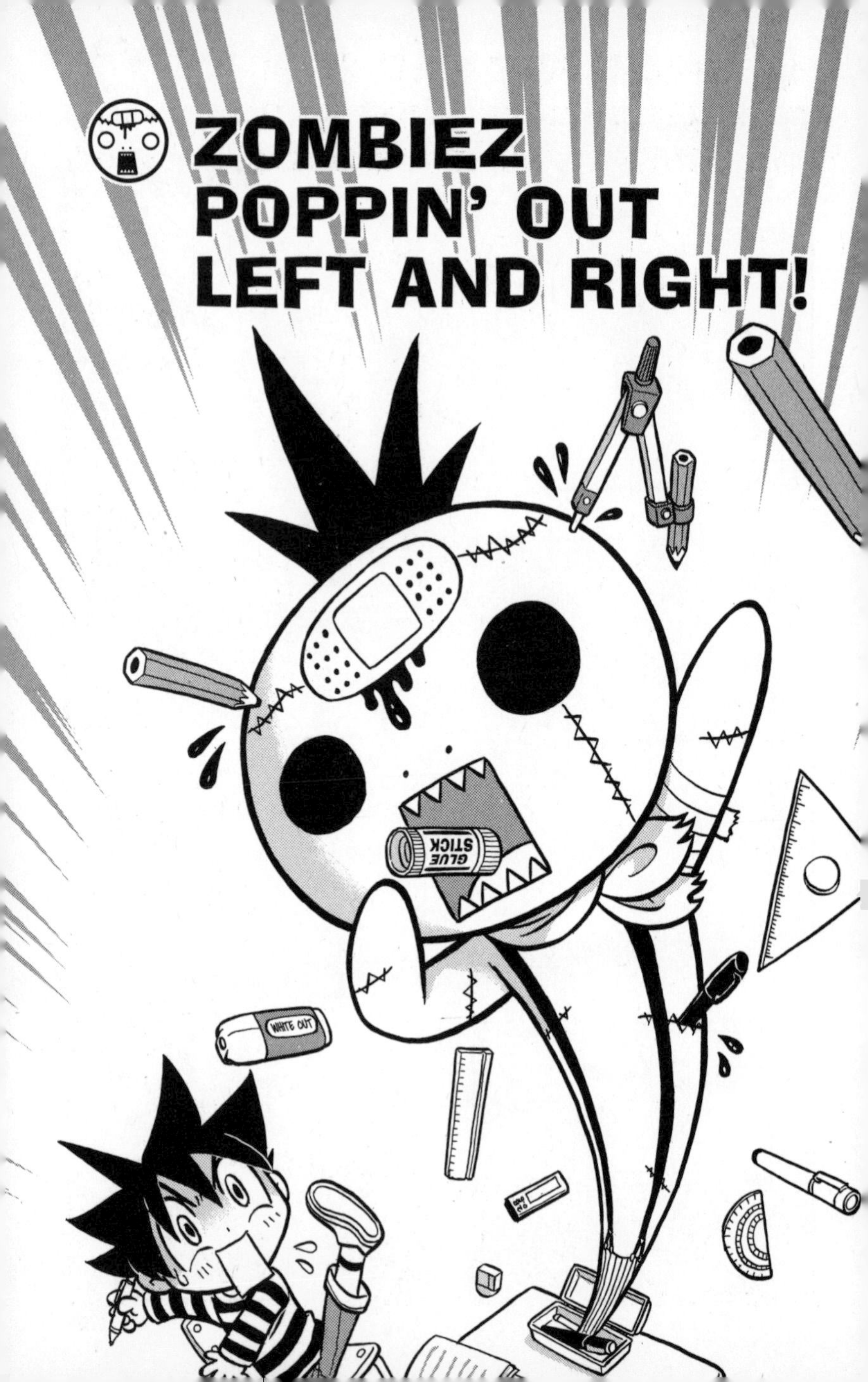
GLUE STICK
WHITE OUT

ZOMBIES...
WHOOOSHHH
CRSSH
...ARE CORPSES THAT HAVE TURNED INTO IMMORTAL MONSTERS.
SCRTCH
SCRTCH
SCRTCH

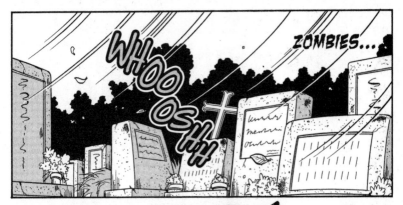

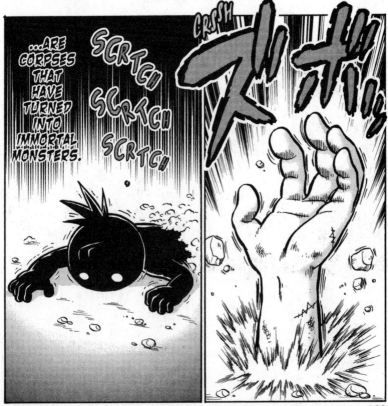

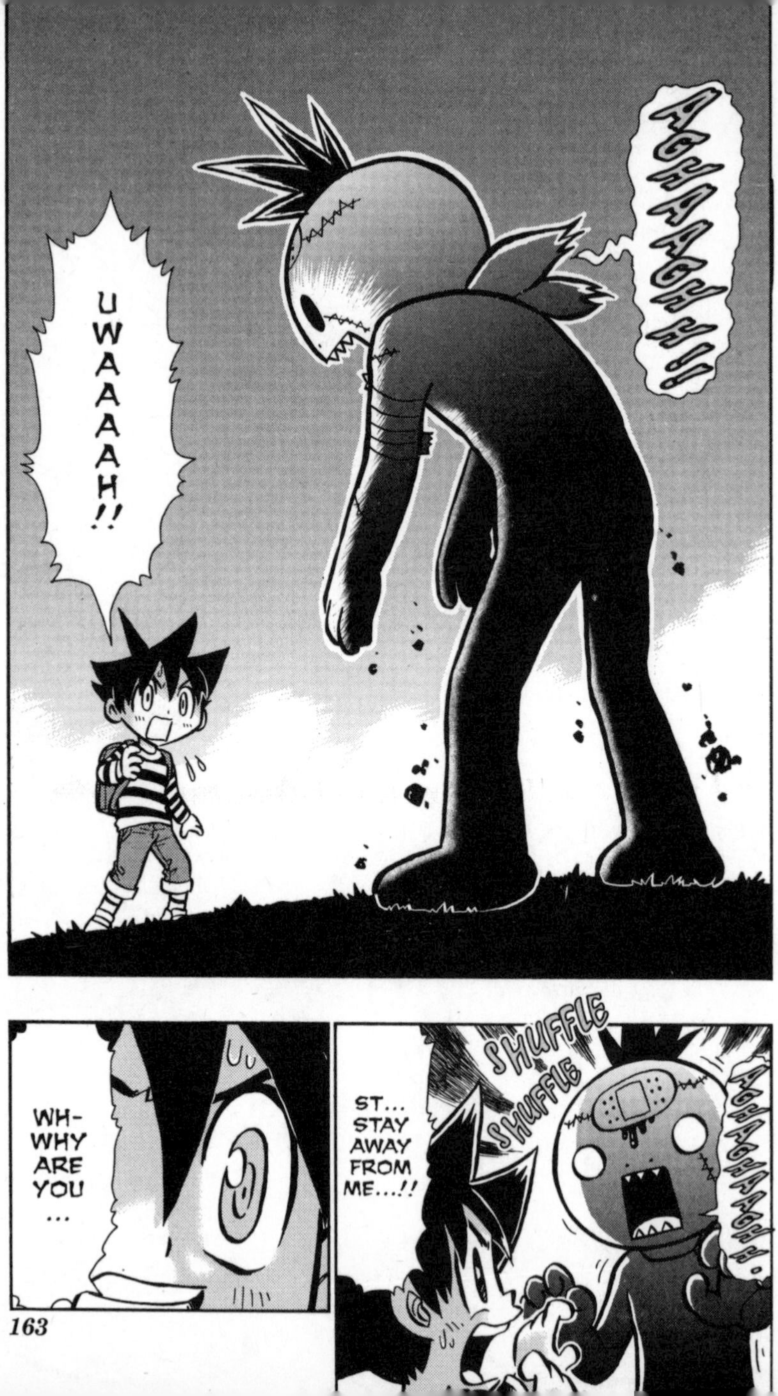
AGHAAAGHH!!
UWAAAAAH!!
SHUFFLE SHUFFLE
AGHAAGHAAAGHH.
ST... STAY AWAY FROM ME...!!
WH- WHY ARE YOU ...

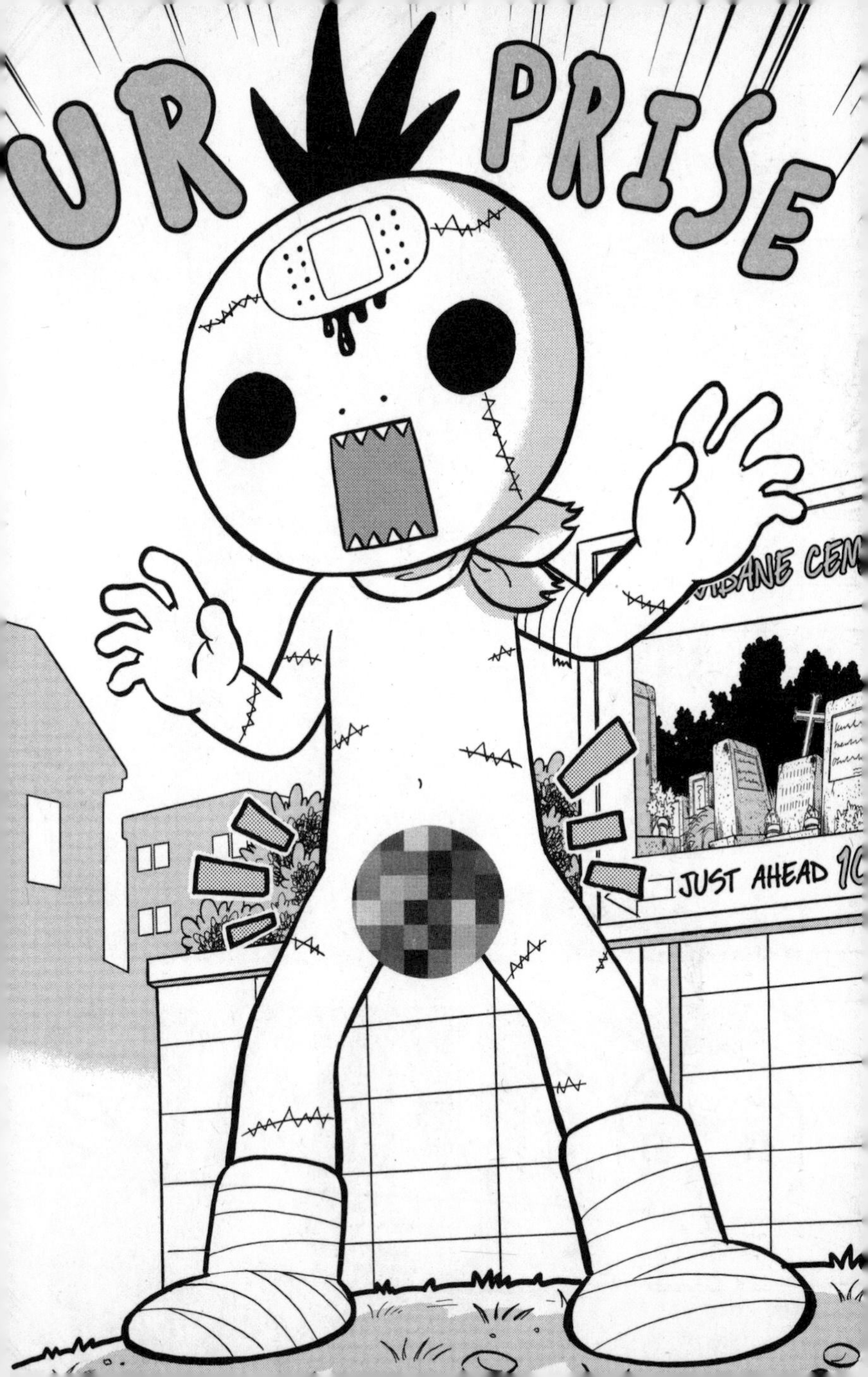
UR
PRISE
...PANE CEM...
JUST AHEAD 10...

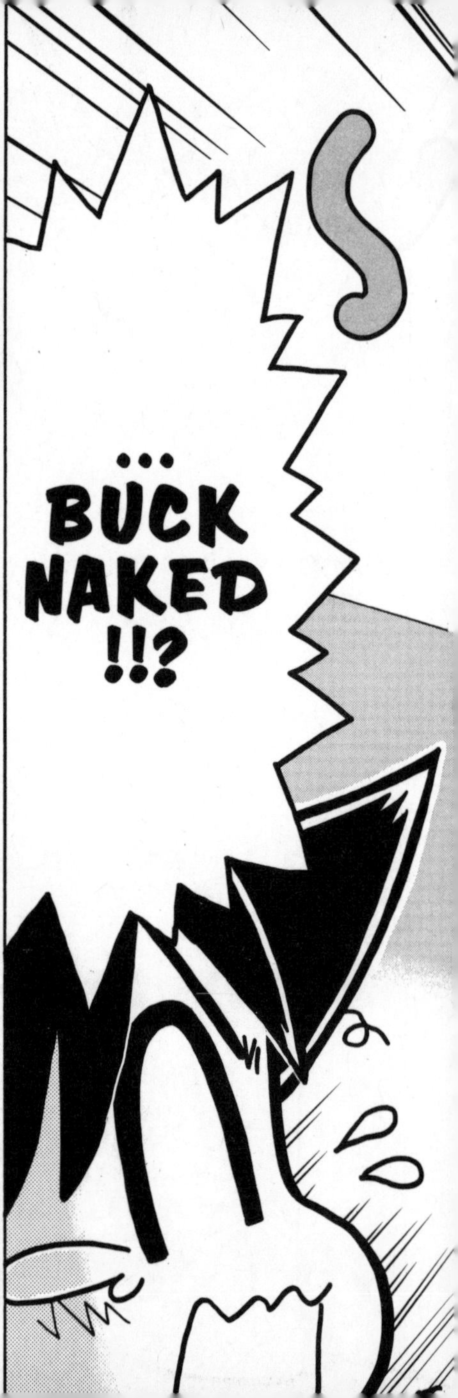
...BÜCK NAKED!!?

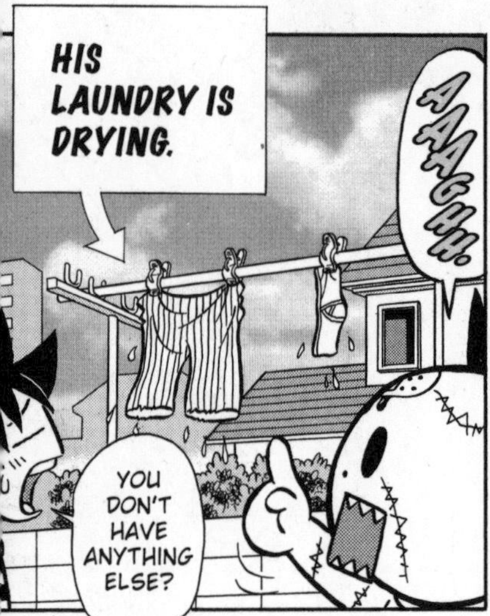
AAAAGHH!
HIS LAUNDRY IS DRYING.
YOU DON'T HAVE ANYTHING ELSE?

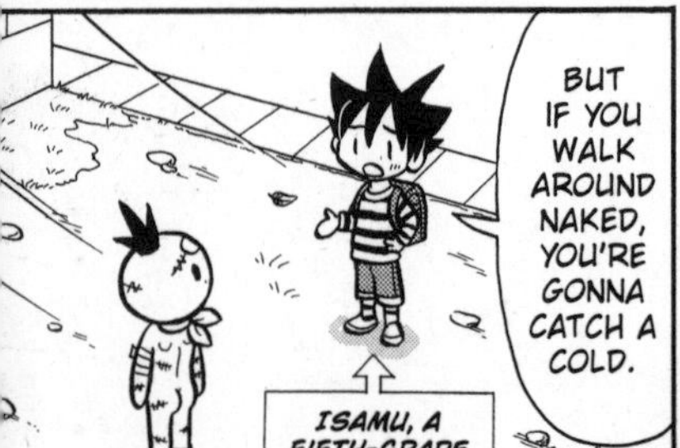
BUT IF YOU WALK AROUND NAKED, YOU'RE GONNA CATCH A COLD.
ISAMU, A FIFTH-GRADE ELEMENTARY STUDENT

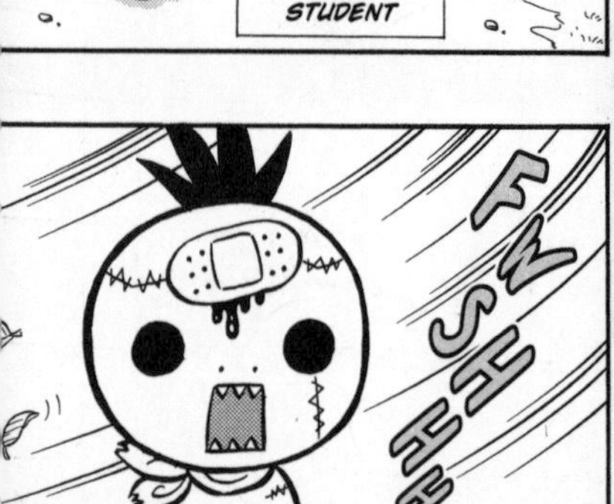
FWSHHH

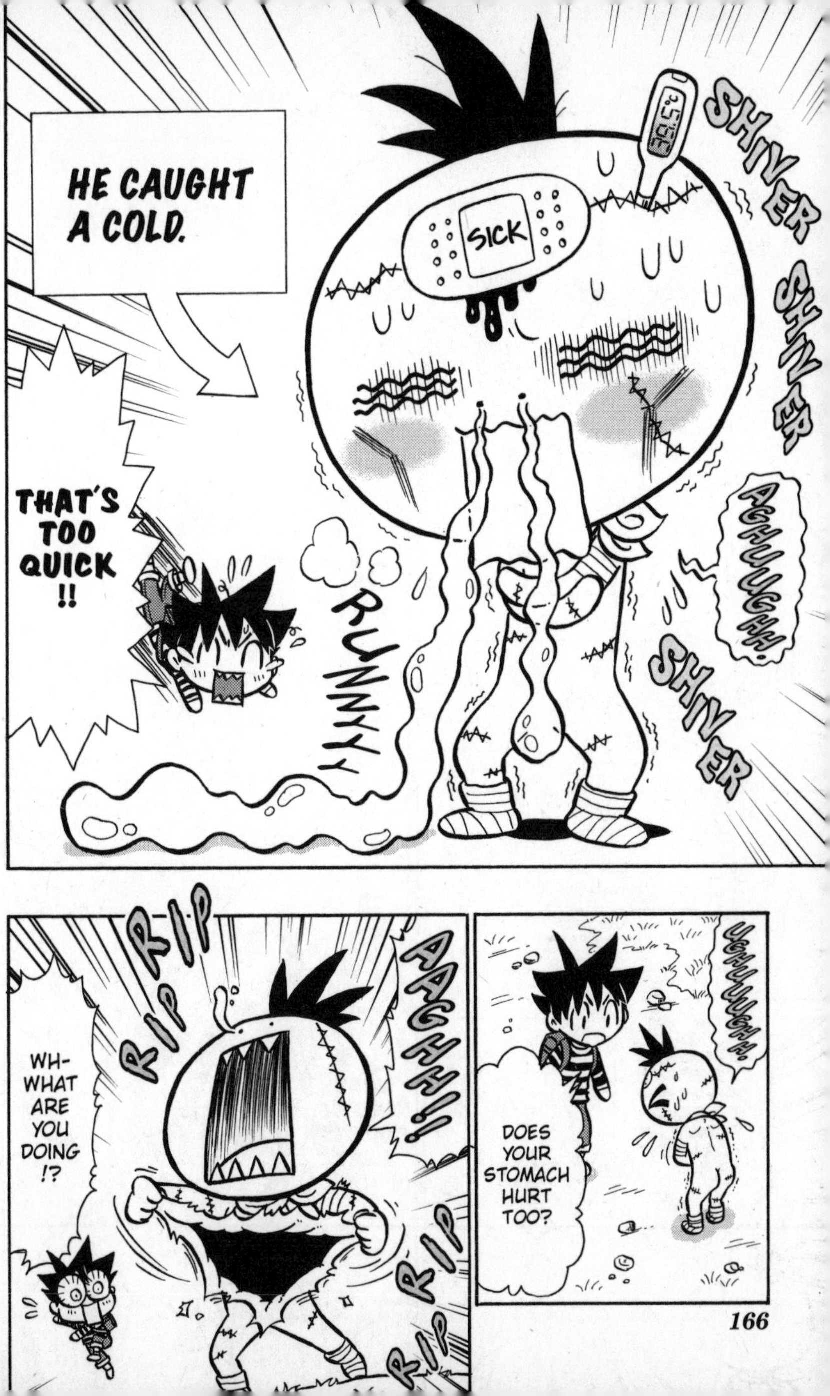
SHIVER
SHIVER
HE CAUGHT A COLD.
SICK
ACHUUGH.
SHIVER
RUNNYYY
THAT'S TOO QUICK !!
UGHUUUGH.
DOES YOUR STOMACH HURT TOO?
AAGHH!!
RIP RIP
RIP
RIP RIP
WH-WHAT ARE YOU DOING !?

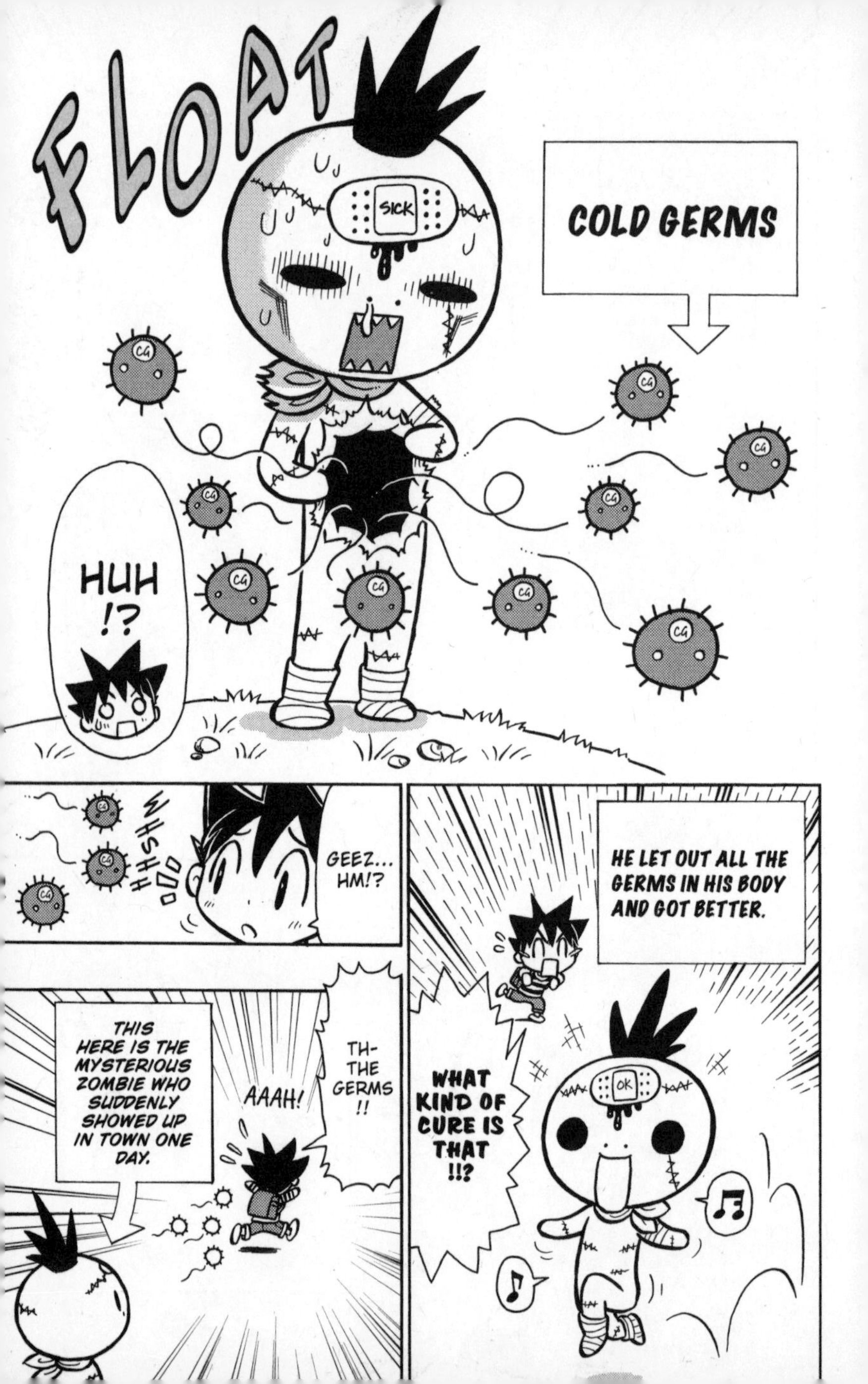
FLOAT
SICK
COLD GERMS
HUH !?
HE LET OUT ALL THE GERMS IN HIS BODY AND GOT BETTER.
OK
WHAT KIND OF CURE IS THAT !!?
WHSHH
GEEZ... HM!?
TH-THE GERMS !!
AAAH!
THIS HERE IS THE MYSTERIOUS ZOMBIE WHO SUDDENLY SHOWED UP IN TOWN ONE DAY.

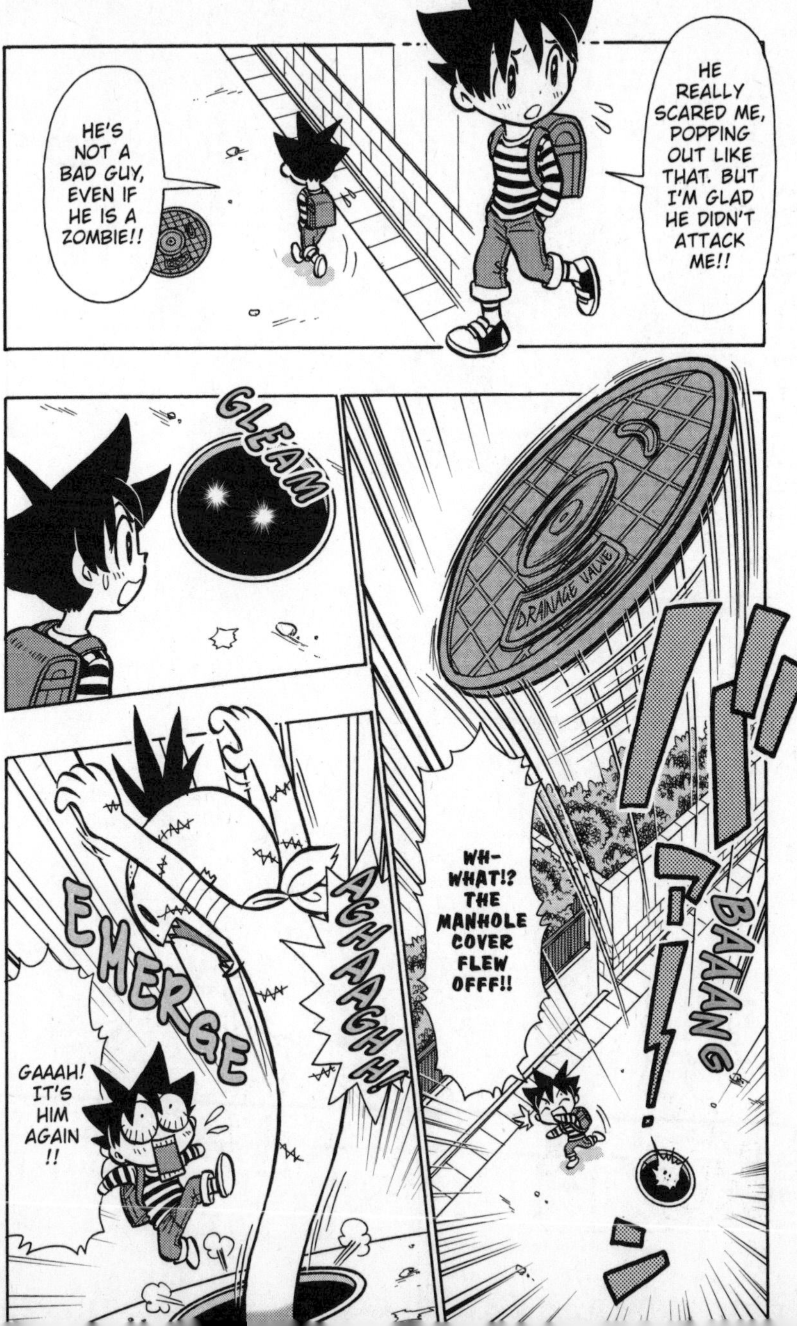

HE REALLY SCARED ME, POPPING OUT LIKE THAT. BUT I'M GLAD HE DIDN'T ATTACK ME!!
HE'S NOT A BAD GUY, EVEN IF HE IS A ZOMBIE!!
DRAINAGE VALVE
BAAANG
WH-WHAT!? THE MANHOLE COVER FLEW OFFF!!
GLEAM
AGHAAAGH!
EMERGE
GAAAH! IT'S HIM AGAIN!!

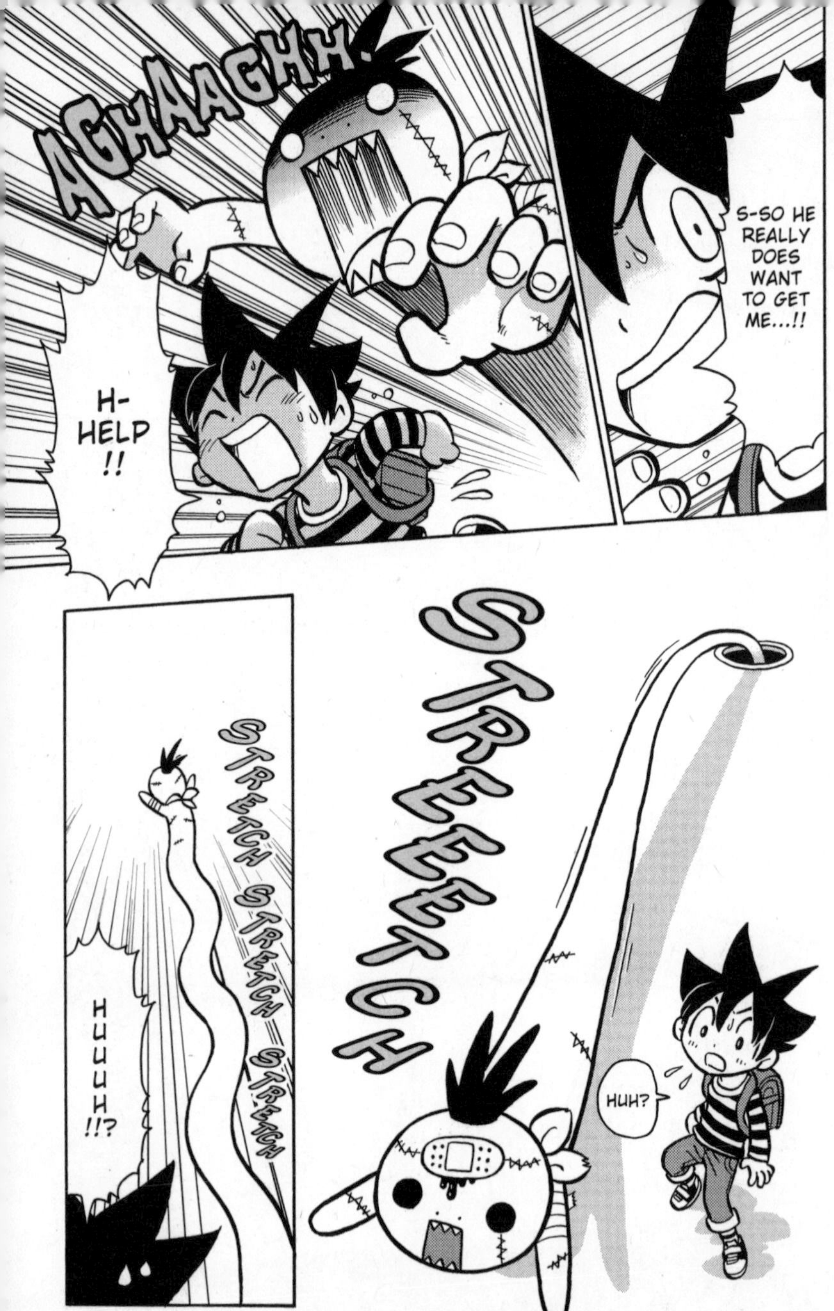
S-SO HE REALLY DOES WANT TO GET ME...!!
AGHAAGHH
H-HELP!!
STREEETCH
HUH?
STRETCH STRETCH STRETCH STRETCH
HUUUUH!!?

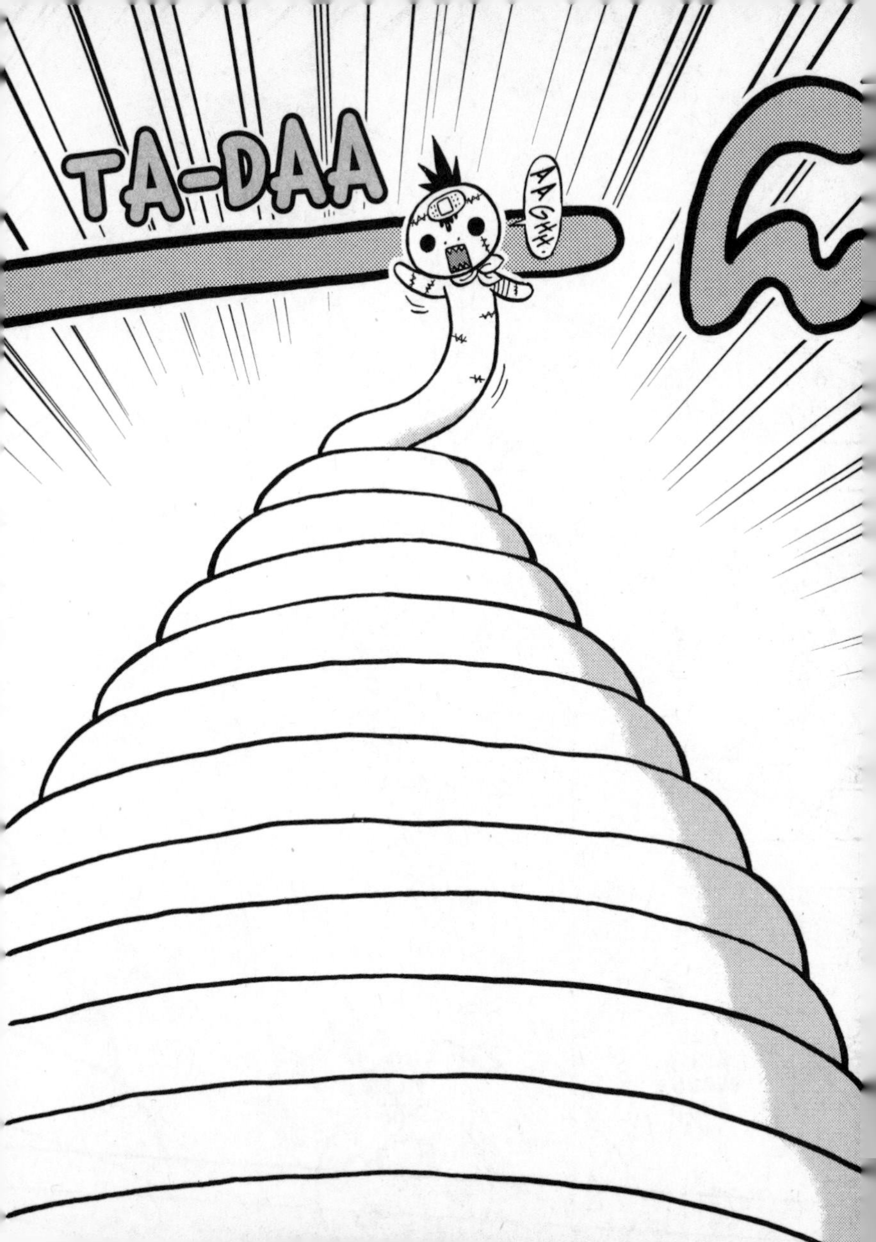
TA-DAA
AAGHH.

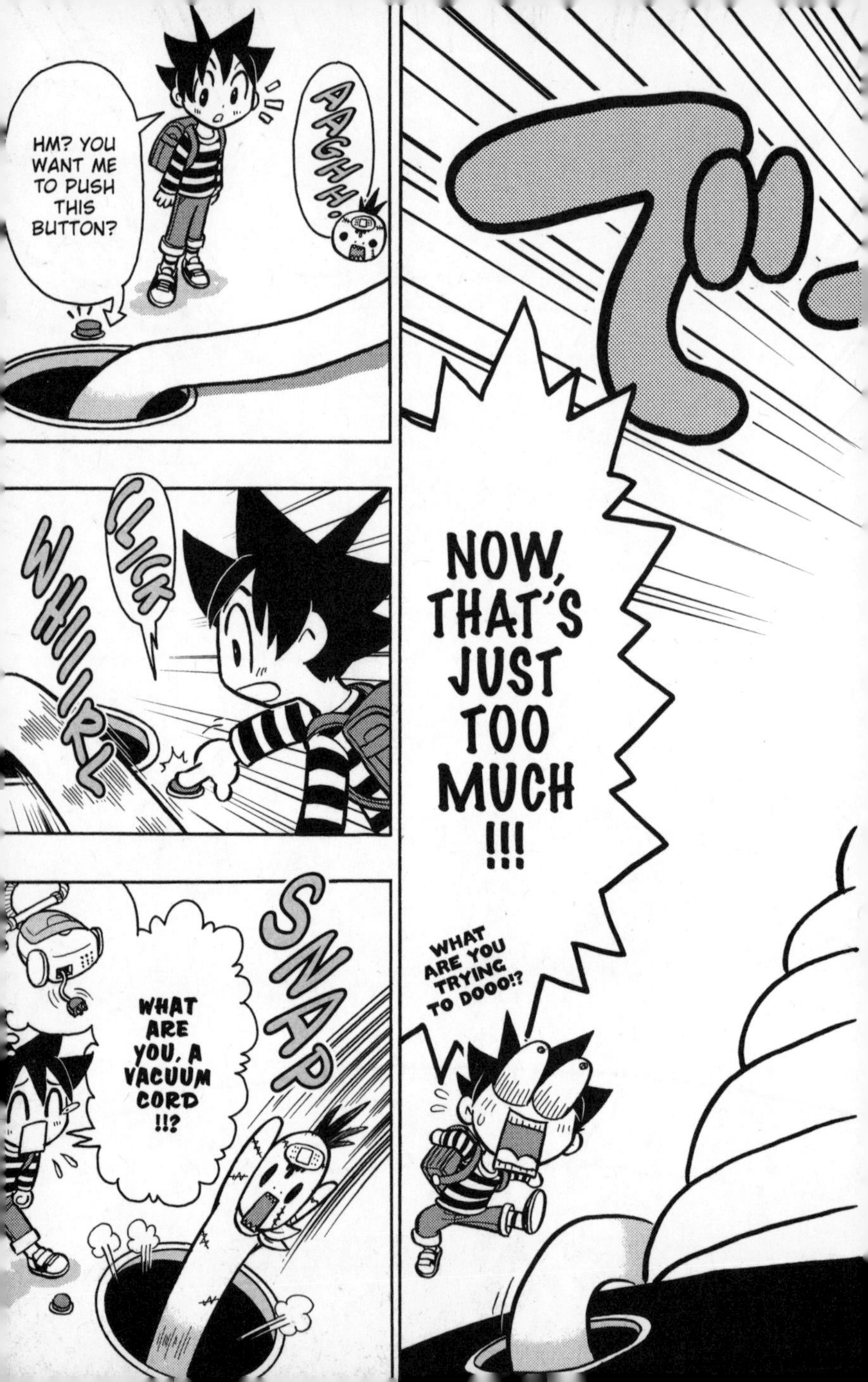
NOW, THAT'S JUST TOO MUCH !!!
WHAT ARE YOU TRYING TO DOOO!?
AAGHH
HM? YOU WANT ME TO PUSH THIS BUTTON?
CLICK
WHIIIRL
SNAP
WHAT ARE YOU, A VACUUM CORD !!?

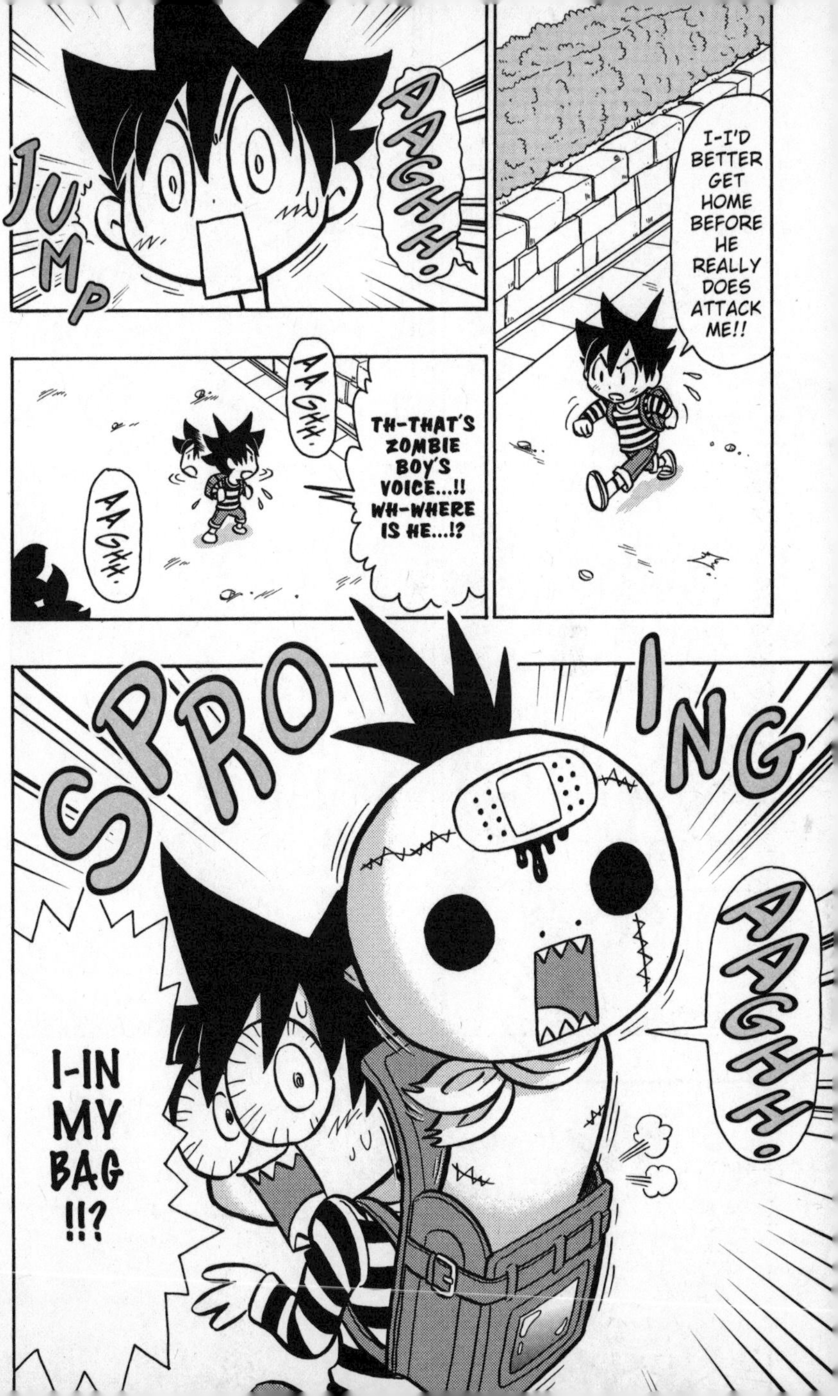
I-I'D BETTER GET HOME BEFORE HE REALLY DOES ATTACK ME!!
AAGHH.
JUMP
AAGHH
TH-THAT'S ZOMBIE BOY'S VOICE...!! WH-WHERE IS HE...!?
AAGHH
SPROING
AAGHH.
I-IN MY BAG!!?

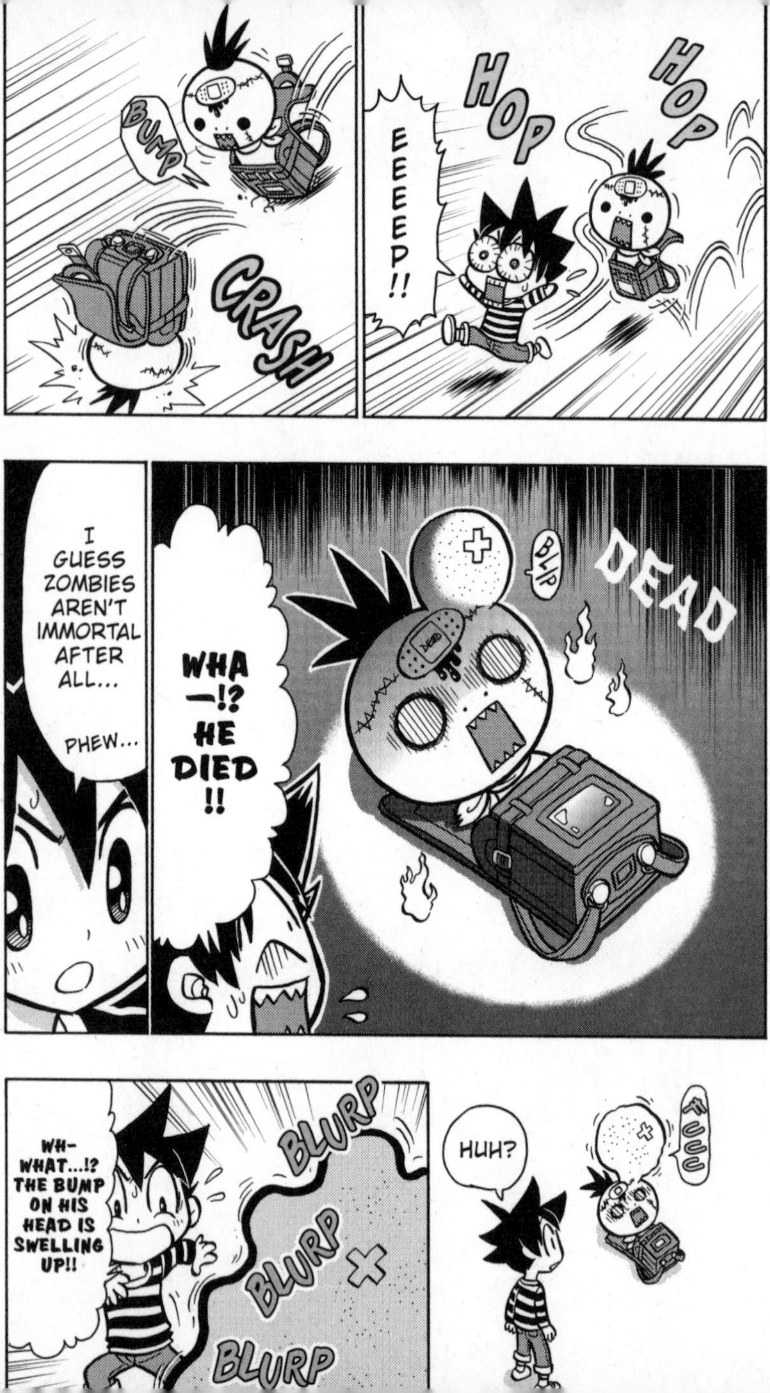
HOP
HOP
EEEEEP!!
BUMP
CRASH
DEAD
BLIP
WHA—!? HE DIED!!
I GUESS ZOMBIES AREN'T IMMORTAL AFTER ALL...
PHEW...
FUUU
HUH?
WH-WHAT...!? THE BUMP ON HIS HEAD IS SWELLING UP!!
BLURP
BLURP
BLURP

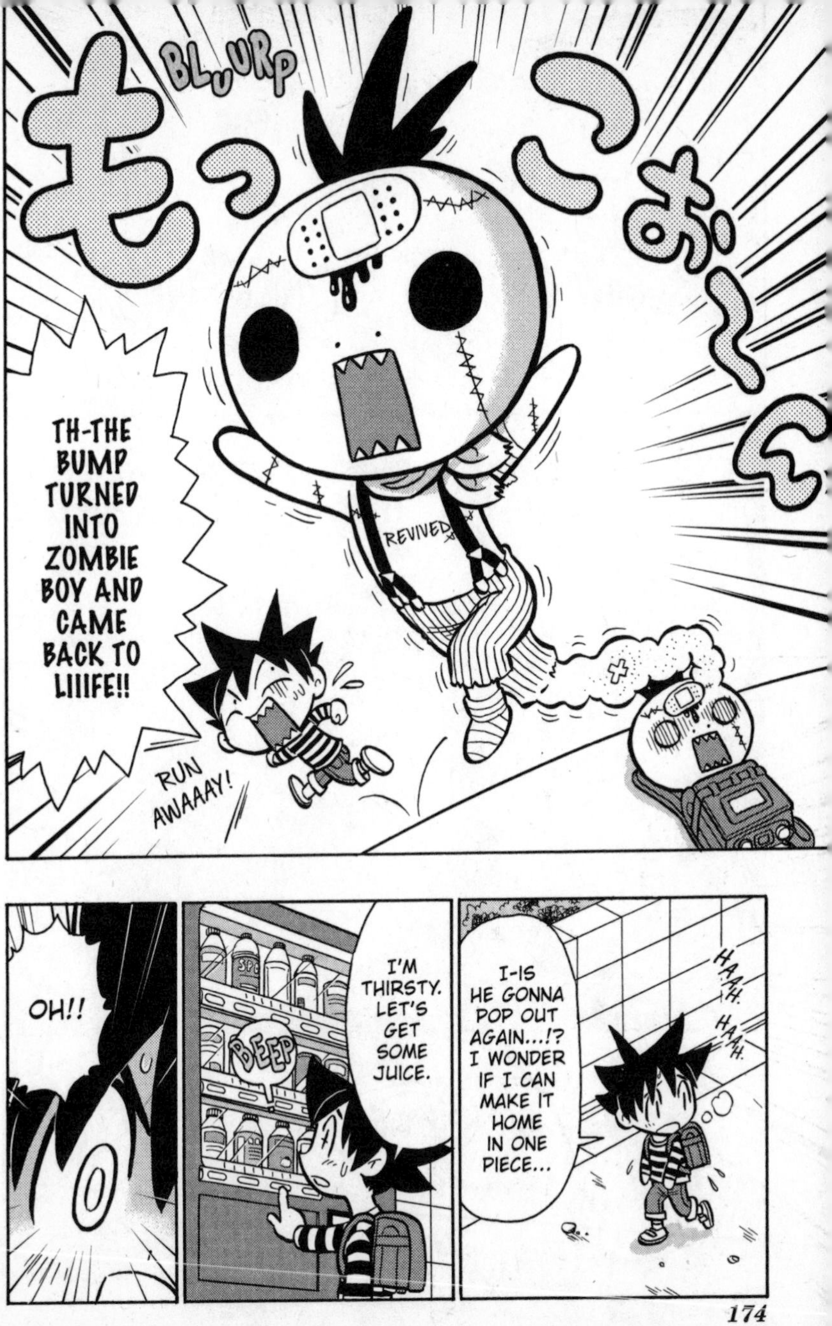
BLUURP
もっこお〜
TH-THE BUMP TURNED INTO ZOMBIE BOY AND CAME BACK TO LIIIFE!!
REVIVED
RUN AWAAAY!
HAAH. HAAH.
I-IS HE GONNA POP OUT AGAIN...!? I WONDER IF I CAN MAKE IT HOME IN ONE PIECE...
I'M THIRSTY. LET'S GET SOME JUICE.
BEEP
OH!!

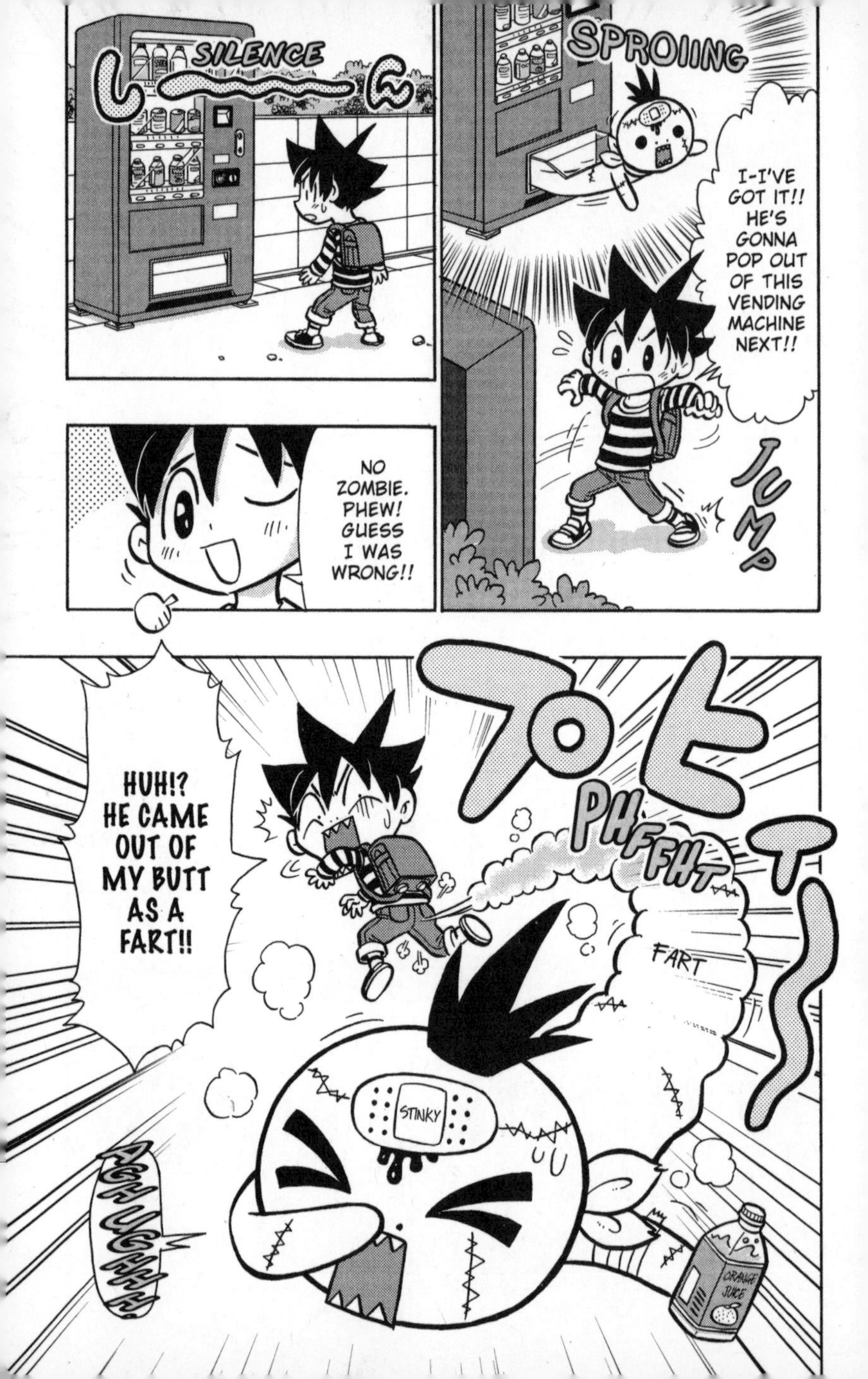

SPROIING
I-I'VE GOT IT!! HE'S GONNA POP OUT OF THIS VENDING MACHINE NEXT!!
JUMP
SILENCE
NO ZOMBIE. PHEW! GUESS I WAS WRONG!!
PHFFHT
HUH!? HE CAME OUT OF MY BUTT AS A FART!!
FART
STINKY
ORANGE JUICE
AGH UGHHH

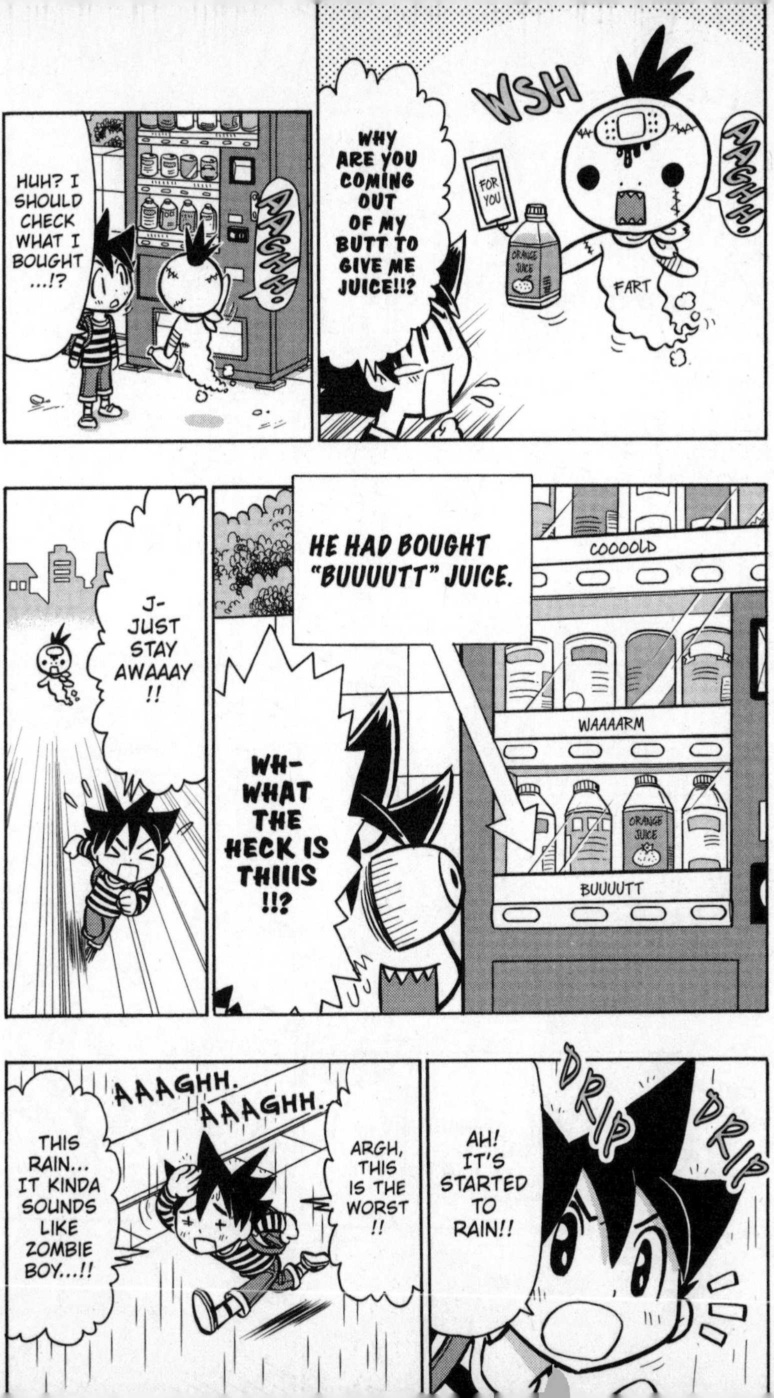
WSH
AAGHH.
FOR YOU
ORANGE JUICE
FART
WHY ARE YOU COMING OUT OF MY BUTT TO GIVE ME JUICE!!?
AAGHH.
HUH? I SHOULD CHECK WHAT I BOUGHT ...!?
HE HAD BOUGHT "BUUUUTT" JUICE.
COOOOLD
WAAAARM
ORANGE JUICE
BUUUUTT
WH-WHAT THE HECK IS THIIIS!!?
J-JUST STAY AWAAAY!!
DRIP DRIP
AH! IT'S STARTED TO RAIN!!
AAAGHH. AAAGHH.
ARGH, THIS IS THE WORST!!
THIS RAIN... IT KINDA SOUNDS LIKE ZOMBIE BOY...!!

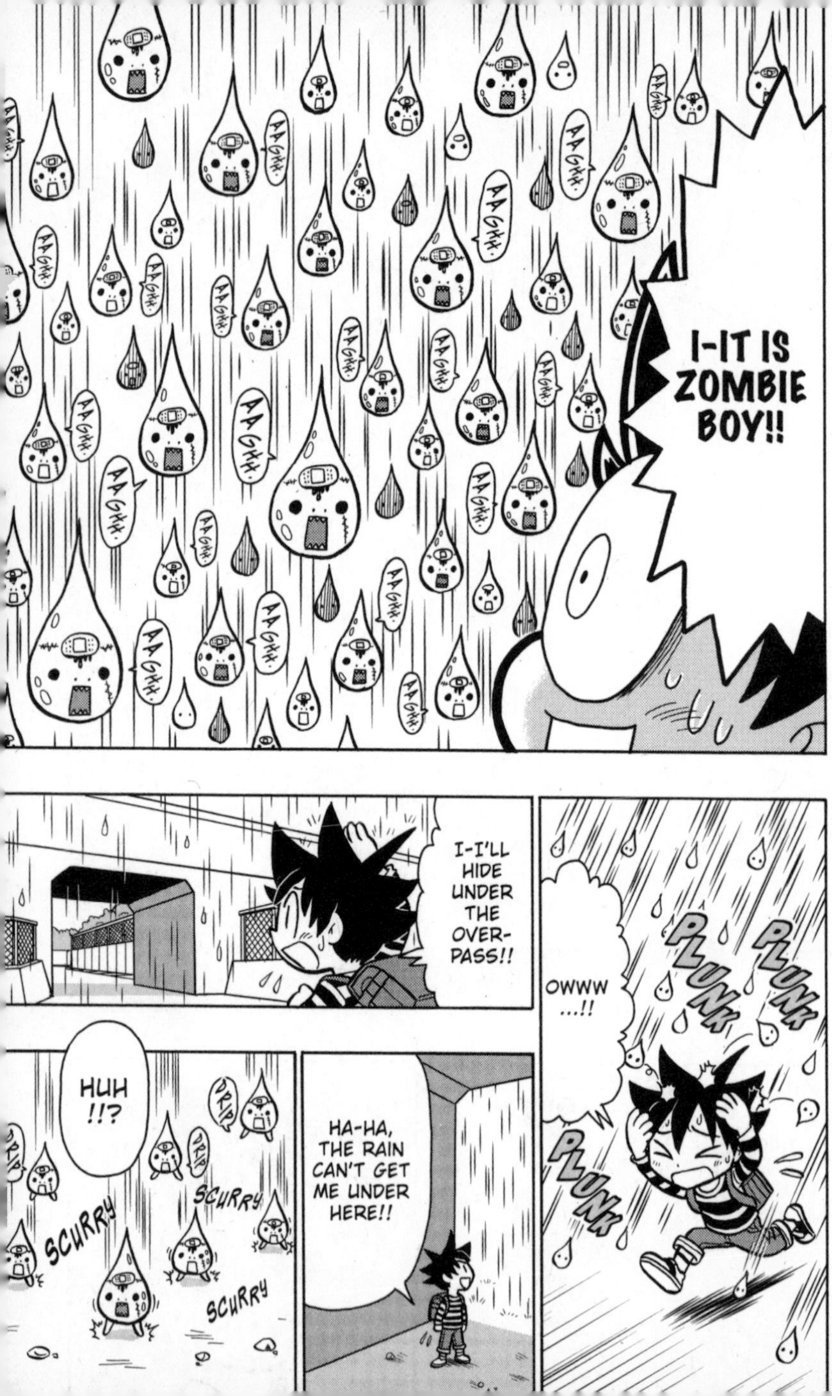
AAGHH.
I-IT IS ZOMBIE BOY!!
OWWW ...!!
PLUNK
PLUNK
PLUNK
I-I'LL HIDE UNDER THE OVER-PASS!!
HA-HA, THE RAIN CAN'T GET ME UNDER HERE!!
HUH !!?
DRIP
DRIP
DRIP
SCURRY
SCURRY
SCURRY

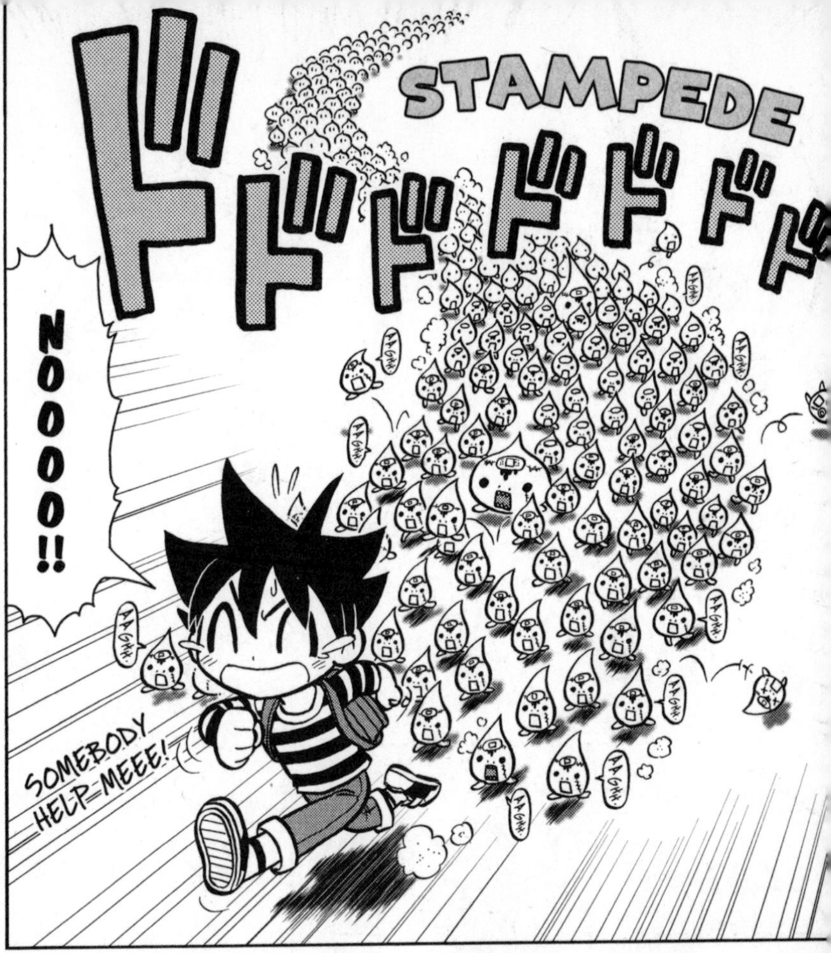
STAMPEDE
ドドドドドドド
NOOOOO!!
SOMEBODY HELP MEEE!
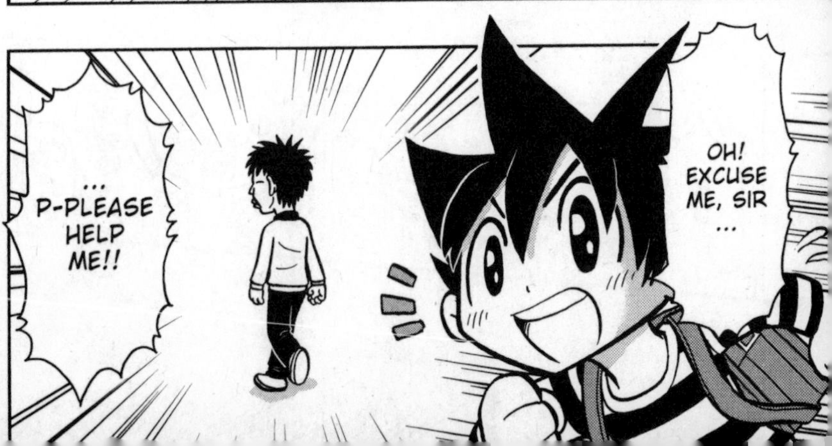
OH! EXCUSE ME, SIR ...
... P-PLEASE HELP ME!!

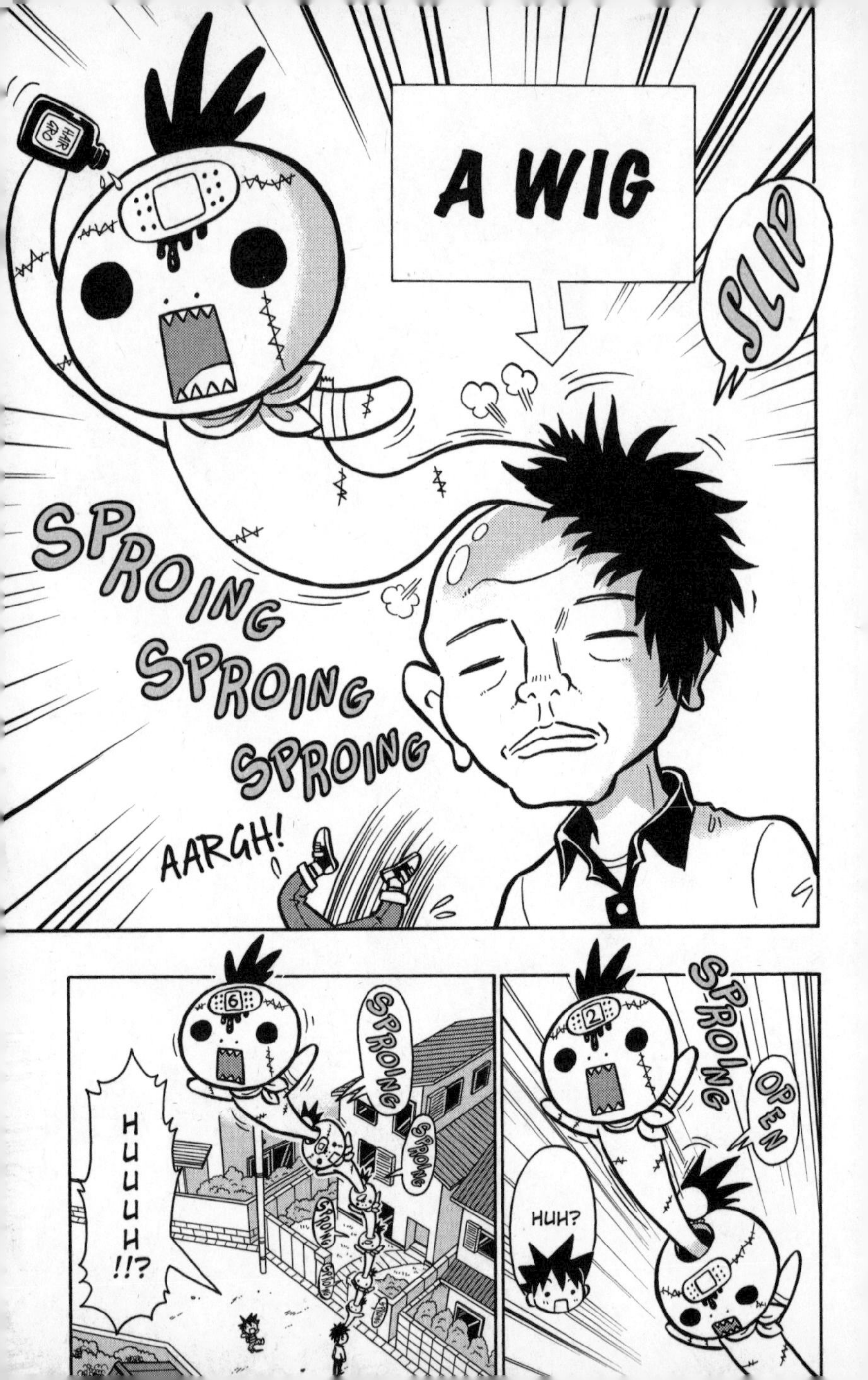
SLIP
A WIG
HAIR GRO
SPROING
SPROING
SPROING
AARGH!
SPROING
OPEN
HUH?
SPROING
SPROING
SPROING
HUUUUH!!?

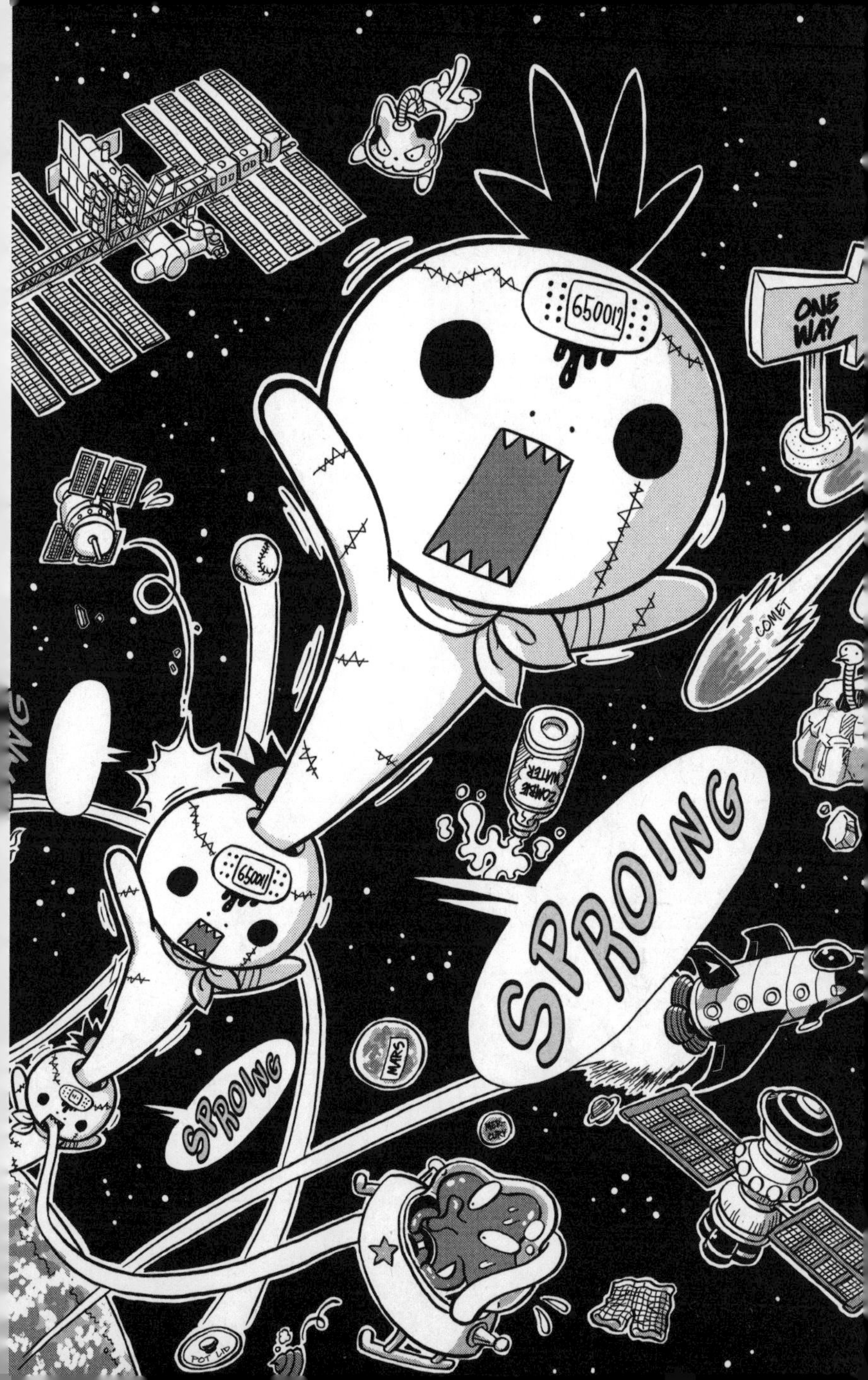
ONE WAY
650012
COMET
ZOMBIE WATER
SPROING
650011
MARS
SPROING
MER-CURY
POT LID

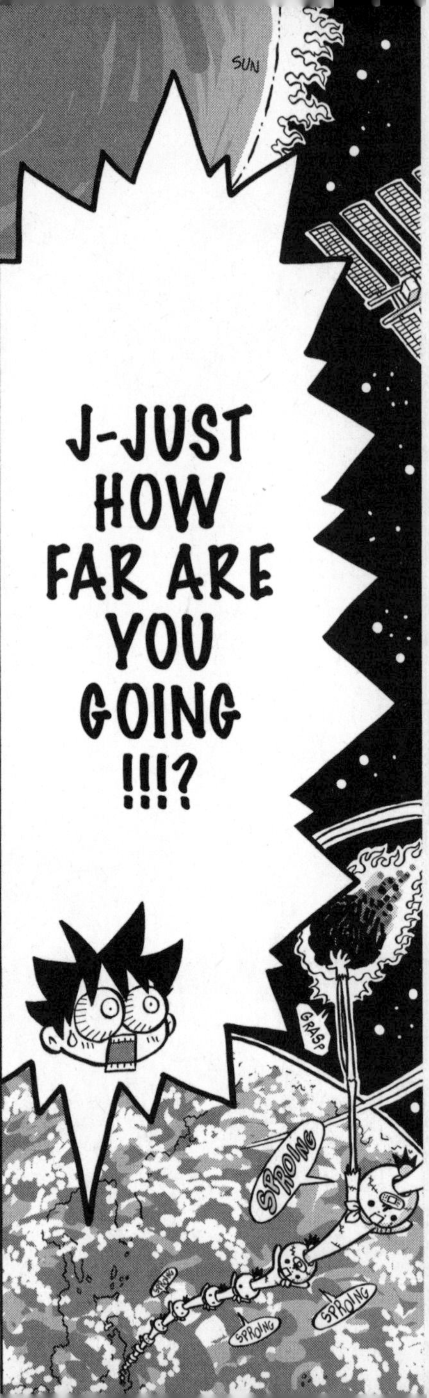
SUN
J-JUST HOW FAR ARE YOU GOING!!!?
GRASP
SPROING
SPROING
SPROING
SPROING
SPROING

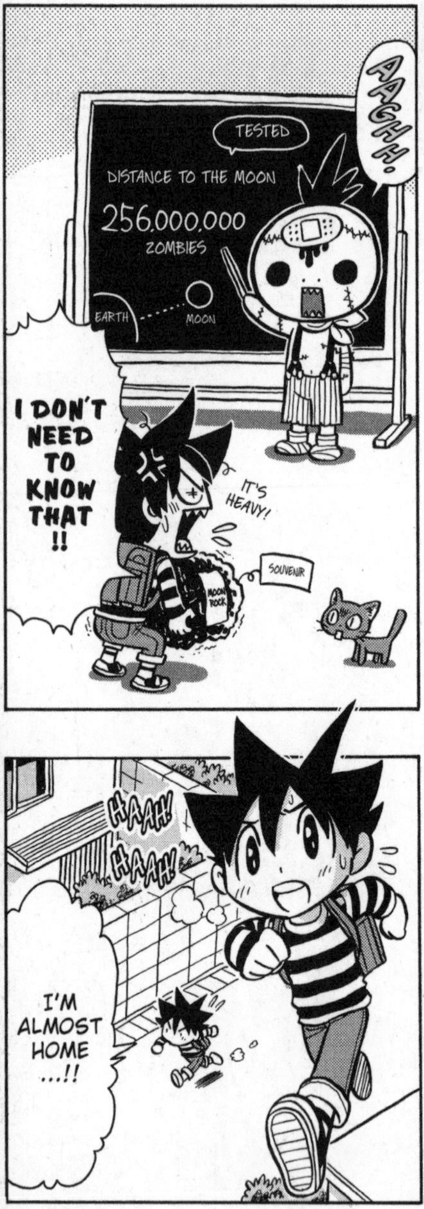
AAGHH!
TESTED
DISTANCE TO THE MOON
256,000,000
ZOMBIES
EARTH
MOON
I DON'T NEED TO KNOW THAT!!
IT'S HEAVY!
SOUVENIR
MOON ROCK
HAAH!
HAAH!
I'M ALMOST HOME...!!

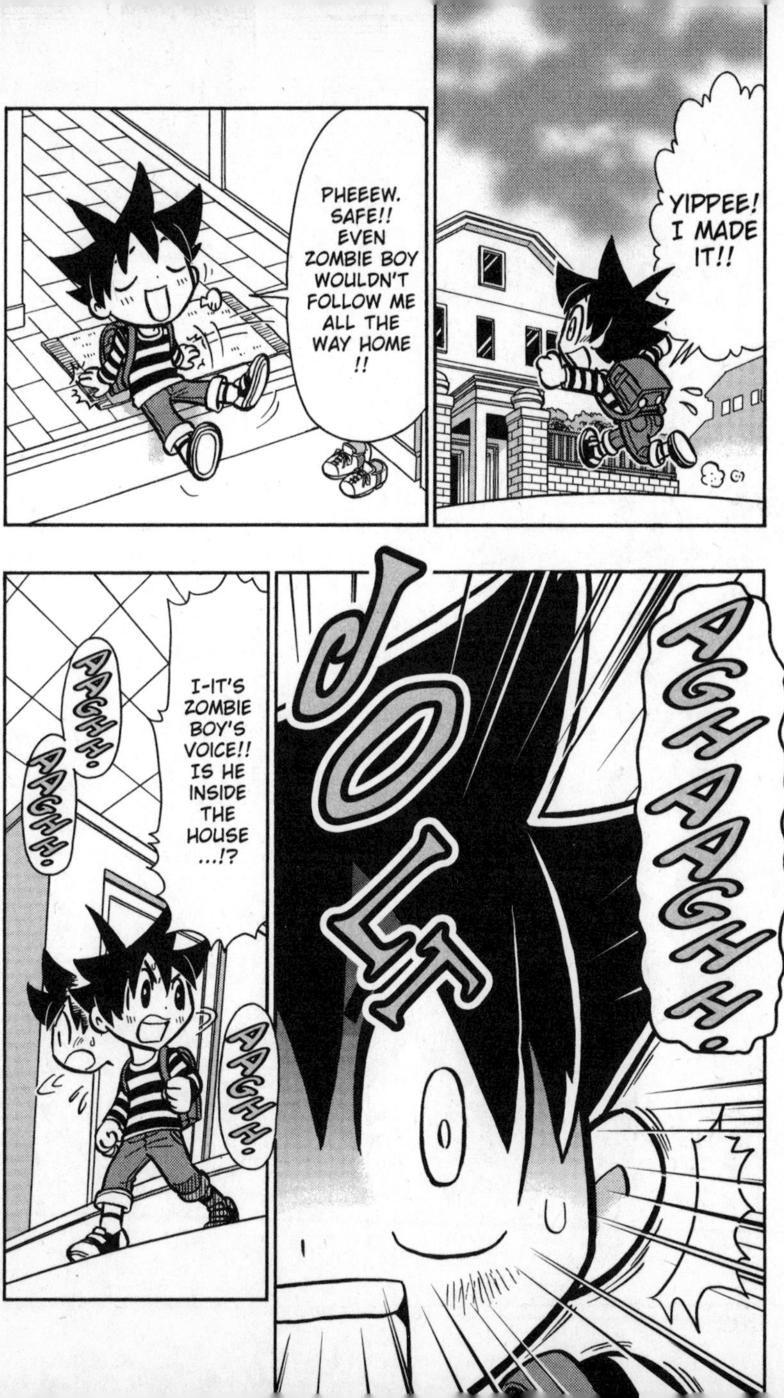
YIPPEE! I MADE IT!!
PHEEEW. SAFE!! EVEN ZOMBIE BOY WOULDN'T FOLLOW ME ALL THE WAY HOME!!
AGHAAAAGHH.
JOLT
I-IT'S ZOMBIE BOY'S VOICE!! IS HE INSIDE THE HOUSE...!?
AAGHH.
AAGHH.
AAGHH.

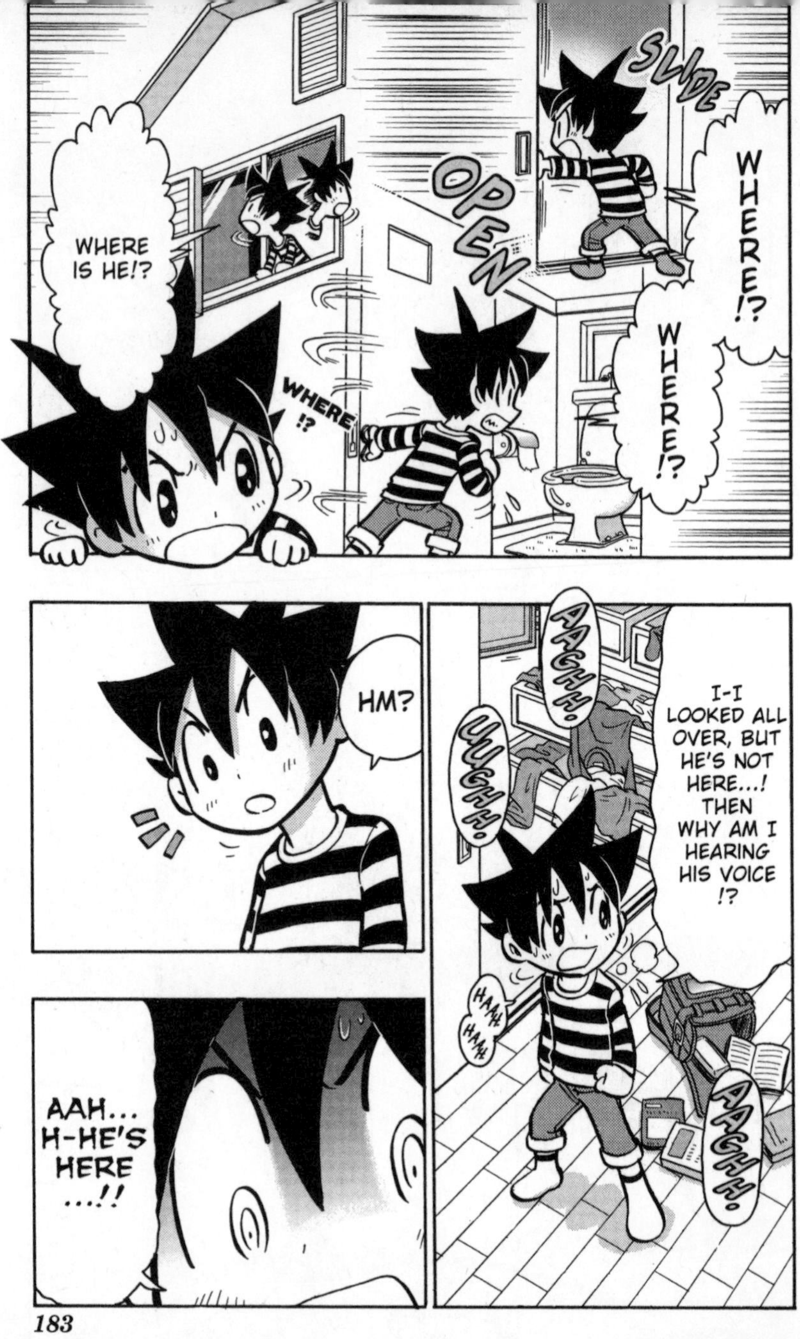
SLIDE
WHERE!?
WHERE!?
OPEN
WHERE!?
WHERE IS HE!?
I-I LOOKED ALL OVER, BUT HE'S NOT HERE...! THEN WHY AM I HEARING HIS VOICE!?
AAGHH.
UUGHH.
AAGHH.
HAAH HAAH
HM?
AAH... H-HE'S HERE...!!

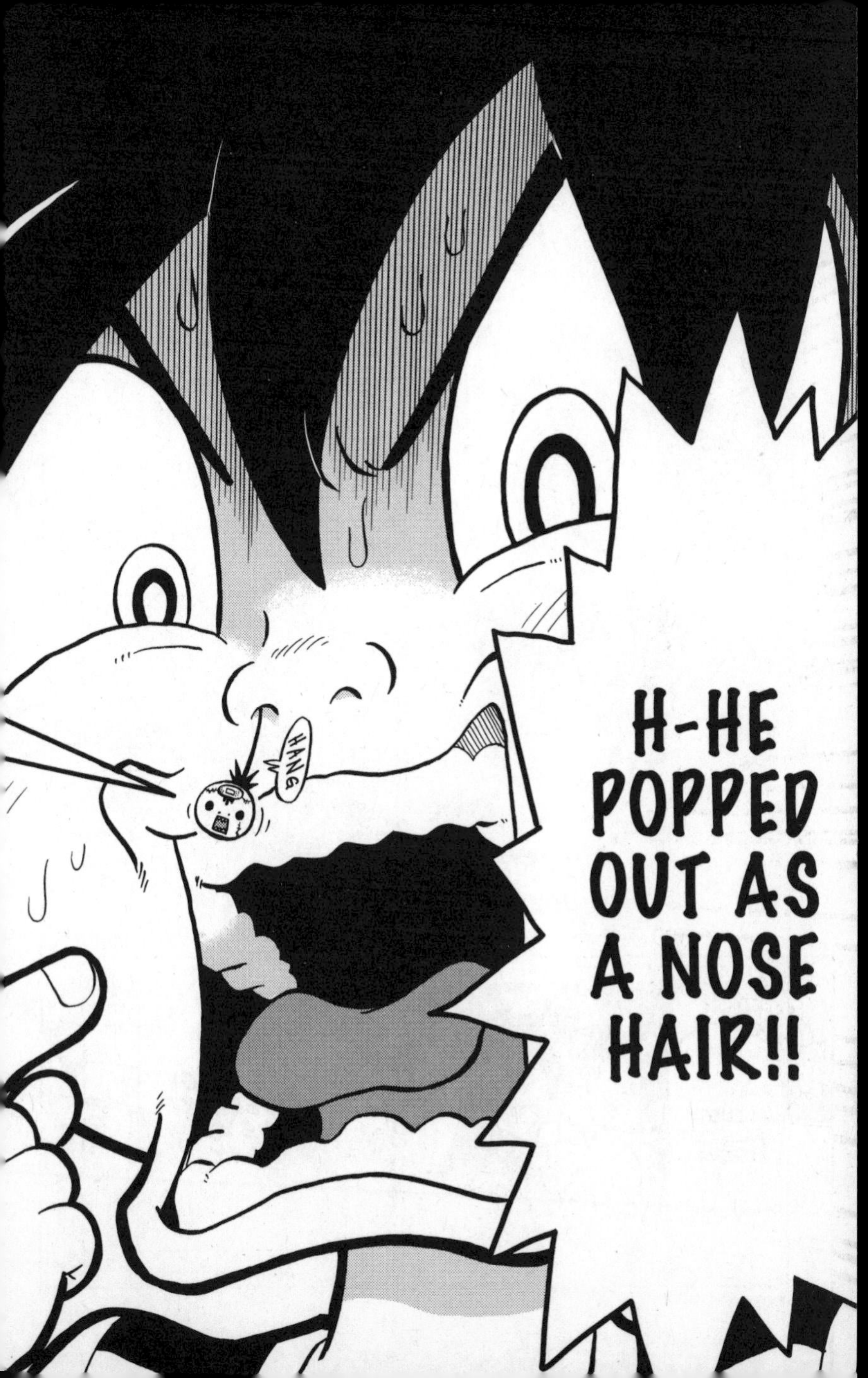
HANG
H-HE POPPED OUT AS A NOSE HAIR!!

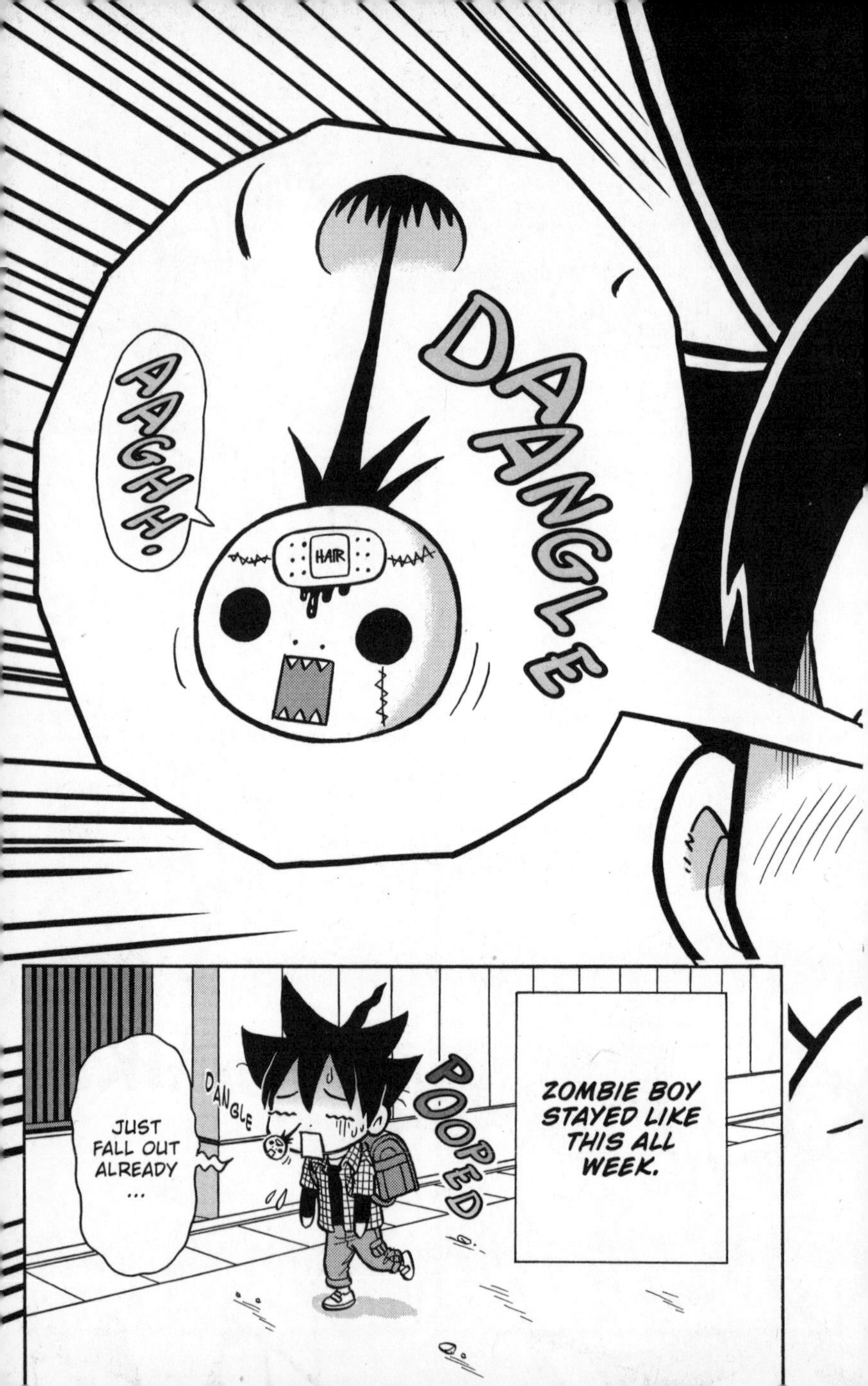
DANGLE
HAIR
AAGHH.
ZOMBIE BOY STAYED LIKE THIS ALL WEEK.
POOPED
DANGLE
JUST FALL OUT ALREADY ...

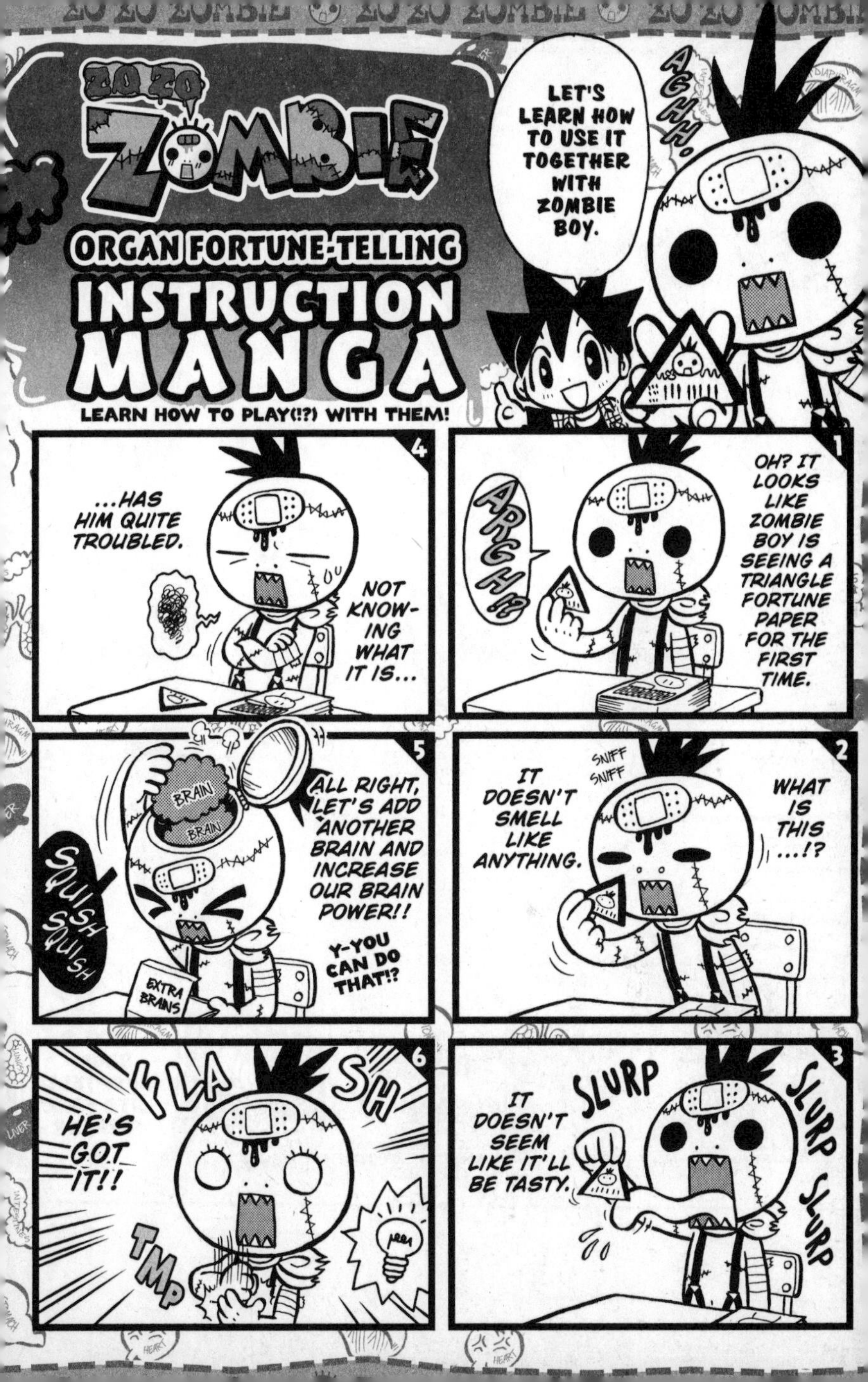
ZO ZO ZOMBIE
ORGAN FORTUNE-TELLING
INSTRUCTION MANGA
LEARN HOW TO PLAY(!?) WITH THEM!
LET'S LEARN HOW TO USE IT TOGETHER WITH ZOMBIE BOY.
AGHH.
OH? IT LOOKS LIKE ZOMBIE BOY IS SEEING A TRIANGLE FORTUNE PAPER FOR THE FIRST TIME.
ARGH!?
WHAT IS THIS...!?
SNIFF SNIFF
IT DOESN'T SMELL LIKE ANYTHING.
SLURP
SLURP
SLURP
SLURP
IT DOESN'T SEEM LIKE IT'LL BE TASTY.
NOT KNOWING WHAT IT IS...
...HAS HIM QUITE TROUBLED.
ALL RIGHT, LET'S ADD ANOTHER BRAIN AND INCREASE OUR BRAIN POWER!!
Y-YOU CAN DO THAT!?
BRAIN
BRAIN
SQUISH SQUISH
EXTRA BRAINS
FLASH
HE'S GOT IT!!
TMP

THIS MANGA EXPLAINS THE FORTUNE-TELLER INCLUDED IN THE APRIL 2013 EDITION OF *COROCORO COMICS.*

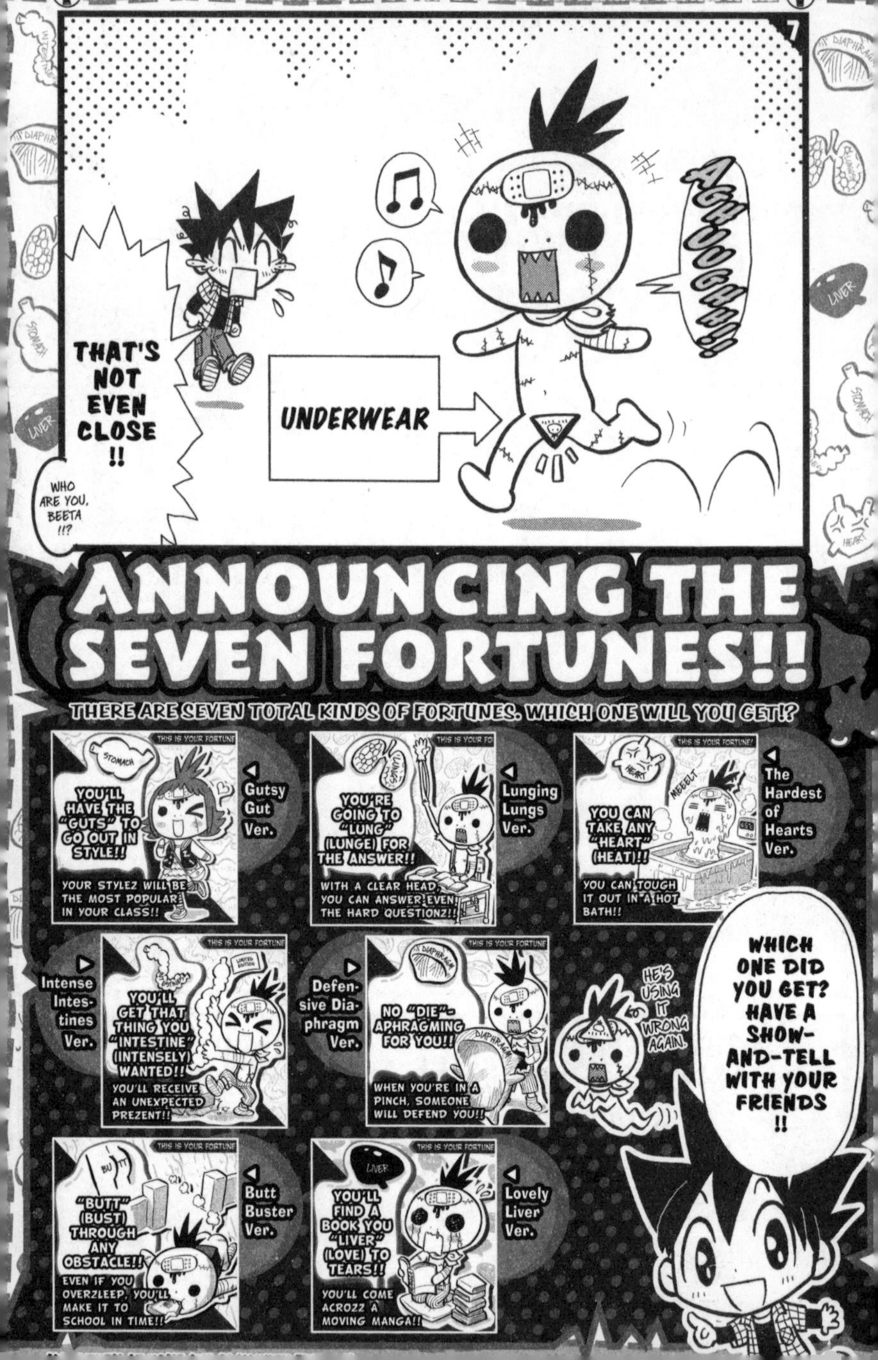

7
AGHUUGHH!!
UNDERWEAR
THAT'S NOT EVEN CLOSE !!
WHO ARE YOU, BEETA !!?
ANNOUNCING THE SEVEN FORTUNES!!
THERE ARE SEVEN TOTAL KINDS OF FORTUNES. WHICH ONE WILL YOU GET!?
THIS IS YOUR FORTUNE
STOMACH
YOU'LL HAVE THE "GUTS" TO GO OUT IN STYLE!!
YOUR STYLEZ WILL BE THE MOST POPULAR IN YOUR CLASS!!
Gutsy Gut Ver.
LUNGS
YOU'RE GOING TO "LUNG" (LUNGE) FOR THE ANSWER!!
WITH A CLEAR HEAD, YOU CAN ANSWER EVEN THE HARD QUESTIONZ!!
Lunging Lungs Ver.
THIS IS YOUR FORTUNE!
HEART
MEEELT
YOU CAN TAKE ANY "HEART" (HEAT)!!
YOU CAN TOUGH IT OUT IN A HOT BATH!!
The Hardest of Hearts Ver.
Intense Intes-tines Ver.
THIS IS YOUR FORTUNE
LIMITED EDITION
YOU'LL GET THAT THING YOU "INTESTINE" (INTENSELY) WANTED!!
YOU'LL RECEIVE AN UNEXPECTED PREZENT!!
Defen-sive Dia-phragm Ver.
THIS IS YOUR FORTUNE
DIAPHRAGM
NO "DIE"-APHRAGMING FOR YOU!!
WHEN YOU'RE IN A PINCH, SOMEONE WILL DEFEND YOU!!
HE'S USING IT WRONG AGAIN.
WHICH ONE DID YOU GET? HAVE A SHOW-AND-TELL WITH YOUR FRIENDS !!
THIS IS YOUR FORTUNE
BUTT
"BUTT" (BUST) THROUGH ANY OBSTACLE!!
EVEN IF YOU OVERZLEEP, YOU'LL MAKE IT TO SCHOOL IN TIME!!
Butt Buster Ver.
THIS IS YOUR FORTUNE
LIVER
YOU'LL FIND A BOOK YOU "LIVER" (LOVE) TO TEARS!!
YOU'LL COME ACROZZ A MOVING MANGA!!
Lovely Liver Ver.

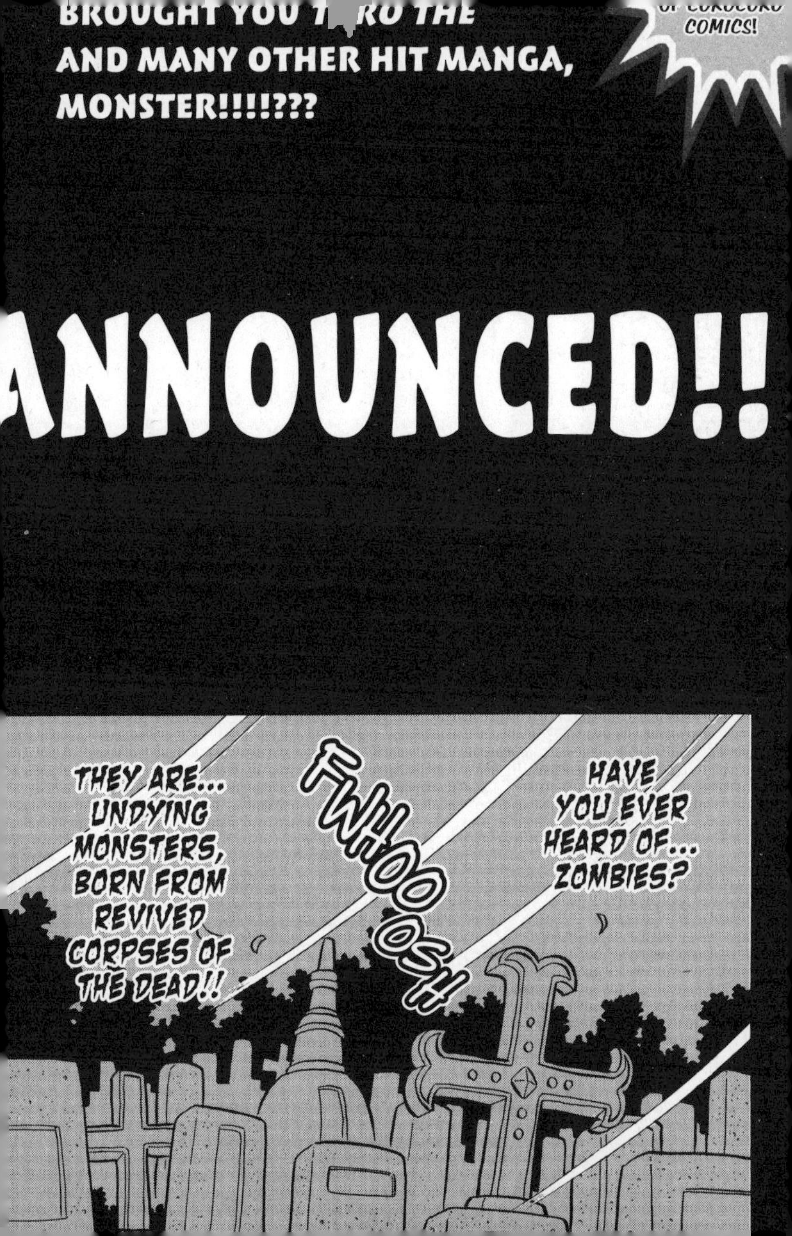
COMICS!
AND MANY OTHER HIT MANGA, MONSTER!!!!???
ANNOUNCED!!
HAVE YOU EVER HEARD OF... ZOMBIES?
FWHOOOSH
THEY ARE... UNDYING MONSTERS, BORN FROM REVIVED CORPSES OF THE DEAD!!

YASUNARI NAGATOSHI SENSEI, THE ARTIST WHO
SPACE ALIEN, MIRACLE BALL, GORORO...
NOW PRESENTS...!! COULD IT BE!? A TERRIFYING

NEW SERIES

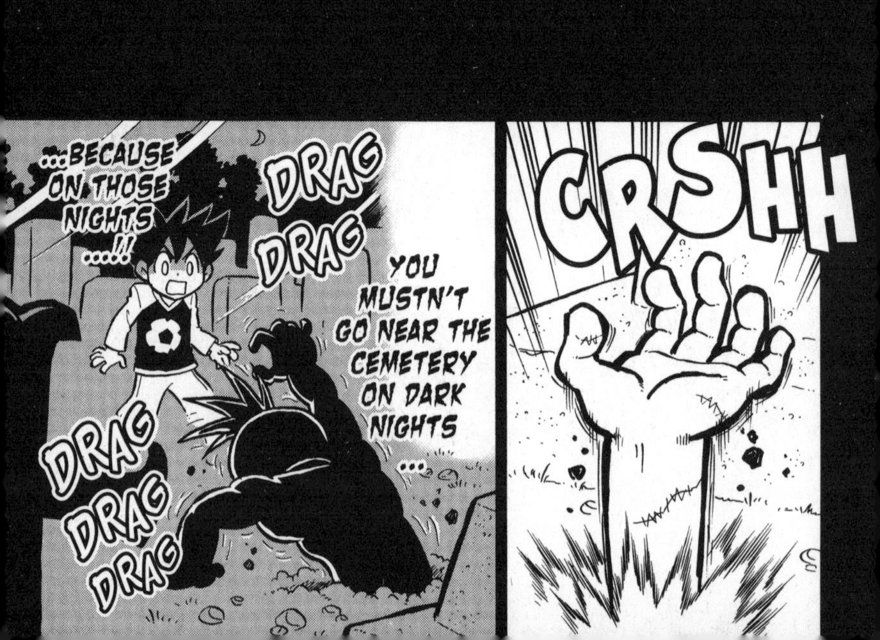
CRSHH
YOU MUSTN'T GO NEAR THE CEMETERY ON DARK NIGHTS ...
DRAG DRAG
...BECAUSE ON THOSE NIGHTS ...!!
DRAG DRAG DRAG

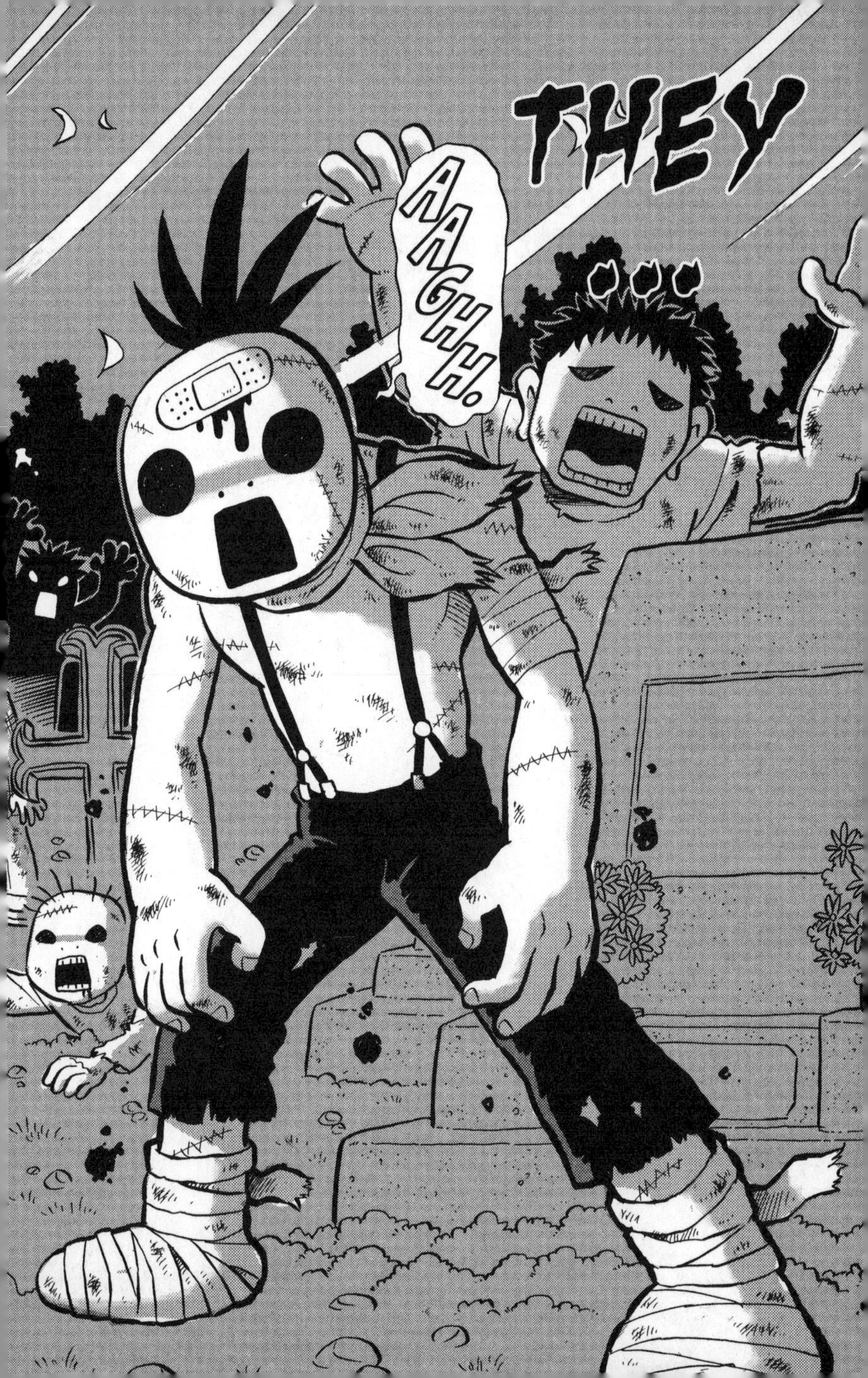
THEY
AAGHH.

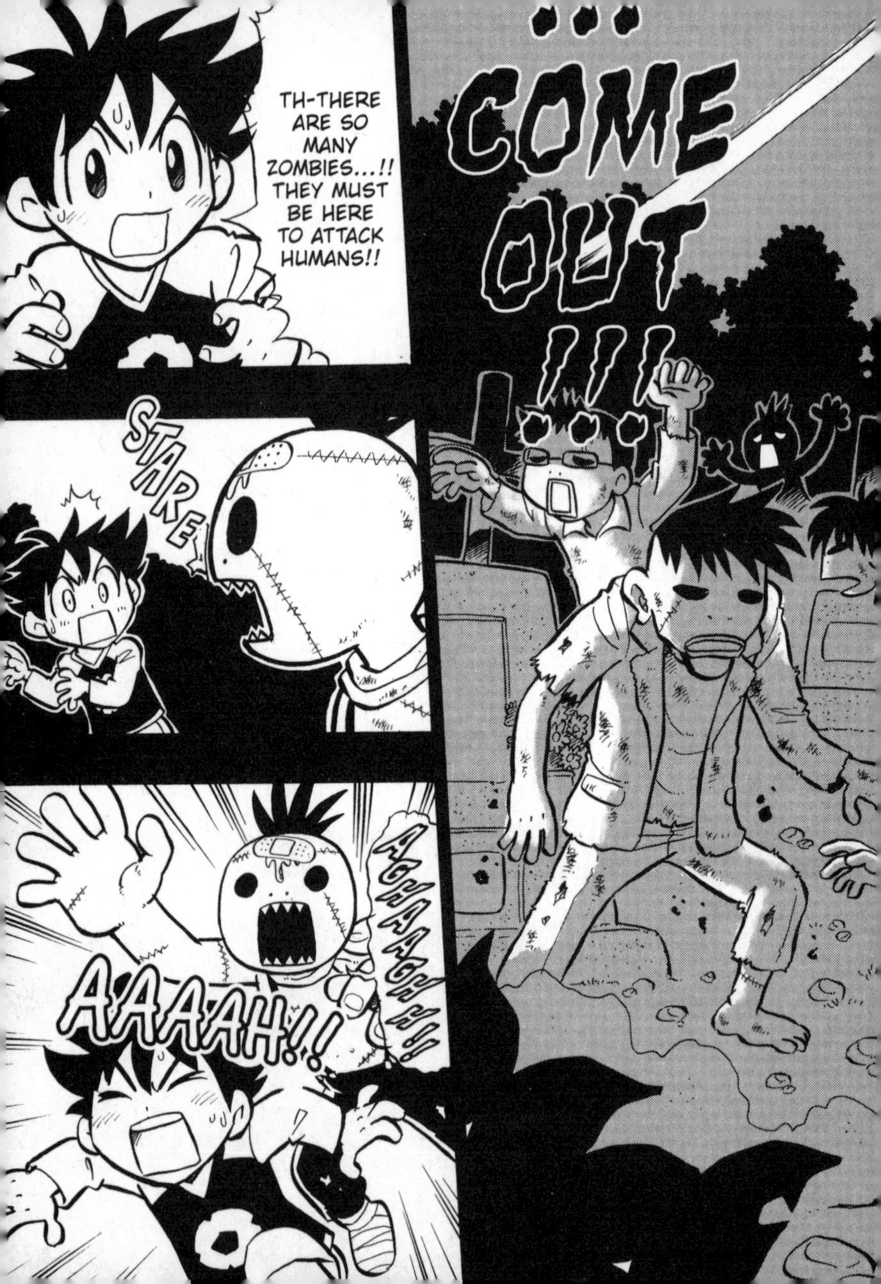
...
COME OUT!!!
...
TH-THERE ARE SO MANY ZOMBIES...!! THEY MUST BE HERE TO ATTACK HUMANS!!
STARE
AGHAAGHH!!
AAAAH!!

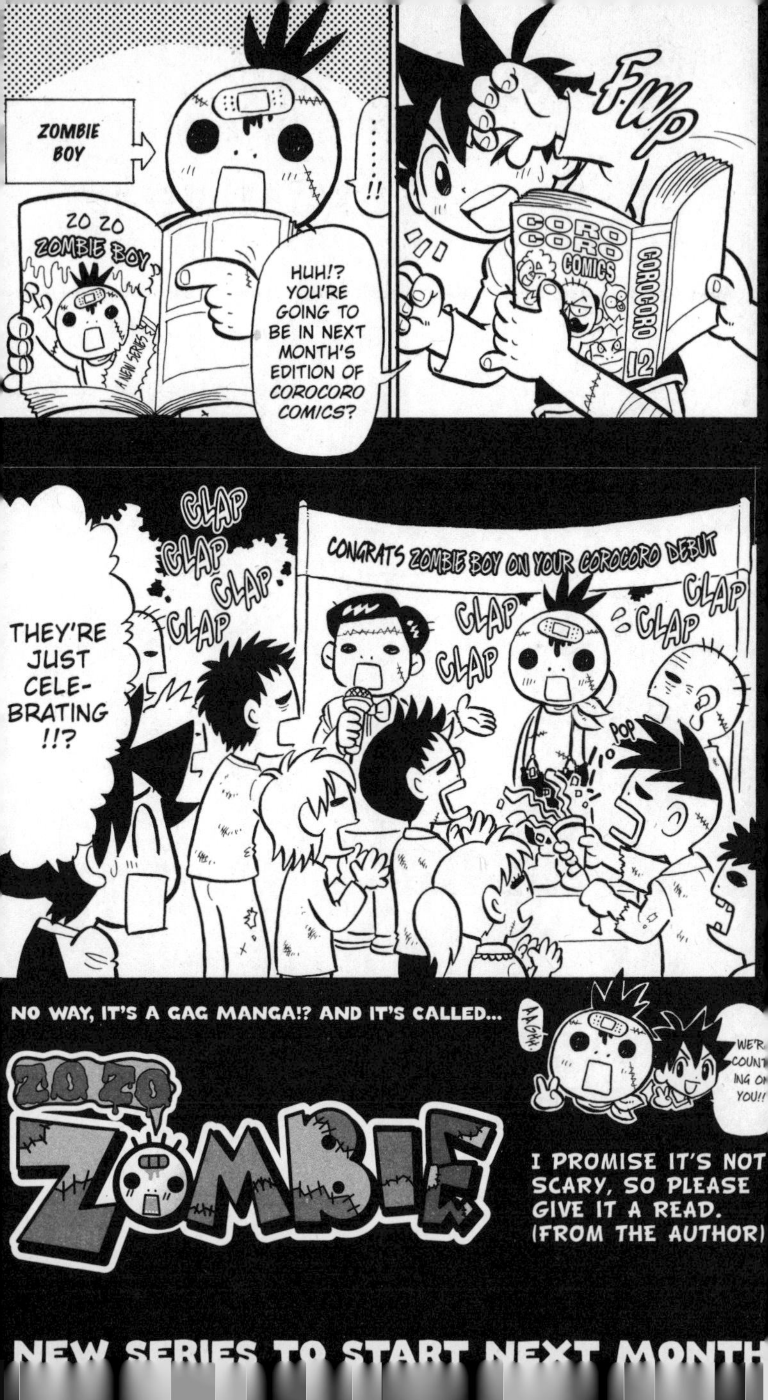
FWP
COROCORO COMICS
COROCORO 12
ZOMBIE BOY
ZO ZO ZOMBIE BOY
A NEW SERIES
...!!
HUH!? YOU'RE GOING TO BE IN NEXT MONTH'S EDITION OF COROCORO COMICS?
CONGRATS ZOMBIE BOY ON YOUR COROCORO DEBUT
CLAP CLAP
CLAP CLAP CLAP
POP
CLAP CLAP CLAP CLAP
THEY'RE JUST CELE-BRATING!!?
NO WAY, IT'S A GAG MANGA!? AND IT'S CALLED...
WE'RE COUNTING ON YOU!!
ZO ZO ZOMBIE
I PROMISE IT'S NOT SCARY, SO PLEASE GIVE IT A READ. (FROM THE AUTHOR)
NEW SERIES TO START NEXT MONTH

ZOMBIE BOY DRAWING SING-ALONG ♫

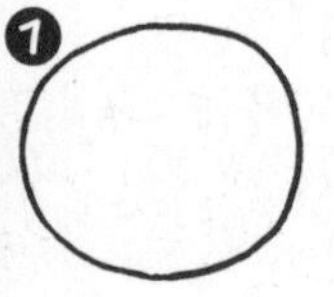

It's a full moon—oh, how nice!

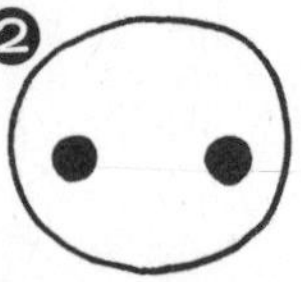

Two shooting stars came falling down.

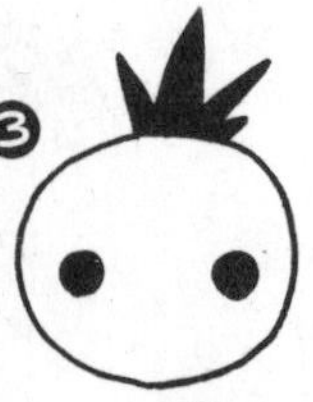

"Bang" go the fireworks into the sky.

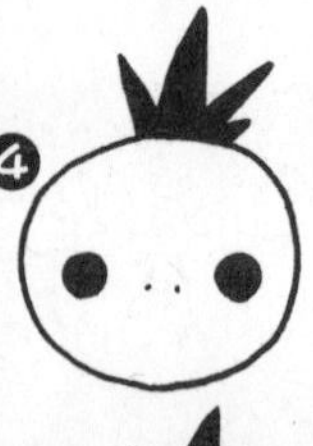

A shake of salt and pepper, a shake of salt and pepper.

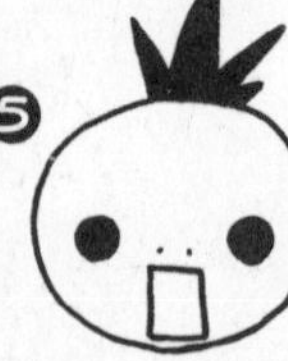

Oops! Into a square hole we fall.

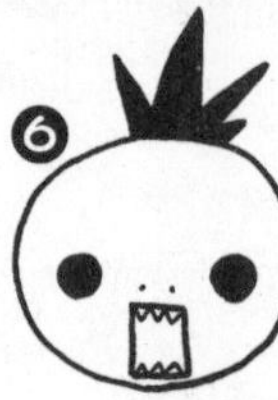

There's a saw in here. What the heck!?

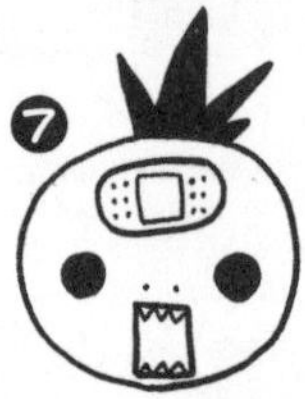

Anybody got a bandage!?

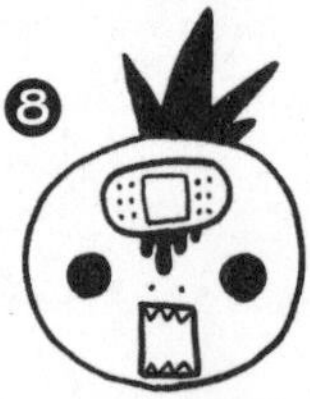

Blood's coming out—this is the worst!!

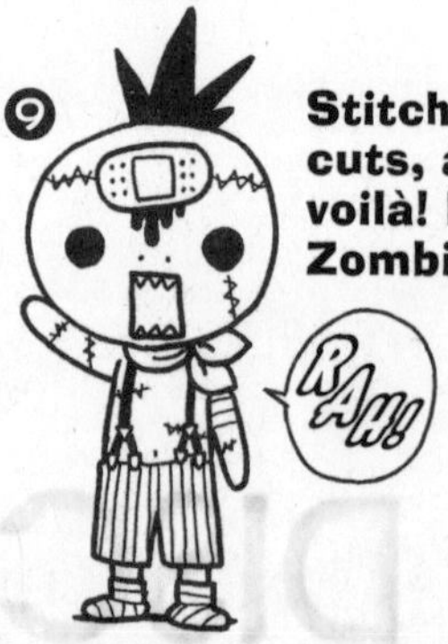
RAH!

Stitch up the cuts, and voilà! It's Zombie Boy!!

ZO ZO ZOMBIE 1 THE END

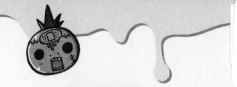
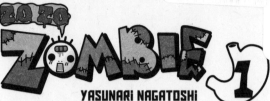

ZOZO ZOMBIE 1

YASUNARI NAGATOSHi

Translation: ALEXANDRA MCCULLOUGH-GARCIA ♣ Lettering: BIANCA PISTILLO

ZOZOZO ZOMBIE-KUN Vol. 1
by Yasunari NAGATOSHI
© 2013 Yasunari NAGATOSHI
All rights reserved.
Original Japanese edition published by SHOGAKUKAN.
English translation rights in the United States of America, Canada, the United Kingdom, Ireland, Australia and New Zealand arranged with SHOGAKUKAN through Tuttle-Mori Agency, Inc.

English translation © 2018 by Yen Press, LLC

JY
1290 Avenue of the Americas
New York, NY 10104

Visit us at jyforkids.com ♣ facebook.com/jyforkids
twitter.com/jyforkids ♣ jyforkids.tumblr.com ♣ instagram.com/jyforkids

First JY Edition: October 2018

JY is an imprint of Yen Press, LLC.
The JY name and logo are trademarks of Yen Press, LLC.

Library of Congress Control Number: 2018948323

ISBN: 978-1-9753-5341-4

10 9 8 7 6 5 4 3 2 1

WOR

Printed in the United States of America

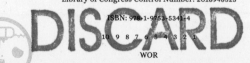